Rebecca's Cove

LJ Maas

Yellow Rose Books

Nederland, Texas

Copyright © 2003 by LJ Maas

ISBN 1-930928-89-0

First Printing 2003

9 8 7 6 5 4 3 2 1

Cover design by LJ Maas

Published by:

Yellow Rose Books
PMB 238, 8691 9th Avenue
Port Arthur, Texas 77642-8025

Find us on the World Wide Web at
http://www.rapbooks.biz

Printed in the United States of America

0807-02-225

To my best mates, *The Misfits*. Their friendship, along with one wild week in Florida, was the inspiration behind the creation of Ana Lia Island.

As always, to the warrior of my heart.

Chapter
1

"That's the best line you could come up with?" The young blonde tapped her perfectly manicured nails on the linen-covered table.

"Well, on such short notice," the dark-haired woman quipped. She took a healthy swallow of the vodka gimlet at her elbow.

Hobie was beginning to enjoy this. She thought dining in a restaurant alone would be dreadfully boring, but the women at the table next to her were unknowingly providing some first-rate entertainment. It was difficult for her not to eavesdrop when her table was only a few feet away from the arguing couple.

"You're a writer and the best excuse you can dream up is that it's just not *working?*"

"Well, you have to give me some credit. I *am* awfully drunk," the brunette slurred. She grinned at her own wittiness.

"I would have thought I rated better. After all, we've been dating for two weeks."

"No, dear, we've been having sex for two weeks. We haven't gone anywhere...done anything. It's just been sex in every elevator and motel in Chicago. Technically," she motioned around her with one hand, "this is our first date."

"You are the most arrogant, shallow—"

"You're calling me shallow? You are by far the most self-involved person I've ever met, and I should know. Up until now, I was the most self-involved person I'd ever met."

"Enjoy your dinner, you bitch!" The next act was textbook and everyone in the restaurant saw it coming—everyone with the exception of the inebriated brunette. The young blonde stood and with one swift movement tossed her drink into the other woman's face.

The recipient of the white wine bath jumped up to keep the rest of the drink out of her lap. She grabbed a napkin and wiped her face, relieved that most of the liquid had missed her. Now standing, the woman towered over the waiters who anxiously scurried around her.

Hobie watched out of the corner of her eye. Obviously, this woman was a somebody. The staff fell all over themselves trying to help her. Although Hobie herself was of above-average height at 5'6", this woman looked well over six feet tall. She had dark hair that fell just to the tops of her ears and which she wore parted on one side. When she looked down to dry off her slacks, Hobie snuck an entire eyeful. Long legs, broad shoulders, and soft gray eyes filled out the package. When the woman glanced back up, she looked directly into Hobie's gaze. A rather pregnant pause lasted longer than perhaps good manners called for, but Hobie felt trapped. The stranger's short hair dipped seductively over one eye in a way that reminded Hobie of a very young Elvis.

Suddenly, she winked at Hobie and shrugged her shoulders as if caught doing something foolish. Hobie felt herself smiling until she realized it felt a lot like flirting. Instantly, her defenses went up and she felt the heat of a blush creep up her neck. She pulled her gaze away from the standing woman and trained her eyes on the work she had brought along to dinner.

Throughout her meal, Hobie couldn't quite get over the feeling that someone was watching her. She didn't dare look over at the tall brunette again. *That's all I need. Remember, Hob, you're going home tomorrow. Do not get crazy in the big city.* Hobie read the journal before her, pausing occasionally to make a note in her Palm hand-held. The five-day conference had been wonderful. Not only had she learned some interesting techniques to take back to her patients, but a week in Chicago had been a much-needed vacation for her.

A message flashed across Hobie's PDA. She stopped chewing on the end of the stylus. One sentence came up on the small screen.

I'd like to know what it feels like to kiss you.

Immediately, Hobie's head jerked up. Fully expecting to run headlong into a leering Michigan Avenue businessman's gaze, she scanned the room. Of course, that was probably what the computer stalker wanted, but she couldn't help herself. It was rather like having someone tell her not to look at the person seated at the next table. Her first impulse had always been to look. Much later, Hobie realized that it was her next action that changed her life completely.

She didn't see a leer, but instead met a set of dazzling gray eyes that caused her lungs to forget why they were there. By the time Hobie caught her breath she realized she was smiling back at the tall woman, who had slipped a slim PDA into her own coat pocket.

Don't smile, Hobie Lynn! Are you insane? This is an order. Do not smile! Do not encourage her. The little voice in Hobie's head kept shouting at her. That voice kept her from doing utterly stupid things in her life—when she listened to it, that is. She was fond of ignoring the little voice. Each time her actions brought about disastrous consequences, she always swore that the next time, she would listen. She rarely did.

This night was no different as Hobie felt a tightening in her abdomen at the beautiful woman's overture. It had been a very long time since she'd felt that sensation. Hobie hadn't really said yes or no when she found the stranger seated opposite her and the waiter bringing them both fresh drinks.

"I couldn't possibly let you walk out of this restaurant without telling you that I'd like to make tonight the most exciting night of your life," the stranger said.

"You're taking me to Disneyland?" Hobie tossed back. She would have laughed aloud at the opening line if anyone else in the world had delivered it. The brunette's charming smile never faltered and she appeared entirely confident, as though being turned down was a foreign concept. Even though the stranger's eyes gave nothing away, Hobie could tell that she had consumed a good deal of alcohol. She wasn't falling down, but there was a definite slur to her speech and an unsteadiness to the way she held her body. Unfortunately, those small defects made her even more appealing to Hobie.

"That's good. You're quick. I like that. I am terribly attracted to you, however."

"You're also very drunk, aren't you?"

"Oh no, not by any stretch. I don't allow myself to get *very* drunk until after midnight. I'm only moderately drunk."

Hobie had no control of the light laughter that escaped her. Drunk or sober, the woman seated across from her was damned charming. Hobie suspected she knew it, too.

The dark-haired woman took the redhead's reaction as acquiescence of a sort and slid her chair closer.

Hobie noticed the subtle maneuver. "Tell me, didn't you just break up with someone over at that table?" she asked.

"Who, me? No. She was my secretary. I had to fire her." She leaned in close and whispered, "She steals. It's a sad case. I'm afraid it's compulsive."

"Steals, eh?" Hobie leaned back and eyed the woman. "What

did she steal?"

"What?"

"Steal. What did she steal?"

"Um...white-out."

"Oh, please!" Hobie laughed and folded her arms across her chest.

"Well, I didn't want to say this...there were Post-it notes, too. You'd be surprised how that stuff can add up, can take a Fortune 500 company right down the tubes."

"You sure you're not on an evening release from some mental health facility?"

"All right, yes." The brunette chuckled and sat up straight. "Not about the release, but I was seeing her. I'm not anymore. I hate to dwell on the pain, though. So, out with the old and in with the new."

"It certainly didn't take you long to get over the unending heartache." Hobie couldn't help but join in the playful banter.

"I'm a quick healer and, after all," the woman's brow furrowed, "it was quite a while ago."

"Quite a while? You call waiting two hours before hitting on another woman *quite a while?*"

"Well," the stranger graced Hobie with that same rakish grin, "I did wait for an hour after eating my dinner before I came over here. An hour's the right amount of time, isn't it? Or is that swimming? I always get the two confused."

Hobie laughed so hard that tears came to her eyes. Wearing a smug expression, the dark-haired woman leaned back in her chair.

"You are incorrigible and I'm sure I shouldn't even be talking to you. I'd say that you're the kind of woman my mother warned me about."

The brunette leaned in close again. "I'd say that your mother was a very smart woman. No, really, come on. At least let me take you out on the town. It's a beautiful night."

"I don't even know your name."

"BJ Warren," she said as she held out her hand.

"Hobie Allen," the auburn-haired woman responded. She shook the offered hand.

"There, now we're properly introduced. What do you say?"

Hobie could hardly hear herself speak over the screaming of the little voice in the back of her mind. "All right, I'll go out with you."

"You won't be sorry."

"You do know that I have no intention of sleeping with you, though," Hobie said.

BJ smiled.

"I have to insist on a verbal acknowledgment of that fact," Hobie added.

BJ paused. "I acknowledge that at this moment, you firmly believe that to be true."

Hobie shook her head. She couldn't understand why she was agreeing to this. It was so completely opposite to the way she lived her life. "You truly are something else."

"I knew you'd come around to my way of thinking." The women stood, and BJ had to still herself momentarily to shake the cobwebs from her brain.

"Tell me you're not driving," Hobie said.

"There are three rules I always adhere to."

"And they are?"

"I always pay my taxes by April fifteenth, I never have unprotected sex with someone I don't know, and I never drink and drive."

"You're a poster for the American way."

"One does what one can," BJ responded with a grin.

They walked out of the restaurant and Hobie was surprised that the tall woman wasn't tripping all over herself. Either she'd had a great deal of experience functioning while inebriated, or the alcohol hadn't affected her as much as Hobie thought. The air was much chillier than it had been earlier when Hobie walked to the restaurant. She rubbed her hands across the goose bumps on her arms.

"Would you mind if I went back to my hotel room for a jacket?" Hobie asked.

"Not at all, I'm sorry. Where are you staying?"

Hobie pointed to the building they were standing next to.

"Well, that's convenient, isn't it?"

"Let me ask you something," Hobie began as they entered the brightly lit hotel lobby. "You act as though you know I don't live here."

The taller woman shrugged. "You have that tourist look about you. Besides, not many native Chicagoans have that good of a tan in April."

"Oh. Um, why don't you wait down here and I'll be right back."

"Why don't I come up with you?" BJ replied.

"I'll just be a sec."

"And you're afraid I'm going to accost you in the elevator."

"No, I didn't say that."

"Maybe you're just afraid that you can't resist me after all."

"I don't see that happening."

BJ made a few clucking noises under her breath. It was the proverbial last straw.

"I am not chicken! Oh, okay. Come on."

"What a charming offer," BJ replied.

Hobie turned to glare at the dark-haired woman and BJ quickly raised her hands.

"Just kidding," she said.

To Hobie, the silence in the elevator was deafening. She nervously cleared her throat as she wondered once again why she was doing this. "In the restaurant, how did you know I was gay?" The question had nagged her from the start.

"I didn't," BJ answered. She leaned against the wall and fixed a gaze on Hobie that she felt all the way down to her toes.

Either this woman has all the confidence in the world or she's really that good, Hobie thought. She let herself become lost in the other woman's penetrating gaze. It was hypnotizing, and Hobie felt as if she would do just about anything the woman asked while she was staring at her like that.

"Oh," she answered softly. The elevator doors opened before she could pursue that line of thought any further.

Once inside the room, Hobie retrieved the white linen jacket that went with her skirt. "Okay, ready to roll."

"Do you mind if I use your bathroom?" BJ asked. She smiled wearily at Hobie.

"Of course not, it's right through there. Do you feel okay?"

"Sure, I won't be a minute."

Hobie stood before the window looking out onto the moonlit landscape of Chicago. She heard the water running in the bathroom and wondered once again what she was doing in her hotel room with a drunken stranger. *I just want the company, that's all. I mean, I made it clear that I'm not going any further than having a few drinks. Oh, good Lord, Hobie, don't lie, especially to yourself. You know damn well that if she looks at you one more time like she did in that elevator, you're going to forget about your resolve. You're going to forget who you are and where you come from, and you're going to jump into bed with her. There's only one answer. I have to call this off and send her on her way, plain and simple.*

"Breathtaking view."

Hobie felt warm breath along the edge of her right ear and she hoped the shiver that ran across her skin wasn't noticeable. "Um, yes. The city's beautiful at night."

"That wasn't the view I was talking about."

Fingertips slid along the skin of Hobie's arms. She closed her eyes to the pleasing sensation and realized just how long it had been since anyone had touched her in that way. Soft lips on the back of her neck snapped her mind back into the reality of the situation.

She spun around in the taller woman's arms and stopped her just as she was leaning in to claim Hobie's lips in a kiss. Hobie pushed against her chest with both hands.

"Oh no, you don't. This is exactly what I don't need," Hobie protested. She escaped to the other side of the room.

"Did that sound as unconvincing to you as it did to me?" BJ's voice flowed across Hobie's senses like warm honey. The dark-haired woman slowly made her way across the room. The redhead looked up with big green eyes that appeared spellbound. "Because, Hobie, I think, deep down, that you think this is *exactly* what you need."

Hobie suspected that was the same phrase BJ used all the time. A few of the words might change now and again, but she had the feeling that the sentiment always reeled them in. BJ smiled in a way that Hobie suspected no woman ever resisted for long before she leaned in once more, but this time Hobie didn't stop her.

The redhead looked like a small, frightened rabbit, too afraid to run and too frightened not to. BJ brushed her lips against Hobie's, gently at first.

The strangled moan that came from Hobie's throat was a dead giveaway. She slipped her arms around the taller woman's neck and they shared a kiss unlike anything either of them had ever experienced.

A sound like sheer delight escaped BJ's lips as the two broke apart for air. Seconds later the small redhead tangled her fingers in BJ's short dark hair and drew her down for another passionate kiss. BJ slipped her hands under Hobie's jacket and pulled her closer.

"Good God, that was—I mean—where did you learn to kiss like that?" BJ stammered breathlessly when they once again parted for breath.

The sound of the taller woman's voice cut directly through Hobie's libidinous haze. "What in the hell am I doing?" She tried to take a step back, but BJ still held her tightly in her arms.

"Well, if you don't know, let me be the first to tell you that you're a natural," BJ replied as her body swayed back and forth.

"God in heaven, what am I doing?"

"Hey, it's not that bad." BJ was slurring her words more than before.

"Not that bad?" Hobie nearly shouted back. "I'm making out with a complete stranger who's so drunk she can barely stand!"

BJ furrowed her brow in genuine confusion. "You mean I'm still standing?"

"Oh God! I don't even believe this is happening to me!" Hobie cried out. She freed herself from BJ's embrace and whirled around. "I do not do this kind of thing. I never let my body think for me. I mean, that's just not me. I'm a hopeless romantic, not the kind of woman who sleeps around. I need time to get to know you, romance...maybe some flowers. I'm so sorry, BJ. You seem like an incredible woman, but I just can't—"

Hobie turned and the sight caused her to freeze. It took a full five seconds before her brain could slip into gear and impel her body forward. "Oh no! No, no, no, no, no!"

Hobie rushed to the bed and BJ, who lay sprawled across it. "Don't you dare! BJ, wake up. Wake up, dammit!" Hobie sat on the bed and lightly slapped the unconscious woman's cheek. "Oh God, please don't do this to me. I swear, I will never, ever do this again. If you help me out of this one, I promise to start going to Mass more and I promise I will never again act like a slut." Hobie looked down at the prone woman and realized that help would not be coming from above, at least not anytime soon. "BJ, please, you cannot stay here." Hobie shook the woman's shoulders one more time.

BJ made a small sound and rolled over, hugging the pillow beside her. She wore a pleasant expression, the corners of her mouth turned up in a slight smile. Hobie gave up in exasperation, her arms falling to her sides and defeat in her eyes. "This is why I don't do things like this," she said quietly to the sleeping woman. "This could only happen to me."

BJ couldn't understand why there was a maid walking on the ceiling until she realized that her own head hung over the end of the bed. The slim brown-skinned woman who approached BJ did so upside down. The sight made the brunette dizzy, which caused her stomach to begin its protestation of the previous evening's alcohol consumption.

"May I clean the room yet, ma'am?" the hotel maid asked.

BJ swallowed and cautiously examined the inside of her mouth with her tongue. She had been sure she would find cotton stuffed there. Finding no such substance, she swallowed a few more times. "Time?" she finally rasped.

"Excuse me?"

"What time is it?"

"It's 2:00 PM, ma'am. The other one said not to wake you until after noon. She said to bring up a meal if you weren't awake by now. Are you hungry?" She lifted the silver domed lid covering a white porcelain plate.

The aroma, which under ordinary circumstances would have been tantalizing, struck BJ like an unseen blow to the stomach. She could feel the small rumble begin. "I'll give you a hundred dollars if you get that food as far away from this room as possible."

"Yes, ma'am."

By the time the maid wheeled the cart to the elevator and had a busboy return it to the kitchen, BJ was sitting up on the side of the bed.

"Bless you," she mumbled. "Here you go." She held out a hundred dollar bill.

"Oh no, ma'am, you don't have to do that. Your friend gave me a big enough tip to make my day."

"I don't have any friends," BJ answered instinctively. She fought to remember who the woman was that she had been with the night before. "Been with" would have to be used loosely since BJ had woken up in bed by herself and fully clothed. *Who the hell was she?*

"Well, this gal checked out and paid me to do what I done for you so far. She even paid for an extra day 'cause she said you would probably sleep late," the maid explained.

Well, it isn't exactly the first time I've passed out, but not even remembering what in the hell I did, that's new. BJ ran her fingers through her hair and massaged her scalp. Her head felt as heavy as a bowling ball. She couldn't believe that a total stranger had gone to that much trouble, especially after she had passed out on her. She had an odd feeling about the encounter. She couldn't remember any particulars, but there was something there. It was something unlike anything she had known before. Thinking back, she drew a blank on the evening after breaking up with... *what was that girl's name?*

"I don't believe this shit," she said aloud. *I can't even remember the girl's name that I've been screwing for the last two weeks.* "You're a case, Warren. This is why I don't do things like this," she said to the uncomprehending maid. "This could only happen to me."

"Look, why don't you just punch a couple of keys and look up the name of the woman who stayed in 8312 last night. I'm sure even someone as mentally challenged as you should be able to do that."

BJ was in rare form as she sparred with the concierge. She had a hangover as big as Wyoming and half of Montana. She wanted to get a name and number, but the hotel staff had been less than cooperative.

"Like I have said, Ms. Warren, we have—"

"And like I have said, Sydney, I don't give a rat's ass for your fucking rules. How much trouble could it possibly be to give me this information?"

"Perhaps if you were family—"

"If she was a goddamn family member, would I need you to give me her phone number?" BJ shouted. The deskman's unflappable demeanor infuriated her all the more. "Okay, here's the deal, Sydney." She started counting out bills from the slim wallet she removed from her inside jacket pocket. She put her billfold away, then leaned across the desk and tucked the wad of bills into the man's front pocket. "Here is five hundred dollars, Sydney. It's *all* yours. All *you* have to do," she enunciated each word slowly, "is push one little teensy button on your computer and give me the name of the fucking woman that stayed in that room!" By the time she finished the sentence, she was shouting again.

The man sighed and looked upward. The clerks and the bellhops were sure he was petitioning heaven for some intercessory assistance. Taking the money from his pocket, he placed it back on the counter and moved toward his computer.

"Now we're getting somewhere," BJ stated smugly.

Sydney turned the computer off.

"Okay, that wasn't really the right button now, was it, Sydney?" BJ watched as the man waved goodbye and vacated the desk area through a back door. "You rat bastard," she mumbled at his retreating figure.

BJ had the doorman hail her a cab. Once inside she swallowed the aspirin that she'd purchased at the hotel gift shop. It took everything she had to get the pills down her dry throat. "Lake Shore Towers," she told the cabbie and pulled out her cellular phone.

She flipped through the stored numbers and selected the one marked "Jules." She listened to the series of tones that represented her agent's work number and waited impatiently, absently staring out the cab window at Lake Michigan.

BJ had known Juliana Ross nearly all her life, since they were in second grade together at parochial school. Juliana's family moved to the US from London, England—Essex, to be exact. Juliana had paid mightily for her place of birth once a thirteen-year-old BJ, vacationing in England, discovered what being an Essex girl meant. Essex girls had a reputation for being airheaded and rather free with their affections, much like stereotypical American blondes. BJ's long-standing dig at her friend was to call her an "Essex girl" even though Juliana was not only highly intelligent, but as ethically and morally upstanding as anyone BJ knew.

If Juliana wasn't BJ's best friend, she would probably have been the last person the brunette would call. However, BJ found herself obsessed with the stranger from the previous evening and she was determined to find her, although she still wasn't absolutely certain why.

"Jules, I need you to find me a girl," she said into the phone as soon as her friend picked up the receiver on the other end.

"I've told you a hundred times, I'm not that kind of an agent. Go down to Rush Street, it's like a smorgasbord down there," Juliana replied. Her accent made her words come out in a quick jumble of dropped syllables, but BJ was used to it.

"That's very cute. I don't mean that kind of a girl. I need to find the girl I was with last night." In BJ's mind, she could see her friend's blonde head shaking.

"I know it sounds strange. In fact, it sounds a little pathetic now that I'm actually saying the words out loud." BJ quickly told her friend the rest of the story. "Look, I know this sounds insane, but all I know is that I have got to find this girl again. I don't understand why, but it's as if my whole future depends on seeing her again."

Juliana thought about what BJ had just told her. This definitely was a departure from BJ's customary cavalier attitude regarding women. Over the years, BJ had grown into a regular beauty and the beast all rolled into one. She was knock-dead gorgeous and could be charming when she wanted something, but she also had the most unpleasant disposition of anyone Juliana had ever known. Their friendship endured because BJ seemed able to let down the walls and be herself with Juliana, who, being a literary agent, was used to dealing with temperamental writers. Their egos needed stroked twenty-four hours a day, and BJ was no different. In fact, her ego was more fragile than most. The irony was that although BJ probably needed, and wanted, love more than anyone else in the world, her attitude, anger, and selfish behavior never allowed anyone the opportunity to get that close.

"Okay, okay, Miss Melodramatic. I've got someone I can put on it. So, where did all this magic take place?"

BJ gave Juliana as much information as she could about the previous evening.

"Hey, speaking of where you were last night, mate, your grandmother called me," Juliana interjected.

"Tanti? Why did she call you?"

"Because you had your phone turned off. Don't you ever check your messages? She said it wasn't life or death, but she did say that she had to talk to you today. Did you need me to ring her back for you?"

"No, no. I'm just getting home now. I plan on soaking in a hot bath and then committing suicide if this hangover doesn't go away. I'll call her before that."

Juliana chuckled at her friend's remark. "All right," she said. "Just remember not to bleed too heavily on the carpet. You'll never get your deposit back if you do."

BJ groaned in pleasure at the feel of the hot bath water on her skin. She stretched her neck out and winced. Passing out and sleeping in a strange bed had twisted her neck and shoulder muscles. They were screaming in retaliation. She sipped the ice-cold Chopin vodka and held the heavy tumbler to the side of her head. The cold glass stopped the pain at her temple for a brief moment, but then the throbbing resumed.

BJ had phoned her grandmother's house six times over the last few hours with no answer, and she was beginning to get worried. Her grandmother lived off the coast of Florida, on an island called Ana Lia. BJ had only been there a few times in her life. She couldn't even remember her last visit. She thought it must have been after her college graduation, when her parents were still alive.

Evelyn Warren was her father's mother. The old woman had always adored BJ, but apparently had some sort of falling out with her son at one time. Neither talked of it, but BJ's father had never encouraged her to visit her grandmother. BJ had always found love and acceptance from the old woman, even though she thought her quite odd most of the time.

Her Tanti, as BJ called her, had been a renowned photojournalist. Evelyn Warren's name had been on numerous *Life* magazine covers from 1940 to 1970. A Jeep accident during an assignment in Guatemala during the early 1970s had left her injured, and she and her best friend Aimee had retired to Evelyn's island home after that. Aimee was a nurse, which worked out well. Evelyn had been a stubborn woman back then, and Aimee's prodding and pushing had been the reason that Evelyn made it through her physical therapy, which ultimately allowed her to walk again.

BJ smiled as she remembered how the two old women used to shout across the house at one another. After Aimee passed away, BJ's grandmother grew more reclusive, content to stay inside her house on the island no matter how many times BJ encouraged her to move to Chicago. BJ talked to her twice a week and saw to her financial needs, although she still didn't go to the island any more than she had when her father was alive. Her absence was due in part to the strangeness of the island itself. The people there all seemed a bit off center, as if they were untouched by modern-day thoughts. The second reason was BJ's fear of the water. She had to either drive over an excruciatingly long bridge across the Gulf or take a ferry to the island. Neither of those options had ever held much appeal for her.

BJ's cell phone rang, even though it sounded a lot more like a shriek to her aching head. She reached out with one hand and pushed the talk button.

"Yes?"

"Baylor?"

"Tanti!" BJ was relieved, yet unconsciously shuddered. Her grandmother was the only living family she had left and the only person to still call her by her given name. "Tanti, where on earth have you been? I've been calling you for hours."

"Well, now, things aren't that bad."

"What do you mean, *that* bad? Why should they be bad at all? Are you sick?"

"No, dear, I had a little accident is all."

"An accident!" BJ sat upright in the tub, ignoring the pain in her back. "Tanti, what happened? Are you okay?"

"I had a little fall, seems I broke my hip and wrist."

"I'm coming to get you. You need to be in a hospital, not some—"

"Baylor, dear heart, calm down. I *am* in hospital."

"Are you on the mainland?"

"No, I'm here on Ana Lia."

"They have a hospital on the island?"

"Why yes, dear heart. It only has five beds, but it's like being in a hotel."

"Tanti, how on earth did you—"

"Baylor...I need your help." The older woman's voice, which had always seemed so strong and confident, was suddenly soft and needy. She had never before asked BJ for help of any kind.

"Whatever you need, Tanti. Just ask."

BJ remembered that promise for quite some time. She blamed much of what happened to her next on that little vow. If she had any clairvoyant abilities or woman's intuition at all, she would never have uttered her next words. "I'll catch a flight first thing in the morning, Tanti. You can count on me."

"I don't understand, Tanti. Did you fall down? How were the conditions there? Do I need to call my lawyer?"

"Baylor, please sit down. You're making me dizzy."

BJ paced the small hospital room from one end to another. Seeing her grandmother in traction, looking small and pale, affected her. Her day hadn't gone well and she felt light-headed from the combination of caffeine and sleep deprivation. Earlier that morning she had three cups of Starbucks coffee while waiting at O'Hare. On the flight to Florida, she briefly entertained the notion of a drink, but didn't want to show up at her grandmother's hospital bed smelling of alcohol. She settled for more coffee instead.

The car rental agency at the Tampa airport had been an experience in itself. BJ wasn't sure if it had been the incredible ineptness of the clerk or the caffeine that had shifted her anger into high gear. It only took an additional year or so to explain to the clerk that she had reserved a car just like the one she owned, a Jaguar XK8, and that a Toyota Corolla was clearly *not* the same thing. She pulled out of the airport calling everyone from the baggage handlers to the car rental clerk rat bastards.

BJ's humiliation for the day reached its zenith when the old man running the ferry remembered her. Of course, it wasn't due to his amazing powers of recall. It had been at least fifteen years since she'd last crossed to the island. BJ guessed that she was the only person he'd seen sitting in the car as the ferry crossed the water with her eyes tightly shut and a death grip on the steering wheel, all the while repeating to herself, "I will not sink. I will not sink."

"Baylor, you're wound up like a clock that's ready to bust a spring. Take a deep breath and come sit here by me." The old woman pointed to the chair beside the bed.

BJ did indeed take a deep breath and sit down beside her grandmother.

"Did you fly or drive?"

"I flew, but I rented a car at the airport."

"Ah, what is it you're driving now?"

"A Jaguar." BJ chuckled. She could never understand her grandmother's interest in her cars.

"And I'll wager it's red."

"You know me too well." BJ laughed outright and then grew serious. "Tanti, I get the distinct feeling you're putting off asking me what you really want to ask."

"Well, not putting off exactly. It's more like...well..."

"Tanti," BJ warned in a slow drawl.

"Oh, okay. I need your help with something."

"Of course, Tanti. You know all you have to do is ask. Anything you need."

"I need you to stay at my house and take care of things until I'm able to do it myself."

"What? Live here?" BJ's voice rose as her body did. "Oh no, Tanti. I can't live here."

"But you just said anything, Baylor."

"Is that what I said? What I meant to say was *almost* anything."

"Baylor..." Evelyn looked up with a pathetic expression. "My greenhouse...little Arturo. Someone has to care for them."

BJ could feel her pushing all the right buttons. "Tanti, you know how I feel about staying on the island. It creeps me out."

"That's your father talking, Baylor Joan Warren," Evelyn chided.

"No, this is something I figured out all on my own. The people in this town are borderline sane at best. They make me uncomfortable."

"That's because you walk around like you've got a stick up your butt."

"Tanti!"

"They just take some getting used to is all. Strike up a conversation sometime. Be *nice* to people."

"Tanti, there's not enough conversation in the whole world to make these people look normal. And I *am* nice."

"Please, Baylor. You're the only family I have."

Evelyn had played her trump card and BJ knew it. "All right," she reluctantly consented. She pointed a finger at her grandmother. "But only until I can hire someone to come in and take care of things."

"Baylor, I don't want strangers in my house."

"Who's taking care of the place now?"

"The sheriff said he brought Arturo to the vet's office, and Mrs. Wedington is taking care of the greenhouse. Please, at least think about it, dear heart." The term of endearment got to BJ every time.

Evelyn pulled a folder from underneath her pillow and held it out to BJ. "I wrote out a few instructions so you wouldn't be lost. You can find the answer to any question you might have right in here."

"Good Lord." BJ hefted the envelope in one hand. "I've turned in manuscripts that weighed less."

"Baylor, tell me you'll look after things and that you won't just run back to the mainland in the middle of the night, at least not before warning me."

"Okay. No promises about staying, though. I'll go there tonight, but if the house turns out to be haunted or anything at all weird happens—"

"Baylor, you've got to give that imagination of yours a rest. What could possibly go wrong?"

Chapter
2

"Okay," the small brunette began as she closed the door to Hobie's private office, "tell me everything and don't skip over the juicy bits."

Hobie laughed at her assistant. Laura had made it her personal mission in life to see Hobie involved with someone...anyone. When Hobie had confided that she had an incredibly romantic experience in Chicago, Laura was ecstatic.

She and Hobie had been friends for years. The wisecracking young woman hadn't been born on the island, but when her parents retired, they had moved to Ana Lia. As soon as Laura finished college, she made the island her permanent home, too. When Hobie had first started her practice, Laura showed up at the door waiting to be hired. They had been best friends ever since.

"Trust me. It's not that juicy," Hobie replied before relating the story.

"I can't believe you were just gonna throw her out. Tall, dark, and gorgeous just doesn't come along every day. What were you thinking?"

"I don't know." Hobie removed the wire-rimmed glasses that were always slipping down her nose. "All those years of Catholic school, I guess. The words 'Whore of Babylon' kept running through my mind."

Laura laughed so hard she almost lost her seat. Eventually she wiped the tears from her eyes and looked at her friend. "Hobie Lynn, you have got to loosen up, girl."

"I know. I'm hopeless, aren't I?"

"Nah. Hopeless would have been never kissing her in the first place," Laura answered with a wink. "Did you sleep in the same bed with her?"

"Well, at $250 a night, I wasn't about to sleep in the bathtub. When I checked out, she was still snoring away. Besides, I think she was lying about who she was."

"Why do you say that?"

"I looked her name up in every online book database I know. There isn't one listing for a BJ Warren."

"Figures. The cuties are usually jerks."

Hobie smiled and looked at the ball of fur snuggled into a wicker basket on the corner of her desk. The only contrast to the snow-white fur was a coal black nose and two equally dark eyes. Hobie scratched under the dog's chin. "Not all the cuties are bad, are they?"

A knock on the main door to the office caused both women to look at their watches. "Is Cheryl coming in to work today?" Hobie asked.

"Yeah, but not till eleven. Must be a patient. They're starting early today," Laura replied.

They both rose and walked into the large waiting room. Laura lifted the shade covering the glass door to reveal an elderly woman, her arms loaded with flyers.

"Good morning, dears." The woman dabbed at her watery eyes with a dainty handkerchief.

"Are you feeling ill, Mrs. Emberly?" Hobie asked.

"Only sick of heart, my dear. I lost my dear Petey."

Laura and Hobie exchanged a look. Petey was the old woman's toy poodle and her only companion since her husband had passed away. Petey, however, had lived long past his prime. He was nineteen years old, blind and deaf, had lost one leg to cancer, and was missing most of his tail due to a neighborhood Doberman who thought the poodle would make a good snack. Petey wasn't much in the frisky department, but he was a first-rate companion to the elderly woman. His sole job in life was to lie on a pillow next to her and wag his nonexistent tail when petted. Since he had never appeared in any obvious pain or distress, no one had ever mentioned that perhaps Mrs. Emberly might want to consider sending Petey to that big doghouse in the sky. It was no surprise to either of the younger women that Petey had finally died.

"I'm so sorry, Mrs. Emberly. You should have called me," Hobie said.

"Well, dear, I did have some of the neighbors helping already. Besides, I am confident he will return."

Mrs. Emberly fancied herself something of an amateur medium. She swore that she could communicate with the dead. On occasion, she came up with the oddest statements, which she said she received directly from those who existed on "the other side." Once, she told Hobie that Winston Churchill was madder than a wet hen because FDR died owing him ten pounds. Those were the days when Hobie nodded and prayed that her own death would take her before senility did. There were times, however, when Mrs. Emberly knew things that would have been nearly impossible to know unless she *had* communicated with someone who had passed.

Hobie, who had lived on the island long enough to know better, never discounted anyone's beliefs. She was an islander, and islanders had seen the strange and the impossible occur on Ana Lia. If Mrs. Emberly said she talked to the dead, then by gosh, that's what her neighbors believed. Everything had its limits, of course, and that included Hobie's gullibility.

Laura and Hobie chanced another glance at one another. They silently negotiated who would ask the inevitable question. Hobie could see that she had lost the coin toss.

"Return?" was all Hobie risked asking.

"Well, of course. You do think there's a chance, don't you?" The old woman looked so pitiful that Hobie and Laura instantly felt guilty over their desire to call the welcome wagon driven by the men wearing white coats.

"Well..." Hobie drew out the word, praying that some words of comfort and wisdom would come to her.

"Oh, I know what you doctors are trained to say, Hobie Lynn. Never give false hope. I understand, dear. That's why I thought I'd ask if you would mind if I put one of these flyers in your office window. In case anyone sees the poor dear just wandering around."

"Flyers?" Laura took the piece of paper from the old woman. Hobie could see that her friend was going to burst into laughter at any moment. "In case Petey...comes back?" Laura asked in disbelief.

"Why yes, dear. This is how it's done, isn't it?"

Suddenly Hobie had a very strange feeling. As if something was right in front of her, but she had been missing it the whole time. It hit her between the eyes just as Laura opened her mouth.

"Actually, Mrs. Emberly—" Laura began.

"Mrs. Emberly, when you say you lost Petey, do you mean that he wandered away?"

"Of course, dear. Whatever did you think I meant?"

"Well, we thought—" Laura started.

"Exactly the same thing!" Hobie quickly interjected. "We'd be happy to put this out front, and I'll keep my eyes open when I go out on house calls."

The old woman closed the door only seconds before Hobie and Laura burst into laughter. "Oh my God," Laura spoke through her laughter. "I thought she meant—"

"Me too!" Hobie laughed. "I got a flash of Petey returning from the dead like something in a bad horror flick."

The old-fashioned bell above the door jingled as the first patients of the day entered the office. "Well, enough fun for one morning, let's get to it," Hobie said.

"You got it, boss. Hey, remember, it's your turn to go get lunch at the Cove today."

"I never forget about lunch." Hobie winked at her friend and the two started their workday.

BJ placed the paper sack of groceries in the back seat of the open convertible. She felt like she was in a time warp of some sort. The narrow main street, along with the rest of downtown Ana Lia, was a nearly exact replica of the fictional town of Mayberry. The one and only stoplight threw her, though. She looked down the street and saw two or three cars quite a distance away, slowly making their way down the crisscrossing and complicated pattern of streets.

"The founding fathers obviously didn't know what a right angle was," BJ grumbled to herself.

A moment later, she lifted her head to a tantalizing odor in the air. She spied the small bakery across the street.

Preparing to cross the street, BJ looked up at the sign that glared accusingly down at her. She was fifteen feet or so from the intersection and the sign reminded her that there was no jaywalking or crossing against the light. "Are they kidding?" She looked down the deserted street. "I haven't seen a sign like that since I was in the third grade."

BJ shook her head as she stepped off the curb. "Yeah, right," she commented to the sign.

Hobie pushed her glasses up the bridge of her nose one more time as she steered the old pickup with her other hand. She downshifted as she approached the turn onto Main Street. Her mind roamed and she wondered if she had told JoJo at the diner to double her order of fries.

After a quick glance at the green right turn arrow, Hobie turned the wheel. Once more, she pushed her glasses firmly up the bridge of her nose. The sunlight blinded her for a split second and she blinked. At the sight of someone in the middle of the street she brought both feet down hard on the brake.

Hobie felt that all action suddenly shifted into an odd mix of real time and slow motion, a lot like a moviemaker's special effect. She heard the squeal of her brakes as the truck's tires worked hard to grab at the dry pavement. Thinking about it later, she decided that what she saw in the middle of that street was simply the product of a libido too long denied. In one instant, Hobie knew that whatever happened after that moment would set the tone for the rest of her life. She had no idea how or why she knew, only that it was a certainty.

A dark head snapped around and flashed startled gray eyes toward the oncoming truck. The glare of the sunlight reflected neatly off Hobie's glasses, nearly blinding BJ.

The battered white pickup screeched to a halt scant inches before making contact with the tall woman, which wouldn't have been a bad thing if Hobie had her foot on the clutch. However, she still had both feet on the brake, and when the truck stalled it jerked forward, hitting the tall woman in the hip.

"Oh my God!" Hobie cried out as she set the brake and jumped from the vehicle. "Oh my God!" she repeated when she looked down at BJ Warren's unconscious body.

George and Maggie, the owners of the local grocery, were the first to hear the commotion. They stood on the sidewalk outside their store, unsure of what to do.

"Call Mack!" Hobie shouted to the couple. George disappeared inside the store at once.

"God, please," Hobie begged. "Please do not let me have killed her." She kneeled beside the dark-haired woman and located a strong pulse in her carotid artery. The tall woman's right leg lay folded underneath her body. Hobie immediately diagnosed the break by glancing at the odd angle of the ankle.

"I can't believe it. I just can't believe it! Is there someone out to get me in life?" Hobie cried out. She could already hear Mack's siren.

In the meantime, Maggie came over and reassuringly stroked the redhead's back. "It's okay, Hobie Lynn. It wasn't your fault. She was crossing against the light. Mainlanders...they never learn."

Hobie nodded at the compassionate words. Maggie had no way of knowing that Hobie already knew the tall stranger. Neither did the grocer have any idea what was going through the redhead's mind at that moment.

This figures. The only woman that I've been attracted to in the last ten years and I go and run her over. God, I have a feeling this is going to be a very long day.

Hobie meticulously scrubbed her hands. She lost herself to her thoughts as she squeezed more Betadine soap into her palm. She added items to the to-do list in her head. She didn't want to call her insurance agent...again. Her auto insurance premiums had increased three times in two years, and adding this incident certainly wouldn't help.

She knew that she had the right of way, but considering that she and the woman lying in the next room had a sort of a past, she would offer to pay for any expenses. Hobie hated dipping into the trust fund her father had set up for her, but she hadn't touched it since paying off her student loans, so she figured she was entitled.

"We're ready for you, Doctor," Cheryl said.

Hobie jumped at the sound. She really had to calm down. "I'll be right in." Doc Elston wouldn't have asked her to step in and set BJ's leg if it hadn't been a clean break and easily reduced. Hobie smiled, thinking that the doc simply didn't want to cut short his vacation. It was a textbook procedure and there was a part of her that always enjoyed this aspect of medicine, stepping in to help someone.

Her brow furrowed as she wondered how she would explain to BJ exactly what had happened. Her stomach twisted into an even tighter knot as she thought of who BJ was. *How could she be Evelyn's granddaughter? God, how could you do this to me?*

The butterflies started another aerial attack in her stomach as Hobie entered the small surgery area of her office and saw BJ's unconscious form lying on a table. She had given her an injection, and BJ had fallen asleep almost immediately.

Hobie's hands uncharacteristically shook. She thought again of what had gone on in Chicago and how she would introduce herself to BJ when she awoke. She shook her head to dispel the negative energy. *Just suck it up and do your job. You've got a patient here who needs you.* That was all it took to bring her focus back onto the situation before her. She took a deep breath and began.

"I'm all finished here...Is she coming out of it yet?...Okay, don't rush her...Lor, let me see that x-ray one more time...be careful of that hip...no, but she has a pretty nasty bruise there..."

BJ heard the soft voice of the woman from the hotel. *Who is she talking to, and why are there other people in the hotel room with us? I remember that spicy, subtle scent of her perfume...God, how good she felt in my arms.*

The perfume disappeared as a harsh antiseptic odor took its place. *Where in the hell am I?* An older, feminine-sounding voice replaced the gentle one in BJ's mind.

"Baylor? Baylor? Wake up for us now."

"Don't call me Baylor," BJ rasped, and then coughed.

"Here, hon. Take a sip." BJ felt a straw placed between her lips and she drank the cool liquid greedily.

"Not too much, Cheryl. Let's make sure she's back from never-never land first," Hobie whispered over the older woman's shoulder. "Try calling her BJ."

"BJ, open your eyes," Cheryl instructed.

BJ did as the voice asked, mainly to find out what kind of dream she was having. As soon as she did, she was sorry. It was as if light and her ability to feel pain were connected. The day's events came rushing into her conscious mind as quickly as the pain registered with her brain.

"Oh God!" she groaned.

"Shouldn't she have something more for pain, Doctor?" Cheryl turned to ask.

"Not yet. The shot is going to have to hold her for a bit. Lor, call Mack and tell him she's awake." Hobie turned back to Cheryl. "I don't want to drug her up any more until we know exactly what we're going to do with her."

"Where in the hell am I?" BJ called out.

Cheryl was the first to answer. "You had an accident and broke your ankle. The doctor set and cast it for you. You'll still be a little groggy from the anesthetic. We didn't give you any more than you'd have for a tooth extraction, but the doctor figured you'd be more comfortable that way. Everything is just fine now."

"I consider that a matter of opinion," BJ responded. She leaned up on one elbow and looked down at the white plaster monstrosity attached to her leg up to mid-thigh. "So, who is this Dr. Kildare who set my leg?"

Hobie knew it was now or never. She stepped forward into BJ's line of sight. "Um, that would be me."

BJ furrowed her brow. The woman looked familiar. "And you are?"

Hobie wasn't sure what she was expecting, but it certainly wasn't that. The question took her by complete surprise. In one hurried epiphany, Hobie understood she'd been granted her reprieve. The writer no more recalled Hobie than she remembered how many vodka gimlets she drank that night in Chicago. That realization didn't exactly make Hobie happy. It should have, but at the same time, she was a little miffed, vacillating between profound thankfulness for her continued anonymity and righteous indignation for being so absolutely forgettable to BJ Warren.

"Oh, I'm sorry," Hobie answered once she realized that BJ was staring at her in a very unamused fashion. "Hobie Allen. Look, I'm so sorry for—"

"So, doc, besides being in complete agony, what's the damage here?" BJ groaned, not having grasped what Hobie was trying to say.

"Well, you broke your ankle. I set and casted it."

"Gee, can you try not to throw so much technical jargon at me all at once?"

Hobie arched an eyebrow at the woman. "All right. Technically, you suffered an oblique fracture of your fibula with the dislocation of the foot. It's commonly called a Pott's fracture. It's a very common injury; as a matter of fact, it's one of the most frequently injured areas of the ankle joint. It was rather textbook, actually. About three inches from the ankle, you had a fracture to the fibula. In addition, the medial malleolus was broken off, but luckily the end of the tibia was not displaced from the corresponding surface of the talus. At the same time, the foot was everted and the muscles in the calf drew up the heel. I repositioned the foot by flexing the leg at right angles with the thigh, which relaxes all the opposing muscles, and by making extension from the ankle and counter-extension at the knee."

BJ leaned on one elbow and stared in silence for a few seconds. "You know, nobody likes a show-off."

"Sorry." Hobie tried not to smile. She attempted to come up with a plausible explanation for what had happened and how she had been involved. She was growing sick at her stomach from the worry and decided to just tell BJ the truth. Unfortunately, before she could come up with a sparkling and witty way to put it, the matter was pushed into the light by her patient.

"You look familiar. Where did you graduate from, anyway?" BJ grumbled.

"Where did I what?" The question took Hobie by surprise. She'd been so focused on explaining the circumstances of the accident that she wasn't sure she'd heard correctly.

"You're not going to say you didn't graduate, are you?" BJ managed a smirk, even though the pain in her ankle had most of her attention.

"Of course not. I happen to be a fully licensed physician. But—"

"No, don't say but. See, whenever there's a but, there's bad news afterward."

"Well, it's not like that, but—"

"See, there's that word again."

"Okay, let me take another route with this." Hobie rubbed her sweaty palms along her rough cotton scrub pants. She knew exactly why she was so nervous. Breaking the news to this woman was going to cause fireworks. Hobie just knew it. She would tell BJ that she had been responsible for hitting her, then the brunette would tell her grandmother, and then Hobie's medical license wouldn't be worth a nickel.

"You are a doctor, right?"

"Yes, I'm a very good doctor." Hobie wondered if she sounded as defensive to everyone else in the room as she did to herself.

Cheryl and Laura exchanged glances with Hobie. Laura shrugged as if to say she couldn't understand why their patient was so obsessed with Hobie's credentials.

"You see, in a way, I'm actually two doctors." Hobie smiled and was just about to make the jest she used with all of her patients.

"In a way? Like in the 'I went to medical school and graduated' way? Or the 'I got my degree out of a box of cereal' way?"

At that moment an ear-splitting squeal pierced the air. It was quite evident that the howl wasn't human. The sound came from the outer waiting room and left all four women in the surgery area in total silence.

"What the fuck was that?" BJ cried out. She shook her head as if the anesthesia still held her in its grasp. The squeal had sounded exactly like a pig.

"Don't worry, that's just our next patient," Cheryl replied.

It wasn't until that very moment that Hobie realized BJ had no idea what kind of a doctor she was. Hobie took it for granted that everyone knew. When she raised her eyes, BJ Warren was staring daggers at her. Hobie cringed. She could see her life falling apart in front of her.

The dark-haired woman took in her surroundings as if for the first time. "Why don't you tell me what's going on here," she said.

"I know this is going to sound a little strange. I am a doctor. Actually, I'm an MD and—"

"Where is your diploma?" BJ asked in a cold, flat voice.

Hobie was proud of that diploma, but at that very moment, words failed her. She could only raise one finger to point to the wall behind the prone woman.

BJ craned her neck and read the framed document aloud. "Yadda, yadda...certifies that Hobie Lynn Allen...Veterinary Medicine...University of Flor—"

Hobie froze. She wished at that moment for an earthquake, a

tidal wave, or any other sort of natural disaster. She wanted nothing more than for the earth to swallow her whole and spit out the
bad parts. When BJ turned back to face Hobie, the redhead swore
she was looking into the face of a stranger. This woman's angry
gaze looked nothing at all like the sparkling gray bedroom eyes
Hobie had been lost in only a day and a half ago.

"Veterinary medicine?" BJ's voice sounded strained yet controlled as she spoke the words.

Hobie finally propelled herself into action. Actually, it was a
lot more like backpedaling and groveling. "Okay, see, that's
what—"

"You're a vet?"

The women in the office could hear the restrained voice
beginning to shred at the edges.

"Technically, yes. But not just a vet. I—"

"A doctor for *animals?*" BJ's voice rose in volume and pitch.
It was apparent the control was showing minute ruptures.

"Well, I wouldn't—"

"A vet!" BJ shouted as any semblance of self-control ripped
wide open and disappeared completely.

Hobie had been trying to get a word in edgewise, but BJ
wouldn't give her a chance to explain. Most people were
impressed once she told them that she'd gone to medical school
and then, years later, studied veterinary medicine. Somehow
Hobie didn't picture BJ being impressed at all.

"Would you quit saying that like it's some sort of crime!"
Hobie finally shouted back.

"Crime? You people wouldn't know a crime if it came up and
bit you on the ass! A fucking vet just set my leg! That's got to be
breaking at least a dozen laws!"

"Let me explain—"

"You can explain to my lawyer!" BJ raved. Her leg slipped off
the sandbags that held it in place and she groaned in pain.

Hobie rushed forward to assist. "Here, let me—"

"Don't touch me! Don't you dare touch me!"

It was about this time that Mack, the local sheriff, walked
into the room. "What the hell is going on back here?" He was a
tall, broad-shouldered man with light brown hair that was speck-
led through with silver, blue eyes, and a physique that strained
against the tailored uniform he wore. He sported a large, well-
trimmed mustache. For all his good looks, he was perhaps the last
one to know. His gentle smile and never-ending supply of wisdom
suited him well for a job in law enforcement. His patience and
sense of humor, however, made him the perfect sheriff for Ana Lia

Island.

"Officer, arrest them." BJ pointed to Hobie and her assistants.

"All of them?" Mack asked in confusion.

"Every last one of them. They're all in on it, but especially her!" BJ looked menacingly at Hobie.

"Her, eh?" Mack's mustache covered up most of his amused smile. "Hobie Lynn?" He looked down at the much shorter woman.

"Mack," Hobie responded dejectedly. Her day had started out so well. She wondered how it had gone so wrong so fast. She didn't know whether to worry over her soon-to-skyrocket insurance rates, cry over the fact that BJ had found her thoroughly forgettable, or scream at the woman's infuriating superior attitude.

"Well, are you going to arrest her?"

"What would you have me arrest her for, Ms. Warren?"

"What for?" BJ shouted. "Look, Gomer, she performed a medical procedure without my consent and to top it off, she's not even a doctor! What the hell do I have to do, draw you a map?"

Mack took a deep breath. He had already spoken with Evelyn and he knew all about Baylor's infamous temper and outspoken attitude. Evelyn called her granddaughter "high-strung." Mack thought the old woman was being kind. He remembered BJ as simply a spoiled, self-centered young girl.

"First off, Ms. Warren, you were not treated without consent. Hobie got a verbal consent from a..." he flipped open a small black notebook, "a Juliana Ross."

"How did you find Jules?"

"Her card was in your wallet." Hobie stepped up to the gurney and held out the irate woman's billfold.

"You went through my wallet?" BJ asked coldly.

Hobie realized that this probably wasn't the best time to mention that fact. "Well, I, um...I guess..."

Mack stepped over and placed a hand on each of Hobie's arms. He gently pushed her back a step to stand with the others. "Don't help any more, okay?"

"She's not a real doctor!" BJ finally blurted out.

"On the contrary, Ms. Warren. Hobie is a licensed physician in the state of Florida." Mack's low gravelly voice had a way of making everything he said sound as though he was talking someone off a high ledge.

"But she—I saw—" BJ finally pointed to the University of Florida diploma hanging on the wall.

"That's right. She's also a doctor of veterinary medicine. She doesn't regularly treat patients, except for her animal practice. In an emergency, though, she always steps up and gives us a hand. Doc Elston, the regular town physician, is on vacation. It was on his recommendation that Hobie set your leg. He said something about healing time and pain. So, you probably should be thankin' these people and not screamin' at them."

Everyone had been lulled into silence by the sheriff's soothing voice. Hobie had known the man all her life and she couldn't ever remember him stringing that many words together at one time. BJ, on the other hand, looked as though the top of her head was going to explode. Hobie could literally hear the words "thar she blows" in the back of her mind.

"You—" BJ raised a finger to the sheriff and met his frank gaze. "She—" The dark-haired woman pointed to Hobie. "They—" BJ didn't even know where to begin with her accusations.

Hobie retrieved her wire-frame glasses from her scrub shirt pocket and put them on. As soon as she looked up, the sun, which was shining in through a west-facing window, reflected off the lenses and directly into BJ's eyes.

The dark-haired woman remembered that she'd seen the exact same image right before the truck had hit her at the intersection. Hobie's eyes met BJ's and the dark-haired woman froze.

"Y-You! It was you. I remember you now!"

Hobie realized that the game was up. BJ had finally remembered that she was the woman from the hotel room. "Yes, it was me," she admitted in defeat. *Honestly, how long did I think I could hide it from her?*

"Arrest her!" BJ cried out again.

"I don't think they can arrest people for that," Hobie responded in a soft, confused voice.

"Do your job, arrest her."

"What for this time?" Mack looked as confused as everyone else.

"She's the one who ran me over!"

Hobie didn't know whether she should be relieved or frightened. BJ appeared so full of righteous anger that she looked like she was having a breakdown.

"Yes, Ms. Warren, she did hit you with her truck, but there's not really anything I can arrest her for."

"Nothing? What kind of town is this? A fine. She should at least pay a fine."

"What kind of fine?" Mack chuckled and Hobie glared at him for egging the dark-haired woman on. BJ was so intent on Hobie's punishment that she hadn't noticed the sheriff was patronizing her.

"Hundreds...thousands of dollars!" Everyone in the room could see that BJ was losing it.

"Now wait just a minute here—" Hobie stepped forward to defend herself. Her understanding and compassion for her patient had come to an abrupt halt.

"Well, let's take a look at this, Ms. Warren. First, you want me to arrest the woman who, on her own time, fixed your leg up so it would heal properly. The woman whose insurance is paying for all your medical bills. You want *me* to fine *her?*"

BJ looked around the room and knew she was getting a bit out of hand. She could see herself as if she were standing off in a corner of the room watching the whole scenario. She could see herself acting like a complete ass, but was powerless to stop her actions. How could so many bad things happen to one person in so short a space of time? *Dear God, is it still Monday?*

"Surely the police force knows how to write out a ticket here in Mayberry?" BJ sneered. In her defense, her ankle was really beginning to hurt and she just wanted to go home and sleep. "You do give tickets here, don't you?"

Hobie winced at the biting remarks and wondered how she could have possibly been attracted to this arrogant woman. She found it almost impossible to believe this was Evelyn's granddaughter. She watched Mack to see how he would handle this attack on his reputation. As always, the man was unflappable.

"Well now, Ms. Warren, that's the first sensible thing that you've said today. I think a ticket is definitely in order. Since I didn't witness the incident, I'm going to go on the evidence I have." Mack reached around to the small of his back and pulled a short, thick binder from where he kept it tucked into his duty belt. He walked over to Hobie, flipped open the book, and extracted a ticket that he had written earlier.

"Hobie Lynn." He handed her the citation. Hobie opened her mouth to disagree, but the sheriff stopped her. "And don't even try to argue. You had the right of way and couldn't have stopped the accident, but she's a pedestrian and you, above everyone else, know the law."

Hobie closed her mouth. She hated it when Mack was right, especially since he so often was. She stuffed the ticket in her pocket and folded her arms across her chest. BJ Warren looked exactly like the proverbial cat after the untimely demise of the canary. Hobie had an intense desire to go over and smack the self-satisfied expression off her face. She had no idea where that feeling came from. She was such a passive, nonviolent person. *Who*

*am I kidding? This woman could make Christ himself come down
from the cross just to smack her one.*

Mack returned to BJ's gurney and pulled out another ticket.
"This one is for you, Ms. Warren."

"Wha—" BJ stared in dumb silence at the slip of paper in her
hand. Everyone in the room knew it was the calm before the
storm.

"I think I better go reschedule some of those patients," Laura
said as she slipped out the door.

Hobie noticed that Cheryl was quick to sneak out as well.
Cowards! she thought.

"Are you insane!" BJ's voice carried all the way out onto
Main Street. "She tries to kill me...vehicular manslaughter, and
you give *me* a ticket for reckless endangerment? I was crossing the
street, for God's sake, and she came barreling—"

"She had the right of way," Mack interrupted. "Ms. Warren,
there's a reason why there is no jaywalking, which you *were* guilty
of, and why there is a stoplight at that intersection. It's a blind
corner. The light turns red for cars in the left lane, but cars in the
right lane have a green turn arrow. If you'd been in the crosswalk,
crossing with the light instead of against it, you wouldn't be lying
here right now. Let me tell you something else. You may not
remember me, Baylor, but I remember you. A few words of advice.
Lose the attitude and try to get along with folks while you're on
the island. If not, I'll personally escort you off Ana Lia."

After a short moment of silence, BJ squinted at the sheriff.
"Should I know you?"

"Not necessarily. I knocked you down when you were eight
years old. You made my sister cry."

They eyed one another for a few seconds more before BJ
backed down from the sheriff's unnerving gaze. "Well, we all do
goofy things when we're kids," she muttered. It was apparent that
BJ had finally run out of steam.

"Well, why don't we see about getting you home. Hobie Lynn,
is that safe?" Mack asked.

"Sure. I'll get her some pain pills and write out some instructions."

"Where are my clothes?" Baylor lifted the blanket to reveal
her attire, a hospital gown.

"Oh, um, I'm terribly sorry, but we had to cut those jeans off
you," Hobie replied.

Before BJ could start another rant, Mack stepped in. "I've got
a pair of sweatpants in the trunk of the car. You can cut off one of
the legs if you want. Don't worry, they were just washed," he

added before BJ could respond.

"Lor," Hobie called out to her assistant. A head peeked into the room. "Run over to the gift shop and get Ms. Warren a clean shirt she can wear home, okay? Tell Allison to charge it to me." Hobie turned back to BJ. "That's okay, isn't it?"

BJ arched an eyebrow. "You buy me a t-shirt and that's supposed to make it better?"

Hobie sighed. "Let's get you fixed up with some crutches."

Twenty minutes and fifty milligrams of Demerol later, BJ was dressed in Ana Lia Sheriff's Department sweatpants and a hospital gown. She had finally quit fighting Hobie and allowed the younger woman to instruct her in the art of walking with crutches. At first, BJ didn't get the idea that just because she had a cast on her leg didn't mean she could put any weight on her foot.

Hobie bit her lip and took quite a few deep breaths to keep from verbally lashing out at the tall woman's outspoken and often cutting remarks. She had learned a great deal about her patient within those twenty minutes, concluding that Baylor Joan Warren honestly had no idea that her remarks were anything other than the truth. She didn't see them as hurtful or cruel. It was as if, somewhere along the line, BJ had become convinced that she was either morally or intellectually superior to those around her. Hobie wondered if BJ had been a spoiled child or if this arrogance had been gradual in the making. She couldn't understand how one woman could feel her needs were so far above everyone else's.

Laura appeared at the door, but Hobie noticed that she hesitated to come much closer. "Um...the gift shop was closed, but the bakery was open." She fiddled with the paper sack in her hands.

BJ fixed one of her patented cold stares on the young woman. "I think wearing éclairs home may cause talk."

"Well, they had this deal. If you bought this," Laura pulled some fudge from the paper package, and BJ's mouth watered at the sight, "then you got this!" She produced a hot pink muscle tee from the sack.

No words were necessary when BJ held the garment up to her chest. Blazoned across the front in big black letters was the bakery's touristy slogan, "I was FU...dged on Ana Lia Island."

"How appropriate," BJ deadpanned in Hobie's direction.

Mack agreed to take BJ home in his squad car. Hobie dispensed enough medication to carry her through until the next day, then gave the pills to Mack and whispered a few words into his ear.

"I'll come by and check on you tomorrow, Ms. Warren. That is, if you can stand the sight of me for a few more days till the doc gets back," Hobie said.

"I'll be counting the hours." BJ winked at Hobie as Mack helped her out to the car. Hobie knew in an instant that the Demerol had worked its way into her patient's system; BJ Warren's charm was back in full force.

"Boy, you sure know how to pick 'em," Laura said. "You were right about that night. She must have been pretty smashed not to even remember you. Good thing you found out what she's really like."

"Well, I guess that little voice of mine was right this time. Dear God, she's like Jekyll and Hyde," Hobie replied. She massaged her temples to combat the slight dizziness she felt. The stress of the entire situation hadn't helped her physical condition. "How about running to the Cove and picking up some dinner? I can't go on till I get some food in me."

"Sure thing, I'll be back in a snap."

Hobie started to clean up the small surgery area. She couldn't keep from thinking about Laura's words. It was true, Hobie should have been glad that BJ didn't remember her. She should have also felt good about seeing BJ's true colors. She didn't feel good at all, though. She hadn't expected to see BJ Warren ever again. Of course, now she had no desire to spend any more time than she absolutely had to with the self-involved woman. Hobie didn't know why, but that thought made her a little sad.

"I'm not sure I feel too comfortable about leaving you to fend for yourself," Mack said. He had pulled the car into the driveway and as close to the front porch as possible. He and BJ sat there in silence for a moment. "You know, if I asked her, Hobie might come out and stay—"

"Not if I were bleeding buckets," BJ answered. "Look," she ran her fingers through her short dark hair and felt it sticking up at odd angles, "I know I'm being a little wacked, but if you piled up every bad day I've ever had, one on top of the other, they still couldn't equal what I've been through today."

"Yeah, I get it. Okay, come on. Let's get you inside."

Mack helped BJ into the house and was surprised when she didn't give him grief about making her comfortable. He figured it was the pain medicine suddenly causing her to be so agreeable. He made up the couch with a sheet and blanket and even fixed a sandwich and a hot cup of tea for her. Before he left, he placed the envelope containing her pills on the fireplace mantel.

"I was told to let you know you could take one of these after ten, but they're not to be left near where you're sleeping."

"What do they do...explode?"

"No." Mack smiled. "Hobie says when patients keep their pain meds near the bed, they wake up in the middle of the night and forget if they took one or not, so they take another. You know the rest of the story."

"Pumping out my stomach would just round this day off nicely, though. I get the picture. The cute redhead doesn't want me to take a dive, right?"

"Yeah, something like that." Mack caught the reference to Hobie, but let it go.

"Hey, Mack," BJ called out to the sheriff as he turned to leave. "What did I say to your sister to make her cry?"

"You told her she was ugly."

"Shit. Kids are so fucking stupid sometimes."

Mack just nodded and turned to go. "You get some sleep—" Before he finished, he noticed the woman was already sprawled along the couch and snoring lightly.

"Do you ever slow down?" Mack directed his question to Hobie, who was running a mop along the surgery floor.

"I can't believe you gave me a ticket!" she said without looking up.

"Hey, it's good to be king."

Hobie reached out and steadied herself with a hand against the tile wall. Her body swayed and she felt the mop handle slip through her fingers. Before she could say anything, strong arms lifted her up and carried her into the other room.

Mack gently laid the younger woman on a worn leather couch in the office. "Hobie, when's the last time you ate?"

"Um..." She struggled to remember. "Laura's gone to get something. I'll be okay, just give me a sec." She slowly sat up, then moved into her desk chair, reached into the desk drawer, and pulled out a candy bar.

"Hey!" she cried out when Mack plucked the candy from her fingers just as she was ready to take a bite. He tossed it into the garbage can before pulling a plastic bottle of milk from the small refrigerator that sat in one corner of the office.

"Mom told you a thousand times not to eat chocolate when your blood sugar bottoms out. Geez, Hob, you'd think a doctor would know better. Drink this."

Hobie chugged the entire bottle. Five minutes later she was feeling more like her old self. "Thanks," she finally said. "Did you get Miss High-and-mighty home all right?"

"Yep. She thinks you're cute."

"Oh, stop that."

"I'm not kidding. Those were her exact words."

"She was high on Demerol," Hobie said. "What?" she added in response to the sheriff's amused stare.

"Are you gonna tell me the whole story with you two or what?"

"First, there is no story. Second, there most definitely is no 'us two'!"

Mack nodded and stretched his legs, crossing them and resting his boots on the corner of Hobie's desk.

"You're not going to leave until I tell you about it, are you?"

"Nope." Mack grinned evilly.

"Why have you spent my entire life torturing me?"

"Because you're my kid sister and that's just what us big brothers do." Mack laughed as Hobie lowered her head until her forehead rested against her desk.

"This has been the longest day of my life," she groaned.

Chapter
3

Hobie peered through the front door window, past the lace curtains, and met a sight that made her smile despite what she'd been thinking about BJ Warren. The tall woman lay on the couch. Her injured leg took up more room than the old sofa had to offer. It seemed that at some point, she had moved the coffee table closer and rested her casted leg atop it.

Hobie didn't want to wake the sleeping woman so she crept back down the porch and walked around to the back of the house. She produced a gold-colored key from the front pocket of her blue jeans and let herself into the kitchen. She placed a cloth-covered basket upon the kitchen table and said, "You stay here."

She began to put away the few grocery items she had bought at the store, unsure why she continued to go the extra mile for someone who probably wouldn't appreciate it in the first place. *She'll probably wake up and shoot me for trespassing.* It was after that thought that Hobie heard the scream.

What Hobie didn't notice while she was puttering around the kitchen was the snow-white ball of fur in the basket that wriggled free from under the cloth. He appraised his surroundings as his little bottom moved back and forth at the sight of hearth and home. He silently hopped out of the basket and looked at the immense distance to the floor. He was rather small, being the runt of the litter, and it looked like a long way down. The Bichon Frise may not have been known for athletic ability, but he had a first-rate brain. The cotton-ball replica padded to the end of the table, jumped down to the chair, and safely moved on to the next level. Once on first-floor territory, he was off.

New things were lying on the living room floor. He loved new smells. After inspecting the luggage on the floor, he moved on to his new housemate. He could see that she was very big and just knew that she would have some nice soft parts against which he could snuggle. In fact, she liked to sleep just as he did. He noticed with appreciation the way the blanket and sheet were wadded up and tangled around her body. He looked longingly up at the fluffy mass of covers. The way he figured, that was his couch, and that blanket was just too inviting to resist. He carefully jumped to the coffee table and picked his way across to the couch. From there, it was just a matter of finding the softest spot. He knew he'd made a good decision as he settled on the woman's belly.

BJ now roused her mind to a semiconscious state and convinced herself that she was having an allergic reaction to the pain medication. She'd never had an allergic reaction to anything before, but the pressure on her chest was making it difficult to breathe. In all the stories she'd ever written, that was the first symptom. A few minutes later, she was fully awake and wondered why the couch was shaking. It wasn't so much the couch as it was her body. It was actually more than shaking. It was a rhythmic sort of movement, as if...

BJ opened one eye and peered down the length of her body. She didn't get far. About ten inches from her face, she ran into a pair of beady black eyes, midnight black nose, and a tiny pink tongue. The tongue moved in and out of the equally small mouth with the same rhythm BJ felt moving her body. She later blamed it on a residual effect from the pain medication, but she chose that moment to yell. More than just yell. BJ could hear herself scream like a girl.

"Aah!" BJ yelled out again when she saw a figure run into the room. She stopped when she realized it was the vet. "What the hell are you doing in here? No, don't answer that, just get this...thing...off of me!"

Hobie quickly scooped the dog off the woman's chest. Now that she knew there was no real emergency, she was trying desperately not to laugh at the prone woman. "It's just Arturo. Did he scare you?" she asked, grinning in amusement.

BJ, realizing that she'd just made a total fool of herself over a dog, quickly tried to cover her own error in identifying the small animal. "I thought it was a rat."

This time Hobie did laugh; she just couldn't help it. "You get a lot of five-pound albino rats in Chicago, do you?"

BJ fixed a cold stare in the redhead's direction. It was quickly becoming the tall woman's trademark expression. "We're lousy with 'em," she replied flatly. "Look, what in the hell are you— Whoa!"

BJ had turned her body to look up at the standing woman and suddenly felt the coffee table sliding away from the couch—with her injured leg still on it. She tried to pull back, but the blanket wrapped around her legs prevented proper movement. It only took another five seconds for her to end up face down on the carpeted floor.

"Oh my God!" Hobie let go of Arturo and bent down to help.

"Shit, that hurt," BJ said. Attempting to rise, she felt the crown of her head connect sharply with the underside of the coffee table. Once more, she sank to the floor and groaned.

"Geez, you're going to kill yourself. Let me help you."

"Don't touch me! Please, just don't touch me."

BJ rolled over and lay there. She looked up at the vet with an expression similar to amazement. "You *look* so normal, but you're really the harbinger of doom. Are you an assassin? I mean, did someone put a hit out on me or something? And maybe they requested it to be a slow, torturous death?"

"I'm really so sorry." Hobie wasn't sure why she was apologizing, but it seemed the thing to do.

"Why are you trying to kill me?" BJ asked in a small, defeated voice.

"Really, I'm doing no such thing. I can't explain it," Hobie said with a sympathetic smile. "At least let me help you up."

"No! No, please don't help me." BJ started to get up on her own. "Frankly, I don't think my body can take any more help from you."

Hobie only felt worse at seeing the tall woman struggle to a seated position on the sofa. It did indeed seem as though BJ's physical well-being was in danger whenever Hobie came near her. She walked out of the room and returned a moment later with a steaming mug.

"Do you drink coffee?"

"Thank God!" BJ accepted it eagerly.

"I'll take that as a yes and thank you."

BJ paused before taking a sip, the mug inches away from her lips. "Aren't you having any?" She glanced up at Hobie suspiciously.

"Oh, for crying out loud. Here." Hobie grabbed the mug. She raised it to her mouth and took a healthy swallow. "See, no arsenic or anything." She handed the mug back.

BJ silently stared into the black liquid.

Hobie thought the woman was actually pouting. "Now what?" she asked.

"Well, it's got your germs all over it now."

"Will you just let it go already?"

"Hey, I haven't completely given up the assassin theory yet."

"Good Lord, you're worse than my—" Hobie stopped

abruptly.

"Who? Worse than who?"

"Never mind." Hobie left the room and returned with a fresh cup of coffee.

BJ cautiously sniffed it before taking a small sip.

"Are you always this paranoid?" Hobie asked.

"You have the nerve to ask me that after what you've put me through in the last twenty-four hours?"

"What—I've—Okay, stop!" Hobie ran the fingers of both hands through her short auburn hair. She struggled to control her own temper. She had always thought of herself as a quiet and reasonable woman, but BJ's whole attitude seemed to awaken every quarrelsome bone in her body. "We can do this, I know we can."

"Do what?" BJ asked in confusion.

"Be nice to each other!" Hobie nearly shouted in exasperation.

"Maybe you should begin first, considering you're the one who ran me over yesterday."

Hobie placed one hand on her hip and held back her harsh reply. She took a deep breath and then spoke. "Okay, maybe nice is too much to hope for. How about we shoot for civil? Surely we can both manage that."

BJ sat there with her arms folded across her chest, apparently mulling over the request, but not at all convinced of the other woman's sincerity.

"Look—"

"I'll try," BJ said at last.

"Oh. All right then," Hobie replied. "See, this isn't so bad."

BJ arched an eyebrow.

"Well, it's a start, anyway. Why don't you let me look at your leg? How does it feel?"

"It hurts like hell."

"You need to get some food into your stomach and you can take a pain pill. I picked up a few basic groceries, all poison free." Hobie ignored the dark-haired woman's smirk. "I didn't get much, but if you give me a list, I can pick up anything you need."

"No offense, but I'd rather do it myself. Oh man, my Jag."

"Mack brought it over early this morning. It's in the driveway." Hobie examined BJ's leg as she spoke, noting that the swelling had lessened considerably. "Can I ask a question?"

"Can I stop you? Okay, okay, don't blow a gasket," BJ said in response to Hobie's look of exasperation. "What?"

"How do you plan on driving that car with this thing on?" Hobie gave the plaster cast a gentle tap.

BJ stared down at her leg. "Shit."

"I'm obligated to tell you that not only is it dangerous to try it, it's also illegal."

"I bet you brush after every meal too, don't you?"

"All I'm saying is—"

"I know, I know. Damn, I have to get around. I'll go insane stuck in this place. I have to see my grandmother, and I need clothes. Preferably, ones I can cut one leg off without too much trouble. I wonder what Jules is up to? I know. I'll call a cab."

Hobie shook her head in reply.

"Let me guess. There are no taxi services on the island."

"That's right."

"Bus, shuttle, golf cart?"

"Nope, not one. Guess I'm looking a little more indispensable than you thought, huh?" Hobie teased while wearing a mile-wide grin.

"Do not push your luck." BJ's acidic reply quickly wiped the smile from Hobie's face.

"Sorry, I didn't mean to gloat."

"Sure you did, but I guess I can't blame you. It's what I would have done."

"That's reassuring," Hobie replied. "Okay, before we get into it again..." She saw BJ gearing up for another acerbic reply and quickly headed her off. "I don't open the office till one o'clock on Tuesdays. Why don't I take you to town? I can show you where to shop so the locals won't think you're a tourist, but first stop will be Rebecca's Cove to get you some breakfast."

BJ didn't answer, but just kept staring at the small redhead. Finally, she asked a question that Hobie didn't expect. "Are you doing all this for me because you feel guilty or what?"

The direct question took Hobie by surprise. "Actually, I'd like to think I'm just that kind of a person, but I admit, I do feel somewhat responsible for your present condition."

BJ didn't know what to make of the woman. Her first reaction was one of skepticism. She had always been a consummate cynic, but she knew that no one could be as sweet and unassuming as Hobie. BJ decided the woman was either a practiced liar or clinically insane. She wondered about being alone with her, but didn't have much choice. *I have to get off this island...soon!*

"All right, you're on," BJ responded uneasily.

By the time the two women started on their way, Hobie began to think their uneasy alliance just might work. BJ had refused any help in getting herself cleaned up, although Hobie did teach her the trick of tying a garbage bag around her cast in order to take a quick shower. The dark-haired woman now wore a faded "No Lights in Wrigleyville" t-shirt and Mack's sweatpants.

"You're a Cubs fan?" BJ asked in surprise as Hobie placed the blue felt cap with its red *C* on her head.

They had just walked out of the house and Hobie knew what was coming next. She had taken grief most of her life for her undying loyalty to her favorite, albeit consistently losing, baseball team. "Is that a problem?"

"Hey, not with me. I just thought us Chicagoans were the only gluttons for punishment."

"Well, I guess it goes to show you there's no accounting for taste and that the Midwest doesn't hold the patent on masochism."

"Touché."

"Your car or mine?" Hobie asked as they came to the driveway. "I'd be happy to drive your Jaguar."

"I'll just bet you would. No way. You know how much they hit me up for insurance to rent this thing? Even the surcharges had surcharges. Besides, I've seen the way you drive. Close up, remember?"

"Very funny. Then it's the truck." Hobie tried to hide her disappointment.

"Ah, the deathmobile," BJ remarked as they came closer to the white Ford truck. She pretended to pay no attention to Hobie sticking out her tongue at the comment.

Hobie pulled open the driver's door and immediately began to pick up some garbage and brush off the seat. "It's a little messy, I admit. I usually try to have it cleaned before I go anywhere, but spring is my busy season."

BJ stared into the open window on the passenger side. Animal hair, leaves, twigs, and dirt covered the cab. She picked up something that looked like a tuft of cotton from the seat.

"What the hell was in here last?"

"Um...sheep."

BJ looked through the window at Hobie, who was standing on the other side of the truck. No words were necessary during the long, painful seconds that BJ glared at Hobie.

"Come on, Dr. Doolittle, we're takin' the Jag."

"You are the angel of death; you know that, don't you? I have never had so many terrible things happen to me in such a short space of time. Are you sure your last name isn't Mengele?"

BJ folded her arms against her chest and leaned against the

red Jaguar. She glared down at Hobie, who was kneeling on the ground.

"Oh, for God's sake, it's only a tire and it wasn't even my fault," Hobie snapped. She was hot, and having to justify her driving skills to BJ Warren was more than she could take. "It was a nail. I'm sorry, but these are just normal glasses. I forgot to wear my amazing vision glasses so I could see a roofing nail in the middle of the road."

It dumbfounded Hobie that she had gone thirty-eight years without wishing grievous harm to anyone, but one hour with BJ Warren and Hobie wanted to throttle the woman. "I can't believe you don't know how to change a tire," she said.

"I didn't say I didn't know how. I simply said that I *don't* change tires."

Hobie paused long enough to glare at the tall woman. She didn't understand what happened next. She certainly didn't know why. Everything seemed to catch up to her at once. She tried to tell herself that she was hot and grumpy from changing the tire and that she hadn't eaten breakfast yet. She reasoned that the past twenty-four hours and running into BJ again—literally—had been a chaotic mixture of delight and irritation. No matter how Hobie tried to rationalize her next action, the simple fact was that she threw the tire iron to the ground and began to cry.

Almost instantaneously, BJ looked as though she'd been thrown into a tank full of sharks. An expression like panic settled on her face. "Wha—what are you doing?"

"I'm crying, okay? Is that all right with you?"

"No, it's not all right...stop it," BJ requested softly. "Please. Come on, stop," she pleaded.

"Why the hell do you care if I cry?"

"Because I don't like it when women cry," BJ answered. She inched herself forward, leaning on the car for support, then reached out and barely touched Hobie's shoulder. "I especially don't like it when I'm the one that's responsible. Look, I know I can be...difficult."

That little declaration seemed to make all the difference to Hobie. Just a few tender words and her tears instantly quieted. She thought twice about what she had heard, thinking that maybe her ears had been playing tricks on her. The BJ Warren that Hobie knew was not the kind of woman to apologize—to anyone. Hobie wiped her cheek with the back of one hand and looked up. She had never seen a more contrite expression.

"Okay," BJ said. "I can be more than difficult. I can be a bitch some of the time; I know that. I really didn't mean to make you cry, though."

For Hobie, in that one instant, BJ Warren became human. She could be bitchy, annoying, and selfish, but in that small space of time, she had displayed her own human frailty. There was also her awareness of her own actions. For the first time since she'd met BJ, Hobie wondered if the tall woman's behavior wasn't simply masking her own insecurities. "Thanks," she said. "That helps more than you know."

"So, you're done now? I mean, you're okay?" BJ asked, although she couldn't make herself look at Hobie.

"Yeah." Hobie wiped her eyes with a tissue from her pocket. "I'm done." She picked up the tire iron once more and tightened the last nut. She stood up and replaced the tools in the car's small trunk. "Don't worry. It's probably just PMS. I'm about two days from my period."

"Okay, TMI, TMI."

"Huh?"

"Too much information. I mean, I'm sorry and all, but I don't want to know any more than that."

"Sorry. I didn't know you had such a weak constitution."

Hobie smiled weakly and BJ breathed a small sigh of relief. "Are we ready then?" she asked.

Hobie nodded. She was a little more than embarrassed at her sudden, and unexpected, tears, but she was also stunned at BJ's reaction. The tall woman had gone from arrogant to groveling in a matter of seconds. *So, tears are your kryptonite, eh? You are so lucky I'm not manipulative.* She smiled to herself as she realized that some day, someone would come along and capitalize on BJ's secret weakness.

"I wish you would have let me call the auto club to change that," BJ said as they got into the car.

"Are you kidding? And have Bubba from the mainland go back and tell all his buddies that he had to change a tire for some helpless woman on Ana Lia? Come on, when you're healthy you do this kind of stuff, right?"

"What kind of stuff?"

"This—change a tire, the oil, an occasional headlight."

"Are you insane?"

"Thank you."

"Sorry," BJ mumbled. "I just meant that, well, I live in the city, born and raised. Most of the time I don't even drive my car. I take a cab or the train unless I'm leaving the city."

"Seriously?" The admission truly surprised Hobie.

"Hey, I'm still pissed that they did away with full-service gas stations. I barely know how to unlock the cap to get gas in the thing. I do hope this will remain confidential, however."

"The fact that you're a total cherry when it comes to cars will go with me to the grave."

Hobie's wide grin was the only sign BJ needed to see that the redhead felt better. "Very funny. Just drive, Doc."

They both agreed that food should be their next priority. Three minutes later, Hobie pulled the Jag into the small parking lot beside the diner.

"I didn't realize it was so close," BJ commented as she carefully extracted her long limbs from the vehicle.

"Yeah, once you get your sea legs under you, so to speak, you could probably walk into town."

"Gee, I'm counting the days."

Well, contrite didn't last long. Hobie decided she would ignore BJ's little digs. Her philosophy was that perhaps, like a schoolyard bully, BJ Warren would eventually tire of tossing her underhanded comments if they no longer received the desired response.

BJ took in the sight of the wooden building with its white-trimmed balcony. She had expected cheap neon with a few sections of the light burned out. Instead, a brightly painted wooden sign on a pole by the street declared the structure to be "Rebecca's Cove, the Golden Key of the Gulf." She'd seen those types of slogans on restaurants in tourist areas around Florida but never thought twice about them, since they usually only meant anything to the owners or the founders of the establishments. She wondered about this one. Perfectly manicured sago palms and yucca plants surrounded what looked to have once been a two-story home. Two massive palm trees shaded the sidewalk up to the door.

Just as they were about to enter the restaurant, an older man stepped in front of BJ.

"Hey, can we say 'personal space,' bud?" she asked.

"Did you see the game last night?" he demanded. He looked to be in his late seventies. His hair was white under his blue-and-gold baseball cap. He wore slacks and a windbreaker, which BJ thought odd considering the heat.

"What the hell—" she said in surprise.

"Didn't ya see the game?" he repeated.

"Yes, Coach Cassidy, we were there," Hobie stepped in to say.

"Ah, good...good." The old man looked BJ up and down. "Injured it during the game, eh?" He indicated her leg.

BJ looked to Hobie for help. "Yes, Coach," the vet answered. "It was last night's game." She gave a pleading look to the tall woman, hoping her expression conveyed the idea that BJ should simply go along with their charade.

"What position?" he asked BJ.

"Huh?"

"Position! Football! What are ya, deaf? What position do ya play?"

"Um...middle linebacker?" BJ answered weakly.

"Hah! Ya certainly got the build for it." The old man slapped BJ's arm and the tall woman arched an indignant eyebrow. Hobie had to cover her mouth with one hand to hide her smile.

"Hobie Lynn, right?" The old man turned his attention to the redhead.

"Right, Coach."

"You a cheerleader?"

"No, sir, marching band."

"Ah. Good, good. Well, carry on."

"Thank you, Coach," Hobie answered.

"What the hell was that all about?" BJ asked as they watched the man walk away.

"That was Walter Cassidy. He went a little off the deep end a number of years back after his wife died. He was the football coach when I was in high school. His family has always been sort of a big deal on Ana Lia."

"A big deal as in the places we passed on the way here, like Cassidy High, Cassidy Football Field, Cassidy Library?"

"Exactly."

"The guy's a nut. Why don't they have him locked up somewhere?"

"Because when you're rich, you're not a nut—you're eccentric. Actually, he's harmless enough, just a little detached from reality is all."

"'A little detached'? I can't believe you people just let him walk the streets like he's...*normal.*"

Hobie paused and looked at the tall woman with a guarded smile. "I don't know. I'm beginning to believe that 'normal' is a rather subjective term."

Before BJ could respond, Hobie held the door open to allow BJ to enter first. "After you," she said. "One of those tables in the back should be the easiest for you to sit at."

BJ felt like a goldfish in a glass bowl. It was as if all action in the entire diner had come to a complete standstill when they entered. The tall woman couldn't help herself. She stopped walking about halfway to their table and stared back at the patrons.

"What are you doing?" Hobie asked.

"Letting them get a good, long look," BJ said loudly enough for those seated around them to hear.

Dozens of embarrassed faces snapped back to their own plates and conversation once again filled the diner.

"You enjoy doing that, don't you?" Hobie asked.

"Doing what?"

"Calling attention to yourself," the vet replied as they sat down.

"It's the only way to stay ahead of the crowd. Besides, I don't like people looking at me like I'm some kind of freak."

Hobie noticed that BJ spoke that last part with a hurt edge to her voice. "You sound like a woman who's had that happen before."

BJ looked at the redhead, not sure if she wanted to reveal anything of her personal life. She gave in a small bit. "A woman who's 6'1" gets used to being stared at, but just because I'm used to it doesn't mean I like it."

"Understandable. They don't mean to treat you badly. They're only curious. I think the whole town knows who you are by now. Word travels fast in Ana Lia, and it's not because they think you're a freak. They're nice people, but it's a relatively small community. Everybody knows everybody's business here. If you gave some of them a chance you might find that you actually have a lot in common."

"I find that highly unlikely," BJ said with her typical haughty flair. "I bet you're one of those who'd rather blend into the background, aren't you? Just do what's expected. Don't make waves and never rock the boat."

"For the most part...well, I suppose I am. Is there anything wrong with that?"

"Not if you're a lemming."

A waitress sat two glasses of ice water down on the table, abruptly halting their conversation. "Mornin'. We wondered where you got to, Hobie Lynn."

"Good morning, JoJo," Hobie answered. "This is Evelyn's granddaughter, BJ Warren. Ms. Warren, this is Joanne Hart, the owner of the Cove."

"It's very nice to finally meet you, Ms. Warren. Your grandmother talks about you all the time."

"Thanks. You've got, um, a...nice place here."

"Thanks right back. The restaurant's been in my family for years."

"Her grandmother is Rebecca Ashby, the woman the Cove was named for," Hobie explained.

"I see." BJ nodded. It always surprised her, but for a woman who made a living with words she was never good at small talk, and she wondered what she should say next.

"Yep. She'll be 95 this summer. She gets around a whole lot slower these days, but she's still got it all up here." JoJo tapped an index finger against her temple. "You get Hobie Lynn to bring you around to the house sometime."

"Uh, sure. Thanks," BJ answered.

Neither BJ nor Hobie knew how to tell the woman that this was the most civil they had been to one another since their accidental, yet brutal meeting. The furthest thing from each woman's mind was becoming friends and socializing with the other.

"So then, what'll it be for you ladies?" JoJo asked. She held a pen and a pad of receipts.

"How about a mocha java with double espresso and extra cinnamon?" BJ wished aloud as she looked at the menu.

"Sure thing. You want skim, 2 percent, or whole milk in that?"

Hobie laughed at the dazed expression on BJ's face.

"Um...2 percent."

"Orange juice, Hobie Lynn?"

"Yes, please."

"Let me get your drinks and I'll be right back for your order." JoJo headed for the kitchen. On her way, she scooped up dirty dishes and exchanged a few jibes with the customers.

"And you thought the island was backwards." Hobie smiled. "Are you a little happier now that you know the Cove is Ana Lia's answer to Starbucks? May I say, as a medical professional, I honestly think that you've been experiencing the beginnings of espresso withdrawal."

"Very amusing."

"Okay, folks." JoJo returned to take their order. "What can I get for you?"

BJ ordered poached eggs, whole-wheat toast, and fresh fruit. She then sat in stunned silence as she listened to Hobie give her order to the waitress.

"Um...three eggs over easy, ham, toast, hash browns—wait, hold the toast. I'll have a side of pancakes instead, and can I have another juice with my meal—oh, and can you add another egg to that?"

"You got it." JoJo left to place their order.

BJ looked under the table at Hobie's feet.

"What?" Hobie asked.

"Nothing. Just looking to see if you had any starving orphans under there you were planning to feed."

"Very funny. I have an extremely high metabolism. I burn everything off too quickly. I can be standing on a street corner and wham! My blood sugar bottoms out and I'm down for the count." Hobie tried to stop herself. She felt as if she was giving BJ much too much information, but she couldn't seem to stop talking. Finally, she cleared her throat nervously and waited for the mocking tone she was sure would come.

"Marching band, eh?" BJ surprised Hobie by changing the subject. "Was that true, what you told the old guy?"

"Oh, that. Yeah."

"Let me guess. Either flute or clarinet."

"Flute, smarty. How did you know that?"

"It figures. I knew it had to be some kind of girly instrument."

"Girly? Were you even in band?"

"High school class of 1977. Actually, I played in school bands for eight years. You just try marching in Chicago. I froze my ass off during the winter and practically collapsed from heat exhaustion every summer. I seriously hold marching band responsible for the aversion I developed to seasonal celebrations. It's probably why Halloween is my favorite holiday...no parades."

"And what was this butch instrument you played? The tuba?"

"Oh, you're such a comedian. No, it was the trumpet."

"Geez, how hard can the trumpet be? You only have three keys on the thing and you can *see* them!"

"It's a lot of work when you hate it."

"Why'd you play if you hated it?"

"Some rat bastard told me that being in band was an easy way to get girls. That little theory turned out to be a major disappointment. I can't begin to tell you how sorry I made Joey Bruder throughout the rest of junior high and high school."

"So you spent eight years playing an instrument you hated? How miserable."

"You're telling me. Actually, I liked the thing when I first got it. I had the usual 'bright shiny object' infatuation, but that only lasted for about two months. Once I realized they wanted me to practice for thirty minutes a day, the party was over."

"It's funny what educators learned from our generation, isn't it? Kids who take an instrument now have band or orchestra practice every day, just like math or English. That way they don't end up being forced to practice at home."

"Really? Little rat bastards don't know how good they have it. How do you know that?" BJ asked.

"Oh...um...I see a lot of the kids in my office with their pets. So, you hated it yet you kept on with it."

BJ shrugged. "My mother made me. She literally locked me in my bedroom for half an hour after school every day. As I got older, I figured it would look good on a college application. What?" she questioned when Hobie shook her head.

"I've just never known anyone to go about something with such a generous helping of apathy before." BJ actually laughed at the remark, and Hobie breathed a sigh of relief.

"Apathetic and proud of it. There were four trumpets in the middle school band. I was fourth seat trumpet until high school. Always last, but being last is highly underrated. When you're on the bottom rung of the ladder, people don't expect quite so much from you. My freshman year, I moved up to third chair. The only reason was because the kid ahead of me moved away."

"I would have thought you were the kind of person with more ambition than that."

"Why?" BJ hurried on to explain, "Ambition is decidedly overvalued. Besides, it only serves to disappoint."

"You sound more like a bitter woman than a philosopher."

BJ smiled briefly. "None of the above. Simply a realist."

The conversation lagged suddenly and both women looked as though they were revisiting their own personal memories of their youth. The sounds of JoJo delivering their breakfast pulled them from their deep thoughts. Once she had moved away from the table, BJ continued.

"I've found that having little or no ambition lends to a more spontaneous way of life. I don't know if I'll always be successful. It's not that I don't care; it's just that it takes more energy than I want to expend to ensure that I'll remain on top. Perhaps it's simply that I haven't found the one thing in life worthy of all that work. On the other hand, maybe it's just that I've never been able to put off my own self-indulgences."

Hobie was only slightly surprised at the hedonistic attitude with which the dark-haired woman lived her life. She was curious as to how much of BJ's way of thinking was truth and how much was simply a cover-up for her own insecurities. Neither woman appeared anxious to continue the conversation further. They concentrated on their food, but in the back of their minds, they both had a nagging feeling that there was more to say.

The art deco style of the restaurant made BJ feel at home. It reminded her of all the diners she had gone to, growing up on Chicago's south side; the kinds of places that served breakfast twenty-four hours a day. The décor included lots of stainless steel and colorful plastic. She had sobered up from many a night on the town in those establishments.

Once she'd finished her meal, BJ spent the next hour keeping up her end of the conversation. They stuck to safe subjects like sports and computers, realizing that other topics touched on too many controversial points. The writer thought it odd that the one person in town who could manage to get on her nerves at the drop of a hat was the same person with whom she suddenly found it so easy to converse.

She found herself people-watching most of the time. Rebecca's Cove certainly seemed to be the hub of operations for the island. People not only came there to eat, but to meet, hear news, even catch a tidbit of gossip or two. There always seemed to be enough room, even though the diner always appeared full.

Hobie had been right when she said everyone knew everyone else in Ana Lia. Nearly all of the patrons stopped to say hello and exchange a few pleasantries with the vet. Hobie had a smile and a good word for every person she met, which annoyed BJ. People who were too friendly had always annoyed her.

"I said, are you about ready to go?"

BJ realized that her own thoughts had so thoroughly captured her attention that she hadn't heard a word the vet had said. "Oh yeah, sorry. I'll just—" She reached for her wallet, which she always carried in the back pocket of her jeans, quickly realizing that her wallet wasn't there because her jeans weren't there. She was still wearing Mack's sweatpants. "Shit!"

"What?"

"I forgot my billfold."

"Oh, is that all. Don't worry, I've got it." Hobie reached for the check that JoJo had placed on the table.

"I'll pay you back," BJ said in embarrassment.

"I'm not worried about it."

"Yeah, but the clothes I wanted to pick up. I just don't want to—"

"Owe me?" Hobie finished the writer's thought.

"Nothing personal. I just don't like being indebted to anyone. It makes me feel...I don't know, obligated."

"Heaven forbid," Hobie responded. "Look, let's not make a big deal out of it. It's not as if you plan to buy Versace sweatpants, right?"

The dark-haired woman smiled in spite of herself. Then she remembered that such accommodating and unpretentious behavior annoyed her. She couldn't let herself become enamored of the redhead's disarming smile. BJ tried to remember the last time she had to guard herself against such a thing. When had it ever been easy to like someone, especially when that someone was a woman? The thing was, she couldn't ever remember a time.

Chapter
4

"I thought we were getting clothes?" BJ looked confused.

"We are."

The tall woman followed Hobie's lead and eased herself out of the vehicle. They stood before an old Victorian home. Cedar shingles on the roof, bay windows, and bright white paint made it look exactly like the sort of place BJ had always dreamed of turning into a bookstore. Unfortunately, there weren't many of these sorts of structures in downtown Chicago. A large bay window presented a display of best-selling books. BJ smiled to herself when she saw the latest Harriet Teasley novel out front. "This looks like a bookstore."

"It does, doesn't it," Hobie responded. She grinned and continued. "Let's just call it a private clothing store. The owners are the Dilby sisters."

"What, those books in the window are just fakes and the whole front of the store opens up like a garage door, right? It opens up into some sort of bat cave?"

"Are you ever serious?" Hobie asked.

"Let me think a minute. Hmm, no," BJ answered.

"The Dilby sisters do run a small bookstore, but it's sort of a store within a store."

"You mean a front."

"A private store."

"Right. A front."

Hobie let out an audible sigh. "You make it sound like they make book on the horses in a back room."

"Sorry," BJ said with a sheepish grin. She hadn't expressed regret over her actions in years, yet this was at least the third time that day she had apologized to Hobie.

"Let me explain. If the locals bought their clothes in the same spots as the tourists did, we'd go broke. It's either that, though, or go to the mainland. Our answer is the Dilby sisters' shop. It's where we buy our clothes."

"I feel like I'm in a surreal spy novel."

"Come on," Hobie directed as the two made their way up the stairs to the large porch.

"This house is a work of art. It's magnificent."

Hobie didn't expect such a sincere tone from the dark-haired woman. Everything was usually a joke to her. She turned her head to look up at the dreamy expression on the writer's face.

BJ suddenly realized that Hobie was staring at her and she lowered her head. "I guess it's just 'cause you don't see homes like this in the city."

"I suppose it's just what you're used to. It's probably the same thing I felt when I visited Chicago. I got off the train at the Daley Center and just stood on the street corner like some hick, craning my neck to look up at the tall buildings."

"You've been to Chicago?"

"Yes, I was just—" Hobie quickly shut her mouth, having forgotten to whom she was speaking. "Um, I go there occasionally for seminars and such."

BJ's face took on an odd expression. "Huh," was all she said in response.

They stood before the door with its etched glass window, and BJ couldn't help herself. "Is there a secret knock, maybe a Morse code signal I should use? Will I have to know the handshake?"

"Shut up," Hobie responded with a smile. She opened the door and they stepped into the air-conditioned shop.

"Hobie Lynn!" An older woman, perhaps in her seventies, waddled up to the redhead. She was short and squat. Not exactly fat, but built in a compact fashion. She had close-cropped hair so black that it was apparent she colored it. She wore a blouse and skirt that clung around her middle a little too tightly. "What can we do for you today?"

"Hi, Helen. Actually, I'm here with—" Hobie was unable to finish the sentence. She had no idea what to call BJ Warren. What was she to Hobie? She could hardly call her a friend. Luckily, Helen Dilby saved her the embarrassment.

"Evelyn's granddaughter. We were over to see Evie yesterday and she told us all about you, Miss Warren. It's so good to finally meet you." The old woman turned and shouted toward the back of the shop. "Katie, come and see who's here."

BJ turned at the sound of a creaking door. Another woman, about the same age as Helen Dilby, walked through a set of book-shelves that parted mysteriously. BJ had to do a double take in order to see that what the older woman came out of was actually a strange-looking sliding door. The *trompe-l'oeil* design resembled an elegant library with a sitting area. It was amazing and BJ realized that because of the quality of the work, it must have cost the owners a pretty penny.

"See, I told you there was a bat cave," BJ murmured to Hobie.

"Stop," Hobie whispered back.

"Katie, this is Evie's granddaughter, BJ," Helen said.

"Katherine Dilby," the other woman said in a gravelly voice. She grasped BJ's hand and shook it brusquely.

Although the two older women looked to be about the same age, their physical appearance was as different as night was from day. Katherine was tall and lean. Her hair looked to have been blonde when she was younger. It was cropped so close to her head that it rose in even spikes. She wore a polo shirt and cotton slacks, but her clothes looked wrinkled and worn in comparison to Helen's sharply pressed outfit.

"BJ needs to get a few things, especially some pants that she can cut one leg off," Hobie said, nodding her head toward BJ's cast.

"Oh my. Evie didn't say anything about that," Helen said.

"Well, it's a rather recent event. My grandmother doesn't know about it yet."

"I'm sure we can take care of everything you need, dear. Why don't you follow Katie into the back? She's the clothes expert, and she can show you where everything is."

Katherine led the way through the sliding door. BJ looked in astonishment at the racks of clothing around her, then let out a low whistle as she looked around, taking in the wide selection. She spent the next thirty minutes picking out an assortment of clothes. Katherine's no-nonsense and at times gruff attitude appealed to BJ, and the older woman was helpful in selecting just the right sizes.

Hobie walked around the shelves of books. She spied the large display of romance novels and picked one up, examining the jacket. After reading the synopsis and a blurb about the book's author, Harriet Teasley, Hobie tossed the book back onto the table. "Who buys this stuff? They call this writing?"

"Oh, you'd be surprised, dear. I can't keep Teasley novels on the shelf."

"Go figure. So, how was Evelyn when you saw her?" Hobie asked. "It's been a couple of days since I've seen her."

"You know that gal. All she does is talk about her granddaughter." Helen looked toward the back room and lowered her voice to a whisper. "I heard that...well, that BJ isn't exactly...um, she's a little different from the quiet girl that Evie described."

Hobie chuckled at the remark. "That's the understatement of the year. I can hardly believe that woman is related to Evelyn."

Helen smiled, almost as if to herself. "Well, you didn't know Evie when she was your age. She was a lot different than she is now."

"She couldn't possibly have been anything like her grand-daughter. One minute she's so arrogant I just want to punch her lights out, and then she gives you one of those charming looks or goes and says something nice or sweet, and I...I—"

"Just can't help being attracted to her," Helen finished.

"Yeah," Hobie answered in a distracted fashion. "No!" she quickly cried out. "Not in a million years, Helen. Get that smile off your face right now. That woman is just too, well, just too *too* for me. I can't believe that Baylor Warren could ever change enough for me to want to spend more than passing moments with her."

"Hmm, that's understandable. There's Noah, too. It's funny, though. When I see the way that girl and you get on, it reminds me of Katie and me. Like fire and water most of the time, complete opposites. We spend more time snapping at one another, but it's really only teasing. Funny the way life is, eh?"

Hobie smiled at the older woman. "Well, Katherine seems to be able to deal with her well enough. She must be buying out the store back there. Oh, that reminds me, can you charge me for BJ's things?"

"Oh?"

"She forgot her wallet. It's nothing more than that."

"Well, we can bill it directly to her if that would help."

"Actually, I think she might like that a lot better. She's not very big on having others do for her. I'd be surprised if Katherine wasn't tearing her hair out right about now."

"Speaking of which, you did tell BJ about Katie before you left them alone, didn't you?"

"What about her?"

"I mean Albert. Did you tell BJ about Albert?"

"Oh, shit!" Hobie cried out. She tore through the book shop and into the clothing store. She just hoped she was in time.

"What in the hell are you talking about? I don't see anyone there." BJ was about near the end of her patience when she saw Hobie rushing toward them.

"What do you mean you can't see him? He's sitting there as plain as the nose on your face!"

"There is no one there, you stu—"

The moment that Hobie ran up to the two women, they both nearly pounced on her. "Hobie!" they exclaimed in unison.

The vet looked from one woman to the other. Katherine and BJ were both red in the face. The writer wore an expression that Hobie was learning to recognize. The look meant that in another five seconds she would be cutting through someone with that sharp tongue of hers.

"Will you tell this woman to just give me my clothes so we can—"

"She sat on Albert!" Katherine nearly screamed.

"Who the fuck is Albert?" BJ shouted back.

BJ knew she probably shouldn't be cursing at an old woman, but her patience had ended. Katherine had been placing the new clothes into bags when BJ decided to rest her leg and sit in the comfortable-looking chair beside the cash register. She hadn't a clue as to what was wrong when the usually silent old woman had begun shouting hysterically at her.

BJ had jumped up, only to become embroiled in one of the most inane arguments in which she'd ever been involved. The old woman insisted BJ had sat there on purpose, eventually telling her that even Albert had better manners.

"I'm sure she didn't even see him, Katherine," Hobie said soothingly.

"How could she not see him?"

"See who?" BJ shouted again. The tenuous grasp she had on her temper was rapidly slipping away.

"Do you see what I mean? She's just like those doctors in Tampa. I don't know if we can do business with your friend, Hobie Lynn."

"Hobie," BJ said calmly—perhaps too calmly, in Hobie's estimation. The vet could practically hear the writer's teeth grinding together. "Do you see this *Albert* in that chair?"

Hobie bit her bottom lip as she looked between the two women once more. If she told BJ the truth, she risked losing Katherine's trust. "Um...yes?"

BJ just stared down at Hobie as Katherine snorted in triumph. BJ looked at the chair once more, beginning to feel as though she were the crazy one. "So, you actually *see* something...*here*?" She waved her hand in front of the seemingly empty chair.

"Of course she does, and it's not *something*, it's Albert!"

Katherine interjected. "And quit slapping him in the nose with your hand like that, you twit!"

"Speaking of slapping someone in the nose..." BJ took a step closer to the angry woman.

Hobie stepped between the women. "Can I see you over here for a second?" she whispered, pulling on BJ's elbow.

"She can't see him. People like her never will," Katherine added.

"I bet it was just the light, Katherine. Look how dark it is back here." The convincing tone to Hobie's voice made the older woman pause to look around. During those few moments, Hobie managed to maneuver BJ a few feet away.

"If you even think about saying you really saw anything over there, I'm going to throw you out the window and run for my life," BJ hissed through her teeth.

If the situation hadn't been so serious, Hobie would have laughed aloud at the sheer confusion coupled with uncertainty on BJ's face. "Look, have you ever seen that old movie with Jimmy Stewart?"

"Dear God in heaven! You are not seriously going to tell me that Albert is a six-foot white rabbit?" BJ whispered.

"Of course not. Don't be ridiculous," Hobie responded. "He's only three feet high, and he's a hamster."

"What?" BJ raised her voice. "What is this island, lunatic central?"

"Shh. Please, just go along with this and I'll explain later, I promise. Please?"

Hobie looked up at BJ with such a pleading expression that the dark-haired woman realized that, at that moment, she couldn't have refused the vet anything. Large green eyes tugged at the tall woman's heartstrings. That bit of insight made BJ uncomfortable. She'd never felt like that before.

"You owe me big time," was her response.

Ten seconds later BJ was standing beside the same comfortable chair. She gestured with one arm. "Of course. I can't believe I missed him!"

"Bullshit!" Katherine exclaimed. "You're making it up now."

"Okay, that's it. I'm going back to Chicago." BJ turned to leave.

"What color is he?" Katherine suddenly spoke up.

BJ quickly looked to Hobie. The redhead tugged on the neck of her t-shirt.

"Brown."

"What color are his eyes?" Katherine raised one eyebrow suspiciously.

Hobie and BJ both panicked, but for different reasons. A quick look over to the vet showed that she seemed to be pointing to her own eye. At least that's what BJ hoped it meant.

"Green," BJ answered with a confident smile.

"There ya go." Katherine slapped BJ on the shoulder enthusiastically. BJ just knew she would have a bruise there before the day was over. It was as if the older woman had completely forgotten that moments earlier she had been in a screaming match with the writer. "Guess it was just too dark for you to see him. I'll have to talk to Helen about more lights back here."

The fact that BJ knew the color of her eyes hadn't been lost on Hobie. It was such a little thing, but it stuck in her mind in a way that worried her. So far, it fit into the same category as many of her other dealings with BJ Warren. She didn't know whether to feel flattered or concerned. "Thanks for the backup," she whispered sarcastically to Helen as she and BJ were on their way out of the store.

"I think you two did very well. Besides, I have to live with Katie. It's always best if I stay out of the Albert debate unless it gets too far out of control."

"Goodbye, you two," Katherine shouted after them. "Come back soon."

"Not in this lifetime," BJ muttered so that only Hobie could hear. Looking back at the two older women, BJ arched an eyebrow at the way Katherine had placed her arm around Helen's waist. In BJ's opinion, there seemed to be more than a sisterly familiarity to it.

Once they were well on their way to the hospital, BJ turned to Hobie. "You owe me one very big story about Albert the giant, yet invisible, hamster."

"I know. Let me explain."

"Oh, and by the way," BJ added, "if those two dykes are sisters, then I'm Mother Teresa."

"So you met the Dilby sisters," Evelyn Warren said.

Hobie and BJ sat beside her bed. The elderly woman had been heartsick upon seeing her granddaughter's cast. When Hobie explained what happened but left out the fact that she was the driver of the vehicle that had hit Baylor, Evelyn just raised an eyebrow at her. Hobie's remorseful expression apparently conveyed more than words could manage, because Evelyn patted her hand affectionately. She spent the next twenty minutes treating BJ like a helpless invalid, going so far as to call the nurse to make her more comfortable. BJ, of course, lapped up the attention as shamelessly as Arturo receiving a belly rub.

"Yes, I met the Dilby sisters, and I use the word 'sisters' loosely."

"It's not for us to judge, Baylor."

"I'm not talking about judging, Tanti, I just think it's a crime that they have to hide who they are. Why don't they move away? There are a lot of places more progressive in their thinking. Shoot, Key West isn't that far away."

"They were young women who lived in a different time, dear heart. It has nothing to do with *where* they live. It's something they grew used to doing out of necessity. It's not an acknowledgment of right or wrong. Some things in life, well, you continue to do them because you've grown comfortable with things that way. Change can be hard on the soul. Sometimes, you just accept things, and people, the way they are. So," she continued with a mischievous look in her eye, "did you meet Albert?"

Hobie laughed and BJ glared at her. "She sat on him," Hobie blurted out through her laughter.

"Oh, my. What did Katherine do?"

"Her eyes bugged about, her head spun around, and smoke came out her ears," BJ replied. "I thought she was having some kind of an attack."

Hobie couldn't stop laughing.

"And this one," BJ pointed to Hobie. "She stood there and encouraged the delusional woman."

"I had to," Hobie responded soberly.

"I agree, Baylor. It took Katherine a long time to get where she is today. It would have done more harm than good for Hobie Lynn to deny Albert's existence," Evelyn said.

"You said you'd tell me the whole story," BJ said to Hobie.

"I suppose I can tell that one best, considering I was there when it all happened," Evelyn said.

Hobie nodded.

"It's not as much of a story as you were probably hoping for, Baylor. Katherine Dilby was a research scientist, quite a feat in the 1950s. There weren't many women doing that kind of work in those days. I suppose no one knows what makes folks go a little loopy. I think Katherine finally dissected one lab animal too many. She had a breakdown of sorts and refused to speak or eat. They had her in a hospital in Miami for a number of years. She never said one solitary word to anyone. That's where she met Helen."

"Why doesn't that surprise me," BJ interrupted to say.

"Helen wasn't a patient at the hospital, she was a volunteer. She started coming by every day to read to Katherine. Just as quickly as it had started, it ended. One day Katherine woke up and she was her old self. There was only one small change."

"Let me guess. Albert was born," BJ said.

"Correct. The doctors thought the creation of Albert was simply Katherine's way of compensating for the years of experiments on the animals she loved. They released her a short time later and she and Helen began their relationship."

"I can't believe it. A woman tells the doctors at a psychiatric hospital that she sees a three-foot hamster everywhere she goes, and they release her?"

"Honestly, Baylor where did you come by all this lack of compassion? Didn't seeing what your father did teach you anything? Katherine hurts no one. She is a wonderful and faithful partner to Helen and a loyal friend to those who take the time to get to know her. Learn to accept, dear heart. Accept people the way they are, all their flaws included."

"Sorry. I'll try, Tanti, but frankly, the people on this island are just giving me too much to work with right off the bat."

"So, what do you think about the rest of our island?"

"I think that if what I've seen of the people so far is as deep as the gene pool gets, then somebody is gonna bash their head open by diving in."

"Oh, Baylor, stop. I'm glad to see the two of you have made friends," Evelyn said with a nod in Hobie's direction.

"Yeah, well," BJ smirked. "We kind of...*ran* into each other."

Hobie returned BJ's half smile and breathed a sigh of relief when she didn't elaborate. It was one more thing for Hobie to ruminate over, however. BJ seemed to love humiliating people. Why hadn't she told her grandmother that Hobie was to blame for the broken ankle?

They sat and talked for another hour until Evelyn grew tired. Hobie mentioned that they should be going anyway, since she had to be in her office in a couple of hours.

Evelyn thanked her granddaughter once more for caring for her cherished home. "Take good care of Arturo," she said just before the two younger women left. "And take better care of yourself, Baylor. You sound as if you're becoming accident prone."

BJ ground her teeth together. She detested having her grandmother think the broken ankle was her own fault, but for some reason, she didn't have the heart to implicate Hobie. The funny thing was that she had no idea why she felt that way. She kissed her grandmother's cheek and said she would be back as soon as she could.

Chapter
5

"So, where to now?" BJ asked once they settled into the red Jaguar.

"Well, after I take you home, I was going to swing by the Cove and get some lunch, and then I have to get to the office."

"Oh." BJ sounded disappointed. "You just ate there a few hours ago."

"I have to eat a lot of meals. They're not all as big as breakfast, but I usually eat about every three hours. You're welcome to join me."

"Nah, I'm not too hungry yet."

"Look, if your leg feels up to roaming around downtown, I could eat lunch while you browse. Then I can take you back home and get my truck."

"Hmm, I'm sure that would be about as exciting as watching grass grow, but I guess it's better than looking at that cotton ball of a mutt for the rest of the day."

"That reminds me. I fed Arturo while you were taking a shower this morning. His food is in the cabinet over the fridge. He gets fed in the morning and at dinner time."

"Check. So, what do you think about the Jag?"

"I think I'm spoiled after one morning of driving it."

"Yep. You really do get what you pay for with these things. It moves like you're sliding along silk."

"I know, it handles great. Earlier this morning I thought I was in heaven."

"What do you mean, earlier?"

"What?"

"You said it handled great earlier. What do you mean? Earlier when?"

"Um..."

BJ straightened up in her seat. "Mack didn't drive it over to

Tanti's house, did he?"

Hobie shook her head.

"*You* did!"

Hobie slowly nodded.

"Holy shit, woman! What is wrong with you? Every time we talk, I catch you in a lie. Is this a compulsive problem?"

"When have I lied?"

"Every single time we talk! Let's start with the whole 'I am a doctor but' conversation, then there's that coach you delude, the nutty woman and her hamster. And you didn't tell my grandmother why my leg was really in a cast."

"Well, you didn't tell her to start with."

"You sure weren't jumping in to make any admissions."

"Look, I didn't mean to lie about the car. It's just that I'd never driven a Jag before, so Mack took my truck and—shit! I'm sorry."

"Sorry you did it, or sorry you got caught?"

"Well, both, I guess, if you're gonna put it that way."

"How did you ever get a medical license?"

"I'm a very good doctor!"

"Who can't tell the truth."

"I bet no one tells the truth when they're around you."

"What in the hell is that supposed to mean?"

"It means that you wouldn't know the truth if it was right in front of your face on a billboard written in letters fifty feet high! The *truth* is, Baylor Warren, you are *the* most opinionated, self-centered, unfeeling person I have ever met."

"Stop the car," BJ cried out.

"What?"

"I said stop the goddamn car!"

Hobie looked in her rear-view mirror and pulled over into a deserted sandy lot. "Are you okay?"

"Get out."

"What?"

"I said get out of my car, right now!"

"Are you insane?"

"I am not going to sit here and let some hick animal doctor from jerkwater USA tell me—"

Hobie removed her seat belt, shoved open the car door, and jumped out. "You know what? You *do* have to listen because you don't have a choice. For once someone is going to tell you just what they think of you!"

"Shut up!" BJ shouted.

"Oh yeah? Who's gonna make me?"

"I swear I'll hit you with this crutch."

"But you can't reach me, can you?"

"Don't make me throw this thing at you."

"I'll bet you couldn't hit the broad side of a barn with it!"

"Hey, I played softball."

"I'm surprised! Seeing as it's such a *girly* sport!" Hobie shouted at the top of her voice. "I am not going to walk two miles back to town just because of your...your...bruised ego!"

"It's my car! I'll be the one to decide who drives and who walks. Let me tell you another thing—"

"Forget it! I'm outta here! You can have your fancy car and the attitude to go with it. If I never see you again it will be too soon!"

"Good, go!"

"Fine!"

"Fine!"

They glared at one another, neither wanting to be the first to admit defeat. Each woman had apparently concluded that she was in a fix without the other.

"Okay, I think we're gonna need to re-think this, temporarily at least."

Hobie silently sat down and slammed the car door. "Okay, but the minute we get back to town, I am never speaking to you again."

"That's just fine with me."

Moments after they were underway both women felt foolish—not that the emotion did anything to dull their anger, but they did at least feel a small amount of regret. Of course, being the rational women they were, neither was willing to admit it to the other. They looked at one another, but quickly looked away.

Hobie took a deep breath. Even when she was a child it had been up to her to play peacemaker. She and Mack had fought incessantly as children. It usually started because of his unmerciful teasing, but Hobie's mother had taught her that it took a much stronger person to extend the olive branch first.

Another deep breath and Hobie knew what she had to do. "Um...do you still...you know, want to walk around town?"

"I don't know. Will I be safe? Do you plan to do much driving?" BJ replied sarcastically.

Hobie closed her eyes and gripped the wheel tightly. *I can do this. I will not let her goad me into another fight.* "Okay, Baylor, here's the deal."

"Must you always call me that?"

"What, Baylor? I thought that was your name."

"It is, but I detest it. Tanti is the only person I can tolerate it from."

"Oh, sorry. I didn't realize. Well, Bay—um, BJ, what I was going to say is that it seems pretty obvious, from the interaction we've had so far, that we grate on each other. I don't know why, but I guess it happens. We're in a situation, though, where we're kind of stuck with one another for the time being. This is a small town and I don't see either of us getting far without interacting with the other at least once in a while." Hobie could hear BJ grinding her teeth, but the other woman still sat with her arms folded across her chest, staring straight ahead.

"I propose that we do our level best to avoid one another. Again, I understand that it's a small town and that we may run into each other eventually. It may even be more than we care for, but I ask that when we are in the same company, we treat each other with a small amount of respect and keep a civil tongue. Even ignoring one another may be easier on our stress levels than what we've been experiencing. How does that sound? I mean, how do you feel about my offer?"

"Like I'm making a deal with Satan," BJ replied.

Hobie sighed. "So, you disagree?"

There was a long pause before BJ answered. "I...suppose not."

"Okay then. Do we have a deal?" She held out her hand.

BJ counted to ten before she answered. It wasn't that she was still mad at the vet, but something inside her never let go of an argument. When BJ took a step back, inside her head, and looked at the situation, she realized she really didn't want to fight with Hobie.

"Deal," she finally said. Perhaps staying away from Hobie was the best thing after all.

"Okay," Hobie said. "Do you still want to look around while I eat?"

"Yeah, why not. Beats a sharp stick in the eye."

They agreed to meet back at the car an hour later. Hobie walked off to the Cove and BJ grabbed her crutches and decided to explore the town.

"Well, that was fun." BJ leaned against the car and glanced at her watch. She shook her wrist to make sure it was running. "Now all I have to do is think of something to do for fifty more minutes."

BJ yawned, stretched, and listened to her stomach rumble. *Damn!* She looked longingly at the Cove's entrance. She stopped a passerby and asked the man if there was anywhere else to eat in town.

"Anywhere else?"

"Yeah, besides Rebecca's Cove," she answered. The conversation didn't hold a lot of promise.

"The Cove's open," he replied in confusion.

"I know, but...it's a long story. I just want to find out if there's anywhere *else* to eat in town."

"Why would ya want to eat somewhere else when the Cove's right there?"

BJ sighed and seriously thought about asking the man if he was Rod Serling, but she figured the sarcasm would be lost on him. "Right you are," she said loudly. "What could I have been thinking? The Cove it is."

Walking into Rebecca's Cove for the second time that day was an entirely different experience. No one seemed to notice her, except for the man who held the door open for her.

"Whaddaya say, Coach."

"Middle linebacker." Walter Cassidy pointed a finger at her.

"Right again."

Once inside, BJ saw that nearly every person in Ana Lia came to the Cove for lunch. Two additional waitresses scurried around the tables and booths, while JoJo minded the counter. The sounds of noisy conversation and dishes banging together filled the air.

She scanned the entire restaurant for an empty seat, but there were none available. A narrow booth opened up, but she knew she could never get her casted leg inside the tiny space. *Amazing. This place seemed to have enough room earlier, but when I need a seat...* She was about to turn around and leave when she spied an empty seat at the counter. She was halfway across the restaurant when she realized who the empty seat was next to. *This is the story of my life.*

Hobie turned to smile at whoever sat down beside her at the lunch counter. The smile froze on her face. She arched one eyebrow.

"Look, I don't like this any more than you," BJ explained. "I'm only sitting here because it's the only seat available."

Hobie shrugged and turned away. "It really doesn't matter."

"I'd sit somewhere else if I could."

"S'okay."

"It's just that with this cast, well, the booths are kinda out, and—"

"Look, I really don't care!"

"Okay, okay. Touchy. What's good to eat here for lunch?" BJ asked, looking around at the surrounding patrons' plates.

"Duck's breath burgers."

"Well, if you're not going to even be serious—"

Hobie grabbed the menu from BJ's hand and pointed to the sandwich section.

"Oh...duck's breath burgers. Okay, now what's good to eat that wasn't quacking around in the back yard yesterday? Okay, okay...don't give me that look. What the heck is it, anyway?"

At that moment, JoJo set a plate down on the counter in front of Hobie. It contained a massive hamburger and a generous helping of thick-cut French fries.

"It looks good, but why the name?"

Hobie lifted the plate and held it under BJ's nose.

"Whoa, mama!" BJ declared at the overpowering odor of garlic. "I hope your patients don't mind."

"I'm a vet. I see animals all day. They probably just think I'm one of them."

Hobie went back to ignoring BJ, and the writer continued to peruse the menu. The distinctive strains of conversation lifted above all the other background noises and BJ looked above the register to see a television mounted on the wall. Her eyebrows came together after she had listened for just a few moments.

"Is everyone watching that TV?" she asked Hobie.

"Yes."

"Are you watching it?"

"I'm trying.*"*

"Very funny. What's this show called?"

"El darkside del amor," Hobie answered.

"'The Dark Side of Love'?" BJ smiled.

"Is that what it means?"

"Yes. Is everyone watching this particular show?"

"Pretty much everyone."

"Every day?"

"For years now."

"And you?"

"Since I moved back to Ana Lia," Hobie said. "It's kind of a tradition."

"You do know it's a Spanish soap opera? That they're not speaking in English."

"Of course I do!"

BJ paused, but couldn't let it go. "Hobie, do you speak Spanish?" she finally asked.

"No."

BJ waited a few heartbeats before asking her next, inevitable question. She wasn't exactly sure she wanted to hear the answer, however. "Does anyone here speak Spanish?"

"Mmm, not that I can think of."

JoJo stepped up to take BJ's order. "What'll it be, Ms. Warren?" she asked, followed by a bright smile.

"A healthy dose of sanity, please. Oh, what the *hell*, a duck's breath burger, heavy on the garlic."

"Good morning, Dr. Allen. Good morning, Miss Grant."

Hobie and Laura mentally groaned. Lisa Carini was a precocious ten-year-old who yearned to be a veterinarian. She had a small menagerie of animals at home, and whenever she brought one of her pets into the office, it turned into an all-day question-and-answer session. She was intelligent and knowledgeable, but the most infuriating child around. Inside her Red Ryder wagon was Percival, her five-foot green tree python. Mostly green with a bluish-white stripe down his back, he lay there, unmoving, a large lump in his middle.

"What have we here?" Hobie turned on her doctor's voice.

"What we have here is Percival. Your memory isn't too good, is it?"

"Lisa!" Mrs. Carini reprimanded her daughter.

Hobie took a deep breath and began again. She couldn't find much fault with Lisa. She had been the same way as a child.

"Okay, why don't you tell me why Percival is here," Hobie said.

"He won't move. I don't understand it. I had him in the back yard yesterday and I went to clean the pool. He was wrapped around his tree when I left, but when I came back, he was like this. I did read that males can become lethargic at certain times of the year."

Laura and Hobie looked at one another and braced themselves for one of Lisa's zoological tirades.

"However, since I'm not breeding Percival, I don't understand it." Lisa scratched her elbow and continued. "I understand that if a snake sits all day he can grow obese and constipated, which is why we are here today, Doctor."

Hobie did a cursory examination of the reptile. She poked and prodded him, tickling his belly with the tip of a blunt hook until he loosened up and removed his head from inside his coils.

She easily saw the problem, but Lisa and her family had probably never seen him in this shape because they fed him nothing larger than small rats.

"Well, the good news is that there's nothing wrong with him that another few days won't cure," Hobie said.

"I don't think he's constipated. I track all the dates of his stool defecation for his feeding schedule," Lisa commented in a self-important manner.

Just wait until she grows up. She's going to be fun at parties, Hobie thought. "Lisa, I think the reason Percival is acting rather lazy is that he's eaten a little *bigger* meal than usual."

"But I haven't given him anything different," Lisa countered.

"I'm not sure how to say this, Lisa, but are you missing any of your rabbits, the big ones?"

"No, not one. I would have noticed," Mrs. Carini answered. "Besides, they aren't in the back yard where Percival was yesterday. They have hutches outside the gate."

All at once, Hobie had a feeling, a horrible feeling. She realized exactly what Percival had eaten. The lump was about the right size. She didn't have the heart to tell the girl or her mother.

"Well, it looks as if he got a hold of a small animal. I wouldn't worry too much about it. He should digest in within the next three to five days. In the meantime, keep him out of the sunlight and let him rest. He should do all the work just fine by himself. Worst-case scenario would be that we have to bring him in and soak him in warm water if he becomes constipated or that because of the larger-than-normal meal, he might suffer a rectal prolapse."

"I understand, Doctor," Lisa replied. "We'll follow your instruction precisely."

"Lisa, Mrs. Carini, can I be frank?"

"Of course, Hobie Lynn," Mrs. Carini replied.

"Percival has become a little bit bigger than most males of his species. I know you consider him a pet, but it may be time to think about giving him to someone who has the room for a snake his size."

"He's like one of the family." Lisa looked upset.

"I know, sweetheart, but I would expect you of all people to understand that what really counts is what's best for the animal."

Lisa furrowed her brow and seemed to be thinking about what a real veterinarian would do.

"I guess you're right," she said. "But how do I find someone good to give him to?"

"Tell you what. I have a friend I went to school with that

works at Busch Gardens, in Tampa. I just bet he would be able to find a great spot for Percival. Would you like me to ask him?"

"Busch Gardens, oh, yes. That would be a perfect spot for Percival. It would be like a real jungle for him."

"Very good. I'll contact him on Monday."

Mrs. Carini thanked Hobie and Laura and followed her daughter out of the office.

"If that was my kid..." Laura let her thought trail off as she shook her head.

Hobie laughed, and then grew serious. "What's worse is I think I know what Percival ate that just happened to wander into his yard."

"What?" Laura asked.

"Remember when Mrs. Emberly was in here looking for Petey?"

"Yeah."

"The Carinis live right behind Mrs. Emberly." Hobie stared at her friend, waiting for her to catch on.

"Oh," Laura responded distractedly. "Oh!" she exclaimed as realization dawned bright. "Oh, man. You don't mean—"

"Yep. I'm afraid poor Petey played his part in the circle of life," Hobie said.

BJ unlocked the front door to her grandmother's house and stepped inside the cool interior. She sat down on the familiar couch that had become resting place and bed. The remote control for the television sat in plain view on the coffee table and BJ scooped it up. She flipped through the channels, but it didn't take her long to realize that Evelyn didn't have cable or a satellite dish. She passed by three major networks, one of which was barely visible through the snow, a local channel, and a public television station.

"Life on the edge," she said as she watched a woman on the local Ana Lia station explain how to plant a sago palm.

A sound to BJ's right captured her attention. She looked against the wall where she had left her suitcase. She remembered leaving the top open, but now all of her clothes were arranged in a pile beside it. She sat there staring down at the floor. A little ball of fluff stood in the middle of the clothing. Arturo looked about as happy with himself as one dog could. His backside wiggled back and forth until he sat down again in his nest of garments.

"You little rat bastard." BJ glared down at him. She bent down and easily lifted Arturo with one hand and brought him up to eye level. "You and I have to have a talk, Squirt."

Arturo's backside continued to wiggle until he looked like a vibrating cotton ball. Suddenly, he reached out with a tiny pink tongue and licked BJ's nose.

"Oh, gross. Dog germs!" BJ fell back on the couch, dropping Arturo into her lap. She wiped a hand across her nose only to have the dog lick the top of her free hand. "Okay, now stop that. Stop that, I said."

The small dog then ran back and forth across the couch, leaping over BJ's lap. Finally, he stopped and lowered his nose, his backside high in the air, as if daring BJ to come after him. When she reached for him, he launched himself from the couch and ran along the floor. He grabbed a small toy and sped back toward the couch. He jumped up, deposited the toy in BJ's lap, and then promptly rolled onto his back.

BJ couldn't keep from laughing. She scratched his stomach until his tongue lolled from his small mouth and he looked to be utterly relaxed. "If you weren't so damn cute you'd be in the oven right now."

BJ lay back on the couch and realized how tired she was. She'd taken a pain pill after lunch and was beginning to feel its effects. "Well, I'm beat, how about you?" Arturo hopped onto BJ's stomach and did a little half turn before he plopped the full length of his body down as a sign of his agreement. "Must you?" she asked the dog.

Arturo closed his coal black eyes and let out a long breath.

"Oh, all right," BJ said with a yawn. "But these are definitely *not* permanent sleeping arrangements." She made a mental note to buy additional pharmaceutical stocks as soon as she got home. "Better living through advanced pharmacology," she muttered just before she fell asleep.

It was so quiet and peaceful that she immediately fell asleep. The neighborhood was virtually silent, an atmosphere to which BJ was unaccustomed. Living in the city all her life, she had never known what it was like to sleep without the sounds of cars, trains, and people. Perhaps it was the depth of her slumber that caused her fright when the doorbell rang.

"Whoa!" The jarring sound of the doorbell startled BJ to the extent that she forgot all about her broken ankle. She attempted to roll off the couch, but one leg never followed. For the second time that day, she ended up face down on the floor beside the couch. She groaned in pain as she searched felt around for her crutches.

With some intense grunts and growls, Arturo had his teeth clamped on one of her crutches and was desperately trying to drag it closer to the prone woman.

"Thanks, Lassie," BJ said as her fingers wrapped around the crutch. "I'm coming!" she shouted as the bell continued to ring.

She slowly crossed the living room and entered the wide hallway that led to the front door. "Yes?" she asked the old woman standing on the porch.

"Baylor Warren?"

BJ winced at the sound of her given name. "Do I have a choice?"

"Excuse me? Are you Evelyn's granddaughter?"

"Yes ma'am. What can I do for you?"

"Ida Wedington." The woman introduced herself in the curt manner that BJ had noticed most of the islanders used with mainlanders. "I saw that Hobie Lynn brought you back home earlier this afternoon. I wanted to give you some time to get settled before I came over and introduced myself."

"Oh, yeah, you're Tanti's next-door neighbor. I remember you. Nice to see you again."

"I see Hobie Lynn brought Arturo back home. Have you had any problems so far?"

"Nope," BJ answered. She had a feeling that if she related all the experiences she'd had on the island thus far, the old woman would run away in fright.

"Well, I wanted to let you know that I can continue to take care of the greenhouses and the outside chores, especially since you seem to be flying on one wing." The old woman chuckled.

BJ found the older woman's attitude a little patronizing. The feeling that people might have been laughing at her often set BJ off. Sometimes, as in this case, she realized that she had built the feelings up in her own mind, but that didn't stop her from doing something foolish in response.

"No need for you to put yourself out. I can handle it," she said.

Ida raised one eyebrow in response. "You sure about that? It's kind of...complicated."

BJ chuckled. "I have a college degree. I'm sure I'll be able to manage."

"Well," Ida said slowly. Her expression said that she had her doubts. "Would you like me to walk you through it the first time?"

"No, thanks though. Tanti wrote out some pretty detailed instructions."

"Okay, but if you find it's too much you just give me a shout. All right?"

"Sure thing," BJ answered, wondering why the woman was

making such a big deal out of watering a few plants.

"Here you go then," Ida said as she pulled a massive ring of keys from her canvas book bag.

"What the hell are these?" BJ accepted the hefty set of keys. "There must be fifty of them."

"Fifty-two, to be exact. They're marked at the top of each key. The greenhouses, shed, and all the rest are to the watering system. You sure you don't want me to run through all of this just one time?"

"No, no, not necessary at all." BJ felt as though she was in over her head, but being the wise woman she was, she wasn't about to admit that fact.

"Okay." Ida wasn't exactly convinced, but Evelyn had said that if Baylor wanted to handle things, Ida should let her.

BJ closed the door after thanking Ida, and once again tested the weight of the key ring in the palm of her hand. She looked down at Arturo before speaking. "Looks like we're the keeper of the keys, pal." Arturo wagged his tail and danced around her feet.

"Hey, it's about dinner time," BJ said when the grandfather clock in the living room chimed six. "Are you hungry?"

Arturo obviously knew that word. He spun around in a tight circle a few times, his feet barely touching the ground, then sped toward the kitchen.

"I'll take that as a yes," BJ answered with an amused laugh. Owning a pet had never held any appeal for the writer, but Arturo seemed different. "I haven't even been on this island for two days and already I'm talking to animals. Okay, she said your food was in this cabinet."

BJ pulled out a large can, opened it up, and looked at it in confusion. "How much of this do you get?" BJ asked of her canine companion. Arturo barked once and danced around a stainless steel food bowl on the kitchen floor.

"Hmm...okay, here ya go." BJ emptied the entire can into the dog's bowl. "Now, how about me?"

BJ looked through the cabinets. She was only hungry for a snack and found an unopened box of Cheez-Its in the pantry. She loved nothing better than Cheez-Its and a nice cold beer. She was thankful that she had talked the vet into making a brief stop at the grocer's before coming back home earlier.

Briefly stopping at the refrigerator, BJ armed herself with an ice-cold bottle of Corona. She sat her treasures on top of the coffee table and found the envelope containing her grandmother's instructions for the running of the household. Taking a long swallow from the bottle of beer, BJ opened the massive manual. She looked over at Arturo, who lay curled up beside her on a couch cushion.

"Hah, we can do this, huh?" She took another drink of beer. "Don't tell me it's too complicated. What do I look like...someone who flips burgers for a living?" she muttered to herself.

She started to read and became thoroughly engrossed in the many small tasks necessary to keep the greenhouses functioning. BJ stared in awe at the detailed drawings Evelyn had provided. "She must have been writing this thing for a year."

"Oops. 'Feed Arturo at breakfast and dinner. One-quarter of a can for each meal.' No wonder you acted so happy, you little squirt," BJ said to Arturo. The small dog, upon hearing the name that was quickly becoming familiar to him, stood up and shook the sleep from his body. He looked up at BJ, burped, and nestled back against the couch cushions.

BJ spent the rest of the evening reading her grandmother's missive and talking to Juliana on the phone. She explained the whole story to her agent, who nearly laughed herself senseless.

"You know," Juliana said, "if that doctor hadn't called me, I'd swear you were making this whole thing up."

"Trust me, this is no joke. I feel like I'm living in a surreal mix of Mayberry meets Twin Peaks. I promised Tanti, but I am not going to last out here, I just know it."

"You hang in there, mate. I'm sure you'll find a few ladies who can keep you *occupied* for the summer."

"Are you kidding? Jules, you do not know what this place is like."

"Yeah, well, that doc's voice sounded plenty sexy. She rabbits on a bit, but she had the cutest laugh."

"She laughed? When?" BJ arched an eyebrow at her unseen friend.

"I don't remember what I said. She was probably affected by my wicked charisma and charm."

"Bite me."

Juliana laughed heartily. "Hey, do you have your laptop with you?" she asked.

"Yeah, why?"

"Good. You can get some work done while you're out there."

"You expect me to be creative and write a best seller here? Impossible, I can't do it."

"Yes, you can. You just need to chill out, mate. Get that doctor to give you some Prozac if you have to, but relax, take it easy and work on that damn manuscript."

"Do any of your other clients know what a ruthless, drug-promoting slave driver you are?" BJ asked.

"Yes, and they love me for it," the agent responded.

"That's what you think," BJ muttered as she hung up the phone.

Chapter
6

BJ's third day on the island started out uneventfully. She and her shadow, which just happened to be a small Bichon puppy, started out the day with breakfast. Arturo looked longingly at his bowl after BJ put the prescribed amount of food in it.

"Get used to it, Squirt. I'm surprised you didn't explode after last night."

Hot coffee and the local newspaper sufficed as breakfast for BJ. She took pride in her above-average culinary skills, but found that she had little to work with at the moment. The ringing of the telephone broke the silence.

"Baylor?"

BJ recognized the vet's voice immediately. She grimaced at the imaginary pain the name caused her. "Why do you insist on calling me that?"

"Oh, sorry, I keep forgetting."

"Obviously." There was silence from the other end of the phone. "Did you call for a reason or are you just testing the line?"

"Oh, yeah. Um, I'm off to the Cove for breakfast before I go to the office, oh, in about an hour. I wondered, well, I guess I'd like to make up for flying off the handle like that yesterday. I can give you a ride down there if you haven't eaten yet. We don't even have to sit together, but...well...I thought I'd offer. My treat, what do you say?"

BJ looked down at Arturo, who sat at her feet. He appeared to be listening intently. BJ put one hand over the receiver.

"She's trying to suck up. What do you think? She's offering breakfast."

Arturo stood and wagged his tail happily.

"What do you know? You're just hoping for a doggie bag."

"Um, Bay—BJ? Are you there?"

"Sure, sounds like a plan."

"Great. I'll be by in about an hour. Bye."

BJ hung up the phone and looked down at Arturo. "Yep, she definitely knew she was in the wrong." She grinned at the pup. "I thought I'd give the poor girl a break and say yes. I threw her a bone. Hah! Get it? I threw her a bone. You know, a little dog humor?"

Arturo just cocked his head to one side.

"I gotta get a dog with a better sense of humor," BJ muttered as she went off in search of Evelyn's instruction manual. It was time to water the plants.

She had never ventured inside her grandmother's greenhouses. Evelyn Warren had five acres of land. When BJ was a young girl, the land had consisted of scrub grass and palm trees. Later, when she grew older and her visits became less frequent, Evelyn had created her dream.

Some of the buildings were like big garages, and BJ assumed they had their own independent light sources. From the outside, it appeared that only the ceiling of the long main greenhouse was made of glass. The rest of the building looked just like all the others: clean, untarnished corrugated metal.

BJ wondered why the buildings had never held any interest for her before. Even odder was the fact that Evelyn had never shown BJ inside the buildings. The only thing she would say was that the greenhouses were something that reminded her of her travels around the world with her friend Aimee.

When you understand the key to happiness, Baylor, you'll be able to appreciate my greenhouses.

BJ could hear Evelyn Warren's voice just as if she were standing beside her. "Funny that I don't remember her saying that till just now," she mused aloud.

"Well, you with me, Squirt?" BJ looked down at Arturo. She held Evelyn's operations manual in one hand, the keys in the other, while maneuvering her crutches at the same time.

They went through the back door of the house, which led to the main greenhouse. BJ was surprised to find a four-foot hallway and another door. A sign on the door said, "Temperature-Controlled Environment: Keep Door Closed."

"Well, that's different," BJ said. Arturo barked in apparent agreement.

BJ opened the door to enter the greenhouse and turned to close it without really looking inside. She pressed the door shut and immediately felt a humid warmth surround her. Turning and looking up, she reeled in stunned dismay.

"What the hell...I mean, *where* the hell am I?" The greenhouse was a tropical paradise. "It's a jungle," she said aloud.

BJ took a few cautious steps and watched as Arturo barked and sped off toward a large pool, complete with a fifteen-foot rock waterfall. The dog never missed a step as he launched himself into the water. He retrieved a floating object and jumped out of the pool. The small pup looked even smaller dripping wet until he shook himself with unmitigated vigor, fluffing his fur back into shape. He ran over to BJ and dropped the tennis ball at her feet.

"Ah, you're a regular here, I see," she said. Arturo wagged his tail in reply. "This place is amazing!" Wearing a wondering grin, she turned in a circle. "It's like your own little Shangri-La. Too cool! So, Tanti, why have you been hiding this from me all these years?"

Armed with her grandmother's instructions, BJ followed a stone path to the west side of the greenhouse. The tropical plants were dense in this portion of the building, and she was hot and sweaty by the time she reached her destination. Without Evelyn's detailed drawings, BJ never would have found the hidden plastic and metal boxes that contained the watering system's controls.

BJ looked at key number two. It was marked along the top as "main: lock boxes 1-3." She easily opened all three hinged lids and looked over the contents of the boxes. Each contained ten knobs that appeared to be water shut-off valves. Each row of knobs had a different color of plastic coating. Letters identified each knobs, and each knob had numbers around its base like a clock, one through twelve.

"Allrighty then," BJ said as she leaned in to take a closer look. She squinted and studied the knobs with intense fascination. "There it is, all right...a bunch of totally unidentifiable knobs. Geez!" She pulled out her drawings and scanned them. "What the hell is this, Tanti? What, do I look like an engineer? How do these old broads do this?"

BJ had a quick flashback just then. She was in the house and the old woman from next door had just handed her the enormous set of keys. *Okay, Beej. Note to self. The next time someone asks you if you'd like them to run through the steps involved in anything, you just nod your head politely and say yes.*

"We can do this, eh, Squirt?" BJ spoke to Arturo, who had found a high perch on some twisted tree roots that resembled the bottom of a mangrove tree. "I mean, it's right here in black and white." She indicated the manual in her hand. "How hard can it be?"

Arturo let out a tiny whimper, which didn't seem like a good omen to her. She decided to overlook her new friend's lack of confidence. Usually she would have been the first to admit her own limitations when working with her hands. When she actually thought about it later, she realized she had never really done anything like this before. She paid people to do mundane physical chores, even if they were in her realm of capability. She couldn't remember ever attempting to do something like fixing a leaky sink or changing her own flat tire.

"Okay, let's give this sucker a shot, shall we?" Holding up the instructions in one hand, BJ began turning knobs with the other.

Finally reading all of the small print that Evelyn had added to the instructions, BJ learned that the tightly sealed building was a rainforest, complete with its own storms. When set to exact specifications via the colored knobs, the system controlled every aspect of the watering of the main greenhouse. The system knew exactly how much rain to add and when to add it to the carefully maintained environment. The key was to set the controls differently each day of the week, then begin all over again on Monday.

"Red H-4...Blue C-10...Green F-1. Geez, I feel like I'm playing Twister, or at the very least calling bingo. Okay, only a few more to go." BJ completed the last few turns as the instructions indicated. "Hah! Don't tell me I got no skills." She stood back and folded her arms across her chest, a gloating smirk on her face.

Glancing down at the instructions again to double-check her work, BJ stared in disbelief at the next paragraph. "Under no circumstances should you adjust the last knob in the series before making sure you have a clear path to the outside door. The system begins two and one-half minutes after last knob adjustment."

"Oh, Tanti! Do you think you could have written this *before* you told me how to move the last knob?" BJ cried out in frustration.

A heartbeat later, a siren sounded over BJ's head, causing her to involuntarily duck. "Oh, that can't be good. Come on, Squirt. We gotta book or we could end up in the middle of a typhoon."

That was about the point where things started to unravel for BJ. She was suddenly faced with the unenviable task of grabbing the manual, the keys, and a small wiggly dog and crutching herself out of the dense undergrowth of tropical plants. Everything would have been fine, too, if it hadn't been for the rubber stoppers at the pointy end of her crutches.

BJ had just breathed a sigh of relief, juggling her menagerie of items. The door that exited into the back yard was within sight. Her progression came to a jerking halt, however, when her crutch slipped between the rocks in the path. She tugged once to free herself, but overestimated the strength of her pull. All of the objects that she had precariously balanced within her hands took flight, including Arturo.

"Shit!"

The dog made a perfect four-paw landing and stood barking before the door.

"Oh, fuck this!" BJ threw the trapped crutch to the ground. She hopped on one foot and threw open the door for Arturo to escape. A sound like a distant, rolling thunder came from overhead. "Great, sound effects to boot."

BJ bent to retrieve the manual and tossed it through the door. She turned around to grab the keys and was hit full in the face with a spray of water from a sprinkler jet that lay hidden among the plants. "Jesus Chr—"

It didn't take a rocket scientist to know what would happen next. While BJ was busy fighting off the water, she lost her footing on the now slick rocks. Her good luck continued to hold out, however. She fell, but instead of cracking open her skull on the stony path, she landed in a patch of elephant ear plants. The bad news was that by this time, the misters and sprinklers had all come on full force. The elephant ear patch was much softer than the rocks, but it hadn't taken long for the ground to turn to mud.

"Motherfu—" BJ rolled toward the path, covered in mud and soaking wet, just as another sprinkler hit her in the face with a sudden jet of water. She crawled, rolled, and finally threw her body through the greenhouse door.

She fell to the ground and rolled onto her back. She lay there that way in the heat of the sun for a few moments, which felt a lot longer than they actually were. Opening her eyes, she squinted and held a hand up to shade off the brilliant sunlight. A very familiar head popped into view, towering over her.

"Why did I know you were in the area?" BJ said.

"Good Lord, what happened to you?" Hobie looked down at BJ, who looked as though she had just rolled through a mud puddle.

Arturo picked that very moment to hop onto BJ's stomach to be a part of things.

"Who...us? Oh, nothing much, just doing a little gardening."

Hobie didn't mean to smile at her predicament, but the sight of Baylor Warren—the usually cool, self-possessed woman—lying on the ground covered in mud and bits of leaves with a small dog attached to her was more than she could stand. She smiled and then had to hold her hand over her mouth to stifle her laughter. "Let me give you a hand."

"No, no, I'm good, thanks." BJ dismissed the offer with a wave. She casually wiped some mud from her cheek and clasped her hands loosely across her middle. She lay there as if it was the most natural thing in the world. "Sooo...how are *you?*"

That's when Hobie full-on lost it. She wanted to stop, especially when she noticed that the harder she laughed, the stonier BJ's expression grew.

"Are we all done now?" BJ asked when Hobie finally slowed down to intermittent giggles.

"I am sorry, but you have to admit—"

"Yeah, yeah...laugh at a woman when she's down. I know your type."

"Come on. Let me help you clean up."

"Nah, go on. You'll be late for work."

"Hey, I'm the boss. I get to make the rules. Come on." Hobie held out her hand once more.

"Geez, I'm falling apart," BJ said.

"Yep, it's hell getting old."

"No, I mean I'm really falling apart." BJ held up a small chunk of plaster for Hobie's inspection.

"Wow, that shouldn't be happening." Hobie bent down to examine the top of BJ's crumbling cast.

"Ya think?" BJ's sarcastic words were lost on Hobie, who seemed more concerned with her patient's cast.

"Okay, Evel Knievel, time to patch you up."

"You better take those clothes off at the door or you're going to get mud on everything in sight," Hobie said.

"Um, no I won't. It'll be okay."

"You're covered from head to foot with mud that's an inch thick!"

"It's not that bad," BJ countered.

"Look, I *am* a doctor. You don't even have to take off your underwear if your sensibilities are that delicate."

"I just can't, okay?"

"Geez. Don't be so silly." Hobie made a move toward BJ's waist and the drawstring of her pants.

"Look, I said I don't need any help." BJ quickly slapped at Hobie's hands.

"I'm trying to help you—"

"I'm not wearing any underwear," BJ said loudly.

"What?"

"What, you don't think the neighbors heard what I said the first time?"

"Oh," Hobie replied. Suddenly she had a vision of exactly

what Baylor Warren looked like without the aforementioned garment covering her most intimate of body parts. She could feel the heat rising within her own body, creeping up her neck and settling on her face.

"What's wrong with you?"

"Huh? Oh, um...nothing."

"Are you blushing?"

"No! I most certainly am not."

"Yes, you are." BJ laughed and added a smirk for good measure. "You're thinking about what I look like under there, aren't you?" She leaned closer. "Shame on you, Doc."

"I am not! Besides, why aren't you wearing any underwear?"

BJ arched an eyebrow.

"Oh God, forget I asked that. It's none of my business and I *really* don't want to know."

BJ smiled as Hobie's blush increased. She didn't have the heart to continue embarrassing the flustered woman. She grew serious and lowered her voice, even though there wasn't anyone else around. "I can't get them on. My arms aren't long enough with this cast on. As it is, I have to use a coat hanger to pull up the sweatpants. Between you and me, I've never really considered dressing to be a team sport. I prefer it solo, if you don't mind."

A wave of sympathy passed through Hobie. She realized how hard it must have been for BJ to admit to that. Not that being caught *sans* skivvies would shake the writer's sexual confidence any, but Hobie understood how difficult it was for BJ to acknowledge that she couldn't do everything herself. That admission, more than any other, caused her to appear vulnerable and human.

"Do you have a robe?" Hobie asked.

"Yeah, inside the bathroom on this floor. It's hanging on a hook inside the door."

"Okay, I'll get it," Hobie said.

BJ watched as the redhead left the room. She leaned heavily on both her crutches, thanks to Hobie, who had waited for a pause in the greenhouse's tropical storm and rushed in to retrieve the lost one.

BJ undressed, took a shower, and got dressed in clean clothes. She kept her self-respect, mostly due to Hobie's adept and tactful handling of the incident.

Riding in the vet's now surprisingly clean truck, BJ watched Hobie out of the corner of one eye. Their breakfast outing had turned into a trip to Hobie's surgicenter to re-cast BJ's leg. They rode along in silence, but BJ's mind was anything but still. She could only wonder at the tender compassions that this stranger, whom BJ had done nothing but spar with, showed her. It was true, they seemed to butt heads more often than not, but this woman caused BJ to feel something other than what she usually felt for women. It was definitely a feeling that made BJ feel good, but she wasn't sure why. She didn't enjoy feeling things and not knowing why she was feeling them. And when it came to Hobie Lynn Allen, BJ found that she had an awful lot of feelings she couldn't account for.

"Thanks, Mack," BJ said.

"No problem. Thanks for this." The officer patted the paper sack in the seat next to him. "Hobie Lynn forgets to eat when she gets busy, then she hits the mat."

"Hey, she helped me out this morning." The writer indicated the new cast with a nod. "Her office looked pretty busy, so I came to the Cove, gave you a call, and here you are."

"Well, thanks anyway. Sometimes she needs a keeper, ya know what I mean?"

"Hey, Mack, lemme ask you something." BJ bent down and leaned against the open passenger side window. "The first day I got here you said you knocked me down when we were kids. You said something about it being because I told your sister she was ugly. Mack, you got more than one sister?"

"I always thought one was more than enough, thanks. Besides, Hobie Lynn gave me enough grief for ten sisters when we were growing up," Mack replied with a smile.

"Shit." BJ hung her head. "I was afraid you were going to say that."

"Well, if it helps you any, Hobie doesn't even remember it. She was all of four or five, so I wouldn't sweat it too much. Why do you suddenly care so much, anyway?"

"Well, I guess I just felt like I owed her or something. I mean, she fixed my leg and...you know..." BJ trailed off nervously. Why did she suddenly feel so tongue-tied talking about Hobie?

"Right," Mack seemingly agreed with a small grin. "Well, I better get Sis her lunch. What are you gonna do after you eat? Need me to swing by and give you a ride home?"

"Nah, I'll just wander and then try walking home. I can handle it."

"Well, I do a drive down Main Street again at three-thirty. If you find you want a ride, just park yourself on the bench outside of the bakery around then."

"You got it. Thanks, Mack." BJ waved goodbye to the sheriff

and watched the patrol car pull away from the curb.

Twenty minutes later BJ sat at the Cove's lunch counter. She had discovered a snack from heaven when JoJo set down a bowl of what looked like tater tots along with her cheeseburger. The tidbits were made of potatoes, just like tater tots, but filled with cheese and bits of jalapeno peppers.

"You want some more of these, Ms. Warren? Another iced tea?" JoJo asked.

"Most definitely, on both counts. These are great. What are they?"

"They're called munchers. They just happen to be from a recipe that belongs to Rebecca herself. Matter of fact she asked just this morning to meet you when you came in next, and what do you know...you're here. Funny, ain't it?"

"Yeah...funny," BJ answered slowly. "Um, sure, I'd be glad to meet her."

After BJ finished her meal, JoJo ushered her into a separate apartment behind the restaurant. "Grandmother lives here by herself. Of course, someone's out front until we close, but she spends her evenings on her own. I'd feel better most days if she'd come live with one of the grandkids, but she says she likes to be independent, and I guess I can't blame her there."

The writer recognized that the same hand had decorated the restaurant and the apartment. They both seemed like places reminiscent of another time, as if age had not altered them from their original states.

They walked into the space that in modern-day terminology would have been the living room, but BJ thought the term "parlor" fit this particular room. The wallpaper had very thin hunter green vertical stripes. A large Persian carpet lay on the polished wood floor, and a love seat nestled along the north wall under a large window. Two overstuffed chairs with Queen Anne legs sat with a small table between them.

"Grandmother, this is Evelyn Warren's granddaughter. You said you wanted to meet her."

"Indeed. Thank you, my dear. Please, sit down, Baylor."

The writer sat in one corner beside the fireplace, wondering when it ever grew cold enough for a fire on Ana Lia. She could only think of one word to describe the older woman and that word was "elegant." She remembered JoJo saying Rebecca Ashby was ninety-five, but BJ would have guessed the woman's age to be closer to seventy. She had hair that shone silver in the subdued lighting of the room. She wore a linen skirt and jacket in a champagne color. A stylishly carved walking stick with a jeweled crown leaned against a small table beside her. Rebecca seemed very different from the rest of the island's residents.

BJ suddenly felt out of place. She self-consciously looked down at her cutoff jeans, and Rebecca saw the uncomfortable expression in her eyes.

"Do you enjoy a good tea leaf, Baylor?" Rebecca asked.

"Um, I suppose so."

"This is a Moroccan mint, which I have always found odd considering that the plant is grown in Malaysia."

"I agree," BJ said. "You'd think they would have called it Malaysian mint or something more in keeping with its place of origin."

She accepted a delicate china cup from the older woman, then politely waited until Rebecca took a sip of the steaming brew before doing likewise. The mint flavor was wonderfully subtle and refreshing.

"It's absolutely perfect. Isn't it?"

"Yes, yes it is."

"You see, it merely goes to show you how little, or how much, a name matters. There are some who even refuse to try this brew, simply because they happen to know that mint is never grown in Morocco. How foolish I'm sure they feel when they discover that a name is sometimes nothing more and nothing less than a name. It doesn't have to be the be-all and end-all or even have some hidden meaning. There are times when we affix a particular moniker to something just because it feels right. After all, what's in a name, eh, Baylor? Even Freud said that 'sometimes, a cigar is just a cigar.'"

BJ sat there with her mouth hanging open a bit, her cup of tea still balanced in one hand. She couldn't put her finger on it, even if someone had pressed her to do so, but she had the strangest feeling that Rebecca wasn't just talking about tea leaves from the other side of the world. Then there was the way she kept using Baylor's given name, a name the writer had grown up detesting.

Had BJ actually disliked her name for any reason other than it had been her father's idea? Was it because he had repeatedly told the story of how he expected his firstborn to be a son and how disappointed he had been when a daughter was placed in his arms? Perhaps BJ's extreme dislike for her name had come on the day when she stood toe to toe with the man who had made her life so miserable to confront him over his abominable behavior. His answer had been to turn away from his only child to declare that he was sorry he had given such a pervert his beloved father's name.

"Are you feeling ill, dear?" Rebecca asked.

BJ came back to the present and shook her head to clear away the old anger she felt whenever thinking of her father. "Yes...yes, I'm fine. Do you know my grandmother well, Mrs. Ashby?"

"Oh my, yes. I met Evie and her friend Aimee in Greece in 1947. Very turbulent times back then, but of course, wherever there was political upheaval that's where you would find Evie and her camera. In fact, it was in Havana, Cuba, that we ran into one another again. It was 1953 and I was on my honeymoon. I remember those two weeks as if they were yesterday, you know. My husband, Charles, met a man who told us about Ana Lia on that trip. I suppose the rest is history."

"I had no idea," BJ said in wonderment. "I mean, I don't remember Tanti ever telling me how it was that she came to Ana Lia."

"Sometimes people tell us all sorts of things, and it's not that we're not listening, just that we're not quite ready to hear."

BJ didn't know what to say to that statement. Was it possible that Tanti had told BJ all of these things and she had selfishly paid her grandmother no mind?

"Shall we entertain ourselves?" Rebecca pulled a thick deck of large cards from a small drawer in the table between their chairs.

BJ chuckled. "So, you're a fortuneteller?" she asked.

"Good heavens, no. It's a game, merely something to pass the time. Actually, I have heard that the Tarot came from an Italian game called *tarrochi*. Some say that it was used as a way to pass on stories that the Christian Church didn't want people to know. You see, in the fourth century, one particular faction of the Christian Church was declared 'official.' Up to that point, there were many manifestations of Christianity. Who is to say who knew the truth and who did not? Well, the Roman emperor Theodosius suddenly said that *this* one was real, and all the others were contrary to accepted belief."

"So, where do the cards come into play?" BJ had studied much history and literature of ancient cultures while working on her doctorate, but she had never heard this tale before. She had to admit that she was intrigued.

"Some people say that one of the heretical factions became known as the 'Hidden Church.' It's thought that the cards told the real history of the Church. The game became a way to disguise them yet still pass on the truth. I have no idea if any of what I've just told you is in fact truth, but it would explain why the Christian Church is so vehemently opposed to the Tarot, eh?"

"I guess so. You know, I really don't believe in such things as tarot cards, ouija boards, or crystal balls," BJ said as Rebecca shuffled the cards in an oddly different manner. The ancient fingers seemed quite nimble. "It's not that I think people are goofy who do believe, it's just that I don't happen to think life works that way. I just don't take it seriously."

"Good. That is a prerequisite of mine, Baylor. Frankly, I don't trust anyone who takes the cards too seriously. That's playing a dangerous game." The old woman arranged the cards face down in three piles on the small table. "The worst thing you can do is to take the Tarot too seriously or literally. Then again, I'm not sure I trust anyone who *refuses* to play the game, either."

BJ felt as if the old woman had forced her into a corner with that remark. "Okay, I guess I'm up for it."

"Excellent. Let's begin. The deck that I'm using is a Rider deck. I enjoy the artwork myself. The three piles represent your past," she indicated each pile with one hand, "your present, and your future. The Tarot is not a way to predict one's future. I've seen the very same cards read differently by different individuals. That's why it's good not to take what you see too seriously."

"If not to predict, then what are they used for?" BJ asked.

"Most believers feel they are a tool for divination, for spiritual exploration."

"And you? What do you use them for?"

"Examination. Examination of people, mostly; of human nature. I find it interesting, the things the cards make us think about. Within this first section, we can see your past. More specifically, it's a way to gain insight into past events. Your present will help you to see what goes on right now, and of course, there is what you may expect in the future."

"All of the cards have what looks like a court jester or a joker painted on the back. What's that supposed to mean?" Baylor asked.

"Very observant, my friend. That is the Fool. There are many ways and spreads to the Tarot. I choose a very traditional way called *The Fool's Journey.* It's rather like a story."

"And I'm the fool, I take it?" BJ raised one eyebrow quizzically.

"Don't be offended, dear Baylor. We are all fools when we start out on a journey. Did you know that the word 'fool' used to be used as a term of honor?"

Baylor shook her head. She vaguely remembered her high-school Latin and recalled that the Fool played a big part in medieval literature.

"A fool was someone who was pure...protected. Do you recall the story of Parsifal?"

"Yes. He was the knight who found the Grail."

"Exactly. Parsifal was a knight of the Round Table. He found the Holy Grail, yet he was known as Parsifal, the Holy Fool. His name actually means 'naïve fool.' You see, his mother kept him sheltered and protected from the hurts of the world."

Rebecca turned over a card from one of the piles. "I've selected a very simple way of reading the Tarot for your first experience. Next time we will try something more complex."

BJ nodded, never questioning the fact that there would be a next time. She watched as Rebecca chose a number of cards from the pile that represented the past. The old woman carefully turned them all face up before speaking.

"The Emperor, the Tower, Strength, and Death. You display fairly strong elements in your past. Some would say your past has been an intense journey that has left its mark on you. The Emperor represents your earthly father." Rebecca watched as BJ's upper lip twitched into a sneer. "Sometimes it simply means a person in authority. It can even mean a certain control or structure that you have had to deal with." She pushed the card aside.

"My father and I had a very...strained relationship." BJ had no idea why she said it. The words just seemed to pop out of her mouth as if her voice had a will of its own.

"How unfortunate. Fathers and daughters...those can be such complex bonds. Your father has passed on, hasn't he?"

"Yes," BJ answered with a tightening of her jaw.

"Let's move on. The next card is the Tower. Usually this represents a shattering of the structure in your life. Perhaps something traumatic, something life altering. This seems to indicate that the event centered on your father." She slid the card over next to the first.

BJ's silence told Rebecca all she needed to know. She moved on to the next card. "Strength. It means exactly what its name implies. Given the first two cards, it's no wonder that you had to develop strength to help face the situations in which you were placed."

"Since I'm still alive, I guess the Death card is wrong, huh?" Baylor asked.

"Death can mean an ending or a change. It is not so much about the physical death as metaphorical. Oddly enough, this is one of the three most misunderstood cards in the Major Arcana of the Tarot. Many times, Death can be a good thing, meaning that something you no longer need is gone from your life. It can be a

way of life, a habit, maybe even a relationship, sometimes innocence. The one thing to remember about death as it relates to
change is that when you fight, it can be painful. If you accept it,
however, you can move upward and onward in enlightenment."

"Yeah, well, so much for the past," BJ said uneasily.
Rebecca's reading was doing exactly what she had predicted. It
was making BJ think. She had once believed that she had put all
those old terrors to rest, but clearly that wasn't the case. "How
about the present?"

Rebecca turned over four cards from the second pile. "The
Magician, the Chariot, the High Priestess, and Temperance. The
Magician represents a teacher who tries to help you see your
potential. You have all the tools and abilities to face life, Baylor.
You haven't accepted that fact yet. Your teacher will help you see
the power that lies within yourself."

BJ sat listening intently. She didn't even notice that Rebecca
had begun to personalize the information. "I don't suppose you
see a name there, do you?" she asked as she leaned over to examine the card.

"I'm sorry, dear, but it doesn't work that way. It could be a
friend, a lover, or a relative. The usual pattern is that it's a person
who has earned your trust, someone who believes in you. Suddenly, this person will appear to you in a different light."

"A little vague, but I guess I can live with it." BJ smiled.
"Okay. Next?"

"The Chariot can represent conflicts, decisions, possibly
travel. The conflicts will be *within* you, Baylor. The Tarot is not as
concerned with the battles you fight outside of yourself as the
ones inside.

"Next we see the High Priestess. She is your spiritual mother,
mystery you will never be able to explain. It is she who calls to
you in those moments of intuition when you follow your instincts,
but don't know exactly why."

The writer stared off into space. The old woman's words had
completely ensnared her. She could see herself; not actually see,
but she could *feel.* She was throwing caution to the wind and acting totally on instinct. For the first time in her life, she wasn't
worrying about the consequences.

Rebecca's voice cut through BJ's vision. "Finally, there is
Temperance. It is indicative of the balance between our inner decisions. The mortal lesson that causes us to know that there is more
to justice than right and wrong, guilty and innocent."

"Well, that was pretty painless," BJ commented.

"You see. It can be great fun, even worthy of some honest

introspection when we don't take it too seriously."

"How about my future? Anything I should look out for? Any long trips I should put off?" *Besides the one that got me here in the first place?*

"Let's take a look," Rebecca answered. She drew four cards from the final pile. "The Sun, the Devil, the Hermit, and the Lovers. How very interesting...all entities. What an exciting place your life will be, Baylor."

"Really?" Rebecca's enthusiasm for the cards had infected the writer. "So, what do these mean?"

"The Sun is a most favorable card. It shines upon those who have suffered during their journey. The Sun's brightness indicates finding ultimate joy or prosperity. It shows that happiness will find you, Baylor."

"Don't you mean *I'll* find *it?*"

"No, not this time. Happiness is like the butterfly that constantly eludes your grasp. When you finally sit back, relax, and open your hand, it settles comfortably in your palm."

"Huh."

"Next, the Devil."

"Now that sounds more like me." BJ grinned at Rebecca.

"The Devil isn't so much a person we can blame, but rather the hell and suffering we create in our life. There is an old saying, 'we make our own devils.' Most people don't want to take responsibility for their life by saying they are where they are because of themselves. It's easier to say something like 'the devil made me do it.' That way, they release themselves of any responsibility.

"Some of these cards depict the devil in ropes or chains. You have drawn a card with an image that is free of such bindings. This expresses an ability to escape your hell, to break away from the negativity. We make our own demons, Baylor. We can destroy them, too."

Demons, BJ thought. *I still have plenty of them, all right.* She found herself asking Rebecca a question to which she feared the answer. "Do you believe they can be destroyed, Mrs. Ashby? Can it be that simple?"

"Don't confuse simplicity with ease, Baylor. Yes, I believe it's that simple, and no, it is never easy."

BJ and Rebecca stared at one another. The writer felt there were more questions to ask, but she couldn't think of them.

"Let's see what's next. The Hermit. How very appropriate for a loner such as you," Rebecca said.

BJ didn't even think to ask how the old woman knew that. She had tried to tell herself that she lived that life because she was having too much fun to commit, but besides some great sex and fun times, she never really had very much fun. "So, why is this guy so fitting for me?" she asked.

"The Hermit represents two factors: solitude and a search for the truth. You see, Baylor, you must travel alone when searching for the truth. It's one of those tasks only you can do. You can certainly surround yourself with those you love as support, but ultimately it is up to you to find the key to unlock that door."

BJ looked up sharply. This was the third time since her arrival on Ana Lia that she had heard or read about the key to happiness. She looked down at the last card in her future. "The Lovers. I kind of like the sound of that."

"As with most of these cards, the Lovers are not literally a string of lovers that will make their way to your bed. Instead, they represent lessons you will learn through love—and that includes loving yourself, which is the most important lesson we can ever learn. If we can do that, how can others not love us as well?"

BJ became silent, thinking of all the older woman had told her. She looked up at the mantel clock above the fireplace. "I had no idea it was so late. I've been here for hours. I'm sorry. I didn't mean to monopolize your time."

"Not at all, Baylor. I thoroughly enjoyed meeting you and I do hope you don't mind the small diversion." Rebecca indicated the cards.

"Not at all. I don't go in much for that sort of thing, but this was actually interesting."

"I do hope you'll come back and see me again. I don't get out too much. I have a hip that troubles me some in this humidity. I hear that you've become friends with our Hobie Lynn. Perhaps you'll bring her to tea some afternoon."

"I'd love to talk with you again." BJ smiled. "Hobie and I do seem to keep *running* into each other." She wasn't exactly sure how much to explain to the old woman. "But to say we're friends might be pushing it a tad."

"Well, you two appear to get on so well. I'm sure the longer you stay in Ana Lia, the more you'll get to know one another."

"Yes, well...I'm not sure I anticipate staying on the island too much longer. Tanti's doctor said she was almost ready to come home. Since I'm not able to care for her with my leg the way it is, I thought I'd just hire someone to take care of the place *and* Tanti."

"Well, Baylor, let me say that you will be sorely missed here, by more people than you know."

Once BJ was safely on her way, Rebecca sat down at her

kitchen table and picked up the cordless telephone. She still looked at the object as though it were something foreign, but she had to admit that some changes in life were good; not all, but some. She dialed and waited.

"Hello, Sarah Jane, how is your mother? Yes, I'm so glad you still recognize this old voice. Is Evie awake this afternoon? I wonder if you wouldn't mind checking for me, dear." Rebecca waited on the line for a few moments.

"She is? Marvelous...would you mind? Thank you, and be sure to tell your mother I said hello." She listened to the canned music and began to hum "The Girl from Ipanema" just as Evelyn Warren picked up the line.

"Evie! How are you, gal? You'll never believe who I just spent the afternoon with...Oh, well, you think you're so smart." Rebecca chuckled at her friend's laughter on the other end of the line. "Yes, my dear, it's precisely as you said. We have more important things to worry about right now, though." Rebecca repeated BJ's parting words.

"Yes, I know. Everything will be ruined if she leaves now. Evie, we simply must come up with a way to keep Baylor on this island for a little longer."

Chapter
7

Fatigue caught up with BJ and, as luck would have it, she was rather close to the bakery. Remembering Mack's offer of a ride, she glanced at her watch. Another twenty minutes and the sheriff would drive by. The tantalizing odors coming from the bakery drew BJ inside and she purchased a couple of pieces of fudge. Once outside, she spied the bench and made her way across the street.

She never thought twice about waiting for the light, even though there was absolutely no traffic on Main Street. If she was aware at all that this was a change in her normal pattern of behavior, she certainly gave no outward sign.

BJ arrived at the bench to find a small boy occupying one end. "Mind if I grab some lumber, kid?"

The spiky blonde-haired boy looked up from the coloring book. He wore round, wire-framed glasses that he frequently pushed up with one finger. Holding a small nub of crayon aloft, he looked her up and down with a wary eye. "My mom says I shouldn't talk to strangers."

BJ grinned. The boy had an almost indiscernible childish lisp that made him adorable, not that BJ was partial to children in any way. "Fair enough. I won't talk to you, then, but I'll take a seat right here. Okay, kid?"

"My mom says learnin' to share is good. S'okay."

BJ stretched out her legs and rested her arms along the back of the bench. The youngster went back to coloring a map of the United States. "Hot out, huh, kid," she commented.

"My mom says it's not polite to call someone 'kid.'"

BJ popped a piece of fudge into her mouth. The Florida heat had quickly turned the treat into warm brown goop. She held out the other piece in one hand. "Wan thum?" she mumbled.

"My mom says it's not polite to talk with your mouth full."

BJ rolled her eyes, yet continued to hold the candy aloft. She knew he wanted it.

"Mom says I should never take candy from a stranger."

"Your mom's got a lot of rules, doesn't she?"

"Kinda." He pushed at his glasses, then smiled at BJ. The grin was the kind that showed off two even rows of perfectly white baby teeth. His smile fairly glowed and BJ just knew that this was one of *them*—a kid that was truly happy.

"What's your name?" he asked.

"What's it to ya?" BJ answered with a wink.

The boy shrugged, smiled again, and resumed his coloring. His feet swung in the air and he appeared perfectly content.

"What's your name?" BJ asked a moment later.

"What's it to ya?" he answered without missing a beat.

"Oh, a smart aleck, eh?"

The youngster giggled.

BJ didn't understand the bond she had with children. The last time Juliana had physically dragged her home for Thanksgiving, she'd received the shock of her life. Searching the house for BJ, she eventually found her in the basement lying on her stomach, circled by half a dozen children, playing Candy Land. BJ wasn't more comfortable with the children than with adults; the children merely accepted her biting honesty and somewhat open criticism.

"My name's BJ."

"Noah." The youngster held out a tiny hand. BJ smiled and shook it.

"See, now we're not strangers." She held out the fudge and the boy quickly popped the gooey mess into his mouth.

"Whatcha up to this afternoon, Bubba?" BJ asked.

"My name's Noah," he said and BJ chuckled. "I'm waitin' for my mom. She's in the drugstore."

"Ah, Mom, the one with all the rules. How was that fudge?"

"Real good, thanks! Mom says sugar's not really bad, 'less you eat too much. Mom says—"

BJ held up a hand. "You sure your mom's not the great and powerful wizard from Oz?"

"No," Noah giggled in reaction. "There she is! Hi, Mom."

Noah stood up on the bench and jumped up and down as his mother came into view. BJ could only watch in stunned amazement as she came closer and, finally, Noah wrapped his arms around her neck.

"Hi, sweetheart." Hobie kissed her son's cheek and returned his fierce hug. "I see you have a new friend." She gave a little smirk in BJ's direction.

"I should have known," BJ replied with a wry smile. "So, this is your mom, huh?"

"Yep."

"I see you two have been sharing some chocolate," Hobie said.

"How did you know that?" BJ asked. "Oh," she said upon seeing Noah's chocolate-covered chin.

Hobie wiped her son's face with a Kleenex. "Well, him and then there's...uh..." She handed a clean piece of tissue to BJ.

The dark-haired woman frowned and wiped her mouth. "Thanks," she muttered. She realized suddenly that the boy looked exactly like Hobie when he scrunched his turned-up nose and pushed his glasses up a tad.

Hobie sat down and Noah jumped in her lap. The bond was easily readable. Hobie wore a million-dollar smile while listening to him talk about his day.

BJ felt a little disappointed by this turn of events. First, for some reason, she had assumed Hobie was unattached. The more time they spent together, the more she thought Hobie was gay. Hobie didn't wear a wedding ring, but that didn't mean anything, did it? The second reason was that BJ felt a little in the way. She watched, almost with envy, as Hobie and Noah laughed and hugged. For the first time, she realized that something was missing in her life, something important.

"You never said you had a kid," she said.

"You never asked," Hobie replied. "Thanks for lunch, by the way. That was awfully sweet of you." Noah settled down in her lap and leaned back against her chest.

BJ arched one eyebrow until it reached angular proportions. "Somehow I figured you'd be the last person on this island to call me sweet."

Hobie chuckled. "Okay, it was very nice. How's that?"

"Much better, thanks. I do have a reputation to uphold, you know."

"Oh, that's right. The association might ask for their broom back."

"You're probably the one that dropped that house on my sister, aren't you?"

Noah's head swung back and forth as he watched them take turns talking. He didn't think it sounded like joking, but he felt much better when the two women looked at one another and started laughing.

"What are you doing out here, anyway?" Hobie asked.

"I'm waiting for Mack. He happened to mention he'd give me a ride if I needed one."

"Oh, us too," Hobie answered as she shifted Noah in her lap. "I loaned the truck to my friend Laura."

Both women looked up as Mack's patrol car braked sharply in front of them. The passenger side window opened and Mack appeared, leaning across the seat.

"Baylor, I've been looking for you. I need you to get in the car right now."

Hobie knew that tone to her brother's voice. It never meant good news. "Mack, is everything okay?"

"Sorry, Hob, I forgot about you and Noah. Come on, everyone, get in," Mack instructed. "Baylor, your grandmother's taken a turn for the worse."

"What's going on, Mack?" BJ demanded once they were settled.

"All I know is what the nurse told me. She said something about Evelyn developing a high fever. I guess they called in a doctor from the mainland and he said to contact her family. That's really all I know."

"Christ, that's all they said?"

"Mom, she said a bad word," Noah said.

"Shh, honey." Hobie pulled Noah into her lap and kissed the top of his head. "She's just very worried."

BJ reached out and ruffled Noah's hair. "Sorry, Bubba, don't listen to me, okay? I may say a few more before the day's over."

Noah clamped his hands over his ears, and BJ smiled at him. "'Kay. I can't hear you."

Hobie pulled her son more tightly to her and watched BJ. The dark-haired woman chewed on her thumbnail as she looked out the window. She looked worried and nervous, but Hobie saw something more. Hobie had seen that haunted expression numerous times. She'd seen it every time she walked into a waiting room to talk with a family member. Family who felt the truth long before the physicians would acknowledge it. That expression, a combination of hurt and fear, was one of the reasons she had left full-time medicine. She was used to that look, but found that she didn't like seeing it on BJ's face. She reached out and laid her hand on BJ's forearm.

BJ looked up in alarm, not used to people breaking that barrier, the personal space that she carefully maintained.

Hobie had no idea what to say to the woman who was still more a stranger than anything else. She squeezed the strong arm and smiled, meeting the anxious gray eyes. Much to her surprise, BJ didn't pull away. Even more surprising to the vet was that she left her own hand resting there for the duration of the trip. Neither woman seemed much inclined to pull away.

"Look, if I don't see this doctor pretty goddamn soon—" BJ's voice rose with every word as she shouted at the nurse. She quieted when she saw Noah clap his hands over his ears.

"Ms. Warren," the nurse began, "I know exactly how you feel, believe me, but if Dr. Trenton stops to talk to you now, then your grandmother goes without his care. He's at her bedside as we speak and as soon as he can, he'll come out and talk with you."

The genuine look of concern on the nurse's face, coupled with the calming tone of her voice, caused BJ to take a step back. She took a deep breath, reluctantly nodded, and sat down beside Hobie and Noah.

"Sarah, is that Steve Trenton seeing Evelyn?" Hobie asked the nurse.

"Yes, it is."

"Hey," Hobie said, turning to face BJ. "The good news is that Steve Trenton is a complete alarmist. If he says she's doing terrible, it means she's not that bad."

BJ offered the vet a halfhearted smile. "You sound like you know him."

"Sort of. I did my residency under him in Tampa."

BJ couldn't even believe that at a time like this, she actually felt a little twinge of pain over the idea that Hobie could have possibly had a past before they met. "Did you...um, know him well?" *Geez, Beej, you sound pathetic. Somebody might even think you were jealous. Yeah, right. I may be hard up out here in the boonies, but I don't have a jealous bone in my body. Never had, never will.*

"I guess I did. As well as one *can* get to know a self-centered sexist jerk." Hobie smiled. "As much as I dislike his ego, I know he's good at what he does."

"Ms. Warren?"

BJ and Hobie looked up to see the topic of their conversation standing before them. Steve Trenton was probably fifty years old, but he could have easily passed for forty. He was slim and tan, with a small sprinkling of gray at his temples. BJ disliked him immediately; he reminded her of the slick salesman who had talked her into buying her Jaguar.

"Hobie?"

"Hello, Steve. Good to see you."

"Uh, yes...same here. Are you a member of the family?" he asked.

"No, I'm here with..." Hobie paused. There was that same predicament again. Who was Baylor Warren to Hobie? "I'm with my...friend," she said at last.

If Hobie's words made any impact on BJ, she gave no indication. "That would be me." BJ felt like waving her fingers in front of the man's face. "How is my grandmother and what the hell happened to her?"

"Well, the short version is that she developed pneumonia," Dr. Trenton said. "Mycoplasma pneumonia, to be specific."

"But I just saw her yesterday. She was fine."

"That's the thing with old folks. They're so used to being stoic and ignoring aches and pains that when you need them to tell you what's going on, they don't."

"I still don't see how—"

"Pneumonia can creep up on older patients quickly, especially hospitalized patients," he explained. "The staff first thought infection, which is common. Post-op patients like Mrs. Warren receive spirometry care in order to combat the effects of being prone for long periods of time, but sometimes there's nothing you can do to stop it."

"What are you doing for her now?"

"She's on intravenous medication and we're working to keep her fever down. We've gotten her back down to a more normal temp. She should do just fine from here on in, but I think we may want to rethink her leaving the hospital. There are a great many things that can go wrong with elderly patients. I doubt Medicare or her insurance will approve it, but if you can afford it, I think the hospital here on Ana Lia is a much safer way to go."

"Money isn't a problem," BJ answered. "I just want my grandmother to get the best care possible."

"I understand."

"Is there a set course of treatment? Will she heal fully from it?"

"Yes, it's pretty standard. There's good and bad to pneumonias. Chances of a fast recovery are greatest under certain conditions. In Mrs. Warren's case, she has a few strikes against her, but that doesn't mean she won't have a 100 percent recovery. We caught it before it had a chance to get to the coughing stage, which is about as good as it gets."

"Will antibiotics help?"

"Absolutely. She needs a proper diet and access to O2 to increase oxygen in the blood. She may need medication to ease chest pain and to provide relief from a violent cough if that becomes an issue, which I doubt. Those are the most important reasons to see that she has around-the-clock care."

"Enough said. Can I see her?"

"Yes, of course. She's feeling a bit social right now, but that's because she feels better. Not too long, though. Rest is the best thing for her now."

"I understand. Oh, thanks, Doctor," she added as an after-thought.

She walked down the short hall to her grandmother's room. "Tanti." BJ smiled at the eyes that met her as soon as she walked into the room.

"Baylor," Evelyn rasped. She looked tired, but in relatively fair condition. The rosy tinge to her cheeks was more from the fever than robust health. "I hope I'm not ruining your plans, dear heart."

"Tanti, don't be ridiculous. I'm always here for anything you need, you know that."

"But I know you wanted to go back to your own home and—"

"Don't give that a second thought, okay? Besides, you're my family. Wherever you are is home. You just concentrate all your strength on getting well. I don't have that much on my plate that I can't spend the summer on Ana Lia."

"Are you sure?"

"I can write here just as well as I can in Chicago."

"Thank you, dear heart. What would I do without you?"

"Well, I guess I'm not gonna let you find that out." BJ patted her grandmother's hand. "I'm just really glad you're going to be okay, Tanti. I was pretty worried for a while there."

"I am sorry, dear. I didn't mean to frighten you."

There was a timid knock on the door and Hobie's head popped into view.

"Hello, dear. Come right in," Evelyn said.

"I don't want to intrude, but I wanted to make sure you were doing all right now, Evelyn."

The nurse walked into the room right after Hobie. "I'm sorry, Ms. Warren, but I wonder if I could get you to sign some paper-work for your grandmother's stay?"

"Sure. Tanti, will you be all right?"

"Oh yes, go, go."

"I'll just be out at the desk."

"Hobie Lynn will stay with me, won't you dear?"

"Of course," Hobie answered.

"I want to thank you, dear, for looking after Baylor," Evelyn said once her granddaughter had left the room.

"Evelyn, I'm the last person in the world you should be

thanking right about now. I feel responsible for all of this."

"What? Oh, that. Don't give it another thought. I'm concerned that Baylor may be very down tonight. She spends so much time alone. She doesn't think I know, but I do. Her life consists of her writing, drinking, and carousing."

Hobie tried not to smile, but she was sure she failed. Evelyn's portrayal of her granddaughter was uncannily accurate. "I'm sure there's more to it than that. She seems to have a very full life."

"She thinks that going out to a party every night of the week and sleeping with a dozen women a month is socializing. It's not, and you know it. The kind of people she spends her time with in Chicago—well, she might as well be alone. I worry about her, Hobie Lynn."

"I know, Evelyn, I know. Tell you what; why don't I ask her to come back to Mother's house and we'll all have dinner together? Do you think she'd be okay with that?"

"Oh, thank you, dear. Knowing that you're keeping an eye on Baylor eases my mind a great deal."

"Don't get too excited. I'm not sure she'll even agree. I don't know if you've been keeping up on current events around town or not, but Baylor and I don't exactly get along 100 percent of the time."

"I know that Baylor can be...difficult."

"Evelyn, saying Baylor is difficult is to give a whole new meaning to the word." Hobie chuckled. "I just don't think she cares to have me around much."

"Why, don't be silly, dear. My granddaughter is completely enamored of you."

Hobie laughed. Then, seeing that Evelyn was serious, she froze. "We're talking about Baylor Warren, right? I mean, you don't have any other granddaughters, do you?"

"No." Evelyn smiled kindly at Hobie's dazed expression. "Just one, and Baylor is it. She may seem full of piss and vinegar right now, but she doesn't know what life is all about yet. She doesn't know what the *key* is." Evelyn whispered this last part and Hobie smiled.

"So, what are you girls talking about?" BJ teased as she came through the door. Hobie and Evelyn both wore guilty expressions. Hobie blushed and turned even redder upon BJ's examination. "Oh, please, Tanti, you're not telling embarrassing stories of when I was a baby, are you?"

"Now, Baylor, would I do such a thing?"

"In a heartbeat," came the writer's dry response.

"All right, ladies, I hate to interrupt, but this patient needs her rest," Dr. Trenton said as he strode into the room.

"Tanti, you have them call me for anything you want or need, you understand? Anything."

"I understand and I will, dear heart. Now, where will you eat dinner?"

BJ laughed. "What in the world does that have to do with the price of tea in China?"

"If I know you're not eating properly, I'll just sit here and worry. I'm sure that can't be good for my health. I think you should eat dinner with Hobie Lynn."

"Tanti!"

"Um, actually," Hobie touched her fingers to BJ's elbow, "I did sort of tell her I might kind of ask you anyway. I mean, just so you wouldn't have to be alone tonight," she stammered. "My mom's cooking dinner for me and Mack anyway."

"Oh, I appreciate it, but I really—"

"If I have to worry about you, Baylor Joan, I'll be awake all night," Evelyn interrupted.

BJ raised an eyebrow. The comment sounded more like a threat than an old woman's worried rambling. She had a fleeting thought that perhaps her grandmother was up to something, but the sincere expression on her face convinced her otherwise.

"Sure. Sure, that would be great." BJ turned and offered Hobie a lopsided smile. "I have to stop by and feed Arturo first, though."

"No problem," Hobie replied.

"Uh, Hobie, I wonder if I could ask you a question?" Dr. Trenton sidled up to Hobie. He was trying to be inconspicuous, but he wasn't subtle enough for BJ.

He tried to move in between the two women, but the redhead stood her ground beside BJ. "Yes, what is it, Steve?"

"Well, I..." He looked up at BJ's somewhat intimidating presence. "I thought, actually wondered if maybe you wanted to..."

His eyes once again met with BJ's cold gaze. Her lips had actually pulled back into a sneer. The message was loud and clear to the would-be suitor. "Um...never mind. Nice to see you again."

"You too, Steve," Hobie answered distractedly.

They left the hospital with Mack, who had surprised BJ by sitting in the waiting room the whole time. They piled into the patrol car once more and Noah scooted over to BJ.

She smiled at the youngster. "She's not all better yet, but she will be soon."

"Good, I'm glad." He nodded emphatically one time to punctuate the remark.

"Thanks, Bubba."

The boy surprised BJ by moving into her lap and looking out the window as they drove along.

"Here, let me..." Hobie reached for the boy, but BJ's hand stopped her.

"Nah, he's okay."

They rode that way in silence until BJ spoke. "Do you and Noah...uh, live alone?" She knew of no other way to ask the inevitable question.

Hobie seemed to miss the question's intent. "We live with my mom. Actually, it's a pretty big place. Noah and I live in a guesthouse on her property. It has its ups and downs. There's always a baby-sitter for Noah, and I get home-cooked meals when I'm too tired to make them."

"And the downs?" BJ thought about what would have happened had she and her mother tried to live together as adults. It would have been World War III.

"Well...it *is* living with your mother. Need I say more?"

BJ chuckled and nodded.

"You better tell her about Mom before she gets surprised." Mack's voice sounded from the front of the car.

"Surprised?" BJ got a strange feeling along her spine. "She doesn't see pink elephants or anything, does she? Wait, is there a hamster I should know about?"

Hobie smiled. "Very funny. No, I just need to give you sort of an advance warning before you meet my mother."

"Dear God, what does she see that's not there?"

"My father." Hobie quickly continued when she saw the writer's eyes grow large. "No, it's not like she sees him. My father died when I was a teenager. Mom, well," Hobie gave a tired smile, "she'll act like she doesn't know my father's dead."

"She doesn't know he's dead?" BJ's voice rose an octave.

"It's not that she doesn't know...it's just that she...well, she..."

BJ saw the tension in Hobie's ramrod straight posture and knew then what she was trying to say. Knew all too well. "She doesn't *want* to know," she said.

The vet looked over at BJ with relief written across her features. "Yeah. She just didn't accept it at first, so everyone kind of went along with her charade. It seemed harmless enough. It's rough now. It's getting harder to explain things to Noah."

"Someone should have a talk with her," BJ said. "You need to be honest with her."

Hobie vigorously shook her head. "No. I lost my father, but

she lost her husband. I don't know how it feels to lose the other half of your whole life. I'm not qualified to sit in judgment and tell her what she's doing is wrong."

BJ shrugged. "It's your call."

BJ immediately felt comfortable in the large Allen home. A long hallway led toward the back of the house; on the right was an entrance to the kitchen, and on the left was an opening into the living room, which was darkened by the shade of the tall palm trees in the front yard.

"Grandma, Grandma!" Noah cried out as soon as they entered.

"There's my pumpkin," Theresa Allen said. She bent down and easily lifted the small boy up.

"Hi, Mom," Hobie and Mack said in unison.

The sheriff gave his mother a hug and stepped back beside BJ.

"MacArthur, you looked tired," Theresa said. The sheriff merely shrugged and rolled his eyes.

BJ couldn't resist. She leaned in close to Mack as Hobie greeted her mother. "*MacArthur?*" she whispered under her breath. "Okay, you got no room to talk about my name."

"Very funny. How'd you like me to double the fine on that jaywalking ticket I gave ya?" he countered.

"Mom." Hobie gave her mother a kiss on the cheek and ushered her to where BJ stood. "Mom, this is—"

"Baylor Warren. Yes, I know, dear. How is Evelyn, my dear?"

BJ's eyebrows shot up. She looked over Theresa's shoulder at Hobie, who shrugged, offering up a guilty smile.

"Word travels like wildfire here on Ana Lia," Hobie said.

"I can see that," BJ replied sarcastically.

"Mom knows you...obviously. Baylor, this is my mother, Theresa Allen."

BJ smiled at the older woman, and the smile that graced her features wasn't flirtatious or jesting. It was warm and relaxed. It was honest. She took Theresa's hand within both of her own. "It's a pleasure to meet you, Mrs. Allen. I appreciate you having me here tonight."

"Now, don't even think twice about it. I'm glad my children had the good manners to invite you. Now, if my husband would just get home we could sit down to the table."

Hobie and BJ exchanged uncomfortable glances, but the tall woman smiled graciously.

"You probably want to get off that ankle," Hobie said. "Mom, why don't you two go into the den and I'll set the table."

"Thank you, sweetheart."

Theresa Allen led the way into a room filled with all of the things that BJ had ever imagined a family den might have. Two overstuffed couches and a large leather recliner circled an oak coffee table. Light wood paneling covered the walls and a piano stood in one corner. BJ examined the framed photographs that sat atop the piano, recognizing the young, freckle-faced redhead in many of the pictures as Hobie. A series of small-paned windows took up the entire length of the west wall and the slowly setting sun lit the room with a warm brilliance. The room had a relaxed atmosphere that BJ could feel soaking into her body the moment she sat down on the comfortably soft sofa.

"Tell me, Baylor, how is Evelyn?" Theresa asked.

"It looks like she's going to be fine; that's what the doctor said, anyway. She didn't look bad, but the doctor thinks it would be best if she stayed in the hospital instead of going home to recuperate."

"I know that will be hard on her. I'll go up there tomorrow and see if she needs anything."

"Thanks, I know that would mean a lot to her. My grandmother's not exactly the type to enjoy being cooped up in the hospital any longer than she has to."

Hobie and Mack walked into the room, followed quickly by Noah. The boy launched himself toward the sheriff, who lifted him high into the air.

"Can I get you something to drink, Baylor?" Hobie asked.

"No, I'm good."

"BJ, why does Mom call you Baylor?" Noah asked.

"Did she?" Baylor hadn't noticed. So many people had called her that over the last few days that she surmised she'd become accustomed to it. She thought it strange that it hadn't caused her as much pain as it used to. "Well, Baylor's actually my real name. BJ is just a nickname that comes from the initials of my first and middle name."

"Okay." Noah ran off, apparently satisfied with her explanation.

"Mom, you think that roast is about done?" Hobie asked.

"I just have to mash the potatoes, but I don't want everything to get cold before your father gets here."

Hobie looked over at Mack, who raised his eyebrows, but said nothing. "Um, Mom...I think Dad said he'd be late tonight. We better go ahead and start."

"Oh, well, I don't know...your father might still—"

BJ gently laid her hand over the older woman's. "Mrs. Allen, excuse me for saying this, but I'm going to say it anyway. You don't really think your husband is coming home, do you?"

"Why, I don't know what you mean."

"Baylor," Hobie said in a low warning tone.

The writer ignored Hobie and continued in a sad, soothing tone. "My father died when I was nineteen, Mrs. Allen. My mother never could accept his death. For the longest time she acted as if he were still alive."

Theresa Allen looked frightened, but couldn't turn away from the dark-haired woman. "I really don't see how that is the same, dear. My husband—"

"Was your whole world, wasn't he? At least that's the way it was for my mother. She woke him in the morning, fixed his meals, and cleaned his clothes. She kept his house and looked after him day and night for twenty-five years. She never even knew what it was like to do anything for herself. She had no idea what her purpose in life was, if it wasn't taking care of him. After he died, I suppose she thought she had no purpose. Do you understand what I'm saying, Mrs. Allen?"

BJ understood how her invasive questions would make the other woman feel. She realized that if Theresa acknowledged her questions, then she would have to accept the truth of it all.

After several moments of silence, Theresa slowly nodded.

Mack glanced over at his sister and they exchanged worried glances, but neither appeared to know exactly what to do.

"When your husband died, you wanted to lie down and do the same. Didn't you? That's what my mother finally did. She went to bed one day and she just never got up again. That's what you probably wanted to do, too. You couldn't, though, could you? You had children who depended on you. There was no curling into a ball and giving up. I bet you never even had time to grieve. You just had to keep going until it seemed as if it never even happened."

"Yes." Theresa's eyes teared up and she nodded, then lowered her head.

BJ squeezed Theresa's hand. "I think it's time for you to admit that your husband is dead and that he's not coming back, Mrs. Allen."

"Get out," Hobie hissed. "I want you to leave. Leave right now."

BJ looked up with a sad expression and nodded. "I will if that's what you want." She turned back to the woman seated beside her. "But let me ask you this, Mrs. Allen. Is that what you want? Do *you* want me to leave?"

Theresa Allen looked into soft gray eyes filled with compassion. BJ knew what she was thinking. She could see it in her eyes. Theresa realized that there was finally someone who knew exactly how she felt. At last, someone who understood what had gone on and how she had let it all snowball to this point.

BJ and Theresa both looked over to where Mack and Hobie stood. Hobie was outraged, that was apparent. Mack shifted his weight uncomfortably from foot to foot.

BJ glanced again at Hobie. The vet's arms hung rigidly at her side, her hands balled into fists. Had BJ guessed Hobie's thoughts at that moment, her own demise would probably have been high on the list.

Then BJ saw something then that she previously thought only existed in the prose she wrote. As she watched Theresa's face, it appeared as though a veil lifted from the older woman's eyes.

Theresa looked between her two children and then turned to BJ. "No," she said so softly it was barely a whisper. Her voice then grew stronger. "No, I don't want you to leave. Hobie Lynn, where are your manners?"

"But I-I—" Hobie stammered.

"I think my behavior has gone on long enough. I thank both of you children, but I never meant to put you through this—"

"No, Mom, it's okay." Mack quickly moved to kneel before his mother.

"It's not, but you're sweet to say so. I can't believe I've carried on for this long. Hobie—"

The redhead spun around and rushed from the room. Seconds later the screen door to the back porch slammed.

"I'll go get her, Mom," Mack spoke up.

"No, Mack. I think I'm the one she's upset with. Let me go," BJ said.

"I'm sure not gonna fight you for it."

BJ rose on her crutches, but before she could move away, Theresa reached out to her.

"Thank you, Baylor. It took courage for you to reveal that piece of yourself to me...to all of us. It's amazing, really, after all these years that your words should be the thing to make me see. I don't even understand that. Maybe if you do the same thing with Hobie Lynn, she'll be forgiving. She's a very good daughter."

BJ smiled and nodded, giving the older woman a wink before she walked away. "I know that, and I'll try to take your advice."

She looked through the screen door and saw Hobie pacing across the yard as Noah ran around trying to catch firebugs. He was oblivious to the emotional turmoil around him.

Taking a deep breath, BJ pushed open the door and walked out onto the porch. The look of hurt and anger on Hobie's face when she looked at BJ took any thoughts of fight from BJ's mind. She simply deflated as she sat down heavily on the porch swing.

Hobie turned toward the ocean and stood silently before stalking across the lawn. BJ prepared herself for one of their now infamous confrontations.

"Do you realize what you could have done?" Hobie asked in a tightly restrained voice.

"Yes, and I'm sorry, but I felt that I had to."

"I asked you not to say anything. I specifically asked you not to interfere."

"Yes, I know."

"What is it with you? Do you always go around doing exactly what you want without any thought to the consequences for others?"

"Yeah, pretty much. Up to this point, anyway."

"That makes you incredibly selfish!"

"I know."

You're impossible!"

"I know that, too."

Hobie abruptly stopped her tirade. She looked tired, as if it had been a great effort to hold on to her anger. She took a few more steps toward BJ. "How can I yell at you if you're going to agree with every damn thing I say?" she asked as she folded her arms across her chest.

BJ attempted to look contrite. She wasn't accustomed to answering for her behavior; rather, she was used to letting loose with her form of brutal honesty. Dispensing a truth tempered with compassion was something new to her.

"Would it make you feel better if you could sock me one? Go ahead. Just let me have it." BJ closed her eyes, scrunched her face up, and prepared for a blow.

"Stop that."

"No, really. I'm serious. Nail me a good one. I guarantee it will make you feel lots better."

Hobie shook her bangs from her eyes and sat down beside BJ. "You are *so* strange," she finally said in exasperation, to which BJ grinned.

After a moment of comfortable silence, Hobie spoke. "I'm sorry," she said, then blew a breath of air upward to push her bangs from her forehead. "I shouldn't have gotten so angry, especially at you. I mean, look what you've done for my mom. In just a few minutes you've changed our lives."

"For the better, I hope."

"I think so."

"Why did you get so mad, then?"

Tears filled Hobie's eyes, and BJ didn't think she was ready for this. A month ago, she had dumped a girlfriend and never thought twice about the jilted woman's tears. Now, sitting beside the tearful redhead, she had the inexplicable urge to hold her in her arms. For some reason she couldn't explain, she wanted to protect Hobie; wanted to keep anything bad from ever happening to her. The enormity of that desire hit BJ like a punch in the stomach. It was even stronger than on the day when Hobie had begun to cry after the Jaguar had a flat. *I wonder if she knows just what kind of a weapon she has there.*

"Hey, it's not worth crying over. I'm pretty tough. It'd take more than you yelling at me to hurt my feelings," BJ said in an attempt to comfort the vet.

Hobie wiped at her eyes. "I got so mad at you because I guess I wanted someone to take it out on."

"Take what out on?"

"The fact that I suck as a daughter."

BJ laughed aloud before she could stop herself. "What do you mean? Hobie Lynn Allen, you are a mother's dream come true."

"I'm not, though." Hobie shook her head. "I'm angry at myself, Baylor. Don't you see?" She looked into BJ's eyes until BJ wondered if she was going to continue.

"I should have been the one. I should have been that honest with my mother. I should have had the strength to be that honest with her. I should have loved her enough to tell her the truth."

"Should, should, should...that word can get you into so much trouble. Take it from me, I grew up as the should queen," BJ responded. "Hobie, if you wanted to tell your mom, why didn't you? Were you just afraid?" She quickly continued, "Because I completely understand that. It's much harder when it's your own family."

Hobie shook her head once more. "No, I think I could almost forgive myself if it was a matter of fear. What I did..." She looked over at BJ again. "I think that I stayed quiet out of selfishness. I'm selfish, plain and simple."

"You are about the least selfish person I have ever met," BJ replied. "Why would you even think such a thing?"

"Because it's true." Hobie took a deep breath and waited in silence for a moment. "I think a part of me *enjoyed* the fact that my mother lived in that little fantasy world where Dad was still

alive and nothing about our lives had ever changed. It was like..."
She lowered her head and her voice dropped to a whisper. "Almost
like he was still here, you know?"

There it was, out in the open. BJ couldn't empathize at all
with Hobie's love for her father, but she was envious.

"It was almost easy to believe that he wasn't really gone when
Mom would keep a plate of food warming in the oven for him or
take his suits to the cleaner's. I guess I didn't want him to be gone
either, so I let Mom carry on. I was selfish. I should have been
stronger."

"There's that 'should' word again." BJ reached out to Hobie.
It felt awkward. Physical affection wasn't something that BJ displayed easily. Sex was one thing, but a compassionate and tender
touch, merely offered out of friendship, was something entirely
different.

She laid her palm gently against Hobie's back. "You might
want to cut yourself a little slack here, too. How old did you say
you were when your dad died?"

"Thirteen."

"Geez, Hobie, you were still a kid. Look, it may not help, but
it's natural that you felt the way you did, so quit beating yourself
up over it."

"Thanks." Hobie smiled and looked immensely relieved. "It
does help. Hey, why are you being so nice to me?"

"I could argue with you if it'd make you feel better. The truth
is, I knew how mad you'd be if I laid out the truth to your mom.
It's just that...I had to."

BJ ran her fingers through her hair, leaving her bangs spiked
up into the air.

"Why did you feel you had to?" Hobie asked.

BJ paused before speaking. She temporarily lost her train of
thought as she breathed in Hobie's perfume. It was a spicy scent
that she couldn't quite place, but it somehow smelled familiar. She
wasn't even sure what it reminded her of, only that it was a good
memory.

"Everything I told your mother was true," BJ explained. Her
expression grew somber. "My mother went through the very same
thing. I just wish someone had come along to talk to her, to tell
her the truth. I didn't see what was happening to her until it was
too late. I was so caught up in my own feelings surrounding my
father's death that I couldn't see that my mother wasn't getting
any better. I was so angry with my father for dying before I had
the chance to really tell him how I felt about him. I guess the truth
is that I was a little bit angry at my mother for thinking he was her

whole world."

"Did she eventually come to grips with it?"

BJ shook her head and looked out toward the water. "No, no she didn't...ever. One day she decided to take a bottle of pills and go to bed. She never woke up."

"Oh, Baylor, I'm so sorry. To lose both your mother and father. You must miss them terribly."

BJ shrugged. "My mother...I mostly miss the *idea* of my mother. There were some times, though..." She turned so she could see Hobie and reclined against the side of the porch swing. "We weren't a very close family. When she was available to me, it was good, but most of the time, my father's needs consumed her whole life. The best thing my mom ever did was to convince my dad that it was okay for me to spend time with Tanti. My old man, though...I hope that son of a bitch is burning in hell."

Hobie didn't reply immediately. "I know it's none of my business, but that seems a little harsh, even from you."

BJ gave her a bitter smile. "So it might seem from the outside looking in."

"Sometimes it helps to work through things by saying them out loud. Do you want to talk about it?"

"No." BJ shook her head. She paused and couldn't help the tears that filled her eyes. "Yes," she whispered.

It had been a good long time since BJ had cried over her past. She had vowed never to fall into the self-pity trap, no matter how tempting the prospect. It was impossible to prevent the tears this time, even though Hobie was the last person BJ wanted to break down in front of.

She wiped her eyes and gave a short, ironic laugh. "I don't do well with feelings, as you can see."

"Are you kidding? You're an expert, and I should know. Seems to me that you've spent a lifetime holding them in."

"Maybe, but it's what gets me by."

"Baylor...your father. Did he do something to you?"

"Yeah, he did all right, but it wasn't what you're thinking." BJ wiped her eyes again and brushed her hand through her hair. She pinched the bridge of her nose and wondered once more why she was doing this, why she was opening up to this woman.

"It may not have been sexual, but it was still abuse. My father was an overbearing, controlling madman, to put it succinctly. He made it a habit of telling me, pretty much from the day I was born, what a disappointment I was to him. I think one day I just decided to live up to his warped expectations of me. I figured if he thought I was out drinking and fooling around, then that's exactly what I'd do. When I was fourteen I got caught in bed with one of our housekeepers." BJ raised her head and smiled sheepishly. "Okay, so I got a little wild, I'll admit."

Hobie smiled back and reached out to squeeze her hand.

BJ wondered if Hobie could imagine her as an unruly and rebellious teen.

"Caught by your father, I presume?"

"Of course," BJ answered. "Is there any other way for shit to happen other than in great big piles?" She cleared her throat and grew serious. "To say that my father freaked would be a major understatement. He lost it. Full-on completely lost it. He wasn't the only one. I pretty much snapped, too. To this day, I don't even remember what we screamed at each other. I took off in his BMW. He had me arrested and charged with stealing his car."

"Your own father had you arrested?"

BJ let out a short bark of laughter. "That's not the half of it. When I went to court, no one listened to me about dear old Dad. It was the seventies. Remember? Kids didn't have things like rights then. My father used his lawyer and the services of a judge that his money elected. The old man brought up every mistake and stupid thing I ever did, like he'd recorded them in a little notebook my whole life for just that purpose. They gave me two choices. One, I could do three to five in a juvenile lockup for grand theft auto. Two, I could spend a short amount of time in a rehab facility."

"Which one did you go for?" Hobie asked when BJ paused.

"I figured time in rehab wouldn't be near as bad as prison. I mean, I heard all the stories from other kids. Juvenile detention was prison, plain and simple. I still couldn't even believe it was happening to me, ya know? It's like it wasn't real, like it was happening to someone else. So I took rehab." She shook her head. "Turns out my old man wasn't sending me to a traditional rehab center for drug or alcohol detox. I was there for a behavior adjustment. I ended up in a place that was determined to cure me of all my social ills, including homosexuality."

"Oh God."

"God definitely wasn't in this place. It was the Griffin-Ward Institute."

BJ paused and Hobie frowned. "In Wisconsin?"

"You've heard of it then?"

Hobie nodded. "In med school. Griffin-Ward was a textbook case of the damage that power, money, and the misguided notions of some fanatical therapists could do to teenagers. Every resident who did a psych rotation heard about the Institute."

"Whatever you heard or read wasn't the half of it. I got

beaten on a daily basis as a form of aversion therapy. There were kids, boys and girls, who were raped, shot up with drugs, even lobotomized. You name it and they tested the treatment out on us. The rich parents got their kids back just the way they wanted them. They were afraid of their own shadows, but hey, at least they didn't party anymore. The nuts that ran the joint called it 'alternative treatment.' Any prisoner of war would tell you it was ordinary torture."

Tears fell from BJ's eyes, but she was barely aware of them. She'd learned to block the emotions out, to think of that time as though it had happened to one of the characters in her novels. She never personalized it anymore. She was afraid of what would happen if she did.

"I guess I was one of the lucky ones. I bribed one of the orderlies and he mailed a letter to my grandmother for me. I'll never forget the day Tanti broke into the place." She laughed and this time the laughter was easier, less bitter. "She and Aimee brought along some reporters, and to this day I have no idea where she got those big thugs with baseball bats that came in with her."

"How long had you been there when Evelyn came?"

"Six months."

"I applaud you, Baylor."

BJ looked up in surprise.

"Really," Hobie continued. "I don't know if I could have even held it together, let alone turn out to be a normal functioning member of society after an experience like that."

No one had ever said that to BJ before. Then again, she'd never told anyone about even this small part of what had happened to her. Juliana knew the basics, but even she had never been privy to BJ's thoughts about those six months. "You would have been fine."

"No. No, I wouldn't have," Hobie answered. "We are who we are. If I had been as strong a person as you, I wouldn't have given up on medicine like I did."

"What *did* happen to make you change directions like that?"

Hobie gave the same sort of smile that BJ wore earlier, tinged with regret and pain. "Maybe another time, huh?"

"Sure. It's been kind of an emotional day, hasn't it?"

"You could say that."

"Personally, I try not to have more than one breakdown on an empty stomach," BJ added with a smile. "Do you forgive me for talking to your mom that way?"

"How could I not? You followed your heart and I don't think

that's ever a bad thing. Besides, I've got the strangest feeling that you never do what you're told anyway."

"You're on to me." BJ grinned. "Hey, speaking of empty stomachs, could I ask a big favor?"

"Of course."

"Do you think you could feed me? I'm really starving."

Hobie laughed aloud and BJ realized that she was coming to adore that sound.

"Hey, Mom, Baylor, look what I can do!" Noah stood on the lawn and turned around in a circle. After spinning like a top at least ten times, he took a step forward and promptly fell to the ground. The two women sat and listened to the youngster's giggles.

"That's great, sweetheart," Hobie called out. She hid her face behind her hand and peeked out at BJ. "Would you believe me if I told you that he's really a prodigy in disguise?"

BJ looked out at the boy who was lying in the grass and laughing at his own ingenuity. "How proud you must be."

The two women continued to laugh as they entered the house.

Chapter
8

"Okay, Squirt!" BJ opened her arms and Arturo jumped into her grasp. "I feel like I'm acting out an episode of *Mission: Impossible* every time we do this." She flipped the box closed on the greenhouse's water system controls, then hopped to the door and escaped out into the sunshine before the first drop of water fell.

"Are we gettin' good at this, or what?" she asked her canine companion.

It had been two months since BJ arrived on Ana Lia. She still had a few things to learn about the island and its eccentric inhabitants, but every day she became a little more comfortable. She ate most of her meals at Rebecca's Cove, talking about everything from books to sports with the other patrons. The greenhouse, Arturo, and all the other chores around her grandmother's home had become routine. She even managed to do some of her better writing while lounging with her laptop on the porch during the warm evenings.

A certain veterinarian took up a great deal of BJ's free time. She enjoyed spending time with Hobie and Noah. The boy was quiet and shy, but he had an incredibly free and interesting way of looking at life. Nothing ever seemed to discourage him; he took everything in his stride. The question mark still in BJ's mind was Noah's father. She supposed that she could have asked about him, but that might have been pushing it. She didn't want Hobie to think that she was actually interested in her.

BJ could see where Noah inherited his reserved nature. Hobie was as tender and gentle a person as she had ever met. The redhead had a sizzling temper when provoked, but for the most part, she was patient, even long suffering. That wasn't to say that BJ and Hobie didn't continue to have off days with one another. Hobie wasn't used to having anyone else to talk to or confide in besides Laura. It seemed as if Hobie went out of her way to keep hold of her spirited independence.

BJ was also new to the arena of friendship. So far, she had done little more than the occasional light flirtation with the vet. She wasn't sure why, but every time she thought about pursuing a more intimate relationship with her, she became sick to her stomach. Because having a friend was a rather new experience, she decided to leave well enough alone. Aside from Juliana, BJ really had no other friends she could rely on or share confidences with. Hobie fit the bill on both counts.

BJ looked at her watch one more time. She had to write a few more paragraphs while the characters were still shouting in her head or she would lose the scene. She was due to meet Hobie, who was taking her to Doc Elston for the first time. She prayed that she might finally switch to a walking cast, which Hobie had explained was a possibility if the x-rays looked good. BJ began typing once more. She knew she would be late, but she had one rule when writing: never say no to your muse.

"I don't understand why *you* can't put on the new cast," BJ said. She and Hobie were sitting in the Jaguar outside Dr. Elston's office.

"First off, we don't know for sure whether you're far along enough in the healing process to allow a short cast, let alone a walking cast. That's why you need the x-rays. Secondly, I'm not the town's physician. I only saw you that day because Doc Elston was on vacation. It would be unethical of me to take one of his patients."

"But what if I *wanted* you as a physician? It wouldn't be stealing if I gave myself to you." Both women paused for a moment after that comment. BJ nervously cleared her throat. "Um, you said you have a license."

"Huh?" Hobie answered. Her mind appeared to still be on the visual image of BJ's last thought. "Uh, yes, yes I do, but I really think you should give the doc a chance first. It's what I would want if I were him."

"Oh, okay. Geez, has anyone ever told you how stubborn you are?"

"Well that sounds a lot like the stubborn pot saying hello to the kettle."

"Touché."

"There is a little something I should warn you about regarding the doc."

"Oh, no! What does he see or who doesn't he think is dead?"

"You're just a laugh a minute. Are you thinking about taking this act on the road?"

"Point taken, Mom. So, what's this guy's hang-up?"

"Well, I guess the easiest way to explain it is to say that he's a bit forgetful. He's not a stupid man. He's a very good physician, but you may have to...keep him on track."

"This is going to be fun, I can see it now." BJ reached into the back seat for her crutches. "Well, you coming in with me?"

"Sure, I've got some time to kill."

"I'm going in to see a doctor who you admit is a few bricks short of a load. Do you think you could manage *not* to use the word 'kill'?"

"Oh, come on," Hobie said as she exited the automobile. "Don't be such a scaredy-cat."

"What a mature comment," BJ said, sticking her tongue out at the vet.

The doctor's office was exactly as BJ pictured a small-town physician's office. There were four examination rooms, but by the silence, she guessed that there were never more than two rooms filled with patients at the same time. Pale green and white ceramic tile decorated the walls. The heavy odor of antiseptic hung in the air, the distinctive smell that distinguished medical offices from other workplaces.

It didn't take long before BJ had seated herself upon an exam table in one of the back rooms. The doctor came in immediately.

"Good afternoon, Miss...um..." He referred to the chart in his hand. "Miss Warren-Baylor." He smiled and BJ took a deep breath.

"Just Warren," she clarified.

"Miss JustWarren?" The doctor stared at the papers in his hand in confusion, and BJ took another deep breath.

"My name is Baylor Joan Warren."

"Ah. Technology, eh?" He indicated the computer printout.

"It's a wonderful thing," BJ added.

"Well, what can we do for you today, Miss Warren?"

BJ looked the doctor in the eye and then glanced down at her right leg where a cast ran from toe to mid-thigh. She half expected the man to laugh at himself for missing such an obvious clue. When the silence grew uncomfortable, she spoke.

"I have a broken bone?" Her own disbelief caused the statement to come out more like a question.

"I see. Which one?"

BJ knew that getting out of this would require some desperate measures. "Excuse me, but can I confide in you, Doctor?"

"Why of course, Miss Warren." He sat down on a padded chrome stool and wheeled himself closer. He patted her hand and BJ knew this was what he was good at doing. He was a kindly soul who usually saw nothing more serious than colds, bumps, and bruises during his day. Because of this insight, she didn't have the heart to lash out at him. She decided to play the Ana Lia game.

"Doctor, I wonder...you see, I'm rather used to female physicians where I come from. I know this is a huge imposition, but...would you be very offended if I asked for a female doctor? I'm sure I've just developed some sort of phobia or something, but I'm quite sensitive about it."

The doctor smiled and gently patted BJ's hand once more. "I completely understand, my dear. Now, don't you worry about this at all. It's funny you should ask because there is a colleague of mine in the waiting room right now. Would you care to meet her? She's a fine doctor."

"Thank you, Doctor. That's so understanding of you." BJ put on her most endearing smile.

"Not at all. Why, you just wait here for one moment. All right?"

Not more than five minutes later, Hobie walked through the door of the examination room. She shook her head. "I don't know what you said to the man. Frankly, I don't think I want to know, but he happens to think you're the sweetest, most genteel woman he's ever met."

"Naturally." BJ smiled broadly.

"I didn't have the heart to tell him the truth."

"Oh, that hurts."

Hobie laughed and shook her head again as she put on a lab coat. She called out a few orders to the nurse and prepared to care for her new patient.

The next morning, Hobie sat in her favorite booth at the Cove. She looked at her watch as she sipped her second cup of coffee. She had already ordered her usual breakfast, knowing that BJ would be late. No matter how early BJ started out, she managed to be delayed. She always had one more sentence to type. She held her muse liable. She had explained to Hobie that her muse gave her the thoughts and the inspiration to write. In appreciation and gratitude, she never said no to her muse, alleging that was the reason she was such a prolific writer. While half of her peers suffered from one form or another of writer's block, she turned out a new novel every year.

Hobie smiled to herself. She knew she'd gotten in deep with Baylor Warren when her perpetual tardiness had actually become endearing. Then there was the comment Evelyn had made that BJ had, in a sense, a thing for Hobie. Hobie dismissed it as an old woman's fantasy, but it stayed in the back of her mind. Of course, there was Chicago, too.

Hobie debated with herself on a daily basis whether to confess to BJ about that night in the hotel. Every day that passed, however, made it that much harder to make a clean breast of things. After a few weeks had passed, Hobie gave up her deliberations, realizing that after this much time, BJ was likely to become angry over the buried truth.

Hobie had a smile on her face before BJ entered the restaurant looking like a million bucks. BJ's broken ankle seemed to be healing just fine, and she was ecstatic with the freedom of the new walking cast. She was able to maneuver much easier using only a cane to walk.

"How do I look, JoJo?" BJ asked when she sat down in the booth. She stuck her leg out for inspection.

"Like you're ready for that Boston Marathon race. You want your usual?"

"Thank you and yes, please."

"Morning," Hobie said with a cheerful smile.

"Right back at ya."

They talked as they ate, then continued their conversation over a few cups of coffee. Hobie had learned quite a bit more about the writer's private life, especially her childhood. BJ was surprisingly free with information from that area of her life. Telling Hobie about the Institute had cracked open a dam.

"Do you mind if I ask a personal question, Baylor?"

"Depends."

"Depends on what?" Hobie asked. "Wait. Let me guess. How personal the question is. Right?"

BJ leaned forward. "No. It depends on how nicely you ask." She smiled haughtily.

"Okay." Hobie offered a saccharine smile of her own. "Evelyn has always told me that you're a successful author. You've even said you're a writer, but..."

"But?" BJ repeated.

"I guess I'd like to know why I can't seem to bring your name up anywhere. I've looked under every genre and every spelling of your name that I can think of, but nothing. The library doesn't have one book or bit of info on you. Are you actually a writer, Baylor, or is it all some kind of cover to hide the fact that you're really a CIA operative?"

BJ laughed. "Hmm, CIA? I've actually never thought of that one."

"I'm trying to be serious."

"So am I. Look, don't fly off the handle." BJ saw the beginnings of Hobie's temper. "I'm not being flip. Well, maybe I am just a little, but there are only about two people in the whole world who know what I'm about to tell you. I'm trusting you with my greatest secret, Hobie."

"Maybe you shouldn't. I mean, I'd hate to be the one that—"

"I'm not worried." BJ graced her with an easy smile. "Hobie, the reason you can't find any information about me anywhere is that I use a pen name. I *am* a successful and popular writer, but when I write, I don't use Baylor Warren."

"What name do you use?"

"I'm Harriet Teasley."

BJ watched Hobie's reaction, waiting for that moment of pleasant surprise. It never came. In fact, the vet's face displayed very little emotion at all. It took on a blank look. She just sat there and blinked her eyes a few times, her body frozen.

"Harriet Teasley the romance queen?" Hobie asked.

"The one and only."

"Oh," was all Hobie said before clamping her mouth shut.

Hobie's lackluster response did indeed appear to affect BJ, while Hobie looked as if she were in pain.

"Are you all right?" BJ asked.

"Who, me? Sure, sure. I just—wait a minute! This isn't a joke or anything, is it?"

"Nope. Harriet is my alter ego."

"Wow," Hobie answered, but her words held no enthusiasm. "I had no idea. What—um, can I ask a question?"

"Sure."

"Why straight romances? I mean, writing the love scenes must be hard." Hobie knew the question was inane, but she was trying to get the whole concept clear in her mind. How could she possibly say what she really thought about Harriet Teasley's novels?

"Trust me, I don't work from memory." BJ lowered her voice to a whisper. "I've never been able to do the guy thing. Not that I haven't known gals who did," she quickly added.

"But you're gay. Why not lesbian romances?"

"When was the last time you saw lesbian fiction on the *New York Times* best seller list? My last book, however, sat there for 18 weeks."

"I'm sorry to seem so dense, but I've never actually...well, I've never read any of them."

"What? Oh, come on. Everyone in the world's read at least one. There are nineteen of them. I've been churning them out since I was twenty."

"Well..." Hobie thought about keeping her mouth shut. The little voice in her head was screaming for her to just smile and nod politely. She couldn't do it, though. She couldn't lie to BJ, not again. She wondered if she could manage to be vague enough to appease her friend. "I did start one once."

"You *started* one?" BJ asked. "Well, what did you think of it?"

"What?" Hobie felt herself being backed into the proverbial corner.

"The book that you started. What did you think of it?"

"Well..."

"Did you like it?"

Hobie cringed. "You know, I may not be the best judge. Romance isn't really my genre. Plus, I didn't even finish it."

"Surely you have some sort of an opinion on what you did read. Did you like it?"

"Huh?" Hobie seemed to have lost the ability to articulate as she scrambled for a way out of BJ's inquisition.

"Like it. Did you like it?"

"I really don't think I'm qualified to—"

"You don't have to be a goddamn critic for the *Times* to know if you liked it or not. Did you like it?" BJ's fingers drummed along the edge of the table.

Hobie saw that BJ was beginning to lose her cool. "Okay, I don't think I like where this is going. Somebody is liable to get their feelings hurt," she said.

"Look." BJ paused and took a deep breath. She lowered her voice in what seemed to be an attempt at restraint. "You're my friend. At least the closest thing to a friend I have on this island. I would expect nothing short of honesty from a friend."

BJ paused, and Hobie thought that maybe she was serious. Perhaps writers were used to this sort of criticism of their work. Hobie was still uncertain, but BJ appeared earnest.

"You really want my honest opinion?" Hobie asked in a timid tone.

"No, I want you to lie to me. Yes! I want you to be honest...brutally honest. Now," BJ leaned back in her seat, "you've read more than just a bit of one of my books, haven't you?"

Hobie nodded hesitantly. "My mother has all your books.

Sometimes I would grab one off the shelf..." Her words trailed off as her fingers pulled nervously at the napkin in her hand.

BJ gave what appeared to be a smug grin. "And?"

"Honest, right?"

"Brutally honest."

"Well, if you really want to know, I don't read the novels, as a rule, because I find the characters shallow and unbelievable. The plots are weak and predictable, and the whole book seems like a cheap sex manual thinly veiled as literature. Frankly, I've always wondered why people spent good money on them."

Hobie looked up and met BJ's gaze. Once she saw her face, Hobie realized that she had made a huge mistake. Scarcely before she had started speaking, the little voice in her head reminded her that when BJ asked for an honest opinion, it probably meant she didn't want to hear the truth. Again, Hobie should have listened to that little voice.

"I can't believe you just said that."

"But you—"

"Who do you think you are, a critic for the *Times?*"

"But you said—"

"No, I see how it is now."

Hobie had been frightened, then nervous. Now she was at the limit of her patience. "Look, you were the one who said you wanted *brutal* honesty! I can't help it if you can't take it."

BJ leaned in closer. "I had no idea you didn't know what you were talking about!" she snapped.

"All right, I've had it. This conversation is over. I do not intend to sit here and be treated like this!" Hobie reached for her wallet and threw a few bills onto the table. She gathered her leather satchel and slid out of the booth.

"I cannot believe you have the nerve to act like the injured party here!"

Hobie rose and turned in exasperation. "You were the one who asked me to be honest. I tried to beg off, but nooo. You just had to have your way."

The people seated around the two women had stopped their conversations and focused in on them. Even the waitresses halted their work to listen.

"I had to have my way? Jesus Christ, you couldn't wait to blast me, could you?"

"You were the one who said you wanted my goddamn opinion!" Hobie shouted at the top of her voice. The words echoed off the now silent diner's walls. It was at that moment that she realized that every person in the Cove was looking directly at her. She closed her eyes and willed her blood pressure not to blow the top of her head sky high.

"I'm waiting for an apology," BJ said as she folded her arms across her chest.

"You're wai—" Hobie clamped her mouth shout.

The entire restaurant appeared to hold their collective breaths, waiting for the vet to explode.

"Here's what you'll get from me. I don't want you to talk to me, Baylor Warren. I don't want you to contact me in any way. If you see me coming down the street, I want you to cross to the other side! You are impossible! You were entirely self-serving and arrogant the first moment I met you, and if it's possible, you are even more so now!" She headed for the double doors.

BJ appeared stunned, as if no one had ever talked to her the way Hobie just had, especially with nearly the whole town watching. She was so angry she couldn't even form a coherent thought. She turned red in the face and sputtered as she tried to come up with a response.

"Oh yeah?" was the best that she could do.

Hobie stopped underneath the exit sign with her hand on the door. She spoke without thinking. "I would have expected something a little more articulate from the great Harriet Teasley!"

Hobie leveled her gaze on BJ. The dark-haired woman's gray eyes went round as saucers before narrowing to even slits.

Hobie couldn't believe that BJ had just been outed, but most of all, she couldn't believe that she was the one who had announced it to the world. She had never feared for her life before, but for a brief moment, when BJ's eyes bored into her own, Hobie indeed felt that particular terror.

"Shit," she muttered just before she pushed the door open and was gone.

BJ fell back into the booth, amazed at what had just transpired. There was a miniscule part of her that knew she had brought the whole thing on herself, but being BJ, she was far from ready to admit to such a thing. She could hear the whispers around her. She hoped against hope that the patrons of Rebecca's Cove hadn't understood Hobie's last comment. Her hope was short lived, however, when she looked up and saw JoJo standing before her.

The proprietor of the Cove held a copy of BJ's latest Harriet Teasley novel. "Is it true?" she asked, clutching the book to her chest.

BJ sighed. She wondered how long it would take before Oprah got wind of the news. She could have stalked out, left with some scathing words. Seeing JoJo holding the book as if it were her firstborn child, though, BJ didn't have the heart. She later vaguely remembered thinking this wasn't like her usual behavior.

"Yeah, it's true."

"Would you mind terribly, Ms. Warren?"

BJ sighed deeply once more. "Sure, fork it over." She grinned at her own wit. "Get it? Fork? You know...a little restaurant-type humor." She signed her name and muttered to herself. "Hah! I still got it. Don't tell me I'm no writer."

"Everyone, Tanti! I sat there and listened to her tell nearly everyone on the island that I was Harriet Teasley! Good God, what's wrong with that woman? Is she brain damaged or something? Everything in my life has gone to shit since the very first moment I met her."

"All right Baylor, enough," Evelyn said forcefully. "Sit down, relax, and try to restrict your voice to a four on the Richter scale, especially if you're going to use profanity."

BJ slumped into the bedside chair and pulled at the top of her short dark hair, causing it to spike up at odd angles. "Sorry, Tanti. I didn't mean to embarrass you with my behavior."

"Baylor Joan, you could never embarrass me. I thought you would have realized that after all these years."

BJ smiled weakly. "Thanks, Tanti. Why are you so easy on me?"

"I suppose because you're so hard on yourself. You always have been, dear heart. Your father has been dead for over twenty years, yet you keep him alive."

"What do you mean?"

"I mean, my dear, that my son's abuse didn't stop with his death. He continues to hurt you even today."

BJ knew her grandmother was right. As much as she would have liked to deny it, she couldn't. Her father had been an arrogant, self-centered person. Until she had heard Hobie's cutting remarks that morning, BJ never even knew that her father had left her his greatest legacy. Jonathan Warren III had done in death what he had been unable to do in life: he had turned his daughter into a carbon copy of himself.

"That bastard made me just like him." BJ covered her face with her hands. "I never had a clue. Did you know, Tanti? Did you see it?"

"I think anyone you let near you could see it, Baylor. The problem is that you let so few people within the boundaries of your heart. You don't let anyone get close to you."

"I know. It keeps me safe, though. Keeps me from getting hurt."

"Baylor...my dear. Keeping yourself safe isn't the way life was meant to be lived. It's surviving, not living. You would get so much more satisfaction if you took an occasional chance. Give what you fear a chance, just once."

"I didn't want to be this way, you know. I never even saw it happening."

"It isn't that uncommon to miss the forest for the trees. The real question is, what will you do about it now that you know?"

"Change," BJ answered quickly. "I'm not going to let that son of a bitch do this. I won't let him beat me."

"It won't be easy, dear heart."

"Hey, I'm an ex-smoker," BJ said as she wiped the tears from her eyes. "Don't tell me about hard." She took her grandmother's hand. "This is me we're talking about, Tanti. I mean, will I be able to change?"

"Baylor, my dear, you're not going to become a saint over-night. In fact, some of your haughty behavior got you where you are today, so you shouldn't be in such a hurry to let it go. Besides, my dear, I suspect that you've already begun to change more than you know."

BJ thought about the times over the last few weeks that she'd questioned her own behavior. There were times when she wondered why she was doing something so out of character for her. Was that why? Had she already begun to change?

"Now that you have all this newfound enlightenment," Eve-lyn gave BJ a teasing smile, "would you like to rethink your confrontation with Hobie yesterday? Was she really the ogre that you painted her out to be? Perhaps both of you ought to take a little blame for the words you spoke in anger."

BJ didn't answer. As much as she wanted to quickly deny any responsibility for her fight with Hobie, a small voice in the back of her mind said that she might very well have had a share, albeit a very small one, in the quarrel.

"Why don't you think about it? Go over things a few times in your head. You'd be surprised at the magic that can happen here on Ana Lia, dear heart. I'm sure that very soon, you and Hobie will have a chance to apologize to one another without either one of you suffering too much embarrassment or humiliation."

"How do you know, Tanti?"

Evelyn smiled a Mona Lisa smile. "Because this is Ana Lia."

Chapter
9

Another week passed on Ana Lia. Baylor and Hobie were still feuding, even though it was a rather silent fight. They avoided one another as much as possible. Hobie busied herself with work and spending time with her son. Baylor hated to admit how much she missed Noah. She sulked around the house, and Arturo, who followed her everywhere, sulked as well.

Hobie and Baylor both continued to dine at Rebecca's Cove, each refusing to speak to the other. Most of the time, they just glared over their plates at one another. There were moments when they felt as though they had carried the whole thing on long enough. Of course, stubbornness seemed to be a trait each woman had plenty of, so neither would be the first to give in and apologize.

Baylor's status had risen considerably on the island since Hobie had inadvertently broadcast that she was the ever-popular Harriet Teasley. Baylor knew her books were popular—she could tell by her royalty checks—but it seemed nearly everyone on the island owned at least one Teasley romance. Baylor attributed this to the fact that it was an island and that it was deathly hot and humid in the summer, leaving the inhabitants with plenty of leisure time.

When Katherine and Helen had cornered Baylor on the street one morning, Baylor earned points with Katherine by inquiring as to Albert's health. The sisters made the writer promise to come in to sign a few books and when she showed up, there was a line of people around the store waiting for her autograph.

It was strange indeed, but the fact that Baylor was a beautiful woman, and had been posing as Harriet Teasley for so many years, intrigued her fans. To the people on Ana Lia, she had become an islander.

Very slowly, Baylor's impression of herself began to change. She had been deliberating over Hobie's comments about the Teasley novels. While Baylor knew Hobie wasn't 100 percent correct, she did realize that the vet hadn't been entirely wrong. Why would she be embarrassed for anyone to ever find out her pen name if she was proud of her work? She had learned long ago that pen names were meant to hide behind for one reason or another. Baylor hid behind Harriet Teasley's name because she knew the writing was substandard. It wasn't awful, but it wasn't what she had dreamed of writing when she was in college.

Baylor asked herself the question that she hadn't thought of in years: *Why do I continue to write them?* Was it only the money? When she was younger, she asked herself that question a great deal. The answer had always been the same, but she pushed the reasoning from her mind every time. This time, however, it stayed around to nag her. The answer had always been one word, something whispered in her ear every moment of the day: fear.

She was afraid, plain and simple. Deep down, she was afraid that if she tried to write something else, something she really wanted to write, the world would discover Baylor Warren was a fraud. She was afraid they would see that she didn't have any talent after all. Mostly she was afraid that her father had been right when he had told her she would never succeed at anything.

The doubts seemed to strike most often at night, when she was alone with no one to talk to. She realized that was why she had started partying and drinking in the first place. When she got drunk, she passed out when her head hit the pillow. When she picked up a girl at a club or a party, she didn't have to sleep alone. It struck her one morning that, apart from an occasional beer, she hadn't had anything to drink since she'd been on the island.

She looked at her reflection in the mirror as she brushed her teeth. "Because this is Ana Lia," she said. Her grandmother's words had an odd feeling of comfort to them.

A short while later, Baylor flipped through the six channels that her grandmother's TV received. She went through the channels repeatedly for twenty minutes. The lack of cable or satellite programming did nothing to improve her mood.

"I've about had it with this, Squirt." At the sound of her voice, Arturo popped up from his spot on Baylor's stomach. "We need to do something desperate to keep our sanity here." She pulled the small Ana Lia telephone book from under the coffee table. She carefully punched in the number she wanted and waited.

"Telephone company? I thought this was the number to the cable TV company. Oh, you take care of cable, too. Oh, okay. I need to get cable installed. It's 912 Oyster Bay Road. No, it's my grandmother. It's okay; I'll be paying the bill. Am I what? Fifteen thousand feet from the CO? What the hell is the CO? Oh, central office." Baylor rubbed one hand across her face. She hadn't quite prepared herself for ordering cable Ana Lia style.

"Okay, how would I know how far I am away from the central office? All right, do you know? The guy that comes out can tell me? Okay, that works. How about today? What? Sometime between eight and noon or one to five. Geez, you think you could make it a little more vague? Never mind. So, what day? Thirty days?" she shouted. "If there is a God in heaven, I won't be here in thirty days."

Baylor held one hand over the receiver and shook her head at Arturo. "Civilization this ain't!"

The voice on the other end of the line drew Baylor's attention back to the phone. "Do I still want to order it? Tell you what, you can have them come out if they feel lucky. Maybe I'll be here between noon and one." She slammed the receiver back in its cradle.

Arturo whimpered and barked up at Baylor.

"You're right. It's become critical." Baylor reached for her PDA. She popped open the lid and navigated her address book. Picking up the phone, she smiled at Arturo. "Now we're going to get some action, I guarantee you."

A sweet-sounding voice answered. "Yes, Anthony Falcone, please. Yes, tell him it's BJ Warren." Baylor hummed along with the canned music. *Does everyone use* The Girl from Ipanema? she thought.

"Tony, *compare!*"

Anthony Falcone had been Baylor's friend and partner in crime growing up. His family had money, so Baylor's father accepted the friendship. What he didn't know was where all that money came from. Tony's father ran the kind of business that no one talked about, and it was probably better for their health if they didn't. Tony took over the family business and invested in just enough legitimate businesses to keep the feds and the IRS off balance. Because Baylor's mother had been born in Palermo, the Falcone family welcomed Baylor into their home as one of their own.

"I'm great, how about you? How are your mom and dad?" Baylor listened as he told her about his family. In the past, she would open mail or reach for a magazine when people went on about their kids or spouses. Now, she found herself asking how the kids were doing in school and when the new baby was due. Tony seemed to notice the difference in her behavior, too.

"No, really, I'm fine. I'm down in Florida. You remember

Tanti? Well, she took sick and I ended up down on Ana Lia Island, then I ended up breaking my leg. No, she's not that bad and I'm good, but I have one small problem that I think you might be able to fix for me."

Baylor sat back and put her leg up on the coffee table. "Well, here's the story. I need one of those satellite dishes installed here at my grandmother's house. You know, one of those big-ass things that will pick up talk shows in Bangladesh. Plus, I want it now, like today or tomorrow before I lose my sanity on this island. What do you say?"

She picked up pen and paper and jotted down some figures and names, giving her personal information when Tony asked for it. Finally, she gave him her credit card number.

"Tony, you are the man! *Buona salute e ricchezza,* my friend," she exclaimed before hanging up.

"Hey, Squirt." Baylor rubbed Arturo's head. "This afternoon, we watch television like real people. It's good to have friends in low places."

It was breakfast time at the Cove. Hobie and Laura were sitting at the counter when Baylor entered and took a seat in a booth. Unbeknownst to Hobie and Baylor, most of the Cove's regular patrons had bets going as to how long the two women could last before they exploded. They all knew Hobie and they'd certainly come to know Baylor. They waited every morning on the edge of their seats, wondering if that would be the day.

To the customers' disappointment, the morning turned out to be uneventful. Hobie and Baylor took turns watching one another while trying not to appear as though they were watching. They were both very close to giving in.

"Hobie Lynn, your mother's on the phone." JoJo laid the cordless phone on the counter in front of the vet.

"Thanks, JoJo," Hobie called out to the already retreating figure. "Mom, what's wrong? Is Noah all right?" Her forehead creased as she listened. "Why did they send him home? What do you mean teacher's conference day? They never said anything. What?"

Hobie's voice grew louder. "Mom, what do you mean you can't watch Noah? No, I can't have him with me all day. I have calls to make. I won't be in the office all day. Can Mack watch him? Okay, bring him here to the Cove and I'll find someone to watch him. No, I'm not upset with you, Mom."

Hobie turned the phone off and gave an exasperated sigh.

"Trouble?" Laura asked.

"I think I liked it better when my mom thought Dad was still alive and she had no life."

"You don't mean that."

"Oh, I know. Looks likes we had a miscommunication today. Noah doesn't have school and Mom has plans. She used to never leave the house; now she's in a book club and the Ladies Guild, and she spends two days a week playing cards up at the hospital with Evelyn."

"Uh-oh."

"Yeah, uh-oh is right. Well, I don't have to panic yet. Hey, JoJo." The proprietor turned to face Hobie. "Any chance you can baby-sit today?"

"Oh, darlin', I would if I could. We're catering Sally Armistead's anniversary party tonight and I'm going to be busy running between here and the mainland for last-minute supplies. I'm sorry."

"Oh, nuts, I forgot about that thing tonight. Okay, don't worry. Thanks."

Hobie looked around the restaurant and encountered Baylor's gaze before the dark-haired woman quickly turned away. *Not in a million years will I leave Noah alone with her.*

"Mrs. Emberly." Hobie greeted the older woman, who sat with four other women. "Have you heard anything on Petey yet?"

"No, dear. I'm afraid I may have to give up hope. The poor dear."

"I'm sorry. I was wondering if I could impose on one of you ladies to watch Noah for me for today? You know how good he is, and—"

"Oh dear, you know we would, but we're celebrating Hannah's birthday today. We already have reservations in Tampa for lunch."

"I understand. You ladies have a great day, and happy birthday, Hannah."

Hobie moved from one booth to another, to no avail. As odd as it seemed, nearly everyone she knew on Ana Lia had a previous engagement. After fifteen minutes, she had exhausted every baby-sitting option in town. She had *nearly* exhausted every baby-sitting option in town. Brushing the bangs from her forehead, she looked to see Baylor grinning like a madwoman, her arms resting along the back of the booth. Hobie put her hands on her hips and stared back. She was out of options and time as she spied Noah running into the restaurant.

"Hi, Mom!"

"Hi, sweetie. Have you eaten breakfast?"

"Uh-huh." Noah nodded.

"Okay. How about a glass of milk?"

"Chocolate milk?" he asked hopefully.

"Sure." Hobie chuckled. "Go sit by Laura at the counter and tell JoJo I said it was all right. I'll be right over there."

"'Kay. Hi, Baylor." The youngster waved as he passed by her booth.

"Hey, Bubba."

Hobie stood in front of Baylor and crossed her arms. The dark-haired woman looked like she was enjoying Hobie's predicament much too much. Her smile reached from ear to ear.

"Well, I guess I'm looking a little more indispensable than you thought, huh?" Baylor used the very line Hobie had employed back when Baylor first realized she needed the vet to drive her around town.

"Have you ever watched a child before in your whole life?" Hobie asked.

"Hey, I am a responsible woman, you know. I won't give the kid matches and I won't leave him alone anywhere. How hard can it be?"

"You have no idea. I want you to stay at home, no roaming around, and I expect him to be unharmed and still have all his extremities when I come to pick him up at four o'clock."

"Sure. Can do. Is he...um, you know, housebroken?"

Hobie rolled her eyes and breathed deeply. "He's six years old!" She realized that meant nothing to a woman who had never been around children. "Yes, he is toilet trained. He can manage it all by himself."

"Cool. Any other last-minute instructions?"

"Yes. When I pick up my son this afternoon, I would like it very much if it could be at Evelyn's home and not the emergency room. I'm also rather fond of the innocent boy he is now. I don't want him learning how to spit, swear, or imitate the noises of any bodily functions. Can you manage that?"

"Well, now that you've eliminated all the fun stuff..." Baylor saw the fire in Hobie's eyes and laughed. "Kidding, kidding. Don't worry so much."

"Right. I feel much better."

"Hey, Bubba," Baylor called. "How'd you like to spend the day with me?"

"All right!" Noah jumped up and down. "Can I, Mom? Can I?"

Hobie looked worried, but smiled. "Sure, sweetheart." She

leaned over and whispered into Baylor's ear. "If anything happens to him, I swear I'll hunt you down, Baylor Warren."

Baylor wondered if it was Hobie's soft breath in her ear or the whispered promise that caused a shiver to run down her spine.

They stopped at Hobie's house first so Noah could bring along a few toys. The two women said nothing at all about their argument. In fact, neither said a word until they pulled into Evelyn's driveway.

"You having company?" Hobie questioned Baylor.

Two unmarked white vans sat in the driveway. *Way to go, Tony,* Baylor thought. "Uh, yeah. I'm just having a little...installation work done." Baylor was thankful that Hobie's good manners did not allow her to pry.

"Arturo!" Noah cried out as they entered the house. The pup barked excitedly, turning around in tight circles. Noah knelt down and Arturo licked his face.

"Let me give ya the lay of the land, Bubba," Baylor said as she took Noah's backpack and tossed it in a chair.

"Huh?"

"Where everything is."

"Oh, I know already. Bafroom is over there, kitchen back there, and it's not polite to go upstairs." Noah smiled and pushed his glasses up his nose.

"So, you've been here before?"

"Yeah, lots. Mom comes to see Missus Warren all the time."

"Really? How interesting. I think you and I are gonna get along just fine, Bubba." Baylor grinned at her little fountain of information. "Hey, come on into the back yard with me. I gotta check on something."

"'Kay."

"Hey there," Baylor said to the two men working on settling into place a four-foot satellite dish.

"You Warren?" the taller of the two men asked.

"In the flesh." She shook hands with him. "You guys are fast. I appreciate it."

"I'm Dave and this is Chuck. I got a call from Pete Giamatti up in Orlando. He says you're a good friend of Tony Falcone's. For a friend of Tony's, I haul ass. Oh, sorry, kid." He looked down at Noah, but the boy was too busy watching Chuck adjust the dish's position with a remote-control device to have noticed.

"Can I get you guys something to drink, anything like that?" Baylor asked.

"Nah, thanks. We will have to get into the house, though, to set up everything in there."

"You got it."

Two hours later, Noah and Baylor knew a great deal about installing cable, legal and illegal, along with the ins and outs of the satellite dish business. Dave was more than happy to pass on his expertise. Baylor seemed as intrigued as six-year-old Noah by the whole process.

"You're all set, Ms. Warren," Chuck informed Baylor.

"Thanks, you guys. You did a first-rate job." She slipped a hundred-dollar bill into Dave's hand. "Go have lunch on me."

"You got it. You have any problems," he handed Baylor his business card, "you just call me."

Like a kid in a candy store, the moment the two men were gone, Baylor rushed over to the remote. Flipping through the 250 plus channels, she tousled Noah's hair. "Welcome to heaven, Bubba."

"Wow," Noah responded. "Ooh, Cubs!"

"Right you are." Baylor stopped on Chicago's local station. "We're just in time, this is the pre-game show. You like the Cubs?" she asked, thinking of the baseball cap that Hobie was never without.

"Oh, yeah."

"Your mother's taught you well. Well, let's get comfortable. You getting hungry yet? How about some baseball-type snacks?"

Noah nodded his head enthusiastically and pushed his glasses up.

"Do you like root beer?" Baylor asked as she looked through the refrigerator.

"Yup."

"How about Cheez-Its?"

"What're Cheez-Its?"

"Here." Baylor opened the box and handed the boy one of the orange crackers.

"Mmm, yeah." Noah nodded his head as he spoke.

"Okay, Bubba. You go have a seat in the living room. You can flip through the channels and I'll get our snack together."

"'Kay."

It only took Baylor a little more than five minutes to assemble all of her usual snacks. She loaded a bowl of Cheez-Its, a smaller bowl of thick pepperoni slices, some pepperoncini, and two glasses of cold root beer onto a large tray, which she carried into the other room.

"Wow. Baylor, see this?"

She turned to the TV and her eyes went wide. "Whoa, yeah!" She grinned at the naked woman on the screen.

Quickly realizing who she was with, she reached over and plucked the remote from Noah's hand. "Oh, man. Are you trying to get me arrested?" She sat down beside Noah and rubbed her hand through his spiked hair. "What do you say we watch the game instead, huh?"

"'Kay," he answered, with a red face.

"Now this, my friend, is the way television was meant to be watched." Baylor pointed to the new 52-inch TV that she had ordered along with the satellite dish. She knew it was an extravagance, but she rarely spent her money on such pleasures and it felt good to do so.

"It's like bein' at the show," Noah said.

"You know it." Baylor took a large swallow of root beer. "Are you sure you wouldn't like milk instead?"

"Nope, I like soda."

Baylor was amused at the differences in regional vocabularies. In Chicago, they called it pop. She found that in Florida, people looked at her strangely unless she said soda pop. "Yeah, I guess they make you drink milk every day at lunch, huh? They used to make us, anyway."

"I get milk sometimes."

"Why only some of the time? Oh, man! Sammy, why'd you swing at that ball?"

"Sometimes I got money for milk, but sometimes I don't."

Baylor wondered at that. Surely Hobie didn't hurt for money—or did she? "Why don't you have money all the time?"

"Sometimes I give it to Billy Crenshaw."

"Why?"

"'Cuz he says give it or he'll slug me."

"He takes your milk money?" Baylor sat up straighter.

"He doesn't take it, I give it to him."

"But why, Noah?"

"'Cuz I don't want to get hit. It might hurt."

"Why don't you tell your mom or one of the teachers?" Baylor asked.

Noah scrunched up his six-year-old face. "I'd look like a baby."

"Yeah, I see your point. Ever thought about saying no?"

"Then he'd hit me."

"Maybe, but you could hit him too. Bullies like kids that don't fight back. If this Billy knows you're going to hit back then he'll probably just quit bothering you."

"But how do I hit him, Baylor?"

"Haven't you ever slugged anyone before?"

Noah shook his head.

"We'll work on it, okay? Remember, though, this is just between us. Your mom might not understand."

"'Kay. Thanks, Baylor."

"You're welcome, Bubba. Now, let's get back to this game, huh?"

Hobie knocked on the door for the third time. "That's it. She's done something horrible to him, I just know it."

She heard loud music coming from the front of the house where the living room was. A quick turn of the front doorknob showed that it was unlocked. She thought twice about entering the house, but gave up feeling bad when she thought about what was going on inside. "She's probably got the stereo on and no idea where Noah is at!"

Walking into the living room, she ran into an amazing sight. Baylor and Noah were in the middle of the room; Noah on the coffee table and Baylor on the floor beside him. They both wore black Ray-Ban sunglasses and they were dancing. Well, it was very nearly dancing. Noah was trying to imitate Baylor's moves. The writer, though hampered by her cast, did a very good job. As if on cue, near the end of the Sam Cooke song, Noah and Baylor both went into a fair version of the Jerk.

The two were laughing and singing, leaving a stunned Hobie unable to believe her eyes. Of course, there was something about watching Baylor swinging her hips in perfect time to the song that affected Hobie in a rather direct manner.

The song ended and Hobie couldn't resist. She applauded. Baylor turned quickly and although Hobie couldn't see her eyes, she could see her cheeks turn pink in embarrassment.

Hobie couldn't seem to remove the grin from her face, which caused Baylor's blush to deepen. "You two are good, but it's time to go home, Noah. No more dancing today."

"But, Mom, it's Motown!" Noah looked at Hobie through his borrowed sunglasses, his hands on his hips.

Just as Hobie arched an eyebrow, Baylor scooped Noah off the table. She tucked the giggling boy under her arm and he hung there like a sack of potatoes.

"I have no idea where he learned that," she said in an attempt to appear casual.

"I'm sure," Hobie replied. "Don't you think you might be

hurting him like that?"

"Am I hurting you, Bubba?"

Noah giggled and lifted his head. "Nope." He swung his legs back and forth.

"Where in the world did you get 'Bubba' from? You know, he might prefer his name." Hobie didn't understand why she was being so petty, but Baylor seemed to draw out every small-minded comment that she had in her.

Baylor looked down. "Is it okay if I call you Bubba, Noah?"

Noah laughed again as if he was having the time of his life. He pushed his glasses up and held out a thumbs-up sign.

"See, he's cool with it. So, the question is, what's really bugging you, Hobie?"

"Let him go, please."

Baylor shrugged and released the youngster. Noah rushed over to his mother and she hugged him tightly. Baylor watched as Hobie's demeanor instantly changed. She always seemed to light up whenever Noah was near.

"Sweetheart, would you please take Arturo and go play in the backyard for a little bit, so I can talk to Baylor?"

"'Kay," Noah replied. As an afterthought, he turned back to his mother and tugged on her jeans. "You're not gonna yell at her, are ya, Mom?"

Hobie dropped to one knee and pulled the Cubs hat from her head. She gently placed it atop Noah's head, a special treat. "No, sweetie, I'm not going to yell."

"Good, 'cuz I had such a good time with her."

"I'm glad. Go on, you, and don't wander out of the back yard."

The two women stared at one another as they heard the kitchen door close. They listened to the sounds of Noah's laughter and Arturo's barking.

"So, do you still want to know what's bugging me?" Hobie asked in a quiet voice.

Baylor felt a rising sense of panic, but she tried to appear nonchalant and nodded.

Hobie lowered her head and ran a hand through her hair. There was a long pause. "I'm so sorry! I had no business saying those things about you or your writing!" she blurted out. "I'm just so sorry. Please, I feel—" She raised her head, tears streaming down her face. "I'm just so sorry," was all she could get out.

"No," Baylor said as she waved her hands. "No, no, no. You agreed. You said you wouldn't cry anymore."

"I lied." Hobie sobbed out the words in exasperation.

She sank onto the living-room couch and reached for a tissue from a nearby box. Hobie watched as Baylor stood rooted in place. She was confused until she remembered: this was Baylor's weakness. Hobie didn't want Baylor caving in over her tears, but the fact that she couldn't stop crying made her cry all the harder.

"I'm such a bitch. I'm so sorry," she cried.

"It's okay, really. I think it was all my fault anyway." Baylor finally propelled herself into action. "Come on," she practically whined. She sat down on the sofa beside Hobie. "It's not your fault, not at all. I'm a much bigger bitch than you, just ask anyone."

"Oh, stop it!" Hobie slapped Baylor's arm.

"What?"

"You're only apologizing because I'm crying."

"How do you know that?"

"Because it happened last time. You turn into a tower of quivering jelly when women cry, don't you?"

"Well, up until now I never did, thank you very much. How do you do that and why are you doing it to me?"

"Because I..." Hobie tossed her used tissue onto the floor in confusion and anger. "Because I like you. All right, are you happy now?"

Baylor smiled without knowing quite why. She supposed it was because of the ridiculousness of the whole situation. For some reason, her anxiety disappeared and she heard her grandmother's voice in her ear saying something about taking risks.

Baylor swallowed hard and moved in closer to the tearful redhead. She felt awkward and unsure of herself. Sure, she had put moves on more women than she could even remember, but it was different when it mattered, and this mattered. She put an arm around Hobie's shoulder, and the vet's head seemed to gravitate toward Baylor's shoulder.

"Shh, come on now. You don't have to cry. It's okay. You know, I may not be the smartest gal in the world, but I'm not sure this is how it works."

"What do you mean?" Hobie's voice came out sounding small and fragile. Baylor noticed that her tears had slowed.

"Well, I'm thinking that maybe you better start liking me a little less, or else one of us is going to have a breakdown."

Hobie chuckled and wiped her eyes with a clean tissue. She sat back up and blew her nose. Baylor handed over the box of tissues and when Hobie had dried her eyes some more, she brushed the hair from Hobie's eyes.

"Baylor, I didn't mean to betray you. I'm so sorry I told

everyone about your books. I wouldn't blame you if you never trusted me again. I have no excuse or rationalization to defend what I did. It was—damn, this is so hard to admit, but it was just because I was angry and my anger made me, I don't know, lose sight of everything. Lose control."

"I understand, better than you think, and it's okay." Baylor gave Hobie's shoulder a small squeeze.

"No, it's not okay."

"Really, it is." Baylor tried to find the words to explain. "I talked to my grandmother last week, right after our little to-do. I admit, I was plenty pissed, but being angry isn't all that unusual for me. This isn't going to come as any great shock to you, I'm sure, but a lot of my anger is what has made me a rather disagreeable person to be around at times. It's like, subconsciously, I have to lash out and humiliate people before they do it to me."

"Why? Do you mind me asking?"

"No, actually, you're the first person I've ever talked to about this, apart from Tanti. I'm no psychiatrist, Hobie, but for me, it's fear."

"Fear? What does someone like you have to be afraid of?"

"The man standing behind me," Baylor answered.

Hobie immediately looked past Baylor and furrowed her brow. "Is he there now?" she asked suspiciously.

"He always seems to be there."

"Do you see him right now?"

Baylor looked at Hobie strangely. "Do I see—Oh! No, I don't mean like that. It's not like I see three-foot hamsters or anything."

"Oh, good." Hobie breathed an audible sigh of relief. "For a minute there I thought—"

"That Ana Lia had finally gotten to me, eh?" Baylor laughed aloud.

"Sorry," Hobie said with a sheepish grin. "So, now, what exactly do you mean when you say there's a man behind you?"

"He's been there all my adult life, whispering in my ear. He tells me things like I'll never be good enough or talented enough. Things like how I'll only get hurt if I try, so it's better not to try at all." Baylor fixed a defeated smirk on her face. "He's my father, and he's been standing there as long as I can remember."

"Oh God. I'm so sorry." Hobie straightened up to look into the writer's face.

Baylor shrugged. "Funny thing, until I talked with Tanti the other day, I didn't even know it was him. All this time and I never even knew that the harder I tried to prove my father was wrong about me, the more like him I became."

"So, what are you going to do?"

"I don't know if I can ever get rid of him. He was a big part of my life, and even though it was mostly bad, I don't think you can just rid yourself of some memories. Now that I recognize who he is and what he's doing to my life, though, I have a choice. He may always be standing there, whispering away, but that doesn't mean I have to listen."

"Well, BJ—"

"It's Baylor," the tall woman said, softening her voice. "My name is Baylor." She smiled.

"Well, I think you'll be able to do it, Baylor," Hobie said.

"Thanks. I hope you're right. Hey, feel better?"

"No, but at least I'm not crying like a maniac," Hobie answered. "I get started and I can't stop. It's very embarrassing. I'm really so very sorry."

"Careful, those are the words that got all this started, remember? How about something cool to drink, a glass of water or iced tea?"

"Water would be great, thanks. I can help," Hobie said as she saw Baylor rise from the couch and head for the kitchen.

Baylor turned around to answer and stopped abruptly. Hobie lay crumpled on the floor. "Oh, that can't be good," Baylor said more to herself than to the unconscious woman.

"Hey, sleeping beauty," Baylor said from her perch on the sofa.

Hobie tried to sit up. "Oh God, is Noah still outside?"

Baylor laid a restraining hand against the vet's shoulder. "It's okay, it's okay," she quickly interjected. "He came in and I told him that you were so tired you had to take a quick nap. He seemed to buy it."

"Thanks." Hobie lay back down. "I still think he's a little too young to understand why Mom passes out occasionally." She tried to rise once more.

"Take it easy. I don't want you going down for the count again. What's your brother ask you all the time, 'When was the last time you ate?'"

"Damn!" Hobie rubbed her face. "Could this day possibly get any more embarrassing?"

"Tell me what to do."

"Do you have any cheese or maybe a glass of milk?"

"Yep, you're in luck. I've got both, but I thought you'd need sugar to get going again?"

"That's a diabetic. Contrary to the diabetic who needs glucose when his blood sugar is low, a hypoglycemic needs protein," Hobie responded. "If I ate something sweet, my blood sugar would rise, but then it would just bottom out again within two hours because I produce too much insulin."

Baylor rose from the sofa and headed toward the kitchen. She turned back and pointed at Hobie. "Stay. That's an order."

"Yes, Sergeant," Hobie replied with a weak smile.

Some time later Hobie felt like her old self. A humiliated, thoroughly embarrassed version of her old self. She and Baylor made light conversation, mostly about how Baylor had spent the day with Noah.

"Um, can I ask a question without you going ballistic?"

Hobie chuckled. "I seriously doubt it, but give it your best shot." Both women smiled.

"Well, and I don't mean to be preaching or anything, but I find it extremely odd that, as a physician, you let this happen to yourself so much."

"I know, and you don't sound preachy. In fact, you sound a lot like Mack and my mom. The funny thing is, you're all right. I should and there's no excuse for it. I just have such a goofy personality." Hobie arched an eyebrow at Baylor. "Not a word."

Baylor smiled and held her hands up in a gesture of mock surrender.

"What I mean is I have such an all-or-nothing personality. I just get so focused on things that I can't seem to even remember to make time to eat, even when I know I'll pay the price."

"Aren't you afraid that you'll do it when you're around Noah?" Baylor asked.

"That's funny too, not funny ha-ha, but funny peculiar. When I'm around Noah, I never seem to have that problem. It's weird, I know. It's as if he keeps me grounded in some way. I know, it's all too strange, isn't it?"

"No. Actually, it makes sense in a jumbled-up sort of way," Baylor answered with an understanding smile. "Is there any medicine you can take? I'm assuming that it's low blood sugar."

"Hypoglycemia, yeah. The losing consciousness is called insulin shock."

"Are you a diabetic?"

"That's the rub of it, I'm not. My hypoglycemia occurs as an idiopathic condition—" Hobie abruptly stopped after seeing Baylor's confusion. "Sorry, I didn't mean to go into medical speak on you. That just means that it happens without a known cause. Once, when I was a teenager, I was unconscious for a number of hours until they gave me an injection of glucose. That's never happened again, though. When I eat and sleep right, I usually have no problem."

"It must be scary never knowing when it might pop up."

"A little. I'm just glad Noah didn't inherit those genes," Hobie replied. "I've thought about it a lot lately and I really have decided to take better care of myself, at least for Noah. I don't want him losing me like I lost Dad."

Okay...now I know Noah was definitely not adopted, Baylor thought.

Just then, the object of their conversation ran into the room. "You done with your nap, Mom?"

"Yes, sweetie, thanks for letting me sleep."

"S'okay. I'm hungry."

"Mmm, me too. We better get home, huh?"

"Um...if you want..." Baylor's voice caught mother and son's attention. "I was going to throw some stuff on the grill and, well, I have plenty. You could stay for dinner. That is, if you want to."

"Oh, thanks, Baylor, but we've imposed on you enough for one day."

"It wouldn't be imposing at all," Baylor quickly said. "What do you say to a barbecue, Bubba?"

"Hot dogs?" Noah asked with an excited expression.

"Hot dogs...bratwurst."

"Ooh, bratwurst," Hobie said. "I haven't had grilled bratwurst since I was in college."

"Then it's a date," Baylor said without thinking. Suddenly realizing what she'd just said, she looked at Hobie to see if she had noticed it too. If Hobie did, she gave no indication.

The evening became about as pleasant a night as Baylor and Hobie could ever remember spending. It was nine o'clock before Hobie could drag herself away. Noah slept soundly on the love seat with Arturo curled in a small white ball beside him. He never even woke when Hobie carried him out to her pickup.

"Are we okay again?" Hobie asked, leaning against the open driver-side door.

Baylor smiled. "Yeah, everything is good. Very good," she couldn't keep from adding. She breathed in the now familiar scent of Hobie's perfume, finally recognizing it as Opium.

The two drew closer. It seemed natural to be standing within the same space. There was a force between the two women, something that they couldn't see, but if they could, Baylor imagined that it would have looked like smoky tendrils. The strands wove around and between them, pulling them closer and closer.

The silence hung heavy in the air. Baylor waited, too afraid to take the final risk of actually reaching in to initiate the physical intimacy of a kiss. It was so hard, so awkward. The reality was that she would either be accepted or denied. Why was that so hard to face? Suddenly, Baylor stopped thinking. If she *was* thinking, her conscious mind certainly wasn't aware of it. She was as lost in the luminous, green eyes before her as Hobie appeared to be adrift within the gray of Baylor's eyes.

"I guess...I, um...should go," Hobie said in a dreamy sort of voice.

"Huh? Oh, yeah...um, yeah, I should probably, um...you know, get inside."

"Inside?"

"Inside...the house." Baylor pointed without taking her eyes from Hobie.

"Oh, yeah. The house." Hobie shook her head and the spell was broken. "Well, I really have to go. Thanks so much, Baylor." She quickly kissed the writer on the cheek.

Never in a million years would Baylor have ever thought that one quick peck on the cheek could affect her so. There she stood, however, in the middle of the street, long after Hobie had driven away. She found it hard to believe that her cheek could still tingle with warmth so long after the kiss.

"You kissed her? Oh my God! What happened? What did she do?" Laura asked in disbelief.

Hobie and Laura were having coffee and doughnuts in the office kitchenette, something they always did on Fridays, when they enjoyed their breakfast and then opened the office extra early. That way they closed at noon.

Laura was astounded at the news. "Details, woman, details," she pressed.

"Oh, please. There are no details to tell. It was a friendly 'thanks and good night' sort of kiss on the cheek," Hobie said.

"Oh, yeah. You kiss me good night all the time. I can see how that would happen."

"Very funny. Look—" The bell interrupted their conversation.

"Don't think I'll let this drop," Laura said before going back to prepare the examination room for their next patient. "This conversation *will* be continued."

Chapter
10

"Hey, goombah!" Juliana Ross stood in the doorway, her arms filled with paper bags.

"You rat bastard!" Baylor pulled the woman in and hugged her.

Juliana, at five foot ten, was very nearly as tall as Baylor, but leaner and not quite as muscular. She was an attractive woman with very short blonde hair, blue eyes, and a smile that easily charmed. Baylor had once told her friend if Brad Pitt had been a woman, he would have been Juliana.

"Hey, mate, you're crushing my cookies."

Baylor laughed and released her. She took one of the bags and showed her into the kitchen where they deposited the bags on the kitchen table.

"What the hell are you doing here?" Baylor asked.

"Well, considering that every evening I've called in the last few weeks I've received no answer and that I've written about 20 e-mails and left 800 voice messages on your mobile, I thought I'd fly down, catch some sun, and find out if you were dead or alive."

"Oh, sorry about that, mate." Baylor at least had the good manners to look repentant. "I've been kind of preoccupied the last couple of weeks."

Juliana went to the refrigerator and pulled out a bottle of cold beer. She held it up in invitation.

"Absolutely," Baylor said.

"Preoccupied, eh? What's her name?"

"Very funny. What makes you think it's a girl?"

"Because I've known you for over twenty years. It's always a girl with you. What's her name?"

"Hobie Lynn Allen."

"The nutter who ran you over?"

"That's the one. Look, though, I think I may have been a little, I don't know, angry at the time. She's not as much of a lunatic
as I initially thought. She's a nice girl and we're just friends."

Baylor wasn't sure why she felt the need to add the part about
being friends. What was it about Juliana that made her feel she
had to downplay her feelings for Hobie? She supposed it was
because her friend had been along for the ride while she had slept
her way through the greater Chicago area. Would she laugh?

Juliana smiled. She had a look on her face that said whenever
anyone stressed the fact that they were "just friends," it usually
meant exactly the opposite.

"It ought to be fun meeting her, then," she said.

"Meeting her?" Baylor suddenly looked pale. "Oh, I don't
know if that's such a good idea."

"Relax, mate. It's not like I'm going to try to steal your girlfriend. I just want to meet her."

"She's not my girlfriend. I told you—"

"I know, I know. Just friends," Juliana interrupted Baylor's
objection. "Whatever you say. Hey, don't you want to open the
presents I brought? I figure you must be going through culinary
withdrawal by now. You should have seen the looks I got carrying
all this on the plane."

"I wondered what was in there. I thought you were just getting cheap when it came to luggage."

"Hardy-har-har! How's that leg?"

"Great," Baylor answered as she pulled open the first bag.
"Matter of fact, I may get the cast off this week. Oh my God!" she
exclaimed when she saw the contents. "Cipriani's angel hair pasta,
roasted sweet peppers...Ooh, Cipriani's sauce, too. Oh God, Marconi bread, manna from heaven! You are wonderful!"

"Yeah, yeah, like I've never heard that before. Make sure you
put the last bag in the freezer."

Upon opening the item in question, Baylor found dry ice
packs surrounding the food. "This is it. I can die a happy woman
now. Geno's deep-dish pizza! Wait, which location, Geno's East?"

"Of course," Juliana answered with a smug smile.

"You are a godsend." Baylor hugged her friend.

"Yeah, women tell me that a lot. It's a curse."

"You're also an egomaniac."

"I learned from the best."

"So, what did you do last night?"

Hobie said nothing, just stared at the remnants of her lunch.

"Hello?" Laura waved her hand in front of Hobie's face. "Anybody home?"

"Huh? Stop that." Hobie slapped at her friend's hand. "I heard you."

"Uh-huh. What did I say?"

"Um...shit."

Laura laughed across from her. Hobie hated getting caught doing something goofy. "You were thinking about her again, weren't you?"

"What makes you say that?" Hobie tried to sound nonchalant.

"Well, first of all, you didn't ask who I meant when I just said 'her.' Second of all, you had those dreamy bedroom eyes going that you always wear when I catch you thinking of Baylor."

"You are such a bitch." Hobie laughed. "Besides, how in the world would you know what my bedroom eyes look like?"

"I don't, but if I had to imagine what they would look like, those are it. What I asked, originally, was what were you up to last night?"

"Oh. Not much. Saw a movie with Noah."

"And Baylor?" Laura grinned.

"Yes, smart ass, with Baylor. Noah happens to like her."

"Uh-huh. And the fact that she is over six feet of dark-haired, well-built sexy lady just happens to be a coincidence."

"Exactly. But it's a coincidence I am ever so thankful for." Hobie grinned back. "Hey, we better get going. We do have at least a little work to finish up before calling it a day."

"You got it, boss. Here, I got it." Laura reached for the check. "I'll gladly pay if it keeps food in your belly and your body off the floor."

The two women laughed and were about to get up when Baylor and Juliana walked into the restaurant. Baylor stopped in front of their booth and, as usual in Hobie's presence, found her tongue rather uncooperative. She smiled, and it would have taken a fool not to see what was in each woman's heart.

. "Hey," Baylor said.

"Hey," Hobie replied.

Juliana cleared her throat loudly.

"Oh." Baylor turned to her friend. "This is my friend and agent, Juliana Ross. Hobie, you've heard me talk about Jules. Uh, Jules this is Hobie Allen and her friend Laura."

"How nice to finally meet you." Hobie held out her hand. Laura gave a little wave from her side of the table.

"Well, the old girl told me that there was a beautiful vet and her lovely assistant living on the island, but I wasn't prepared for this."

Baylor blushed slightly and she didn't know if it was due to her friend's flirtation or having Hobie know that Baylor had called her lovely.

Hobie had to pull her hand back, as Juliana still held onto it. "We were just getting ready to leave, but we can stay for a few minutes if you two want to sit. Right, Lor?"

"You're the boss, boss," Laura replied with a smile.

"Oh, I don't think—" Baylor began.

"That would be great," Juliana said.

Baylor had an odd feeling. She was rather getting used to odd feelings. It seemed that Ana Lia put her more in tune with her emotions, and what she was feeling right now felt a lot like jealousy. All of a sudden, she didn't want Juliana to get to know Hobie. She knew in her heart that if she said something to her, Juliana would not even think about flirting with Hobie. She had a great deal of integrity that way, but would she laugh at Baylor? Mock her?

Baylor gave in to the peer pressure and said nothing. Without so much as a glance at Hobie, she slipped into the side of the booth where Laura sat. Juliana looked about as surprised as Hobie.

"So, what brings you to Ana Lia?" Hobie asked.

Baylor was sure that Hobie wondered why she looked so uncomfortable and why she was acting as if Hobie were a stranger.

"I had an incredible urge to see what was keeping my best mate so far from the big city." Juliana offered that charming grin once again. "I see now what kept her," she added, never taking her eyes from Hobie's face.

"So, Jules—do you mind me calling you that?" Hobie asked.

"Not at all, love."

"Where are you from originally?"

"My family moved from London when I was a kid."

"How exciting. I was there for a conference about eight years ago. I loved it. Where in London are you from?"

Juliana's smile faltered and she threw a quick glance at Baylor, who already showed the beginnings of a smile.

"Essex," Juliana answered.

Hobie smiled. "Blonde hair, blue eyes...so, you're an Essex girl, are you?"

Baylor snorted, trying to contain her laughter.

"I'm sorry, I couldn't resist," Hobie said with a sympathetic smile.

"Don't be," Juliana replied. She indicated Baylor with a nod. "She just loves it."

"Well, we better not keep you." Baylor rose abruptly and the three others stared at her.

"Oh, uh, yes," Hobie agreed. "We really do have to get going. Jules, will you be staying for a few days?"

"Yes."

"No."

Juliana and Baylor answered in unison. Juliana smiled amiably at her friend.

"As a matter of fact, I've sort of just decided that a little time on Ana Lia may be exactly what I need," Juliana added.

"Well, I hope we'll be seeing you again," Hobie said.

"I think I can pretty much guarantee that," Juliana replied, moving aside to allow the vet to pass.

Baylor and Juliana watched as the other women left. The writer glanced at her watch and quickly dragged her friend over to the counter.

"Geez, mate, where's the fire?"

"There's something on TV I don't want to miss. Oh, and just what the hell was that supposed to be back there?" Baylor demanded as they sat down.

"What?"

"What? You were practically all over her, and you say what!"

"When you say 'her,' I take it you mean Hobie?"

Baylor looked at her friend with a cynical expression.

"Hey, you're the one who said you were just friends and now you're acting like she belongs to you. Which is it, my friend?"

"I, uh, you...oh, shut up and let's eat."

"Look, BJ—"

"Jules, can this wait till the next commercial?" Baylor held up a hand, never taking her eyes off the television.

Juliana watched as nearly all activity in the diner came to an abrupt halt. It took a moment or two before she realized that everyone in the restaurant was watching the television. It took a few seconds longer to realize that the actors in the program were not speaking English.

"It's in Spanish, right?"

"Yeah."

"Do you speak Spanish?"

"Maybe a little. You know, a couple of classes in high school."

"Seems like a really popular show."

"Oh, yeah. I've been watching it since I got to the island. It's really kind of addictive," Baylor answered distractedly.

"Does somebody else here translate for everyone?"

"No." Baylor turned and looked at Juliana as though she had grown an additional head in the past few moments. "Why would they?"

"Oh, I get it, all right, very funny. You're not serious, right?"

"Shh." Baylor stared intently at the television.

Juliana watched the screen, trying to decipher what was happening. "What are they saying?"

"I'm not sure, but I think the brunette has done something terrible to the blonde, and I think the old guy saw it. Or he knows about it somehow."

Juliana let Baylor order their lunch, although she grew slightly worried at the sound of duck's breath burgers and munchers. By the time their food came, Juliana had become involved in the television show herself.

"Who's he?" she asked, popping another muncher into her mouth.

"He's the blonde's lover, but I think he might be gay."

"How do you know?"

"He kissed the brunette's husband. Of course, that might not mean anything considering the brunette's husband ended up dead the next day."

"Could have been the kiss of death," Juliana commented.

"Exactly what I was thinking."

The two women ate their lunch and watched television. During the commercial breaks, Juliana found herself drifting into thought. She loved Baylor like a sister. Over the years, they had often competed for the same women, but with one big difference: Baylor was interested in the conquest, the game, but she had a bad habit of not caring for the feelings of the women she became involved with. More often than not, Juliana would voluntarily give up in a bet with her to save the feelings of the woman involved. She had seen her friend grow unreasonably jealous when it came to someone that she was interested in, but it was an envy born of possessiveness and ownership, not true love. Juliana wished that, just once, her friend might experience the latter.

She also wondered at her own behavior. Had she really allowed herself be drawn into this world of Baylor's so easily? She attributed it to Baylor's ability to lure her into her schemes and dreams. That had been a talent of Baylor's since they'd been children.

What the hell, Juliana thought. She continued to watch the actors on the screen speak in a language with which she was completely unfamiliar. *When in Rome...*

"Let me ask you something, Jules."

Baylor and Juliana sat beside the pool in Evelyn's back yard, sipping margaritas and talking about nothing and everything, the sort of talk of friends who feel completely comfortable with one another. Juliana splashed her feet in the water, but Baylor's aversion to open water included the pool. She reclined on a lounger in the shade.

"What do you think of me?" Baylor asked.

"I try not to."

"As a writer."

"Absolutely brill, mate."

"And what about my books?"

"What about them?"

"Don't play games with me, Jules."

"You've been thinking again, haven't you? I told you years ago not to listen to that old man of yours."

"It's not that."

"Then what?" Juliana rose and took a seat in the chaise lounge beside Baylor. She toweled her legs dry and tried to pretend that she didn't know what Baylor meant.

"When we were in college I planned to be such a different writer than I am now. I wanted to write novels that would...I don't know, make a difference, or help people in some way. Instead, I write cheap trash. At the very least, I feel like I'm living such a lie. I don't mind writing straight stories, but straight romance? It's far from what I know, that's for sure."

"That trash made you a wealthy woman. Plus, there is no credence to the idea that writing what you know will produce a better novel."

"I don't want to sound ungrateful, to you or anyone. It's just me, I guess." Baylor ran her fingers through her hair and let her head fall against the back of the lounge chair.

"Let me tell you a story, Baylor. Remember when we were in college together? I wanted to be a writer just like you."

"I thought you would be, too. You were better than I was. What happened with that, Jules?"

"I set out to write the great American novel. I wanted to be the female Hemingway. I felt I was above writing romance or mystery. I turned down half a dozen advances to write fiction. I had words of substance inside of me that I bloody well wanted the world to know about. I felt I'd done it, too. I finally hawked my perfect masterpiece to every publisher I could get in to see."

"What happened?"

Juliana smiled at her friend. "They liked it so much that I became an agent so I could tell my authors not to make themselves bonkers over what they're *not* getting paid to write and to enjoy the ride over what they *are* making money to write."

"Very funny."

"It's true, in a sad way." Juliana closed her eyes, enjoying the warmth of the sun on her face. "Look, quit making yourself bonkers, mate. I'm telling you this from experience. If you want to feel good about yourself as a writer, and writing something different will do that, then you go for it. I'll be behind you all the way. Just don't do what I did to myself for the first ten years after I became an agent. I hated that I felt like I was selling out my writing. I was *very* successful as an agent, though. Authors like you helped." Juliana winked. "So, for a long time, I acted like you are now. I beat myself up over the fact that I was working as an agent and not a writer. The money was too good to say no, so I felt guilty most of the time, thereby making me a pretty miserable person to be around nine-tenths of the time."

"That's why you've always known just what to say to me, isn't it? You've been there," Baylor said.

"Boy, have I been there."

"So, how'd you do it? How'd you get past it?"

"I guess I finally made a choice. That sounds simple, doesn't it? Actually, mate, I was thirty-five years old and had just realized that making a personal decision, one that affected my whole life, was the hardest thing I could ever do. I just wish I'd seen the truth of it twenty years sooner."

"I hear you, Jules."

Juliana looked on as Baylor nodded. She had always promised herself that she would have this talk with Baylor one day. She had often recognized Baylor's dilemma regarding her novels. It was very odd, though, that here on an island off the coast of Florida, Juliana should find it so easy to open up to her.

A nervous thought passed through her mind just then. She wondered if she should tell Baylor that Evelyn had talked her into coming to the island. Evelyn had pleaded with her to come and see Baylor, but under no circumstances to tell her who had initiated the visit. Even though they were best friends, Juliana had given her word.

She chose to smile in silence at her friend.

Chapter
11

"Gee, if I'd known there was going to be a party, I would have brought nicer clothes," Juliana said as she fastened a thin gold necklace, followed by a matching bracelet.

They were readying themselves for a social event that Baylor wished she were attending alone, or even with Hobie. It was a fund-raiser for the Ana Lia Public Library. She had donated an entire set of Harriet Teasley novels, and the Ladies Guild insisted she be there for the event.

"You know, this isn't going to be quite like the parties in the high-rises on Lake Shore Drive. I don't picture this as your cup of tea. Maybe you ought to sit this one out."

"It sounds distinctly as if you don't want me to come," Juliana replied.

Baylor looked at her friend's hurt expression. "Hey, I'm sorry. I didn't mean it the way it sounded, mate. Of course you're welcome to come."

"That's better." Juliana smiled broadly.

Baylor hated lying to Juliana, but it was because of their friendship, and the expression on her face, that Baylor surrendered. The reality was that she wanted to keep Juliana as far away from her new friends as possible. *Did I just think of the nuts on this island as my friends?*

She still couldn't get past the idea that Juliana would ridicule her newfound feelings for this place, its people, and most of all, for Hobie. It never occurred to her that Juliana might be perfectly accepting of everything and everyone on the island. Therefore, she did what she had been good at for so many years: she covered up her true feelings. She did have one fleeting thought. *Is it that I don't want Juliana near any of these people, or just Hobie?*

"Now, care to tell me what the deal is between you and the vet?"

"I told you—"

"Yeah, yeah, the just friends bit. I know that's what you said, but was it what you meant?"

"What do you mean, 'what I meant'?"

"I saw the way you two looked at each other. There was, I don't know, like some kind of spark or something. Are you trying to tell me that there's nothing going on there?"

Baylor hesitated for just a fraction of a second, and that was her undoing. Juliana read the vacillation perfectly.

"I like her, all right? As a *friend!*"

"You just like her," Juliana repeated.

"Yeah. I don't *like her,* like her. I just like her. What?" Baylor stared indignantly at Juliana.

"I just haven't heard anyone use that expression since I was in the sixth grade," Juliana said before she burst into laughter.

"You're a regular fuckin' comedian," Baylor responded. She turned her back and pulled a linen jacket on over her tank top.

"It's just that you're about as transparent as glass. Why don't you just tell this girl that you want her?"

"It's not like that between us."

"You mean you're chicken."

"I am not chicken!" Baylor shouted. "We are just friends!"

"Then you won't mind if I ask her out."

If one statement could have ever been the equivalent of dropping a bomb into the middle of a room, that one was it. All Baylor could do was to stare at her friend in disbelief.

"Just what in the hell is that supposed to mean?"

"For starters, no wonder you haven't been on a date down here if you don't understand what asking a woman out means. Secondly, I think she's pretty damned attractive and nice, to boot. If you don't want her that way, well..."

"I think that would be a bad idea." Baylor found her voice at last. "A very bad idea." She began to pace, her cast thumping loudly on the wooden floor.

"And why is that?" Juliana asked. She folded her arms across her chest and looked at her friend with an amused expression, which was lost on Baylor.

"Because—because—because Hobie doesn't need any problems in her life right now." Baylor pointed at Juliana.

"I wasn't planning to marry her. I was thinking more about a little dinner, drinks, maybe a little snogging."

"She is not that kind of girl."

"You said she had a kid."

"What does that have to do with anything?"

"It means she was that kind of girl at least once." Juliana wiggled her eyebrows.

"You are sick, ya know that?" Baylor shouted across the room.

Juliana laughed aloud. "Look, Baylor—"

Baylor firmly placed her palms flat against her ears. "I can't hear you. The crazy woman's mouth is still moving, but I am not listening." She hummed loudly, but couldn't drown out Juliana's next question.

"If you want this girl for yourself, mate, why don't you just tell me so?"

"What? Just because I think that maybe you shouldn't waltz into town and shag my friend, that means I want her?"

"Pretty much, yeah. Unless..." Juliana paused as if remembering something. "Unless you're afraid to admit that you like this girl. Even to me."

Baylor quickly turned pale. "I—I don't want to talk about this anymore." She turned her back on Juliana again, grabbed her wallet, and shoved it into her jacket pocket.

"Oh my God!" Juliana watched the taller woman frantically pace back and forth across the dining room. "Sally Ann Kapinski!" she exclaimed.

Baylor turned to face her friend. "You agreed never to bring her up again!"

"That's it, isn't it?" Juliana shook her head in wonderment. "You were in love with Sally, but you were afraid to admit it. You were afraid that everyone would laugh at you."

"You're full of shit," Baylor snarled.

"Afraid that everyone would make fun of you," Juliana continued. "The most eligible lesbian in Chicago finally having her wings clipped and putting on the old ball and chain. That's it, isn't it? You knew you'd take shit from all of us, so you chickened out. You never told Sally how you felt and she left you because of it."

"You know what? I don't care. I didn't give a damn about Sally Kapinski then, and I don't give a damn about Hobie Allen now. If you want to make a fool of yourself by asking her out, then you go on and do it!" Baylor straightened her jacket and struggled to gain control of her temper. "Just leave me out of your little plan. Now, can we get going or do you want to analyze my fucking life a little more, Doctor?"

Juliana stood in silence for a moment longer. "I'm thinking stress management might be something you might want to look into, mate."

Baylor released a strangled cry of frustration, then spoke in a slow, calm voice. "I'm going to kill you one day. I'm going to make it slow and painful, I swear. No, even better, I'm going to bide my time until one day, they're holding a sanity hearing for you. Then I'm going to explain, in great detail, what a complete and utter lunatic you are."

Juliana grinned and scooped up the Jaguar's keys off the table. "Promises, promises."

The agent's lighthearted laughter followed Baylor as she walked out the front door. She closed her eyes and counted to ten, wondering how her night could possible get any worse.

"You look like a million bucks," Baylor said to Hobie, who wore a sleek pale blue dress that clung to her body in a manner that made it hard for Baylor to concentrate on anything else. She had made it a point to search out the redhead before Juliana had a chance to talk to her.

"Thanks. You're looking pretty sharp yourself," answered Hobie. "You know, I'm glad we have a few minutes alone. There's something I need to talk to you about. It has to do with Noah. You see, he—"

"Hiya, Baylor." Noah tugged on the tall woman's pant leg to get her attention.

"Hey, Bubba. What's up?" Baylor looked down at the youngster and immediately became concerned. "What in the hel—heck happened to you?"

"That's what I wanted to talk with you about," Hobie interjected.

Baylor quickly reached down and scooped Noah into her arms. He sported a broad smile and one black eye.

"Noah, what happened?" Baylor was beyond concerned as she examined his bruise. Her distress over the boy wasn't lost on Hobie.

"Well," Noah began as he gesticulated wildly with his hands, "Billy Crenshaw came up to me and he says, 'Give me your milk money or else,' and I said, 'Or else what.' 'Or else I'm gonna sock you,' he says. So I said just what you told me. I said, 'Forget it, you rat bastard, *my* money is for *my* milk!'" Noah beamed, Hobie arched an eyebrow, and Baylor cringed at the language that the youngster had picked up from her.

"Then what happened?" Baylor looked almost afraid to hear the answer.

"Then he hit me. I fell down, but you know what, Baylor?"

The writer dumbly shook her head.

"When he hit me and I fell down, it hurt, but it didn't hurt near as bad as I 'spected it to. So I jumped back up and I held up my hands just like you showed me, with my thumbs on the outside, and I said, 'You still ain't getting my money, you rat bastard.' He says, 'I'll hit you again,' and I said, 'Just you try.' When he tried, I punched him right in the tummy, just like you said. He cried like a baby. That's when the teacher called Mom." Noah giggled and swung his legs.

"Wow, I...um..." Baylor could feel Hobie's eyes boring into her. She was unsure what to say. She had thought the bully would back down, giving her time to explain the situation to Hobie. Typical of Baylor, however, she hadn't yet been able to find the nerve to broach the subject.

"Noah, sweetheart, why don't you let me talk to Baylor alone. Okay?"

"'Kay," he answered as Baylor settled him onto his feet.

"All right, I'm waiting." Hobie looked up at Baylor.

"Okay...um..."

"Tell me there is a good explanation for this. Tell me that you had a good, solid reason to teach my son to hit someone. Tell me that I'm only imagining that it was a stupid, reckless, even dangerous thing for you to do. Please, Baylor, give me some kind of an intelligent answer to all of this."

Baylor looked rather panicked. This wasn't exactly the way she had pictured the evening starting.

"Baylor?" Hobie pressed.

"I...I...oh, shit. I'm really trying to come up with something solid for you here, Hobie, but man. The truth is I did teach him a few things, but only self-defense moves, I swear that. I honestly thought the bully would back down, you know? Oh hell, I'm really sorry."

"Apology accepted."

Baylor quickly looked up from her shoes. In order *not* to meet Hobie's intense gaze, she had chosen that moment to find something fascinating about them. "Did you just accept my apology?"

"I did."

"Okay." Baylor looked around. "Your brother's around somewhere to kick the shit out of me, right?"

Hobie's laughter eased Baylor's suspicions somewhat. "Why are you always so paranoid?"

"I've usually got good reason."

"Well, I mean it when I say that I understand why you helped Noah the way you did. Frankly, I think I should thank you."

"Thank me?"

"Uh-huh." Hobie nodded. "I admit, you were a little lucky that I didn't run into you this afternoon. My blood pressure was pretty high when I was on my way home from picking up a young boy with a black eye, especially when that boy said you were the one who taught him how to fight."

"Now, about that," Baylor began.

"I'm not through," Hobie interrupted. "I was pretty upset, as you can imagine."

"Understandably so," Baylor added. "I know how you can get."

Her last response was a little too enthusiastic. Hobie arched an eyebrow.

"Sorry," Baylor said.

"Like I said, I was pretty upset. When Noah told me the whole story, though, I asked him why he told you about Billy Crenshaw instead of me. He said that he knew you would get it. I took that to mean that he thought you would understand what he was going through. When I thought about it, I realized that he was right. Any advice I would have given him wouldn't have helped a six-year-old much against a playground bully. I guess I get so concerned with making sure Noah grows up to be respectful of others and a nice boy that I forgot the rest of the world isn't always so nice." Hobie looked at Baylor with the expression that made her knees go weak.

"Thanks for being there for him, Baylor."

"No problem." Baylor gave Hobie a little half smile.

"I owe you one."

Baylor raised an eyebrow and looked down at her casted leg.

"Okay, I owe you a whole lot more than one," Hobie responded. "Now on to more pleasant subjects. How is Juliana enjoying the island?"

Baylor's smile and amiable expression evaporated. "Um, Jules...well...look, Hobie...about her..."

Baylor had a thought. What if she faced her fears and admitted to Hobie how she felt? Would the vet shoot her down? She wondered if she had it in her. As much as she hated to admit it, Juliana had been right about Sally. Baylor's biggest nightmare in life was the fear of being laughed at. It didn't even matter if it was a good-natured ribbing from friends. She feared it as though it were her father himself mocking her. Still, if she didn't say something to Hobie now, she might lose the chance.

"What about her?" Hobie asked with a confused expression.

"Well, actually, it's less about Jules and more about me...you and me."

"You and me?"

"You and me. I think...actually, I wonder..." Baylor paused to lick her lips. All of a sudden, her mouth had gone bone dry. *I can do this. I can do this. I can tell her I love her. Love her? Where the hell did that come from? What happened to "I want to go out with her"? I like her? Love her? Okay, shit, come back to that later. Get her to go out with you first, dipshit. Focus, Baylor, focus.*

"Hobie Lynn," Baylor took a deep breath. "I wonder...I— I...Hobie, would you—"

"Well, if it isn't my favorite old friend and my favorite new friend."

To Baylor, Juliana's voice felt like a bucket of ice water tossed over her head. *Jules, you heartless bitch.* "What do you want?" she asked sourly.

"Did I interrupt something?"

"Yes," Baylor responded.

"Well, I can come back later."

"Of course not," Hobie said, remembering her manners. "I was just asking Baylor about you."

"Well, then it's definitely my lucky day."

Baylor recognized that Juliana had a charming smile and seemed to know exactly what to say to the women. She herself used to be like that. That is, until Hobie appeared in her life. Baylor eyed Hobie and noticed her flushed face. *Great, just great!*

"Excuse me, I need a drink," she said before rushing away toward the bar.

"I wonder what got into her?" Juliana commented.

"I wonder, too." Hobie looked longingly after her. "I guess she'll be back." She turned her attention to Juliana.

"I suppose it gives me an opportunity to get to know you a bit better."

"Me?" Hobie wondered if teeth that white could be anything but caps as she became slightly mesmerized by Juliana's charming grin.

"I always want to get better acquainted with beautiful women."

"Jules, are you flirting with me?"

"If you have to ask I must be doing it wrong."

Hobie laughed at the agent's honest response. "Do I have a sign on my forehead that points me out as the only lesbian in town, or what?"

It was Juliana's turn for laughter. "No, not at all. I figured I'd take a chance and, with a bit of luck, be pleasantly surprised. Actually, I was hoping I could lure you into a little walk on the beach."

"Well, my answer may surprise you, but I'm not sure how

pleasant it will be for you."

"Meaning?"

"Meaning I am gay, but I'm not in the market for a girl-friend."

"I see. You're already spoken for, then?"

"Um...in a way." Hobie was kicking herself for not just blurt-ing out to Baylor that she had fallen for her. *Fallen...in love? Where the hell did that come from? Like her...you like her, that's it. Isn't it?*

"I must have been mistaken, then. I am sorry, Hobie. It's just that when Baylor told me you and she were nothing but friends, well, I guess I figured I stood a chance."

Juliana hated herself right about then. Of course, she still wasn't certain about Baylor and Hobie; there was the outside chance that Baylor was telling the truth and that friendship was truly the only thing that existed between the two. She saw her words explode within the green eyes, which suddenly narrowed.

"Just friends?"

"That's what she said. Am I wrong, Hobie? Are you two more than friends?" Juliana knew what the answer would be. If she'd ever seen a woman surprised at the notion that she was suddenly single, it was Hobie.

Hobie took a deep breath. "If Baylor says we're just friends, then I guess that's what we are. Now, didn't you say something about a walk?"

"I did indeed." Juliana placed a hand on the small of Hobie's back and turned to usher her down the concrete steps to the beach. She saw Baylor walking their way and winked at her. Bay-lor's crushed expression tugged painfully at her heart. *Dear Lord, please let Evelyn be right, or a twenty-five-year friendship just went down the drain.*

Baylor drummed her fingers impatiently on the tabletop. She had selected a spot near the edge of the patio so she could tell when Hobie and Juliana returned. When they did, they looked much too happy for her liking.

"Just where in the hell have you been?" Baylor was on her third vodka, which did nothing to mellow her mood.

"I beg your pardon?" Hobie asked indignantly. Juliana took a step back as Hobie and Baylor stared daggers at one another.

"Do you usually just go off and leave your son?" Baylor could see that Hobie was trying to control her temper. She also knew that her first instinct would be to let Baylor have it with both barrels, but there were too many people at the surrounding tables. Hobie probably didn't feel like making yet another scene in front of the whole town.

"If it's any of your business," Hobie said in a controlled voice, "my mother is watching Noah."

"Oh," Baylor replied, the wind seemingly gone from her sails.

"Excuse me, I think I need a drink. Jules, can I get you anything?" Hobie asked.

"Uh, no, thanks anyway."

Hobie started to leave, but thought better of it and turned back to Baylor. She stood behind her and bent down. Baylor flinched when she felt the vet's hands on her shoulders. Then there was a sexy voice whispering in her ear.

"I'm a little surprised you care so much about where I go and who I choose to see." Hobie stood up and gave Baylor's shoulders a shove. "Considering the fact that we're just friends!" She turned and stalked away.

Baylor glared up at Juliana, who sat down beside her, purposefully ignoring her expression. "Holy shit, mate, is she ever mad at you. Did you see her? I think she had little wisps of smoke coming out her ears." She chuckled at Baylor's predicament, then reached over and stole a sip of her drink.

"Give me that!" Baylor snapped. "You are a rat bastard. Did you have to tell her I said that? God damn it, Jules, don't you know I like that girl!"

"Oh my God, time out, time out." Juliana waved her hands. "Hello! Were you even in the same room when I had that conversation with you earlier? Who the bloody hell was that I was talking to?"

"Oh, don't give me that shit!"

"No, that was definitely you I had that conversation with. I said 'Do you like her' and you said you liked her, but you didn't *like her*, like her. Is any of this ringing a bell?"

"Oh, shut up!" Baylor finished the rest of her drink in one gulp. "I suppose you already asked her to marry you."

"I would have if I thought I had a prayer of her saying yes."

"She seemed plenty eager to go out into the moonlight with you."

"Well, maybe it was my considerable charm."

Baylor snorted.

"Or maybe it was the fact that she was so damned surprised to hear that the woman she really has the hots for said they were 'just friends.'" Juliana used her fingers to make little quote marks in the air.

"Did she say that?"

"Say what?"

"That she had the hots—I mean, that she was interested in me. You know, in that way."

"No, she didn't come right out and say it."

"Then how in the hell do you know that was what she was thinking?"

"I've been around enough women in my lifetime to be able to tell when one is using me because she's mad at the woman she really wants. You know, I don't even believe we're having this conversation. You are forty-two years old, Baylor, and we're talking about your love life like we're still in grade school."

Baylor munched on an ice cube and continued to glare at Juliana. "Like you're some big-ass expert on women. May I remind you that you're the same age and single too?"

"Yeah, but *I've* got a date for tomorrow night."

"You bitch. You're still gonna go out with her, knowing the way I feel?"

"Hey, being an understanding mate only goes so far, especially when a beautiful woman is involved."

"I guess I know where *our* friendship stands," Baylor said, looking away.

"Don't even go there, mate. If I weren't your friend, I wouldn't be telling you that the one way you could get this girl would be to be honest with her."

"Jesus H. Christ." Baylor rested her head in her hands. "How did I let this situation get so fucked up?"

"Baylor, you said a bad word." Noah just happened to be on his way over to their table. He clapped his hands tightly over his ears.

Juliana smiled at his antics. His friendly smile and glasses made him instantly recognizable as Hobie's son.

"Hey there, Bubba. You caught me. Sorry about that."

"S'okay."

"Just do me a favor. Be sure not to tell your mom about that, huh?" Baylor lifted Noah into her lap and Juliana watched, seemingly fascinated at how comfortable she appeared around him.

"I'm kind of on thin ice with her tonight."

"Why?"

"Well, I didn't exactly tell your mom the truth about something."

"Oh," Noah drew out the word. "Mom says don't use bad words and always be honest."

"So far, you're batting a thousand, mate." Juliana chuckled.

Baylor glared at her. "Noah, this woman with the very big mouth, her name is Juliana. You can call her Jules. She's my very best friend in the whole world. Next to you, of course." She tickled Noah, who giggled.

"So," Baylor continued, looking over at Juliana, "you think I should start being honest, eh?"

"Spot on."

"Honesty, huh? Okay, how's this for a start at honesty? Bubba, do you know who your dad is?"

"Uh-huh." Noah nodded. "Oh, Baylor, I gotta go. They're givin' out cake and ice cream now." He squirmed his way out of Baylor's lap.

"Wait, just a sec, Bubba." Baylor caught his arm. "Noah, who is your dad?" ·

"965-2338," answered the preoccupied boy. "Baylor, I gotta go now."

Baylor released Noah's arm and watched as he sped off to the dessert table. "What the hell do you make of that?"

"I don't know. Oh, wait." Juliana counted the digits with the fingers of one hand. "I bet it's the bloke's phone number."

"Shit, I never thought of that. If he doesn't know the area code, it must mean it's local. I wonder..."

"Do not tell me you're thinking about doing what I think you are."

"What?"

"You're gonna call that number, aren't you?"

"Maybe," Baylor answered as she swirled what was left of the ice in her glass.

"Let it go. If Hobie wants to tell you, she will. A gal like Hobie doesn't stroll into your life every day, Baylor. If you really do have feelings for her, you better concentrate on finding the nerve to tell her so."

"I find it extremely interesting that you should say that, considering you're going out on a date with her tomorrow."

"Like I said, mate, the way to stop that from happening is to tell her...tonight. It's not a case of you or me. Trust me on this one. I'm just an alternate. If she knew that you were in the game, I wouldn't even be in the running."

"So, all I have to do is come out and say...it."

"Well, first thing I'd work on is your delivery." Juliana tried hard not to laugh at her friend. "If you can't say the words to yourself, you're certainly not going to be able to say them to her."

"Okay, okay, I'm working on it. I think I need some more to drink first." Without saying another word, Baylor jumped up and headed for the bar.

"Hobie?"

"What now?" Hobie turned to face Baylor and literally stopped breathing for a moment. The tall woman's short hair dipped into her face, covering one eye. She looked exactly as she had on the night the two women first met. Any harsh words that Hobie might have been prepared to say over Baylor's previous behavior melted away on her tongue.

"Baylor?" Hobie only hoped the little catch in her voice hadn't been audible.

"Yeah. Um, you got a sec, because I have something—of—of the...of the...*utmost* importance to speak to you about."

The dark-haired woman's body swayed back and forth ever so slightly. Hobie realized that the rakish charm Baylor possessed was due to the same influence as their first meeting. Baylor Warren was dead drunk.

"Something important, eh?" Hobie asked. She felt herself wanting to smile. It was so difficult to be cross with a woman who looked so adorable.

"Yes, yes...important, very important. *Life threatening,* in fact," Baylor slurred.

Hobie finally smiled, perturbed at herself for it, but only slightly so. Baylor was beautiful and charming. She had a heart, even when she pretended not to, and there was something innocently childlike in her ability to see nothing beyond the task before her. Even though she was so drunk that she had to hold on to the back of a chair to keep her body upright, Baylor still had the ability to enchant Hobie.

"So..." Hobie prompted.

"So, what?" Baylor's brow furrowed together.

"You wanted to tell me something life threatening, as I recall."

"Huh? Oh yeah. No, life *altering,* not threatening."

"I see." Hobie waited again, but Baylor just stared at her with a cute sort of half smile on her face. "And it would be?" she finally asked.

"Oh! Yes. Um, honey—Hobie, I mean Hobie!"

"Yes, Baylor?" Two hours earlier, when Baylor had last approached her, Hobie had wanted to pick up a heavy object and plant it in Baylor's skull; now she wasn't sure how to describe what she felt. It was as though being with Baylor this way took Hobie back to that night in Chicago. The night when every part of her being screamed at her to be sensible, but instead she said "what the hell" and allowed Baylor to kiss her anyway—and that one kiss was something Hobie wouldn't give back for the world.

Baylor brushed the hair from her eyes and tried to focus on what she wanted to say. "Hobie, I...Hobie, will you—"

"Hobie Lynn, can we have just a moment to get your opinion on this?" Peter Mason, the head librarian, called out. He added that he wanted Hobie's opinion as a board member regarding some of the funds they had collected that evening.

"Sure, Peter, just give me a minute," Hobie said. Unfortunately, by the time she turned back to face Baylor, the writer was in a heap on the floor.

"Oh, Baylor," Hobie said to the unconscious woman.

"Hey, mate. Come on, wake up." Juliana lightly slapped Baylor's face a few more times until she saw that she was coming around.

"Stop that!" Baylor pushed Juliana's hand away.

"She's back to her testy self," Juliana said as she looked up at Hobie.

"I guess that means she's fine," Hobie said. "Baylor, can you stand up?"

"I thought I was," Baylor answered.

"Okay, then." Juliana shook her head with a chuckle. "Up you go, mate."

Hobie looked Baylor over and peered into her eyes before declaring that, while she was completely inebriated, she hadn't hurt herself.

"My God, you weigh a lot," Juliana said to Baylor, who leaned heavily against her. "I better get you home."

"Here, let me give you a hand." Hobie moved to Baylor's other side and slipped her arm around her waist. They made their way from the party, Baylor in the middle with her arms around Juliana and Hobie's shoulders.

"I hate to make you do this," Juliana began, "but I'm not sure I can handle Miss Temperance here by myself."

"No problem," Hobie responded. "That's my pickup over there. We can all fit in the front seat."

Baylor's legs had trouble moving at a steady pace. Her knees seemed to turn to liquid with every few steps, and the cast made things even worse. She rocked between her two navigators until she nearly hung on Hobie.

"You smell good," she slurred.

"Thank you."

"I mean you smell *really* good. Doesn't she smell good, Jules?" Baylor quickly swung her head toward her old friend.

"A veritable flower garden," Juliana replied.

"I'm serious." Baylor looked between the two women with the childlike expression that only someone who is quite drunk can muster up. "You always smell so good."

"All right, enough smelling. Duck your head and get in there," Hobie ordered with a smile when they reached the truck.

They rode along in silence until Baylor began nudging Hobie's elbow.

"What?" Hobie finally blurted out in exasperation.

"I don't feel so good."

"Oh, no you don't, Baylor Warren. If you throw up on me I swear I will toss you into the pickup bed."

Juliana laughed at Baylor's expression. "You better pull over, Hobie."

As soon as the truck stopped, it took all of five seconds for Baylor to bolt from the cab and lose the contents of her stomach. A packaged moist towelette and a few mints later, Baylor settled herself in the pickup once more.

"I feel much better. Where are we going now?" Baylor may have felt better, but she continued to slur her words badly.

"I have an idea," Hobie said.

"Cool."

"How about I drop you two off at home so you can sleep it off? Then I go home and go to bed."

"Well, that doesn't sound like any fun at all."

Hobie's laughter was an unexpected surprise. "Yep, it's the curse of being good. Just call me Hobie 'no fun' Allen."

Baylor leaned against the redhead. "Maybe that's because nobody ever gave you a good enough reason to be bad."

Hobie felt her stomach do a little flip. She was thankful that Juliana was in the car with them because if they had been alone, she just knew that she would have pulled over and ravished the woman beside her. Instead, she took a deep breath and gripped the steering wheel even harder.

They eventually reached Evelyn's home. Juliana and Hobie assisted Baylor inside and deposited her on the couch.

Hobie held out two aspirin and a glass of water for Baylor. "Take these, they may help in the morning."

Baylor swallowed the pills obediently. "Don't go yet, Hobie," she pleaded.

"What is it?" Hobie sat down on the couch beside the now

prone woman.

"I...this all started because I had something to say to you...something very important."

"I remember. 'Life altering' I believe is the way you put it."

"Right, right. Life altering."

"And it would be?"

Juliana stood in the shadows watching them.

"Huh?" Baylor looked confused.

"What did you want to tell me, Baylor?" Hobie enunciated each word carefully.

"Oh, yeah. I wanted to say..." Baylor squinted her eyes. "Um...I wanted to say..."

"Yes?" Hobie was afraid to hear what it was, but she was even more terrified to think that it wouldn't be what she was expecting. She didn't have the nerve to come out and say it herself. "You wanted to tell me something important?"

"Yeah. Hobie, I...I...damn, I can't remember." Baylor looked at her surroundings as though something would jog her memory.

"Right." Hobie rose. "If you think of it just holler," she added with a gentle smile. How could she find fault with Baylor's inability to speak when she herself couldn't gather the courage to speak openly about her feelings? How could Hobie take the chance of opening her heart when Baylor might not have had that in mind at all? How big of a fool would she look then?

She grabbed the blanket from the end of the couch. Baylor was already asleep by the time Hobie pulled the covering over her. The vet was almost thankful for that. It gave her the opportunity to look down on Baylor unobserved.

"I better go." Hobie pulled her gaze away from the sleeping figure.

"Let me walk you out," Juliana responded.

The air surrounding them still felt extremely humid as they stood on the porch, welcoming the light breeze that brushed against their skin.

"I appreciate your help in getting Baylor home."

"That's all right." Hobie turned and smiled. "It wasn't a big deal."

"She had a pretty good reason for getting as hammered as she did. Do you want to know why?" Juliana tilted her head and made eye contact with the redhead.

"No. No, don't tell me." Hobie lowered her head to hide a sudden blush. "Actually, I'd kind of like to use my imagination as to what she was going to say to me."

"Hobie, if you'd like to change your mind about tomorrow—"

"No," she answered softly. "I wouldn't. I just hope you won't be too disappointed."

"At what, being second choice? Nah, I've been Baylor's friend for so long that I'm used to losing out to her."

"Look, we're—"

"Dear God, if you say 'just friends' I'll scream." Juliana sat against the porch railing. "Hobie, I'm not looking for anything magical to happen between us. It's just been a long time since I've been out with a beautiful, intelligent woman...a *nice* woman. I'm simply looking forward to seeing that wonderful smile across the table from me tomorrow, nothing else, no strings."

"You two." Hobie shook her head. She paused to push her glasses up. "Between you and Baylor, I swear, you've got more charm than two women ought to be allowed to have. I think a night out with you sounds like fun, Jules. Thanks for asking me. Do you think Baylor will be able to handle you going off on a date while you're a guest?"

Juliana laughed as if that question were an inside joke. "I don't think she'd mind so much if I was going out with someone other than you. No, I fully expect the top of her head to blow off. You know, it's been a long time since Baylor's cared about anyone to get this worked up. Matter of fact, I don't ever remember it being this bad." She then gave Hobie a devilish grin. "I think it'll be good for her."

"I'll see you tomorrow, then." Hobie turned to leave. "Say about six?"

"Sounds good. Baylor doesn't know it yet, but I plan on using her Jag."

"I don't even want to be around for that fight," Hobie said as she walked away. She waved goodbye and wondered for about the millionth time that night why she was going out on a date with the best friend of the woman she really wanted to go out with.

Tomorrow should be an interesting day, Hobie thought.

Chapter
12

"Hobie...Hobie," Baylor mumbled in her half sleep. She had been dreaming that she and the vet were sharing a kiss. The kiss seemed familiar, but even in her dream state, Baylor knew that she'd never kissed Hobie before, and she had no idea why she would remember kissing a woman that she'd never kissed before. She woke from her slumber a little more fully and immediately felt the pain of the previous evening's indulgence. Barely squinting her eyes open, she found the source of the wet kisses.

"Arturo, get off me!" Baylor pushed at the white ball of fluff, but he took that as an invitation to play. "Stop, Squirt. Hey, quit chewing on my ear!"

It took Baylor quite some time that morning to get motivated enough to move. She eventually made it into the kitchen, turned on the coffee maker, and sat at the kitchen table. She rested her head on the smooth wood, which felt cool against her cheek. That was how Juliana found her.

"Good morning, morning glory! Hey, are we going to the Cove for brekky? I sure could go for some eggs and greasy bacon." Juliana poured two cups of coffee as she spoke.

"Eat shit and die," Baylor groaned without raising her head from the table.

"Let me fix you up with my patented hangover cure. It has raw eggs in it."

"Tanti keeps a gun and I'm not afraid to use it."

Juliana laughed, but kept her voice down. She reached out and stroked the top of her friend's head. "Here, this may help, mate." She set the mug of coffee on the table in front of Baylor.

Baylor sipped the steaming brew and massaged her temple with her free hand.

"How many gimlets did you have last night?"

"I think I lost count at ten. How shitfaced did I get? Tell me I didn't do anything to piss off Hobie."

"Um, well..."

"Oh, no. What did I do?"

"Let's see. You cornered Hobie and kept telling her you had something life altering to tell her. Then you passed out on her. She helped me get you home. You threw up—not on her, thankfully— you flirted shamelessly with her in the truck, and that's about it."

"Did I tell her?"

"That you're in love with her? Nah, by the time we got home, you couldn't remember what it was you wanted to say." She easily interpreted the stricken look on Baylor's face. "And, yes, you told me that you cared for her."

"Geez, I must have been drunk," Baylor noted. "God, she must hate me."

"Surprisingly enough, I believe she still thinks you're rather cute. Damned if I know why."

Baylor's head popped up at that. "Cute? Were those her exact words? I mean did she actually *say* I was cute?"

"Can we say pathetic?" Juliana chuckled.

"Oh, shut up. If she didn't actually come out and say she liked me, then how do you know for sure?"

"Trust me on this. I've lost enough girlfriends to you that I pretty much know what it looks like when I've been relegated to alternate status."

"Really?" Baylor asked with a small smile.

Juliana glared. "I'd appreciate a little less enthusiasm at that comment."

"Sorry," Baylor said. "I meant...really?" she added with a somber expression and a low tone.

"That's better."

"So, at least I didn't embarrass her too bad, huh?"

"I didn't say that. I said I think she likes you and that you didn't piss her off."

"What the hell is that supposed to mean?"

"It means that you embarrassed the hell out of her. Don't you remember the dance?"

"Dance? Dance?" Baylor mumbled the words under her breath. "Oh, shit." She looked over at Juliana, her eyes widening.

"I see it's all coming back to you."

"Not all. Refresh my memory."

"Okay, let's see. Not that I meant to eavesdrop, mind you."

"Oh, naturally."

"Well, I think it started when you walked up to the table she was sitting at..."

"Hey." *Baylor walked up to Hobie's table. She was well on her way to inebriated bliss.*

"Hiya, Baylor."

"Hey, Bubba. Hello," *Baylor slowly drawled as she attempted to get Hobie's attention.*

"Hello, Baylor," *Hobie said at last.*

"May I have this dance?"

"Are you insane?"

"What? What'd I say?"

"Women don't dance together on Ana Lia," *Hobie answered.*

"Those old dykes do." *Baylor pointed to Katherine and Helen as they moved together on the dance floor.*

"They're sisters."

"I don't think anyone really believes that, do you? Come on, let's dance."

"Go away."

"Come on, we could be sisters, too." *Baylor grinned.*

Hobie shook her head and tried not to smile. "Somehow, I just don't think the family resemblance is there."

"Sure it is. We're practically identical twins." *Baylor dropped to one knee and put an arm around Hobie's shoulder.* "Bubba, what do you think? Your mom and me look alike, right?"

"Oh, stop," *Hobie ordered.*

"Um..." *Noah pushed his glasses up.*

Baylor offered a wide, toothy grin and nodded for Noah to see. "Come on, Bubba, how 'bout it?" *Again, she nodded.*

"Yes," *the youngster said, then burst out laughing.*

"See," *Baylor said as she turned to Hobie.*

"My own child, thank you very much."

"Hey, my man here only calls 'em as he sees 'em. So, let's dance."

Hobie watched as Baylor used her cane to get to her feet. "There's something seriously wrong with you. You know that, right?"

"What? I bet plenty of gals here would dance with me if I asked."

"Well, by all means." *Hobie smiled and spread her arms wide.* "Don't let me interrupt a master at work."

"All right, smart ass." *Baylor turned toward the tables sur-rounding the dance area.* "She thinks I can't get a dance partner," *she said to herself as she searched the area. She noticed that there weren't many women there who weren't collecting Social Security. She looked at Hobie, who sat there with a smug smile.*

"Okay, so the pickings are a little slim. I bet even the old *broads will dance with me." She spotted a familiar face. "Mrs. Emberly..."*

"Oh God," Hobie groaned.

"Mrs. Emberly, would it bother you to dance with me?"

"Why no, dear. Although you are rather tall, and you seem a little incapacitated with that leg."

Baylor turned and walked over to Hobie. "See," she said with an air of triumph.

"That's because she doesn't know you're gay."

Baylor spun on one heel. "Mrs. Emberly—"

"Don't even think about it, Baylor Warren!"

"Mrs. Emberly, I'm gay. Would that affect your decision to dance with me?"

"Why no, dear. I love to see you young women happy."

"Um, it's not really that kind of—never mind." Baylor gave up when she saw Hobie giggling. "Thanks anyway, Mrs. Emberly."

"Have a heart and quit laughing so hard." A dejected Baylor sat down beside Hobie. "One dance and I promise I'll leave you alone for the rest of the evening," she entreated.

"I should be so lucky," Hobie responded.

"Ow, that hurts. Okay, guess I'll just have to tell a few more of the old broads I'm gay and try to get a dance out of them." Baylor made as if to rise, but hesitated just long enough to hear Hobie's hurried response.

"Don't you dare!" Hobie pointed a finger at the writer. "One dance and then you behave. Right?"

"Scout's honor." Baylor drew a cross against her chest.

"Why do I doubt that you ever did Girl Scouts?" Hobie immediately regretted her choice of words. She waited with a scowl for Baylor to comment in some lewd manner.

"Well, what are you looking at?" Baylor asked.

"I was waiting for you to respond with some sort of indecent remark about what I said."

Baylor smiled. "Hmm."

"What?"

The writer leaned closer to Hobie, who now stood beside her. "Oh, nothing, just wondering."

"Wondering what?"

"Wondering if it's sex you're always thinking about or whether it's me that's always on your mind." Baylor whispered the last few words against Hobie's ear. She put on an arrogant grin when she saw the goose bumps rise on the smaller woman's skin.

"I suggest you concern yourself a little less with what I have on my mind."

"Don't be that way," Baylor teased. *"Even though you are rather cute when you're mad. Come on, how about that dance?"*

"I have an idea."

Baylor knew she'd crossed a line by the look in Hobie's eye. *"Yes?"*

"Why don't you go ask one of your little Girl Scout friends? Better yet, go ask Mrs. Emberly to dance with you!" Hobie turned, grabbed Noah's hand, and walked away, leaving Baylor speechless and badly in need of another drink.

"Oh God," Baylor groaned. "Why do I turn into such an ass when I drink?"

"Only when you drink?"

"And you're supposed to be my best friend."

Juliana chuckled lightly. "Mate, the way you're going, I'm your only friend."

"My life is over." Baylor let her head fall against the table once more.

Juliana had been thinking the exact thing, but in regard to herself. Especially because she knew that very shortly, she would have to remind Baylor that she was going on a date with Baylor's girl.

"Do not do this, Baylor. You said this morning that you could handle this."

"I lied! You of all people should know what a compulsive liar I am."

Juliana and Baylor faced off against one another. The writer was a good three inches taller, but Juliana stood her ground. She knew her best friend would never *really* hurt her, though she wouldn't have been able to tell by the smoldering gaze now leveled at her.

"You want me to stay home?" Juliana asked.

"Yes," Baylor answered.

"Then tell her."

A moment's silence passed while they glared at one another.

"I just need a little more time."

"For what? So you can get drunk again and actually throw up *on* her this time?"

"The time has to be right."

"Well, unless the time becomes *right* in the next five minutes, fork over the keys, because I'm going out to dinner with her."

"You are evil, you know that?"

"Jesus Christ, Baylor, you are driving me out of my mind! I am tired of babying you through this. Either act like an adult or step aside."

"Fine, just fine, but, I'll drive you over there. Try going on a date in that zoo-mobile she drives."

"You can be such a git sometimes," Juliana said in exasperation. "Fine, let's go."

Juliana focused on the road during the short drive to Hobie's house. The women said little to one another, and Juliana hoped it was all worth it. She had placed a quick phone call to Evelyn earlier while Baylor was in the shower. Evelyn had told Juliana that even though Baylor—and their friendship—appeared to be suffering greatly, Juliana should do exactly what she had been doing. It was hard, though; she didn't like to see her friend hurting. Even so, there was another part of her that had to struggle not to kick Baylor in the head for her infantile behavior.

When they pulled up in front of the house, they found Noah playing on the front lawn.

"Baylor!" He ran up to the writer and dove into her arms. "Are you and me goin' out on a date too?"

Baylor laughed in spite of herself. Noah had a way of pulling her out of her funk with his infectious enthusiasm for life. "I don't know about that, Bubba. Where's your mom?"

"She's getting dressed. Hi, Jules."

"Hey there, Noah."

Noah showed Juliana his new bicycle and explained that he planned to have the training wheels removed as soon as he could ride it on two wheels. The agent paid close attention as he took her around the yard. He explained all his favorite toys and play spots. She smiled as he spoke about Baylor and what good friends they were.

Baylor, in the meantime, took the opportunity to slip inside the house. She wasn't trying to do anything funny; all she wanted was a few moments alone with Hobie. Perhaps in that brief space of time, she could find a way to open up to her.

There was no one else in the medium-sized guest-house, but Baylor heard a familiar voice coming from the back. She silently made her way there and listened outside the door.

"Definitely not this dress. I look like I'm asking for something," Hobie said to her reflection. It was the third outfit she'd tried on in the last half-hour.

Part of Hobie approached the evening with trepidation, mostly because she wished it had been the tall, beautiful writer who had asked her out. The disheartening fact was that Hobie was falling for Baylor a little more each day, and Baylor had yet to show any real interest in Hobie. *Why doesn't she say anything? Yeah, right, like you're so much better. But what if she doesn't feel the same?* The only conclusion was that the writer simply wasn't interested in Hobie, at least not anything long term.

Hobie's other half was genuinely looking forward to her night out. It had been a long time since she'd sat across from an intelligent woman, especially one that looked as good as Juliana Ross. She was everything any woman could want in a potential partner. In Hobie's opinion, there was only one thing wrong with Juliana. She wasn't Baylor.

Hobie finally settled on a pale green tank top and cream-colored slacks with a matching jacket to wear inside the restaurant. She casually tossed the jacket over one shoulder and pulled the bedroom door open, nearly screaming as Baylor came tumbling through her bedroom door. "What in the hell?"

"Hi there." Baylor waggled her fingers from her prone position. "I bet you're wondering why I'm here."

"What I'm wondering is how I can shoot you for trespassing and not go to jail!"

"Okay, you're angry, I can understand how seeing me outside your bedroom door might do that." Baylor appeared to be struggling for a way out of the mess in which she now found herself.

Hobie took a deep breath and closed her eyes. How did the woman she had so many good feelings for always make her angry enough to want to inflict bodily harm on her?

"I am going to pretend that there is a good reason for this." Hobie took another cleansing breath and opened her eyes. "I can't talk to you while you're lying there. Get up."

Baylor held a hand out and Hobie folded her arms across her chest. "Okay, I can see we're still a teensy bit angry," Baylor said as she rose. "Look, Hobie, this is going to take a little bit of faith on your part—"

"I don't want to hear it," Hobie said.

"Okay, just a little more faith than that."

"God Almighty, Baylor, I don't know what to do about you anymore."

"I'm sorry, Hobie, and if you knew me half as well as Jules, you'd know that I don't apologize to anyone."

Hobie's anger melted away as quickly as it had appeared. The expression on Baylor's face was one of a kind. Hobie was afraid that she was about to cry.

"It's okay," she said hurriedly. "I mean there's no real damage done, right?" She caught herself and suddenly wondered why she was being so apologetic. "Look, what are you doing here any-way?"

"Oh, um, it's such a nice night that I thought I'd go for a walk, get some exercise. Jules gave me a ride. She's in the yard with Noah."

"Oh." Hobie had almost hoped it was for a more personal reason. "Did you, um, did you remember what it was that you wanted to say to me last night?" she asked as she shifted her feet nervously.

"Did I—" Baylor swallowed so hard it made an audible sound. "Remember? Uh, well, it's like this..." Her mouth felt like the Sahara, she had pains in her chest, and she had the over-whelming urge to vomit. She raised her hand to run her fingers through her hair, but her hand was shaking so badly that she shoved it into her pocket instead.

"Did you remember?" Hobie pressed.

Baylor concentrated on breathing out and breathing in. She was absolutely certain that if she didn't focus on that particular act, she would pass out. She could feel the room shrinking as Hobie waited for an answer. Finally, she looked into Hobie's clear green eyes and realized that if the rest of her life was to hold any meaning at all, she had to bite the bullet and say the words.

"Hobie I—I...no, I don't remember."

"You look pretty, Mom." Noah rushed into the house, fol-lowed by Juliana.

"I second that," Juliana added. "I wondered where you went off to," she whispered to Baylor. She could tell by their expres-sions that Baylor hadn't told Hobie. "Well, I guess we better be off, eh?"

"I guess so." Hobie directed a longing look at Baylor's.

Baylor, you clueless jerk, you, Juliana thought silently. *Sorry, mate, but you're gonna pay for your silence this time.*

"Come on, we can walk Noah up to my mom's place on our way out," Hobie said.

The three women had a short yet silent walk up to the main house. Had they been privy to one another's thoughts, it would have been quite enlightening, considering they were all thinking along the same lines.

"What in the world?" Hobie pulled a note down that appeared to have been hastily tacked up on the back door. "Great!" She waved the note at Juliana. "Mom had to run out. All she says is 'be back soon.'"

"Cool!" Noah cried out. "Does that mean Baylor can stay with me?"

Hobie and Juliana exchanged a look. They slowly turned to look at Baylor.

One last nail in my coffin, eh? Jules, you rat bastard! Baylor's short fingernails dug into her palms as she clenched her hands into fists inside her pockets.

"I know it's a huge imposition..." Hobie left the question unasked.

Baylor opened her mouth to come back with some sort of smart-ass reply when she looked down at Noah. The young boy's face beamed with excitement. He absently pushed his glasses up and hopped from foot to foot in anticipation. Baylor didn't see how she could stand to put a look of disappointment there. "Well, what do you say, Bubba? Pizza from Mama Lia's for dinner?"

"All right!" Noah pumped a fist in the air.

After settling Noah and Baylor into the guest-house, Hobie and Juliana prepared to leave. Baylor kept pretending that it didn't matter. It was her fault, after all. The reality of it was that she was angry and heartsick. She plastered a fake smile on her face.

"You know my cell phone number. Mom should be home any minute, so don't feel obligated to stay. Thanks, Baylor." Hobie gently squeezed the writer's hand. "It's a nice thing you're doing."

Baylor smiled. She couldn't believe what she was about to say. "I hope you have a good time."

Juliana slapped her friend's shoulder and shook her hand. "Thanks, mate. I'll bring you a doggie bag."

Oh, I am gonna hurt you so bad. Baylor's smile turned to a smirk. She lowered her voice so that only Juliana could hear her words. "You, on the other hand, I hope you choke on a very large piece of food."

"So, there I was on one ski and crossing the finish line. It was a miracle I didn't break every bone in my body." Hobie couldn't believe she was telling the story, but Juliana had such an easy manner about her that the words just seemed to spill out. "I've been monopolizing the entire dinner conversation. I'm sorry. I can talk quite a bit, but it's been a long time since anyone's wanted to sit through these stories," she said. "Usually, I have to know someone for quite some time before they hear this stuff."

"You've kept me on the edge of my seat." Juliana smiled, knowing how it affected women. Perfect white teeth were framed by flawless pink lips. She'd endured five years of orthodontic ser-vitude as a teenager to get that exceptional smile. Funny thing was, Hobie didn't seem particularly affected by it. She smiled, laughed, talked, and generally enjoyed herself, but Juliana noticed there was no sexual tension between them. She felt that their big night out had all the atmosphere of a blind date with her sister. The good part was that Juliana liked her sister and they always had a great time when they went out together. "I saw the picture on your mantel, the one of you holding that trophy. I guess I wondered how a teenager who could barely hold up those water skis won first place."

"Well, now you know it was 20 percent skill, 30 percent luck, and 50 percent sheer determination," Hobie laughingly responded.

"I'm betting that determination is something you've always had and that it serves you well."

Hobie blushed and lowered her head. She hadn't expected Juliana to be able to read her so well. "You're a literary agent, right?"

"Yes. Why do you ask?"

"I think you missed your calling as a therapist. I'm not usually one to chat about my past or myself much, yet you have me talking about things I haven't told anyone about, ever."

Juliana smiled an almost sly smile. "That's why I'm an exceptional agent. It takes a certain kind of person to handle the massive ego of a writer or anyone who performs, for that matter. They put everything they have inside themselves out before the world, like a child offering up that first crayon drawing for Mom in hopes of winning a place on the refrigerator door. Most people in the world have no idea that goes on. They think that Grisham and the King don't go through that anymore when they put out a new book. The truth is, they get attacks of paranoia and doubts about their talent, or their latest effort, even more so than a new novelist. 'Is it as good as my last one? Will it make as much money? Will I still be on top?' The list of their fears goes on and on."

Juliana paused to take a sip of wine. "Writers have to talk to someone about all of this, and not many people know just what to say to talk them off the ledge. Family members try, but unless they're writers too, they can't really empathize. A writer can't possibly go to friends or other authors; that would be like admitting weakness. So, at three in the morning when the rest of the world is asleep, they call the one person who understands them. The one person who can stroke their ego, make them feel as though they can walk on water. They call their agent."

Juliana poured them both another glass of '95 Tullio Zamo Pinot Bianco. "So you see, in a way, I am a therapist. My authors tell me the things that they can't even tell their shrinks."

"That's absolutely amazing. I had no idea. Geez, you should write a book."

Juliana opened her mouth for a snappy retort, but saw Hobie's teasing smile. "Very funny...write a book."

"Thanks, I thought it was pretty good. Well, at least now I know why I find myself spilling my guts to you."

"It's my curse, I guess," Juliana replied. "Besides, I know your type."

"My type? What's that supposed to mean?"

"Just that I understand a little bit about people and human nature. I know when someone's not the type to open up of their own accord, so I use a few tricks and techniques to get them to start talking."

"Oh, really. And just what tricks did you play on me?"

"You're not angry about that, are you?"

"I don't know." Hobie sat back in her chair. "Why don't you tell me what you did first and I'll let you know."

"It's no Jedi mind game or anything," Juliana laughed. "You don't like to give out personal information about yourself. You're textbook, actually. I simply created the kind of environment where you felt safe enough to talk. Nothing outlandish."

"But *how* did you know?"

"Sometimes it's just a feeling I get for people. I thought right off that you were someone who loves people. You're caring and giving. Eight times out of ten that's because it draws attention away from you. You like being middle management. You'd rather be a cog in the wheel than stand out. You never fill out questionnaires or answer those annoying e-mails where friends want to know all your favorite things, your likes and dislikes. You feel like you'll give away your power if people know too much about you. Perhaps somewhere along the line someone close to you might have even hurt you because you opened up completely. You're determined not to make the same mistake twice. And last but not least, your favorite books are George Orwell's *1984,* C. S. Lewis' Space Trilogy, and Alcott's *Little Women.*"

"You forgot *To Kill a Mockingbird,*" Hobie added. "Good Lord, I think you better give me your jacket."

"Are you cold?" Juliana started to rise from her seat.

"No, but I feel distinctly naked."

Juliana sat back down. "Touché."

"So, who do you tell your secrets to? Who listens to the listener?"

"Hmm, good question. Baylor, I suppose. She's the one who listens to all my insanity."

Hobie saw the opportunity and carefully baited the hook. "Have you and Baylor known each for a very long time?"

"We met as kids." Juliana's voice seemed tight, which didn't go unnoticed by Hobie.

"I'm sorry, do you feel uncomfortable talking about this?"

Juliana smiled. "No apology necessary. I'm sorry if I seemed abrupt. I guess I feel a little strange talking about Baylor to you."

"Strange...to me?" Hobie stammered. *Oh God. What did Baylor tell her? Maybe she warned her about giving me personal info. What if Baylor put Jules up to asking me out just to get me out of her hair? Have I been a pest? Wait a minute, Hob. Baylor is the one who's always nipping at your heels whenever you turn around. It's like she's following you. Don't get paranoid here.*

"Hello?" Juliana tried to make eye contact with Hobie. She didn't want to admit that she was a little worried about her glazed-over expression.

"Geez, I'm sorry. I was in another zip code for a minute there."

"More like another time zone." Juliana laughed.

"Sorry. Where were we?"

"I think you were going to tell me about your work."

Hobie raised one eyebrow. Juliana felt her heart twitch slightly. It was an exact reproduction of Baylor's trademark move, and when Baylor used it, it was never a good thing.

"No," Hobie drawled slowly. "You were about to tell me why you feel uncomfortable telling me about Baylor." She wasn't certain what was going on, but it was apparent that she had done something to shake Juliana's usually unflappable demeanor.

"I was?" Juliana struggled to remember how the conversation had suddenly gone so wrong. Only a moment ago she'd been nicely in control, and now Hobie had taken charge. She'd not given the vet enough credit. Evelyn had been explicit in her instructions, telling Juliana not to interfere directly when it came to Hobie and Baylor. Juliana remembered laughing when she had said that manipulation was okay, but actually talking about the relationship with either woman was a bad thing. *Jesus, I should have never gotten myself into this bloody mess. Note to self, leaving Chicago is a bad thing.*

Juliana unfastened the top button of her blouse. It had suddenly grown warm inside the restaurant. "Well..."

Hobie decided to put an end to her own doubts. Whatever Baylor Warren felt for her, it was a sure bet that Juliana knew what it was. She reached across the table and covered Juliana's hand with her own. "Jules, tell me something about Baylor. Something maybe she's keeping hidden."

"Um...she doesn't like peas?"

Maybe it was the nervous tension, or perhaps it was that Juliana could be as charming as Baylor ever was, but Hobie smiled. Then she laughed, and Juliana laughed right along with her.

"You are as bad as she is, you know that?"

"Oh, now, there's no need to insult me," Juliana replied.

"Do you play golf?" Hobie asked suddenly.

"Golf? Yeah, I try to get in a few holes when I can. Why?"

Hobie smiled at her suddenly suspicious expression. "Let's go have some fun. You know, forget about Baylor and everyone who makes us crazy. What do you say?"

Juliana realized that Hobie was indeed like her sister, who could find a way to have fun in the middle of a snowstorm. The agent showed off her perfect smile again. "I'm game if you are."

"Great. Let's go."

"Wait a minute," Juliana called out as she tossed some bills onto the table. "Where are we going?"

"A place I know where we can be kids again. Come on." Hobie took Juliana's hand and pulled her along.

"What do you say, Bubba? Ya got room for one more piece?" Baylor and Noah sat on the floor surrounded by empty soda bottles and a cardboard pizza carton.

"I'm gonna explode, I think," he said.

Baylor chuckled. "I'm with you. I can barely move."

"Hey, Baylor?"

"What's up?"

"Do you like my mom?"

"Of course I like her. Did you think I didn't?" Baylor stretched and lay down on her stomach, cupping her chin in the palms of both hands.

Noah mimicked her posture. "I mean do you *like her* like her? Like for a girlfriend."

Geez, kids are way more advanced nowadays. The funny thing about Noah's question was that Baylor felt none of the panic she had when standing before Hobie, faced with the same question. It was as if Noah was a pal, like Juliana. She didn't feel that lying to the youngster was even an option.

"Yeah," Baylor answered. "I do like her."

"Cool."

"That doesn't bother you or anything?"

Noah grinned displaying all of his perfect baby teeth. "No

way, man! You're so cool, Baylor. I wish you lived here all the time. Anyway, I think Mom likes you, too."

"Really?" As usual, Baylor's ears were at attention with that statement. "Did she actually say that she liked me?" *I am so pathetic. Milking a six-year-old for info about his mother.*

"She didn't really say so, but she acts like it. You can kinda tell when Mom doesn't like ya. She goes around the house yellin' your name."

"Has she ever yelled my name?"

"Nope. You should tell her."

"Yeah, well, about that..."

"You afraid?"

"Yep."

"I know how you feel."

"Are you sure you're only six years old?" Baylor asked with an amused grin.

"Uh-huh."

"So, what makes you so knowledgeable?"

"Huh?"

"How do you know how I feel," she translated.

"Madison Riley. She's in Mrs. London's class with me. She's super pretty and she's nice, too. She says hi to me every day at the monkey bars."

"So, what do you want to do about Miss Riley?"

"I don't know. Ask her if she'll sit with me at lunch?"

"That's a good start, Bubba." Baylor was relieved to know that at six, that was all Noah knew how to do with a girl. She was constantly amazed to hear the language and sexual propositions from the mouths of ten-year-old boys when she walked down Chicago streets. She thought back to her own youth. Her sexual career had begun early; much too early, by most accounts.

"So, why don't you just tell this girl? Go right up to her and ask her to eat lunch with you." Baylor rolled over onto her back. She rested her hands on her stomach, and when she turned to look at Noah, she saw that he had again imitated her pose. Both of his eyebrows raised above his wire-rimmed glasses at Baylor's question.

She laughed. "Point taken. Are you sure you're only six?"

"Yes," Noah answered before he burst into a fit of giggles.

"I guess it's because you're scared, huh?"

"Yep. What if she thinks I'm a goof? What if she laughs?"

"What if she doesn't feel the same way?"

"Yeah."

"What do you think we—I mean, *you* should do?"

"Um...I could wait. Maybe if she likes me she'll say something first."

"Nah." Baylor shook her head dejectedly. "You can't do that, Bubba. Trust me on this one. Your girl will end up going on a date with your best friend."

"Huh?"

"I mean lunch. She'll end up eating lunch with someone else."

"Oh. What should I do, Baylor?"

"You're gonna have to tell her, Bubba." Baylor realized that she was actually talking to herself. "If you like this girl, I mean really like her, then you've got to speak up. You might be scared, it may even feel like you can't breathe or you're going to throw up, but you have to suck it up and tell her. See, the crazy thing is, she's probably just as scared as you are. Yeah, I bet that's it. Maybe she's afraid that you don't feel the same way she does. One of you has to say something, though. I guess it all comes down to how badly you want her."

"I guess I can try. I sure hope I don't throw up on her, though."

"Yeah," Baylor chuckled. "Take my word for it, they don't like when you do that. Hey, Bubba, can I ask you a question?"

"Yep."

"What else do you know about your dad?"

"He's 965-2338."

"I know that you know his number, but what else can you tell me about him?"

"Nothing."

"Nothing at all?"

"Well..."

"What? Bubba, what is it? What do you know?"

"Follow me," Noah commanded as he jumped to his feet and ran off toward his mother's bedroom.

Baylor hesitantly walked in as Noah was struggling to push a wooden chair up to the open closet. She felt as though she was violating Hobie's privacy by being there. She looked around nervously. "What the devil are you up to over there?"

Noah put a large, thick book on the chair and began to scale his self-made mountain. Baylor rushed up behind him to hold him steady.

"Thanks," Noah said. "Here it is!" He scrambled back down and laid a brown folder on his mother's desk. He pulled out an envelope and removed its contents, then smoothed the paper as if it were a map to some long-buried treasure.

"Mom showed me it once and said this was my dad. She doesn't know I figured out where she keeps it. You won't tell, will ya, Baylor?"

Baylor looked down at the paper and smiled. In fact, her smile couldn't get much bigger, or brighter, or happier. "Your secret's safe with me, Bubba."

They both looked down at the faded page. In the center, someone had taped a small white appointment reminder card. On the card two dates had been handwritten under the headings "first insemination" and "second insemination." Lastly, there was the number that Noah had so dutifully memorized: Sperm Donor #965-2338.

Nobody else in the picture. No guy...ever. Happy days. Shit, it would be if she weren't out on a date with my best friend. Okay, some people might see that as a down side.

As they put away the document, Baylor began thinking about Noah and how all this affected him. Did he understand that his mom didn't know who his dad was?

"Hey, Bubba, you don't mind, do you? I mean, not really having a dad around?"

"Nah. Mom told me when I was real little, like last year. She said I was more special, 'cuz she went out looking for me. She wanted me so bad, but she said some families have two moms or two dads instead of a mom and dad. Leroy is in my class at school and he only has a dad. His mom went away when he was a baby."

Once more Baylor was amazed by the way Noah seemed to take everything in stride. She knew that was Hobie's influence.

A knock on the door brought them both out into the living room just as Theresa Allen opened the front door.

"Goodness, Baylor. I'm sorry I'm late. Thanks so much for watching Noah until I could get back. Hobie doesn't know how lucky she is to have you around."

"Yeah, I think the same thing some days," Baylor teased. "Hey, Bubba, you mind staying with your grandma for the rest of the night? I just thought of something really important I need to do. I'll make it up to you, okay?"

"'Kay, Baylor." The youngster held out his arms and Baylor scooped him up easily. She gave him a big kiss on the cheek and tickled him until he squirmed and giggled, then deposited him on the couch.

"You know, Baylor," Theresa Allen began as the writer said goodbye, "it's a shame Hobie can't see what she has in you." She smiled and Baylor responded in kind.

"I'm gonna try and do something about that, Mrs. Allen.

Wish me luck."

"Good luck, Baylor," Theresa shouted. "With Hobie Lynn, you'll need it," she whispered under her breath.

Chapter
13

"Okay, think things through. Don't go off half assed here."

Baylor drove along in the Jag, talking to herself all the while. It wasn't easy to drive with the cast on, but with the lighter walking cast, at least she could operate the pedals.

Baylor turned left down Oceanside Road. The seafood restaurant there was the best on the island and Baylor, in an unusually benevolent moment, had given Juliana that information.

"Okay, when I see her, what do I say? No, don't get hung up on the words. Just remember, don't lie, don't panic, don't forget to breathe, and whatever you do, don't throw up on her."

Baylor saw Hobie's pickup from a block away. It was parked on the street, directly in front of the restaurant.

"This is it. I don't even care if she laughs in my face, but I am going to say my piece and pray. There's nothing that's going to stop me this time."

Baylor pulled over in the shadows about five car lengths behind Hobie's truck. She watched as Hobie and Juliana left the building laughing, joking, and worst of all, hand in hand. Baylor's heart sank onto the floor of the Jag. She went from elation to heartbreak in a matter of seconds. Juliana opened the driver's door for Hobie, bowed, and kissed her hand. The two looked so...happy.

As she looked upon the scene, Baylor's mood changed. She was tempted to wallow in self-pity. For nearly a full minute, she did indeed sit there feeling sorry for herself. Then other emotions kicked in, first jealousy, and then anger. The anger was a feeling that she could really wrap her teeth around.

Those bitches. They're acting like I'm not even alive. I don't believe I ever thought Hobie was such a sweet girl. That tramp's letting Jules put her paws wherever she wants. Unbelievable...and I thought Jules was my best friend. Shit! She knew how I felt and she's still all over Hobie! Some friends...they're both sluts!

A plan formulated in Baylor's head at that very instant. Sometime later that evening, she looked back on that moment and realized that perhaps the plan hadn't been the best of ideas. However, sitting there in her car, she could think of only one thing to appease her jealous nature. She would follow the two women. She would listen to their conversations, watch their behavior, and confront them. She would confront the Jezebels and throw their own actions into their faces. Baylor would see that, like Hester Prynne, both women ended up with a scarlet *A* on their chests.

"Treat me like a fucking idiot. We'll see about that!" Baylor roughly shoved the gearshift and followed the white pickup. "Careful...no need to hurry or lose control," she said aloud.

If she could have seen herself, Baylor would have either stopped the car and turned around or laughed hysterically at her own ludicrous behavior. Instead, like a character in a poorly written spy novel, she followed a short distance behind Hobie's truck, intent on catching the two women at something.

"Okay, let me get this straight," Juliana said as she rolled up the sleeves of her blouse. "Up the ramp, bank into the clown's mouth, and then it will roll right down the giraffe's neck?"

"Exactly!" Hobie clapped. "Give it a shot, come on."

"Hey, just you try and keep up, hotshot. Three iron," Juliana ordered as she held out one hand.

"Three iron," Hobie responded as she slapped the handle of a golf club into the other woman's hand.

Juliana bent her knees and tested the club's swing before actually hitting the bright orange golf ball.

What in the holy hell are they doing here? Baylor asked herself as she slipped into the brightly lit park. She passed under the sign that said "Ana Lia's Fantasy Island: Putt-Putt Golf." *Either they're trying to make this look innocent, or they've both slipped a gear or two.*

"Like this, right?" Juliana asked.

Hobie smiled at the blonde. Tall and muscular, the agent had a look of concentration as intense as any Nancy Lopez might have conjured up.

"Wait a minute. Make sure you line it up with the clown's right eyeball. Here..." Hobie put one arm around Juliana's waist and ran her right hand along the agent's arm and down to her wrist. She didn't even realize how closely she had her body pressed against Juliana's back. "Aim right along there."

Oh, yeah. Tramps on parade. Baylor slipped behind a ten-foot ice-cream cone and watched. *One date. One fucking date and she's all over her!*

Juliana felt the other woman's body against her, but even if she had wanted something to happen between them, even if she hadn't thought of Hobie as Baylor's girl, she was having too much fun to spoil it with sex or even innuendo. She couldn't resist one little tease, however. "You know, I can't ever remember having this much fun with my clothes still on."

Hobie's laughter rang out. "Absolutely incorrigible. Come on, sexy, let's see if you're all hot air." She smacked Juliana across the backside and stepped away.

"Oh, baby, now you've got me fired up." Juliana pulled her arms back and swung the golf club with a gentle force.

The ball sped up the red-carpeted ramp and bounced against one of the octagonal borders. The ball shot into the clown's mouth, and the women watched as it spiraled down until it eventually reached the giraffe tunnel that was its destination. The ball circled gracefully and dropped with a resounding plunk into the metal cup.

"Oh, yeah. I'm good!"

Both women doubled over in laughter. Juliana swept Hobie into a hug and placed a quick kiss on her cheek. "Thanks to my excellent caddy," she said to more laughter.

Baylor watched the two women walk away, now arm in arm and still laughing. She turned to discreetly follow and tripped over an oncoming golf ball.

"Hey, dude, you playin' or peepin'?" Three young men now stood before her.

Baylor arched an eyebrow and put on her most intimidating look, which wasn't hard considering the mood she was in. "Do I look like a dude?"

"Uh, matter of fact, yeah!" The three boys laughed.

Baylor took a step closer to the young man who had spoken. She towered over him. "How'd you like to have a ten-foot ice-cream cone shoved up your ass, funny man?" she demanded, glancing up at the statue beside her.

He swallowed hard and backed away until he stood with his friends. Baylor walked off after Hobie and Juliana. "Sometimes it's good to be king," she said with an evil smile.

"Okay, all I have to do is ace this one hole and I will be the undisputed putt-putt champion of the world." Juliana waved to an imaginary crowd.

Hobie laughed. "Well, the whole world may be pushing it. Let's just say Ana Lia. Besides, that one's harder than it looks."

Ten minutes later Juliana was still trying for the same hole, swearing profusely. "God damn it! It did it again!"

"You know this is supposed to be fun, remember?"

"I am having fun," Juliana said as she ground her teeth together. "Can't you tell?" She finally looked up with a sheepish grin. "It's that stupid hippo. Every time my ball gets close to going into his mouth, those stupid teeth pop out and knock it out of the way."

"Okay, quit pouting, it makes you look like Noah. Step aside." Hobie gracefully pushed the agent to one side of the green. "It's all in your timing and the wrists. Are you watching?"

"Oh, yeah." Juliana grinned as she crouched down on one knee. Her unintentional stance afforded her a picture-perfect view of the vet's backside.

"Asshole!" Baylor muttered to herself. "Jules is doing exactly...well, what I'd do. Okay, I can't fault her for sneaking a peek, but that is definitely not going to stop me from beating the living crap out of her tonight."

"Jules, I asked if you were watching my wrists, not my ass."

"No, as I recall, you said, 'are you watching?' You didn't specify any particular body part."

"Touché. How's the view?" Hobie asked with a sly grin.

"Bloody good, if I may say so without getting my face slapped."

"You certainly may not!" Baylor hissed under her breath.

"You certainly may. Say so, I mean, not get your face slapped. As a thirty-eight-year-old mother, I'm happy to know someone still looks," Hobie replied. "Okay, here goes." She swung the club in a gentle arc. The timing was perfect as the ball ricocheted off two chomping plastic teeth and rolled into the hippo's mouth.

The vet held her hand up to her mouth and blew on her nails, then polished them on her blouse. "What can I say?"

"Come on, Tiger, let's see how you do over the water hazard. I'm taking a par for this hole," Juliana said.

"Cheater," Hobie cried out as Juliana dragged her away by one arm.

"Cheater is right," Baylor said. She stood up from her place within the shadows where she had hidden behind a massive version of the birds that bob up and down in order to drink from a glass of water. She stepped away from the brightly colored bird just as a group of girls in Scout uniforms entered the green.

Baylor thought later that she should have moved faster, but at the time she was intent on watching Juliana and Hobie walk away. She didn't anticipate that one of the eight-year-old girls would get a hole in one.

"Ow!" Baylor cried out as the bird dipped and its beak hit her shoulder. She tried to move away, but the bird turned as she did and pecked her sharply on the top of the head.

"Jesus Christ," she screamed and punched at the bird, which only resulted in knocking the red bowler hat from its head. The hat fell to the ground with a great deal of clatter, but the bird succeeded in hitting Baylor two more times before she could anticipate in which direction its head would move next.

Baylor could feel something—was it blood?—running down the side of her face, but she couldn't stop the attacking bird long enough to check. Unfortunately, at the precise moment she finally achieved her bearings and could duck the bird's advances, her casted foot stepped directly into the open bowler. Unable to right herself, she spun around as the hat slid against the concrete.

"Motherfu—" The last thing Baylor remembered about the putt-putt golf course was the way her body felt as it flipped over the three-foot hedge surrounding the greens. She lay in the dirt, and right before passing out, she saw the bird's face. Later she would swear that it had been smiling.

"What was that?" Hobie asked Juliana. The two women looked back in the direction from which they had come.

"Must be some bloke fooling around," Juliana answered as they walked toward the exit.

"I had a great time tonight, Hobie. In fact, I can't even remember the last time I had that much fun," Juliana said.

Hobie slipped an arm around the agent's waist and walked with her back to the guest-house. "I had a great time, too and boy, did I need one."

They stopped at the bottom step to the wooden porch. "No offense, but I'm not even going to try to kiss you good night," Juliana said. They parted, but she retained her hold of Hobie's hand.

"Well, there's none taken." Hobie smiled and her brow furrowed. "Mind telling me why not, though?"

"Please don't take this the wrong way, because I mean it as a huge compliment," Juliana began. "It's just that going out with you has been amazingly similar to going out with my sister. Don't get me wrong, I love my sister. In fact—"

"Jules," Hobie interrupted. "It's okay. I don't have a sister, but I think I know what you're driving at. It was nice going out with a friend and having fun."

"Spot on," Juliana answered in relief.

"We're in perfect agreement then?" Hobie asked.

"We make great buddies and nothing more." Both women chuckled.

"Want to sit for a while?" Hobie asked, indicating the porch swing.

"Yeah, sounds good."

"Can I get you anything to drink, maybe a glass of wine?"

"Only if you're having some."

Hobie quickly returned with two glasses of Pinot Grigio and lit the bamboo torches.

"Thanks. It's beautiful out here. I didn't realize this place was that close to the water."

"It's only about two hundred yards. When it's quiet like this I love to sit here and listen. You're right; it is beautiful. Hot, but beautiful."

They talked for a while about nothing of great consequence, just relaxing and enjoying the evening. Juliana was amused by how often Hobie brought Baylor's name into the conversation. It was always something interesting or funny that the writer had said or done. What made it so amusing was that Juliana was sure the vet had no idea that she was doing it. She wavered regarding her next move, but she simply couldn't resist.

"So," she turned and put her arm on the back of the chair, "tell me about Baylor." She cupped her chin in the palm of her other hand.

"B-Baylor? Tell you what about her?" Hobie suddenly felt a warmth creeping up her neck that had very little to do with the tropical evening.

"Tell me about you...and her."

"Well, I'm sure I don't know what you mean." Hobie chuckled slightly to make light of the question that had already affected her deeply.

Juliana directed a knowing look toward Hobie.

The vet tried to laugh again, but no sound would come. She rolled her eyes and turned her head as if she could play the whole thing off as a joke. Juliana's perceptive expression halted her ruse.

"Do you want me to tell you about me and Baylor?" Hobie sat her glass of wine on a small mosaic table. She stood and began pacing. "The woman is certifiable."

Juliana lowered her head in order to hide her smile.

"I turn around and she's there. She's like some little puppy, nipping at my heels. One minute she hates me, the next minute she does something so—so, well, so wonderful and sweet that it makes it nearly impossible not to—" She stopped abruptly, but apparently Juliana knew how to finish the sentence.

"To love her."

Hobie looked as though she'd been slapped, then she looked as though she was going to cry. She sat down heavily in the swing next to Juliana. "If you think for one moment that I'm in love with Baylor Warren...she's nuts, do you know that?"

Juliana smiled. "She's eccentric."

"That's just a rich person's way of saying nuts," Hobie countered. "The scary thing is that she thinks the rest of the world is crazy. She's, oh God, I don't even know where to start."

"Let's see if I can help. She's smart, but she knows it. She's talented, which she doesn't know, not how much, at least. Children and animals adore her and although she has the patience of a saint with them, she won't give most adults the time of day. Plus, she has an ego the size of a small third-world country and she never sees her own faults."

"But she's so...so...well, so the opposite of all that some days. When she's not trying—"

"She's sullen and brooding," Juliana said.

"Beautiful. Compassionate," Hobie added softly.

"Sarcastic. Caustic."

"Tender. Gentle."

"And finally, she's the biggest pain in the ass in the whole world," Juliana said.

Hobie looked over at Juliana. With a stricken expression, she covered up her face with her hands. "Oh God, Jules. I'm in love with the biggest pain in the ass in the world! How did this happen?"

She looked about ready to cry. Juliana wrapped an arm around her and held her for a few moments.

That's when Baylor returned.

The writer had suffered what she would remember as a harrowing, rather traumatic experience. The most embarrassing point had been regaining consciousness surrounded by a group of eight-year-old Junior Girl Scouts. Too embarrassed to explain what happened, Baylor had made up an extraordinary story about how she suffered from seizures, and the girls were thrilled to get credit for finding her and saving her life. The older woman with them looked a little skeptical, but the lie served its purpose. Baylor tossed the girls enough money for ice cream and gingerly made her way back to her car.

She cleaned herself up as best she could with a travel package of Kleenex and a bottle of water. She wondered if she had a concussion; the plastic bird had hit her hard enough to draw blood.

She was dirty, sweaty, and bloody, but there was only one thing to do at that point. She decided to go back to Hobie's house and wait for her two-timing friends.

She parked the Jaguar, hoping fervently that the other women hadn't noticed its absence. The guest-house was not visible from the street. It was set behind the main house and surrounded by a privet and bougainvilleas. That's where Baylor decided to set up watch.

She could hear the sound of voices, but not what they were saying. She angled over in order to better see the front of the guest-house. What she saw was her best friend with her arms around Hobie, who didn't look like she was doing much to change that situation.

"Son of a bi—ouch! God damn it!" Baylor had no idea that the beautiful red bougainvillea flowers, whose petals looked like rice paper, had thorns the size of small railroad spikes. She had leaned a bit too close and the shoulder of her jacket snagged on the spiny thorns. Unfortunately, the more she struggled, the more entangled she became.

"Did you hear something?" Hobie lifted her head from Juliana's shoulder.

"No," Juliana answered. "Did you want me to take a look?"

"No, it's probably just an alligator."

Juliana's eyes opened wide and she nervously looked around the dark area surrounding the porch.

"Just kidding. I haven't seen one since I was a kid." Hobie's smile returned. "It's really probably just a raccoon or something equally as harmless."

"Oh, love, you've got a well-evil sense of humor."

"Sorry. Jules, I don't want you to think I'm using you, but could I ask you just one thing about Baylor?"

"I am the world's foremost authority on Baylor Warren, my dear. Ask away."

"What's wrong with her? Was she dropped on her head as a baby or what?"

The question was such a serious one, and Hobie's expression so earnest, that Juliana hated to laugh, but she just couldn't help it. She tilted her head back and roared with laughter.

"I'm sorry," she replied. "I can't stop myself. You're the first person who's ever had the guts to ask a question like that about Baylor."

"I'm serious," Hobie countered with a smile and a light chuckle. "My God, it wasn't bad enough that she had Noah fighting on the playground and calling other six-year-olds rat bastards.

Last week, she taught him how to spit because she said that every big-leaguer should know how."

Juliana's laughter increased.

"I was over at Evelyn's house for lunch once. An alarm went off and she rushed out to the greenhouse with Arturo right behind her. I swear she's trained that dog to do the oddest things. She grabbed a clipboard, rushed out of the kitchen, and fifteen minutes later came back as if nothing ever happened. I told you about Katherine and Helen, right?"

Juliana stopped laughing long enough to mutter, "Yeah, the gals with the big rat."

"It's a hamster, but that's not the point. When Baylor first got here, I had to beg her not to offend those women."

"What's she doing, being mean to them? That doesn't sound like Baylor," Jules asked, wiping tears from her eyes.

"Mean? She goes around acting as if Albert is real. Not just to be polite to Katherine, either. She talks about that goddamn rat to everyone who'll listen!"

"I thought you said it was a hamster?"

"Whatever! You know what I mean! The coach is another example," Hobie added. "She only sees the coach when she goes to the Cove. He hangs around the restaurant."

"Yeah, she told me about him. The football geezer."

"Right. I found her one afternoon on a park bench with the man. She was drawing up plays for the team."

"Maybe she was just trying to help the bloke out."

"He hasn't coached football in twenty years! There is no team!"

"Oh."

"I just don't know what to do about her anymore," Hobie added as she slumped into the porch swing once again. "I'm afraid I'm in love with a crazy woman, Jules."

Juliana made a sound that was half coughing and half laughter. "Funny, she says the same about you."

"Baylor's in love with me?" Hobie asked.

Juliana looked up, a fearful expression on her face. "No, no, I didn't say that."

"Yes, you did! I knew it. I just knew it! That's what she wanted to tell me yesterday."

"No, it didn't come from me. Don't you dare repeat it. Something bad will happen, I know it."

"Oh, please."

"It will. Evelyn said—"

"Evelyn? What's she got to do with it?"

"Oh my god! I didn't say that. Shut up...don't talk to me any more about it."

"Will you stop?"

"No," Juliana covered her ears with her hands. "No, no, no, no, no—"

"Will you stop!" Hobie slapped the agent's arm sharply. "My god, you and Baylor are exactly alike. What am I getting myself into?"

Juliana looked over at the vet with a contrite expression. "Sorry. Just—just pretend like you don't know. I promised Evelyn—"

"What in the hell does Evelyn have to do with all of this?"

"Nothing, nothing at all."

"God, maybe it's not Baylor who's crazy. Maybe it's me. I feel like I'm losing it."

"Look, Hobie," Juliana began calmly, "Baylor's always been a bit different. The interesting thing is that she doesn't see it that way. She sees herself as perfectly normal and everyone else as slightly bonkers. Maybe she's just found a place in Ana Lia where it's okay to be different. Maybe you and Evelyn are even responsible for taking our eccentric, slightly lovable, forty-two-year-old kid and making her see that different is acceptable."

"So you mean I'm to blame?"

Juliana chuckled. "In a way, I guess. I'm just trying to get you to look at the other side of that coin."

Hobie smiled back, a look that was part exasperation and part resignation crossing her face. "I don't think I could pry her out of my heart now with a crowbar. Trust me, I've tried. God Almighty, Jules, do you want to know the absolute craziest part?"

"And that is?"

"I'm in love with the woman who, at this very moment, is spying on us from the bushes."

"You're kidding."

"I'd know the sound of her cursing anywhere," Hobie answered dryly. "Listen."

Juliana paused to listen to the night sounds around them. Faintly, from the ocean side of the house, she heard Baylor's mutterings.

"Goddamn son of a—" Then there was a ripping sound, followed by more muttered curses.

"I don't believe it," Juliana said.

"I do. Just what in the hell did she expect to catch us doing is what I wonder."

"With Baylor, there's no telling." Juliana was trying very

hard not to laugh, which made her look as though she was struggling to hold her breath. "What do you think she's doing back
there to be cursing so much?" She gave up and allowed her laughter to escape.

"I don't know, but I know what she's going to see up here."

"What's that mean?"

"Just follow my lead. Okay?"

"This sounds like trouble. Careful, Hobie."

"I'm just going to give her what she came here for."

"All right, boss."

"So, want to come inside for a nightcap?" Hobie asked loudly.
She rose from the swing and held out a hand. "We can get *much*
more comfortable inside."

"Uh, what about Noah?" Juliana asked, playing along.

"Don't worry, he's staying the night with my mother."

By this time, Baylor had thoroughly entangled herself
amongst the spiny thorns of the bougainvilleas. She heard what
was transpiring on the porch, which made her fight all the harder
to get out of her current predicament. Of course, the harder she
struggled, the tighter the long, vine-like branches held her in their
grasp.

Juliana rose and took Hobie's hand. When they reached the
door of the guest-house, Hobie turned around. Her next action
took Juliana completely by surprise. She reached up and kissed
her. It was no quick peck on the cheek, and Juliana's whole body
melted into the kiss. In a matter of seconds, the kiss was over and
Hobie pulled Juliana through the open door.

That was about the time that Baylor went ballistic. She aban-
doned her jacket to the bloodthirsty branches and launched herself
with amazing speed toward the guest-house.

Juliana was still trying to catch her breath when Hobie closed
the door. She leaned against a chair. "You know when I said that
going out with you was sort of like dating my sister?"

"Yeah."

"I changed my mind. I don't think my sister would snog anything like that."

"You're gonna have to explain that one."

"What, snog? Oh, kiss."

Hobie slapped Juliana's arm, which brought about a smile.
"How long do you think it will take her?"

"Twenty, thirty more seconds," Juliana answered.

"And you say you know the woman. Five more seconds, tops.
Five...four...three...two..."

Baylor pounded on the door. "Hobie Lynn, open this door

right now!"

Juliana turned to Hobie. "You're bloody good."

"I am, aren't I?" Hobie tossed her hair to one side as she slowly walked to the door. She laughed at her own behavior before opening the door to face down her wounded would-be paramour.

"Baylor, my god, what happened to you?" Hobie asked.

Dirt and bits of leaves clung to Baylor's clothes, and her hands were covered with bruises and scratches. The worst of it looked to be a streak of dried blood running from her hair and down one side of her face.

"You owe me three hundred dollars!" Baylor sneered.

"What in the world are you talking about?" Hobie asked.

"Your shrubbery just ate my linen Armani jacket."

Hobie crossed her arms. "And what, may I ask, were you doing in my shrubbery?"

Baylor opened her mouth for an angry reply. She watched as one of Hobie's eyebrows arched up and disappeared under auburn bangs. "I—she—" She couldn't decide who to blame first. In her mind, she wasn't to blame for any of the evening's events. She was an innocent bystander. "You're confusing me!" She pointed an accusing finger at Hobie.

"Good Lord. Sit down before you fall down." Hobie shook her head. "Let me get the first-aid kit." She walked out of the room.

Baylor sat down heavily in the wooden chair. "Come here," she all but whispered.

Juliana drew a step closer. "What?"

"Come here a minute."

The agent crossed the small living room, but stopped before reaching her friend. "Why?" she drawled out suspiciously.

"Because I'm going to beat the crap out of you!" Baylor shouted out as she lunged toward her. By the time Hobie returned with the first-aid kit, Baylor and Juliana had nearly come to blows.

"Stop it." Hobie moved between the two women. "Stop it!" she screamed. "What the hell is going on?"

"She—" Juliana and Baylor spoke at the same time. They each had a hand raised and a finger pointed at the other.

"Just stop it. Stop it now," Hobie ordered. She stood between them, one arm against each woman's chest, trying to keep them from attacking one another. "Has anyone ever told the two of you that you're very high-energy friends to be around?"

"I thought they meant it in a good way," Baylor answered.

"Trust me." Hobie pushed Baylor back into the chair. "They

didn't."

She took a wet cloth and carefully began cleaning the cuts on the writer's hands. She then moved to clean the dried blood from her face and neck.

"Do you mean to tell me that my bushes did all this to you?" she asked. "What the hell did you do, dive into them?"

"No. If you must know, I was attacked by a very large bird."

"You're kidding. Baylor, why didn't you say so?" Perhaps the attack had caused Baylor's apparent disorientation. Maybe that was why she was in the bushes in the first place. "Was it a gull or a pelican?"

"I think it was a chicken, or maybe a parrot, I'm not sure. I'm sure it was yellow, though," Baylor answered.

Hobie paused, and she and Juliana looked at one another.

"Not only are they both rather small birds, they are quite dissimilar by comparison," Juliana said.

"This thing was at least nine feet tall," Baylor said.

"What?" Hobie laughed. "I think she might have a concussion. Baylor," she continued loudly, "how many fingers am I holding up?"

"I'm not mentally incapacitated and I also have not gone deaf, so quit yelling at me."

"Well, then, you're quite insane. There are no nine-foot birds roaming around Ana Lia. I'm certain something like that would have made the papers. It would have been on all the news stations. I'm a vet. I would have been called."

"So I'm a liar. I bet if it was her saying it, you'd believe it," Baylor countered.

"Oh, for God's sake," Hobie said. "Just look at what you're saying. I mean, the only nine-foot chicken on Ana Lia is the one out at the miniature golf—"

Baylor picked that moment to find something fascinating about the floor.

"Oh, I just don't believe you would stoop that low," Hobie said.

Juliana, in the meantime, finally realized what Hobie was talking about. "Baylor." She took a deep breath. "Tell me you didn't. Tell me that you didn't follow us around tonight like some bleeding nutter. Tell me that you didn't embarrass me like that."

"Embarrass you?" Baylor's voice rose. "I was the one that was attacked by that damn parakeet and had to be pulled from certain death by a bunch of Green Scouts!"

"Girl Scouts." Hobie couldn't stop herself from correcting the writer. She had seen the troop of girls behind them at the putt-putt course.

"Move out of the way, Hobie," Juliana ordered.

"Why?"

"Because I'm going to beat the crap out of her!" Juliana rushed toward Baylor and the two were at it once again.

"I can't believe you didn't trust me!" she shouted as she took a swing at the writer.

"Trust? After that kiss I saw, you have the nerve to talk to me about trust?" Baylor tried to put a headlock on her friend.

Meanwhile, Hobie, who was a good four inches shorter than either woman, found herself caught in the middle of their desperate attempts to reach one another.

"Stop it!" she practically screamed. She managed to push them apart once more, but by this time, she was thoroughly exhausted. "I have had enough! Jules, it's been great fun, but maybe you should go home."

"But—"

"It's okay," Hobie interrupted. "I think Baylor and I need to talk."

Juliana agreed with a short nod of her head. Just because she understood didn't mean she had to like it. "Give me the keys." She held out her hand to Baylor.

"Forget it, use her jalopy."

"Give her the goddamn keys," Hobie hissed.

Baylor immediately complied. "How am I supposed to get home?" It came out as more of a whine than she had intended.

"I bloody well hope she makes you walk," Juliana said as Hobie led her to the door.

Baylor took a step toward her friend.

"Sit!" Hobie barked.

Baylor's eyes went wide at the command. She silently sat down.

"Try not to kill her," Juliana whispered to Hobie. "She may be the biggest pain in the ass in the world, but it's really hard to break in a new best mate."

"I'll see what I can do," Hobie said with a smile. "I make no promises, however. Thanks, Jules." She gently squeezed the agent's hand and closed the door behind her.

"Now, as for you," Hobie said as she turned to face a suddenly tongue-tied Baylor. "Geez, you're a mess."

"I know," Baylor answered with an exasperated sigh. "You know, I'm really a rather normal person. I work, I pay my taxes, millions of people buy my books—"

"Baylor?"

"People *like* me. Okay, they don't actually like me, but they respect me—"

"Baylor."

"I'm not usually this—this—"

"Baylor!"

The writer paused and raised her head as if hearing Hobie for the first time.

"I meant that you're a dirty mess. Filthy. You need a shower."

"Oh." Baylor looked down at her clothes. She casually brushed a small twig from her slacks and, just as nonchalantly, pulled up a piece of her blouse that had ripped at the shoulder.

"Come on, you can take a shower here." Hobie dragged Baylor into her bedroom. "There are clean towels in the cabinet. Everything you need is in the bath. My robe is on the back of the door; feel free. I'll see what I can do about some fresh clothes. Need anything in particular?"

Baylor shook her head dumbly. She was accustomed to being in charge, but when Hobie was in the room, she felt as though her control simply disappeared.

"I'll be in the living room, then," Hobie said as she closed the bedroom door.

Baylor stared at the closed door for a few moments longer. *Okay, there's something wrong here. Why is she being so nice to me? A woman I've just pissed off being overly nice to me? That can't be good.*

"Baylor, old girl," she muttered to herself as she turned on the tap, "you are in a great deal of trouble."

Chapter
14

Baylor spent twenty minutes in the bathroom, and she managed to worry herself into a frenzied state. She had never known it was possible to ruminate over so many different topics in such a short span of time. Looking into her reflection in the bathroom mirror, she ran her fingers through her wet hair and wondered once again how her life had gone so far off course in the two months since she'd been on Ana Lia.

She cautiously stepped from the bathroom into Hobie's bedroom. A small pile of clothes sat on the end of the vet's bed with a note attached. "Mac must buy these things by the gross, but he assures me that they're freshly laundered." Baylor grinned when she unfolded the Ana Lia Sheriff's Department-issue sweatpants and t-shirt.

As she dressed, she thought about what, if anything, she should tell Hobie. Would they all be better off if she simply went back home and pretended she'd never been trapped on the island in the first place? Baylor had always had issues, especially concerning her love life. Years in therapy had shown her the source of her difficulties, but no amount of analysis had managed to exorcise the memory of the way her father had treated her. She knew that she alone had the power to change her inability to commit. The question was, did she have the nerve to take the first step? Would it be worth it?

She stepped into the living room and found the answer to that question directly before her. Hobie sat cross-legged on the thickly carpeted floor. She had changed into a royal blue sleeveless blouse and a pair of mid-thigh-length cotton shorts. Her bare feet tapped the floor in time to the music as she leafed through her CDs. Her shoulder-length auburn hair took on a deep, rich color that Baylor thought any runway model would envy. The sight of Hobie, so relaxed and beautiful, struck Baylor like an arrow through her heart.

Hobie looked up and into Baylor's gaze. "Hey, you look like you feel much better."

The bright smile disarmed Baylor. She had thought Hobie would be angrier, but she looked almost tranquil. "I feel cleaner, at any rate," she answered.

"Good. How does your leg feel?"

"Great, just great."

"We ought to be able to take that cast off this week."

"Fantastic. No complaints from me there."

Baylor wondered how long she could, or should, keep up the casual conversation. She had a feeling that if Hobie didn't dig in and begin, they would still be standing in the middle of the living room the next morning. As fate would have it, Hobie read her mind.

"Baylor, why don't you sit?"

Here it comes, Baylor thought. "If you don't mind, I think I'll just lean here," she said. She rested her backside against the edge of one of the four tall stools along the breakfast bar.

"I hope you agree that we need to talk," Hobie said.

"Um, yeah. I guess I figured you'd be a lot madder at me than you are, though."

"Mad?" Hobie got to her feet.

Okay, maybe reminding her that she's supposed to be mad is a bad thing. Shit, looks like she's losing it now. Actually, she kinda reminds me of...well, shit...of me.

"I'm not sure you can appreciate just how mad I am at your actions tonight, Baylor. I'm pretty sure I don't even know the whole story yet. I'm not certain I even want to, but what I do know is enough to piss me off from now until the very moment that hell freezes over."

She paced back and forth across the small living room. "The lack of faith, of trust that you must have had, either for me or Jules, to follow us around like—"

"Okay, now about that—" Baylor attempted to tell some small part of her side of the story.

Hobie continued as if she hadn't heard Baylor. "—like some sort of deranged stalker! This is crazy. You know, I turn around and there you are—"

"Well, in all defense—"

"I don't know how much longer I can put up with this. You come into town and first you hate me, then you like me. I just—"

"Okay, I admit I've been a little inconsistent, but—"

"Inconsistent?" Hobie acted as though she had finally heard something that Baylor said. "You've turned me into a crazy woman. I don't know what to think when I'm around you. I don't know how to act or what to say. What do I wear? Do I put on perfume, or is that sending her some kind of a hidden message?"

"I like the way you smell. I mean, I like the perfume you wear." Baylor offered a small grin.

"See what I mean? Baylor, you say things like that and it makes me think—God, I don't know if I can do this. I feel so—"

Hobie's eyes began to tear and that, as always, affected Baylor more than anything else in the world could. She opened her ears and began to really listen to what Hobie had been saying. When she actually *heard* the words, she finally understood. All the time she had been worrying about Hobie rejecting her, and here the vet was afraid of the very same thing.

"You know, my life has a certain order to it. I'm usually very in control," Hobie went on. "I never thought I'd like you so much, Baylor, but then you do something or you say something and I just don't even know how to describe how I feel anymore. I mean, one minute I—"

Hobie continued to babble, even after Baylor stood before her calling her name. The writer placed both hands on Hobie's shoulders. Baylor knew right then that there would be only one way to do it, only one way to convince Hobie as well as herself. For once in her life, she had to live and not just survive.

Baylor took one deep breath and kissed the girl.

It took a number of seconds for Hobie to even realize that she was being kissed. Just as swiftly as it had begun, it was over. Baylor pulled back slightly to look into stunned green eyes. Hobie's shock was short lived, however. She felt the pull of Baylor's loving gaze and the corners of her lips drew upward in a smile. In a synchronized move, Baylor's hands went to Hobie's waist as the vet slipped her arms around the writer's neck. On tiptoe, Hobie returned Baylor's kiss with even more fervor. It wasn't rushed, but slow and lingering, powerful in its intensity. It seemed as though each of them had waited a lifetime for that kiss. Oddly enough, Baylor felt as though this had all happened before. One kiss turned into many until the need for air pulled the two women apart.

"Wow," Hobie said with a grin.

"Yeah," Baylor said with a matching smile. She bent her head to eliminate the distance between them, and their lips met once more.

A soft warmth enveloped Baylor's senses. Her brain swam as though she were high on drink. Hobie's kisses brought her to a place that she hadn't visited in ages. It was a safe spot, a place where it was okay to feel vulnerable, to feel good, to simply feel. Had she ever really been there in any woman's arms before Hobie? There was one time. There must have been. Kissing Hobie was so familiar. Baylor was certain she had felt this kiss before.

Her brow creased as she continued to share tender caresses with Hobie. When had Baylor experienced these feelings? Images flashed through her mind. A glass of wine tossed into her face...a smiling stranger...a hotel room...the hotel room where she awoke the next morning...a beautiful but unseen face...slowly coming into focus.

Baylor opened her eyes and abruptly pushed Hobie away, holding her at arm's length. "You! It was you!"

She didn't have to say more than that. Hobie knew exactly what Baylor meant. She had hoped she would never to have to explain the situation, but, then again, she had never expected to be making out a second time with Baylor Warren.

"If you're talking about Chicago, yes. It was me," Hobie answered.

"I—I don't understand. I looked for you!"

"Oh, right." Hobie laughed.

"Really. I had Jules trying to find you."

"Wow, she's good."

"Hobie, why didn't you say anything when I got here?"

"Well, excuse me, but if you think back, you'll remember that you were less than pleased with me when you got to Ana Lia."

"Oh," Baylor answered. "Okay, I can see that, but wasn't there some moment since then that you could have mentioned you spent the night with me?"

"When was I supposed to say that? 'Um, yes, I think we'll be putting on a walking cast today, and oh, by the way, did I mention that I was the woman you passed out on in Chicago?'"

"Okay, I can see where timing was probably an issue," Baylor replied.

"You do remember that nothing happened between us. Nothing, you know," Hobie said.

"I figured as much when I woke up fully dressed."

"Well, I suppose I should admit that having you *not* recognize me when you got to the island wasn't very flattering or good for my self-esteem, I might add. Part of me was disappointed, but the other part was happy that you didn't remember me."

"Happy?" Baylor asked in confusion.

"I think you know that I don't do things like take women back to my hotel room." Hobie smiled. "Well, at least not in a strange town. I guess I was embarrassed. I felt like some major slut."

"Hobie, that's about the furthest thing from my mind when I think of you."

"What *do* you think about...when you think of me?" Hobie probed.

"I think about how wonderful you are, what a caring, loving woman you are. How special you make people feel, without even doing anything out of the ordinary. I think about what a great mom you are, and I think that everyone in this world should be so lucky as to spend time with you. If they did, they'd discover what I already know. That no one comes as close to absolute beauty as you."

"Boy, have I got you fooled," Hobie answered self-consciously. She shook her head. "You have no idea what you're getting yourself into when you get me."

"Do I?" Baylor asked as she reached out and let her fingertips slide against Hobie's tan cheek. "Get you, I mean."

Hobie smiled at yet another perfectly phrased response from Baylor. "I'm thinking you're pretty much stuck with me. I love you, Baylor." Silence hung in the air after Hobie's last statement. "It's okay if you don't feel the same way. I—"

"No, but I do. Feel the same way," Baylor hurriedly added.

"Oh," Hobie let out a sigh of relief. "Wow." She indicated with her eyes and a subtle tilt of her head that Baylor should carry that acknowledgment a step further.

"Baylor," she commented at last. "Are you sure you feel the same way? Because it's okay if you don't. I've just been so afraid to be the first one to say it that I guess it all came out at once. If you need time to—"

"No, really. I—I..." Baylor wore a pained expression. "Do you really have to hear the words?" she asked, already knowing the answer.

"Yes, I really have to hear the words. I *need* the words, Baylor."

"Okay...here goes. Hobie, I—I—"

Suddenly Baylor's face became ashen. She felt as if there was a tremendous weight on her chest. She looked down in terror as she felt her left arm go numb. "Oh my god."

"What?" Hobie asked in fear.

"I think I'm having a heart attack."

Hobie had seen many an MI during her residency. It was always possible that Baylor was indeed having one, but Hobie's expression said that it was doubtful.

"I can't feel my arm." Baylor looked down at the limb in question. "Holy shit, I'm gonna die."

Hobie rolled her eyes, then sharply pinched Baylor's arm.
"Ow!"

"Did you feel that?"

"Yes, dammit. That hurt," Baylor replied in her customary tone of voice.

"Then your arm isn't numb, you're not having a heart attack, neither are you about to die. See how that all works? You have to actually feel nothing to say that your arm is numb."

"Well, I can see why you got out of medicine with a bedside manner like that." Baylor rubbed the spot where Hobie had pinched her. "That was hard." Her face formed into a childlike pout.

"I bet you don't feel like you're having a heart attack anymore, though. Do you?" Hobie asked with a smile.

"You are not a nice woman." A tiny smile formed on Baylor's face. "I love you, Hobie." Just like that, she said the words, before she had the chance to think about them any longer. She didn't want to wait to see what her father's memory would whisper in her ear. She shrugged off the ghost for the first time in her adult life and it felt good. Damn good.

It only took that simple admission to open the floodgates of emotion for Baylor. She pulled Hobie into her embrace and kissed her with a passion that made their previous kisses seem ordinary in comparison.

"I want you to stay here tonight," Hobie breathed against her neck.

"Yes, oh, yes." Baylor murmured her assent as she and Hobie lowered themselves as one onto the overstuffed couch.

"Oh, yes," Hobie moaned as Baylor's weight pressed on top of her. "Ow, ow."

"What?"

"Your cast. Watch where you're swinging that thing."

"How about you on top?" Baylor could think of no delicate way to put it.

"Good idea." Hobie squirmed as Baylor slid her back against the couch. "Hmm." She paused. "You sure you're ready to give up the power and control of the top position?"

Baylor grinned. "I'll risk it. Now where were we?"

"Right here." Hobie covered the writer's mouth with her own.

"Mmm," Baylor moaned. Suddenly the groans became short and sharp. "Mmm-mm!"

"What?" Hobie finally translated the sounds to mean Baylor was in pain.

"Don't put your hand there, it hurts."

Hobie immediately lifted her hand and pushed up Baylor's t-shirt. Just underneath her ribs was the beginning of a nasty bruise. "How on earth did this happen?"

"Putt-putt course," Baylor answered as she tried to get Hobie's mind on other things with her caresses. "I think it was the swinging monkeys. One of them waylaid me."

"God, Baylor," Hobie said, still examining the large bruise. Baylor's hand slipped under Hobie's blouse and snaked around her waist, stroking the smooth skin. "Oh God, Baylor!" Hobie exclaimed again, with more enthusiasm this time.

"Ow! Just don't lean over that way," Baylor directed, unwilling to end her kisses.

"Hey!" Hobie cried. "Okay, now you've got my hair."

"Ow, shit! Sorry, baby, but the cuts on my hand sting. Let's try this..." Baylor tried to move out from under Hobie so they could at least lie on the couch, facing one another.

"Ouch!" Hobie cried out as a strand of hair caught on Baylor's ring.

"I almost got it...just a sec...there, that wasn't too hard. Whoa!" Baylor had moved just a little too far toward the end of the couch. Her weight carried her until she was lying flat on her back on the floor.

"Jesus, Baylor! Are you okay?" Hobie asked in alarm. It was apparent to Baylor that Hobie was trying very hard not to laugh at her, especially before she found out if she had injured herself.

"Who, me?" Baylor tried to appear casual. "Oh, yeah. Cushy carpeting you have in this place. I'm getting rather used to falling, actually. I really think there's an art to it."

Hobie covered her mouth to stifle her laughter.

"I feel at this point I probably should make something very clear," Baylor said. "I don't usually run into this many problems when making love. It usually goes much smoother than this."

Hobie burst into laughter at last. "Are you always this...this..." She searched for a word that wouldn't offend Baylor.

"Clumsy...a klutz?" Baylor finished. "That's the funny part. I'm considered downright graceful by most people. This seemed to start when I arrived here on the island. For some reason, it appears to be accentuated whenever I'm around you."

Hobie leaned over the side of the couch and reached a hand down to stroke Baylor's cheek. "I'm sorry, sweetheart."

Baylor responded with a sloppy grin. The term of endearment made its way straight to her heart. "Um, you could come down here. It's pretty comfy," she pointed out as she patted the carpeted floor.

"I have an idea," Hobie began. "What would you think if I said I wanted to wait?" She crinkled up her nose as if expecting a blow.

"You don't want to?"

"No! That's not it at all." She brushed a stray lock of hair out of Baylor's eyes. "I do. Trust me, I do. I just want it to be...I don't know, not perfect, but damn close. I was thinking if we waited until I took that cast off and when you healed up a little bit—"

"Not a long bit?" Baylor asked.

"No, sweetheart, not a long bit at all."

"Sounds practical, which kind of sounds like you." Baylor grinned. "I guess I should—"

"I don't want you to go, though. Would you still stay tonight?"

"Think we can manage it without killing each other?"

"I'll take my chances."

"Then yeah," Baylor answered softly. "I want to, if only to be next to you."

"I can arrange that. Come on," Hobie said as she slid off the couch and helped Baylor to her feet.

Hobie led the writer to the now familiar bedroom. "Do you want to sleep in these?" She gently tugged the drawstring on Baylor's borrowed sweatpants.

"I think if we plan on just sleeping, then I'd better. It's that no-underwear thing again."

"Spoilsport," Hobie replied with a teasing smile. "I'll be right back."

Hobie returned a short while later, her face freshly scrubbed and her breath smelling of mint. Baylor had seated herself on the end of the bed, unsure of where to go from there. The redhead stood in front of Baylor and it seemed the most natural thing in the world for the writer to slip her hands around Hobie's slim waist.

"This is my usual sleep attire." Hobie looked down at the faded blue Chicago Cubs t-shirt. "Is it going to...bother you?"

Baylor swallowed at the sight of the white lace bikini underwear that peeked out from under the shirt. She pulled Hobie in closer to her. "I think if you were wearing flannel from head to toe, you'd still turn me on."

"You always know just what to say to me."

"I am a writer, after all," Baylor replied with a pretentious air.

Hobie rewarded her with a slow kiss. A slight wince and a pained moan from Baylor alerted the vet to stop where she was.

"No strenuous activity for you tonight," Hobie said, ignoring the charming pout on Baylor's face. "I'd say a week before all those bruises heal."

"A week?" Baylor nearly shouted. "Five days?"

"Actually, I meant seven. There are still seven days in a week, right?" Hobie scrunched up her face and began counting with her fingers.

"Four."

"I said seven."

"Wait...five."

"Seven."

"Six!" Baylor pleaded.

"You're under the mistaken impression that taking advice from your doctor is like an evening at Sotheby's."

"Oh, please. Come on, baby..." Baylor ended the thought by running her hands along the backs of Hobie's thighs, pulling her closer.

"Oh, no, you don't." Hobie laughed as she extracted herself from the writer's suddenly octopuslike grasp. She had been seconds away from giving in to Baylor's sensual bargaining.

"One thing you better learn right now." Hobie held the writer's chin in her fingers. "I already know how charming you are, and I know how much you like to use that charm, Baylor Warren. That sexy little pout and those magic hands may have worked on those girls you went out with before—we are talking before, right?"

Baylor held up three fingers in a Scout salute. "I only have eyes for you."

"Good," Hobie said as she grinned slyly. "As I was saying, that routine may have worked with the girls, but you're dealing with a woman now."

"Don't I know it." Baylor returned the smile and the light kiss that Hobie had placed upon her lips.

She settled into bed, propping a pillow under her cast. After she got comfortable, she opened her arms and nodded to Hobie, who snuggled in against her as though they had been doing it that way for years.

"Good night," Hobie said as she kissed Baylor's neck.

"Night," Baylor responded. She kissed the top of Hobie's head. She thought Hobie had already fallen asleep when she heard her lilting laughter. "You okay?"

"I was just wondering..."

"Yeah?"

"I wonder if I could get a copy of the security tape from putt-

putt. You know, to see the bird when you—"

"Good night, Hobie Lynn," Baylor said through clenched teeth.

Hobie didn't say another word, but long into the night, Baylor heard her occasional chuckle.

"Mmm, you okay?" Hobie asked as she felt Baylor slip back into bed.

"Just had to make a pre-dawn pit stop." She carefully situated her cast so that she could roll onto her side and curl up behind Hobie.

"Feels good," Hobie mumbled sleepily as she felt Baylor's body against her own. "I forgot to warn you that I have to get up later and cook Noah breakfast."

"Won't your mom fix him breakfast?"

"It's kind of a Sunday tradition. Noah likes a disgusting breakfast, his favorite treat, so I make them on Sundays."

"What's the treat?"

"Chocolate-chip pancakes."

"Really?" Baylor said excitedly, lifting her head off the pillow.

Hobie turned slightly to look into the writer's face.

"It's chocolate. Chocolate always sounds good," Baylor responded defensively.

Hobie rolled back over and mumbled into her pillow. "You and Noah will get along famously. He likes chocolate almost as much as you do." She felt a soft, and unexpected, kiss on her neck as Baylor settled against her.

Baylor was surprised at how natural it felt to be lying there with Hobie. There wasn't any of the usual discomfort related to sleeping in the same bed with someone for the first time. *We must be meant to be*, she thought just before she drifted off to sleep again.

Sunrise came sooner than she thought possible. "Arturo, get off my stomach," she commanded sleepily.

A giggle followed Baylor's command.

"It's not Arturo," Noah whispered. "It's me, Noah. Noah Allen." He lifted Baylor's eyelid with a tiny index finger. "You in there, Baylor?"

"No, there's nobody home."

Noah laughed again. "Yes, there is."

Baylor struggled to open her eyes, with some success on the second attempt. "Hey, Bubba. Why are you so wide awake at this hour?"

"Pancakes." He said the word and then smiled his large, toothy grin before pushing his glasses up. "Mom makes 'em."

Hearing Hobie's name, Baylor looked to the other side of the bed. The vet lay asleep on her stomach, buried under a mound of sheets and blankets.

"Tell you what." Baylor lowered her voice. "Why don't you and I start breakfast and let your mom sleep a few minutes longer. What do you say?"

"Do you know what my favorite breakfast in the whole wide world is?"

"Chocolate-chip pancakes, of course."

Noah's eyes widened. "How'd you know that?"

"I know everything," Baylor whispered and then winked. "All right, give me a few minutes and I'll meet you in the kitchen. Deal?"

"'Kay. Baylor, do you know how to make pancakes?"

"Well, I've never actually made chocolate-chip ones before, but how hard can it be, right?"

"Right." The youngster smiled and clambered off the bed.

As promised, it only took Baylor a few minutes to wash her face and try to smooth out her morning hair. Hobie had left her a toothbrush, still in its packaging, on the bathroom sink. On her way out of the bedroom, Baylor couldn't resist going back to the bed and looking down at the sleeping redhead.

What a lovesick dyke I've turned into, Baylor thought just before she bent down to place a gentle kiss on Hobie's cheek.

"Hmm?" Hobie muttered. "What time is it?" she rasped in a throaty voice.

"It's really early. Go back to sleep." Baylor kissed her again.

"'Kay," Hobie replied and instantly drifted back to sleep.

Baylor almost laughed aloud at the resemblance between mother and son. She walked into the kitchen to find Noah perched upon one of the high stools.

"Mom always lets me sit here and watch. I could help, though."

"Have you ever helped before?" Baylor asked hopefully.

"Uh-uh." Noah shook his head.

"Then I think it's probably better to have only one person in the kitchen at a time who doesn't know where anything's at."

"You go for it, Baylor." Noah had a giant smile, as if he thought this was the most adventurous thing in the world.

Baylor reached out and mussed the boy's hair. "You know it, Bubba."

It only took a matter of moments to realize she was in over

her head. Now, Baylor prided herself on her culinary abilities, but Hobie's kitchen was a lesson in futility. It was difficult enough to find all the necessary utensils, let alone the ingredients.

"Doesn't your mom have pancake mix anywhere? Or maybe flour?"

Noah shrugged.

Baylor finally admitted defeat when she found buttons in the flour canister and a can of baking powder that looked like it had last been used during the Carter administration.

"You sure your mom is the one who makes these pancakes you always have?" Baylor muttered to herself. "Okay, Bubba, I have an idea. Your mom likes her coffee as much as I do. I know a surefire way for us to wake her up. Where does she keep the coffee?"

Hobie smiled and stretched as the morning sunlight sliced across the bed. She breathed in and smelled the rich odor of freshly brewed coffee. That was when she recalled just who else was in the house with her. She remembered a time when she would have dashed into the shower, brushed her teeth, and put on a little makeup before letting her new bedroom partner see her. She couldn't really understand why she didn't feel that same urgency now. It all felt so natural with Baylor.

She replaced her sleeping shirt with a longer one and went in search of the source of the delicious aroma. "Good morning," she said.

"Mornin', Mom!" Noah hugged Hobie when she bent to kiss his cheek.

"Morning, Mom," Baylor added, holding out a steaming mug of coffee.

"Thanks. Nice hairdo you've got going there." Hobie pointed out the cowlick that Baylor couldn't keep plastered down.

"Speak for yourself, bedhead." Baylor smiled and ran her fingers through Hobie's unruly locks. She was actually a bit surprised. She had expected Hobie to walk out of the bedroom, but she wasn't sure who this woman was. The previous evening's confessions had caused her to look different today. As sappy as it sounded to Baylor's own ears, she thought the redhead looked much more angelic.

She leaned in for a kiss, only to have Hobie pull back ever so slightly.

"I, um..." Hobie began.

Baylor quickly looked at Noah, who was calmly watching

them. She hadn't thought about him being in the room, but Hobie obviously had. "Oh, I'm sorry, I—"

"No! No, it's not that at all," Hobie said with an embarrassed grin. She sat down her coffee cup and backed away toward the bedroom. "I haven't brushed my teeth yet. Be back in a sec."

Baylor chuckled. She leaned against the counter beside Noah and sipped her coffee. She turned to him. "Women. Go figure," she said and shook her head.

"Yeah," Noah agreed, shaking his head the same way. He wasn't absolutely certain what it was about women that Baylor didn't understand, but he liked Baylor. If something bothered her then Noah figured it should affect him, too.

Hobie returned a few minutes later wearing a sheepish expression. "Do you think it's humanly possible for me to embarrass myself any more this morning?"

"Not if you don't count the fact that the back of your shirt is tucked into your underwear," Baylor replied casually.

"Aw, geez!" Hobie exclaimed, her face turning red. She quickly reached around and pulled it loose. "I must look—"

"Beautiful," Baylor finished. "Right, Bubba?"

"Yep! You look beautiful, Mom," Noah added.

Hobie leaned her forehead against Baylor's chest as the taller woman wrapped her arms around her. "Thanks, guys. You two are good for my ego." She tugged on Baylor's t-shirt to get her attention. "Hey, you. Come on down here."

Baylor bent down and Hobie sweetly kissed her lips. Noah giggled and Baylor opened one eye, finally pulling away. "What are you laughing at, huh?"

Noah pointed at Baylor. "You like Mom!"

"I do not!" Baylor winked at Hobie and mustered up a false expression of disgust.

"Do too. Baylor and Mom, sittin' in a tree k-i-s-s-i-n-g..."

"Oh, now you're gonna get it." Baylor moved toward the boy just as he leaped from the chair.

Hobie watched as the two ran screaming and laughing through the house. "Hey, who wants chocolate-chip pancakes?" she asked after a few moments.

All action in the living room stopped. Baylor had let Noah pin her to the ground, but both turned their heads and answered, "Me, me!"

I'm not sure whether I just gained a lover or another kid, Hobie thought as she moved around the kitchen. The thought frightened her, but then again, the future always frightened Hobie. She smiled as she listened to Baylor and Noah in the other room.

How often did a woman find a partner who loved her child, and whom her child loved in return? Did some kisses and a declaration of love necessarily mean a lifetime commitment, though? Would Baylor move to Ana Lia? Could she? Hobie thought about Chicago. The city was wonderful, with opportunities unavailable anywhere else, but did she want to raise Noah there?

Hobie sighed deeply. Now she wondered if falling in love with Baylor was a good thing or not.

Chapter
15

"Hey." Baylor slumped into the chaise lounge beside the pool, Arturo in her lap. He had been happy to see her, leaping into her arms the minute she had entered the house.

"Hey." Juliana raised an eye from the manuscript she was reading. "Well?"

"Well what?" Baylor asked.

"Don't make me hurt you."

"Hurt me? Oh, yeah. Like you tried to do last night? You hit like a girl."

The two friends paused to look at one another and burst into laughter. They had been through much worse over the years than the previous night's encounter. They had, and always would, remain friends, no matter what idiotic things they might say to one another in the heat of the moment.

"About last night," Baylor began, "you know...Well, I'm sorry, I just—"

"Don't sweat it, mate. So," Juliana drawled with a leering grin, "how was last night?"

Baylor grinned without realizing she had done so.

"I guess that smile says it all. About damn time."

"No thanks to you." Baylor laughed.

Juliana just kept smiling. One thing she would never reveal to Baylor was that she had played a part, albeit the tiniest part, in setting the two women up. Baylor didn't like to be pushed. If she felt that she'd been manipulated in any way, she'd ruin her life and hurt Hobie just to spite everyone.

"So, tell me the good parts," Juliana said.

"It was all good, but not in the way you're thinking."

"Did you tell her?"

"Yep."

"Atta girl."

"We spent the night together, but we slept...that's all."

"Right," Juliana said sarcastically. "I bet there was some

major snogging going on over there."

"Nope, that's the honest truth." Baylor cleared her throat self-consciously. "We sort of agreed to wait, you know, take it slow. Till the cast is off, and then we can—"

"You mean she said no."

"Yeah, pretty much. I did everything but get on my knees and beg."

Juliana laughed. "It'll be good for you. Build up your character. You know, women like this aren't just flings, mate. Hobie's the real deal."

"I know," Baylor stretched in the chair. "You'd think I'd be more, I don't know...scared of that. Wouldn't you?"

"Knowing you, I'd have to answer a big fat yes. Usually you're running for the hills about this time."

"I know. I can't figure it out. I just know I'm not going to let that son of a bitch beat me anymore."

Juliana looked at her friend. She knew the writer was referring to her father. Baylor lay stretched out with her eyes closed and the white pup already snoring in her lap. The agent couldn't remember a time when Baylor had looked this comfortable in her own skin.

"You deserve this girl, mate," Juliana said softly.

"I don't know about that, but I've got to try. Hey, I better get cleaned up. Hobie's coming by and we're going to see Tanti. Want to come with?"

"Nah," Juliana answered. She wasn't sure she could keep from spilling any secrets in a room with Evelyn, Hobie, and Baylor. "I'm gonna work on my tan. I'll go up this afternoon and visit with her."

"Check. Thanks for taking care of Arturo while I'm out, too."

"No problem. He's a lot of fun once you get used to being his puppy pillow."

Baylor chuckled. "Yeah, I kind of got him into some bad habits. Okay, I'm off to get cleaned up. See ya later."

"Later," Juliana echoed.

"Thanks for going with me to see Tanti," Baylor said. For the first time in her life, she was enjoying being a passenger in her own car. It gave her the opportunity to play voyeur and watch Hobie as she drove.

"You don't have to thank me. I've been Evelyn's friend for years."

"I guess it's just an excuse for me to spend time with you,

then." Baylor stretched her arm along the back seat and played with the loose hair at the back of Hobie's neck. The redhead offered up a bright smile before turning her attention back to the road. Baylor knew her heart was in deep when her stomach did a little flip at the sight of that smile.

"You know that Evelyn is going to give us the third degree, don't you?"

"Not if she doesn't know, she won't."

"So we don't say anything about us?" Hobie asked.

"Unless you want to answer a lot of personal questions. I don't know, how's your embarrassment tolerance?" Baylor asked with a smile.

Hobie returned the laughter. "I see your point, but we are going to get asked. You know how folks are around here."

"I guess." Baylor's brow creased.

Out of the corner of her eye, Hobie saw Baylor's expression. It didn't look as though she was entirely pleased at the idea of their relationship becoming common knowledge. Immediately Hobie's defenses went up. "Is it that you don't want people knowing you're in a relationship or that you don't want them to know it's with me?"

"What?" Baylor stopped her wandering mind. "No, no, baby, it's nothing like that at all. I didn't mean it like it sounded. I guess I'm just lousy at being in the spotlight. That's the part I was dreading."

"Oh," Hobie answered quietly. "I thought maybe—"

"Don't think that. It was the furthest thing from my mind," Baylor quickly added.

"So, do you think we can treat each other like nothing's different between us?"

"You mean can I look at you without revealing how absolutely lucky I feel, without showing to every single person in the room how much I love you?"

Hobie smiled and shook her head. "You do have a way of saying just the right thing at times."

"Besides, I don't know how Tanti will react to us, you know, being a couple."

"Why do you think she'd have a problem with it?"

"Well, she's never said anything. She's actually been pretty accepting of my sexual preference, but we've never really talked about how she feels about me being gay."

"I think Evelyn's probably the last person on the island to have a problem with that." Hobie chuckled.

"There's a first time for everything."

"Yeah, but wouldn't that kind of be like the pot calling the kettle black?"

"Huh?"

"Well, because of her and Aimee."

"What about her and Aimee?"

"What do you mean, what do I mean?"

"I mean, what do Evelyn and Aimee have to do with the price of tea in China?"

"I just meant that since Evelyn was gay, or at least had a female lover in her life, I'm sure she wouldn't come down on you. What did you think I was talking about?"

"Excuse me?" Baylor's mouth went dry and her mind shut down.

"I said, what did you—"

"I heard what you said, what I don't get is why you said it."

Hobie pulled the car into the hospital parking lot. She turned off the ignition and turned in the seat to face Baylor. "We are having a huge gap in communicating here. Aren't we?"

"I think so," Baylor laughed nervously. "Why would you say that Tanti is gay?"

"Um...because she is," Hobie replied slowly.

"She is? My grandmother? We are talking about Evelyn Warren, right?"

"Of course. Baylor, didn't you know this?"

"No," Baylor answered as she sat back into her seat. "I had no idea. Are you sure?"

"Baylor, that's not the kind of thing you can mistake. Surely you were around Evelyn and Aimee when you were younger?"

"Yeah, but Tanti never said anything. All they did was joke around and yell at each other a lot. They acted like...well, I don't know. They argued all the time!" She paused and looked over at a smiling Hobie. "That sounds like us, doesn't it?"

"Kind of," Hobie replied.

"Holy shit! How could no one have told me?"

"I guess they all figured you knew. Did your parents ever say anything when you were a kid?"

Baylor realized with startling clarity why her father had disowned his mother. "Yeah, that sounds exactly like something he'd do," she muttered.

"What?"

"Oh, sorry. I was just remembering. As far back as I can remember, my father never spoke to Tanti. Mom said they had a falling out, but I'll bet you anything it was over that."

"Some son," Hobie said. "Oh, sweetheart, I'm sorry. I

shouldn't have said that."

"Don't be. It's just what I was thinking. I can't believe Tanti never came out and told me."

"Maybe she thought you knew. Maybe she even felt that you weren't ready to hear that kind of thing about your father." Hobie laid a gentle hand on Baylor's arm. "Whatever it was, you know that Evelyn must have been thinking of you."

"Yeah, you're right. Tanti's always been there for me."

"Just do me one favor?" Hobie asked.

"Sure, anything."

"Just make sure you don't, well, pounce on Evelyn with this news the minute we get there. Okay?"

"Give me a little credit, hon. I can be the epitome of tact when I want to be."

"Well, if it isn't my two favorite girls!" Evelyn exclaimed heartily. She looked positively healthy and glowing.

"I can't believe you never told me you were gay!" Baylor blurted out.

Hobie let her face fall into her open hand. "Smooth," she said once she raised her head. "What happened to tact?"

"Oops, I forgot," Baylor admitted. "Still," she refocused her attention on her grandmother, "Tanti, why didn't you ever tell me you're a lesbian?"

"Because I'm not," Evelyn replied.

"See," Baylor turned to a surprised Hobie. "I told you she was straight."

"Oh, but I'm not that either, Baylor."

Baylor stood there looking at her grandmother. Suddenly her eyes lit up. "Oh. I get it." She looked at Hobie and waggled her finger back and forth. "Because she was married once...she's bi."

"Uh-uh," Evelyn answered, shaking her head.

Baylor stood silently. "Okay, I'm confused."

"Baylor, you know how much I detest labels. I cared very much for your grandfather while he was alive. Then, I met Aimee and...well, I fell in love with her. If I call myself this or that, it seems as though I'm putting limits on love. We all know that sometimes love just happens, whether we mean it to or not."

Baylor and Hobie exchanged a guilty look.

Evelyn watched the two women closely. They hadn't said a word about it, but she could read all the signs. Not only were they in love, but they also had finally shared their feelings with one another. There were subtle changes in their behavior; their chairs sat just a tad closer than usual, their eyes occasionally locked. Evelyn nearly jumped for joy. She couldn't wait to phone Rebecca.

"If I'd ever thought you didn't know, Baylor, I would have surely told you. Some things about me never seemed to interest you. Like my being a Wiccan, for example."

"You're a witch?" Baylor's voice rose considerably.

"I think they prefer the term 'Wiccan,'" Hobie added.

"You knew about this? Are you one, too?" Baylor asked with a suspicious glance.

"Don't be silly. Of course I'm not," Hobie replied. "Some of the...well, older women on the island are."

"I'm afraid it very nearly is just us old women any more, Hobie Lynn. Your mother is probably the youngest member of the Ladies Guild."

"My mother?" Hobie stood alongside Baylor at this point. "That's what the Ladies Guild is, and my mother is a...a...witch?"

"I thought you said they liked to be called Wiccans," Baylor said smugly.

"That's before I knew my mother was one of them," Hobie shot back. "I think I need to sit." An expression like amazement fixed itself upon her face. "I don't understand. I mean, I've heard rumors, but—"

"Hobie, I'm sure it's not what you think. Tell her, Tanti." Baylor looked to her grandmother for support. "I mean," she looked at Hobie, "it's not like they dance naked under the moon or anything." She laughed.

"Well, as a matter of fact, we do, dear," Evelyn interjected. Two sets of eyes on her prompted her to continue. "But only once a year. It's more tradition than anything else."

"I think I'm losing my mind," Hobie said.

"Welcome to my world," Baylor said as she rested a reassuring hand on Hobie's shoulder.

"You girls act as if I've lost my mind. Hobie Lynn, these practices have gone on for more years than even I've been on this island. There's nothing to be afraid of or worried about. Most of the younger women on the island think we're just a bunch of loony old women, but we're absolutely harmless. We never hurt anyone and we don't share our views with anyone but the most open-minded. Just the thought of witches living on the same block does frighten some." Evelyn whispered the last sentence.

Hobie looked up at the kindly old woman and instantly felt guilty. She had done what people had been doing to her all her life—judged. "I'm sorry, Evelyn. I shouldn't have sounded so disapproving. I had no right."

Evelyn reached out to squeeze Hobie's hand. "Being different comes with a price. I think we all know that. Eh?" She looked up at Baylor.

"I guess we should know most of all," Baylor finally admitted with a wry grin.

"Baylor, I wonder if you could get me some water?" Evelyn asked.

"Sure, Tanti." Baylor reached for the pitcher on the bedside table.

"No, dear, that water isn't any good."

Baylor eyed the plastic pitcher. "No good?"

"The best water is in the vending machine in the lobby, just near the entrance."

"All the way over there?" Baylor raised her voice.

"I suppose I could call a nurse to take me over..."

"No, no. I can go get it. Anything else you want? Like some unsalted Brazil nuts that I need to actually go to Brazil for?"

Hobie slapped her playfully on the thigh. Baylor grinned down at her and Evelyn looked on, certain she had never seen her granddaughter quite this happy before.

"Okay. Hobie, want anything?"

"No, I'm good."

"I don't suppose you have a broom I can use to just fly over there, do you?" Baylor grinned at her grandmother. Evelyn returned her granddaughter's comment with an arched eyebrow.

"Okay, okay, sorry. Geez, can't anyone take a joke anymore?"

As soon as Baylor left the room, Evelyn laughed and reached for Hobie's hand. "Tell me everything."

"What?" Hobie asked with a confused chuckle.

"You and Baylor."

"I have no idea what you mean," Hobie replied.

"Hobie Lynn, I know that Baylor likes to hide her emotions, but that's never been quite like you. Now, am I right about the two of you?"

"Yes, Evelyn," Hobie said. "You're right."

"Well then, tell me all the juicy details."

Hobie laughed. "There are no juicy bits to talk about yet, and even if I had some, I don't think I'd feel entirely comfortable talking to Baylor's grandmother about our sex life."

"Such a spoilsport," Evelyn teased. "I can't tell you how happy I am for you both. You deserve this, Hobie Lynn, a love that will last a lifetime."

"I'd like to think it will last a lifetime, Evelyn, but as to deserving it, that's debatable."

"You're not still worried about that, are you?"

"Evelyn, I haven't told Baylor. I should have before because now it's too late. She'll be so angry. I just don't know how to handle it."

"Honestly, it's not as if it wasn't an accident."

"You know how paranoid Baylor can be. She's certain to think the worst, something terrible, like there's some sort of conspiracy behind it all."

"I honestly don't see why she would be that upset," Evelyn protested. "I think you should just come right out and tell her. She'll understand it coming from you."

"Oh, you think that, do you? And, just how am I supposed to phrase it? 'Oh, Baylor, has your grandmother told you how she ended up breaking her hip? No? Well, let me be the first to say that I ran her over with my pickup at the very same intersection I hit you! Small world, huh?'"

Hobie looked up into Evelyn's face and noticed her stricken expression. She didn't understand until she realized that Evelyn was looking past her. She turned, but she already knew what she would see. Baylor was standing in the open door staring, open-mouthed, at them.

"Oh God," Hobie breathed.

"Was that supposed to be a joke?" Baylor asked. She walked slowly into the room and deposited two bottles of water onto the bedside stand.

"Now, Baylor..." Evelyn paused, uncertain what to say next. She wanted to make a joke, say something light to break up the stormy expression growing on Baylor's face. That look stopped her, however.

"I don't believe it. Tell me it's not true. Hobie, I can't believe you would hide something like this from me."

"Now, Baylor—" Hobie began.

"Will you both quit saying 'now, Baylor'!"

"Well, it's just that we can see that you're getting upset—"

"Then you're both goddamn clairvoyant!" Baylor shouted. "You're damn right I'm getting upset. I can't believe that you purposely hid this information from me."

"Baylor, stop. It was me who told Hobie not to say anything."

"No, Tanti, don't try to cover for her."

"Cover for me?" Hobie's voice rose about two octaves. "I'll have you know that I don't need your grandmother to take the fall for me."

"Oh, yeah? Who usually does it?" Baylor shot back. There was one moment, one brief moment, when she had thought that perhaps calming down and listening to reason would be a smart thing. That point had passed her by about twenty seconds earlier. Now, the writer only had one thought: Hobie Lynn had purposefully deceived her. Of course, in Baylor's mind, the infraction grew quickly from simple deception to betrayal. Perhaps it was her past, her natural mistrust, or the fact that her temper could strike faster than lightning. Whatever the reason was, it only took a matter of seconds to transform Hobie from lover to enemy.

By this time, the little voice inside Hobie's head, the one that told her she had gone too far, was having fits of apoplexy. She knew she had one last chance to think rationally. She took a deep breath, her hands clenched into fists. "Okay, I can do this. I can behave like an intelligent adult. Now, Baylor—"

"I swear, I'm going to smack the next person who says that."

"Baylor, you must stop!" Evelyn could see all of her hard work and planning slipping away because of the two strong-willed women. "Think about what you're saying. Hobie, you too."

"That's the problem, she never thinks before she speaks. Her thoughts drop down onto her tongue and out her mouth like a Pez dispenser!" Hobie cried out.

"Oh, yeah?" Baylor returned, frustrated that Hobie had caught her off guard.

"Ooh, what a sparkling retort."

"Baylor, please..." Evelyn's words sounded fatigued as she made one last halfhearted attempt to calm the two women, who now stood toe to toe. "I certainly didn't plan it this way," she muttered under her breath.

Unfortunately, Baylor heard the comment. "Planned?" Baylor looked between Hobie and Evelyn. "Holy shit! I don't believe it, but it all makes sense. You got me on this island on purpose," she said to her grandmother. "This whole thing was some—some—setup."

"Oh, please!" Hobie rolled her eyes.

"And you're in on it, too!" Baylor took a step backward as she pointed at Hobie. Her paranoia kicked into high gear. "You're a witch, just like the rest of them, aren't you?"

"Oh, you're about to see what a witch I am!" Hobie took a step closer to the writer.

"You ran over Tanti to get me here, and then *you,*" Baylor pointed to her grandmother, "put a spell on me."

"Oh...my...God! Do you hear yourself?" Hobie asked.

"It sounds reasonable," Baylor rushed to reply.

"The idea that the moon is made of green cheese probably sounds reasonable to you!" Hobie shouted back, as though she had never declared her love for the writer, as though they were strangers in a street fight.

"Is that a dig about my intelligence? You know, I have a PhD. You should be calling *me* doctor!"

"Oh, for Christ's sake!" Hobie turned to pick up her jacket. "I can't believe I seriously entertained the idea of a relationship with you. How desperate can one woman get? I don't know how I fell into this. You are insane!"

Hobie moved toward the door and there were tears in her eyes when she turned to face the women in the room. "I don't want you to contact me again, Baylor, and I want you to stay as far away from my son as possible. Noah doesn't need this. I'm sorry, Evelyn," she said before she walked out the door.

Baylor looked at her grandmother, contemplating how odd it was that sometimes the smallest things made the biggest impact. The mention of Noah's name had snapped her brain back into reality. She realized that the last few moments—because that was actually all the time that had passed during their argument—were going to change her life. As she watched Hobie disappear down the hall, she also understood that change wasn't going to be for the better.

Baylor's countenance appeared to clear. She felt a pressure in her chest, an old familiar weight that sat heavily where her heart should have been. The reality of what she said, and to whom she'd just said it, came crashing in on her.

"Oh God. Tanti, what have I done?" Baylor said to her grandmother, sitting down with a heavy sigh. She lowered her head into her hands and muttered, "Shit, shit, shit."

"I don't think cursing is going to help any," Evelyn said gently.

"Oh God, Tanti. What's wrong with me? How could I have said those things? I'm so sorry, I didn't mean—"

"Are you under the impression that you're the only one to blame here?"

"Well, I...What do you mean? Yeah, of course it was my fault."

"Why do you think that, dear heart?"

"Um, I, uh...I don't know. I guess because when things like this happen it's always my fault. Me and my big mouth."

"Is that you talking or your father?"

Baylor looked up in surprise.

"From where I sit," Evelyn said, "all three of us had a hand in making a rather cosmic mess of this whole day. I shouldn't have asked Hobie to stay quiet about the accident. I do apologize for that deception, Baylor."

"Tanti, it's not necessary. I—"

"I think it is necessary, and I'm an old lady. You shouldn't argue with old ladies."

Baylor grinned.

"There, that's better. At least I can still make you smile." She held out her hand and Baylor engulfed it in her own strong grasp.

"Hobie may have been doing as I asked, but she was as guilty as you in perpetuating that argument. Sometimes that girl has the temperament of a rattlesnake on a hot day."

"Are we talking about the same person?" Baylor asked.

Evelyn's only answer was a cryptic smile.

"I don't know how I'm going to make this one right, Tanti. I hear what you're saying, but I don't think Hobie is looking at this in the same way you are."

"What are you most afraid of, dear?"

"That she won't forgive me. That I'll lose her," she added softly. "I don't know how I'll handle that."

"You love her that much?"

"Yes. I don't know how I'm going to do this, Tanti. I don't know how I'm going to keep going without her. Geez, how pathetic does that sound?"

"Baylor Warren, you sound as if she's left the country. You haven't even tried to talk to her yet."

"Did you see the look on her face? See that anger in her eyes? She thinks it's all my fault...and it is." Baylor pulled at her forelock. "I don't know why I'm like this."

"Like what, dear?"

"Like...like me," Baylor answered. She rose and paced around the small room. "Hobie's right. I'm selfish and arrogant. I think I'm so superior to everyone else I meet. I don't even know why I act so mean to people. I guess I'm just a lost cause."

"Baylor, dear heart, show yourself as much compassion as you're learning to show others."

"Me? I'm the least compassionate person on this earth!"

"That's not what I hear. People tell me that you sit for hours in the bookstore having tea with Katherine and Albert."

Baylor felt a prickly heat gather around her collar.

"They say you sit with the coach, just to keep him company, that you watch out for Hobie's boy, Noah. Theresa Allen said that in one night you brought her family closer than they've been in twenty years. Are those the actions of a selfish woman, Baylor?"

The writer refused to look up from her shoes.

"Baylor, there are a lot of reasons why people do the things they do. Many of yours have to do with the way your father treated you, the anger and the feelings of inadequacy that his treatment instilled in you. I'm so sorry for that. I would have done more if I could have."

"Tanti, I never blamed—"

"I know that, but that's not why I bring this up now. I'm telling you these things to make you see that you may have been one way for a very long time, but people can change. You've changed, Baylor. You've changed for the better, and I've never been more proud of you."

"Are you forgetting how I just acted?"

"Well, we all have our weak moments," Evelyn deadpanned.

Baylor finally smiled as she sat down.

"Are you happy, Baylor?"

"Not as this moment I'm not."

"You need to work at finding the key, then. The key to your happiness."

"That's funny. Rebecca Ashby was the last person to say that to me. Seems like I hear a lot about the key to happiness around here."

"You'll find that the people who are the most comfortable with themselves have discovered what it is. Maybe that's why we have so many content people on Ana Lia."

"So, what is it, the key to happiness?"

"First of all, it's up to you to discover that. Second, it's different for everyone. What makes you happy, Baylor?"

"Hobie. Hey, maybe she's the key to my happiness, huh?" Baylor asked.

"As lovely as that sounds, dear, let me give you one bit of advice about your happiness. Don't take this from your grandmother; take it from an old woman who has lived an awful lot of life. Don't ever let your happiness depend upon another person, even one as lovely as Hobie Lynn."

"I guess that makes sense," Baylor replied.

"What makes you happy, my dear?" Evelyn repeated gently.

"I was just trying to think of that. I have to say that looking at my life, I don't recall too many times when I was actually happy. I wouldn't say that writing does it for me. I mean, I love it, but it can become work, ya know? There's Hobie. Noah," Baylor added with a smile. "But if I couldn't say people, I don't know. I feel like it's right here, ya know?" She grasped at the air. "I just can't verbalize it. Like it's a feeling of things. Damn, that makes no sense at all, does it?"

"It will come. Usually when you're doing something mundane or something you've done a thousand times before. Suddenly you'll realize that this is the thing that truly brings you happiness."

"Do you know yours? Did you figure it out?" Baylor asked.

Evelyn nodded, that same Mona Lisa smile on her face.

"Well, is it a secret? Can you tell me or is it a witch thing?"

"You are a little stuck on that, aren't you?"

"Oh, no, not at all. You know me; open mouth, insert foot. Sorry. Come on, tell me."

"I'm surprised you don't know what brings me the greatest joy in my life, aside from my headstrong granddaughter, that is."

"Aimee? No, you said not to depend on other people for your happiness. Um, Arturo? No, you just got him." Baylor's brow furrowed in concentration.

"You've been taking care of them for me since the first day you arrived," Evelyn hinted.

Baylor's eyes lit up as the pieces fell into place. Framed *Life* covers and photos of her grandmother's adventures filled her house. Cambodia, Thailand, Peru, Colombia, Brazil, Guatemala, Mexico.

"You've been in every jungle from—" Baylor looked into her grandmother's eyes. "Your greenhouses."

Evelyn smiled and leaned back on her pillows. "I finally realized it when I couldn't go on assignment anymore. The jungles and rainforests were what I missed most of all. Unless you've been there, you don't know what the early morning dew sounds like as it drips from leaf to leaf. There's a smell...wet, loamy earth that's all humid and still." Her eyes took on a faraway expression. "Aimee and I worked to bring the rainforest to Ana Lia."

The argument with Hobie came rushing back at Baylor. "I won't ever be that happy, not without Hobie."

Evelyn shook off her dreamy thoughts. "You won't unless you find that girl and at least try to apologize."

"Me? Shouldn't she apologize to me?"

Evelyn raised an eyebrow, looking remarkably like her granddaughter.

"Okay, that was a stupid thing to say, wasn't it?"

"See, you *are* learning to change. In the beginning of a relationship, you'll find that one person may have to initiate apologies. It's not always like that, but there are some people who...well, they're too afraid of appearing vulnerable. Given enough time and love, they'll overcome that. In the meantime, you may need to be the first to extend the olive branch, even when you know that you're right. After all, does it really matter who did what to whom first? Isn't it more important to have Hobie Lynn back in your life?"

Baylor realized the truth of it. Getting Hobie back was the most important thing. *I guess my pride can suffer a few bumps and bruises to make that happen. Right?*

"Is Hobie one of those people you just talked about, Tanti? Is she afraid?"

"Hobie Lynn is very afraid, Baylor. Remember when I told you that our past experiences shape who we are?"

Baylor nodded.

"Hobie's life was shaped by her father, too. When he died, he left her with the feeling that people aren't permanent. She fears living without love, but just as strong is her fear of loving someone who will leave her."

"I have to find her." Baylor jumped up from her seat and crossed the room to the window. "The car's still here. Maybe she walked."

"What would you do if I said I knew where to find her?"

"Kiss you." Baylor grinned before growing serious. "Then grovel, I guess."

"Help her confront her fears, Baylor. She is a master at sweeping her emotions into a corner. If you're serious about this girl, you have to make her admit to it; in the end, it will be worth it. One more thing, Baylor."

The writer turned.

"Don't do this unless you really are serious about committing to one woman and helping to raise a son. You'll do harm to everyone, yourself included, if you don't know yet whether this is what you want."

Baylor nodded slowly, her brain now working overtime. "Hobie is what I want, her and everything about her. Noah, this island, these crazy people—all of it, and I'll do whatever it takes to get her."

Evelyn's smile fairly lit up the room. Her happiness at that moment had nothing to do with her hopes for Baylor's future on Ana Lia. Rather, it came from seeing her only grandchild finally become the woman she had always hoped she would one day be.

"Very well, then. I think you'll find Hobie Lynn at the west end of the building. There's a small atrium across from physical therapy. She loves flowers. You'll also discover that she is as miserable over her actions as you were."

Baylor smiled from ear to ear. "Thanks, Tanti!" She was almost out of the door before Evelyn's voice stopped her.

"Wait a minute!" Evelyn pointed to her own cheek. "Aren't

you forgetting what you just promised?"

"Oh, yeah." Baylor blushed and came back to her grandmother's bedside. She leaned down and planted a gentle kiss on the old woman's cheek. "Thanks, Tanti. I'll be back. You're the best."

"Yes, that goes without saying," Evelyn said as Baylor rushed out the door.

The entrance to the atrium was through stained-glass doors, making it look more like a chapel. As Baylor approached, she saw a small plaque bolted into the wall. It read, "Many thanks to Evelyn Warren for the design and funding of this special part of our hospital."

Baylor smiled to herself. It figured that Evelyn was responsible. How she knew Hobie would be there, Baylor didn't even want to guess. She silently pushed open the door. Sure enough, Hobie sat alone on a stone bench near a bubbling water fountain. Baylor stared open-mouthed at the beautiful surroundings. It was a miniature version of the greenhouses Evelyn had at home. There were even some small birds flitting among the branches.

Baylor's plan was to quietly walk up to Hobie, who appeared lost in her own thoughts. She stepped into the room and was startled by a loud squawk. "Jesus Christ!" she cried out, swatting at a brightly colored macaw on its perch. The bird raised its wings and squawked again.

Hobie quickly turned to see the exchange. "That figures," she muttered. She turned away. "What do you want?"

"I, um, I guess I came to find you...to apologize."

"Apologize?"

"Well, yeah."

"Why on earth would you want to apologize to me?"

Baylor looked surprised. She had expected Hobie to be mad, but this seemed like something more. "Um...because I like you. I care about you," she answered uncertainly.

"You shouldn't."

"Huh?"

"Care. I'm not worth it."

"I disagree. Look, Hob, I'm confused. Why do you sound so weird?"

"If you'd known me long enough, it wouldn't sound weird at all," Hobie answered, wearing a bittersweet smile.

"I don't get it."

"I'm mad! All right?" Hobie stood and crossed to where Baylor stood. "I'm just mad!"

"At me?"

"No, at me," Hobie answered. "You're just...in the way."

Baylor concentrated on not smiling. She had a feeling that it would only make Hobie angrier, but it was so hard to keep a straight face. Hobie looked cute, too damn cute. Even if Baylor had wanted to remain angry, she couldn't resist that face. "Can I do anything to help in this little war you seem to have going on between you and you?" Baylor couldn't help it. She smiled the tiniest bit.

That action brought about a much-needed change in Hobie, whose features relaxed for a moment until her brow furrowed. Suddenly she covered her face with both hands.

"I'm so sorry, Baylor. I didn't mean those things. I didn't mean any of it. I didn't mean it when I said I didn't want to see you again, I can be such a bitch. I—"

"Honey, honey." Baylor quickly moved to envelop Hobie in her arms. "It's okay. You know, I did have a small part in all of that nonsense."

"No, no." Hobie shook her head as she buried her face against Baylor's chest. "I'm just that way. I can be such a failure."

"A failure at what?"

"I don't know. Life. Everything."

Baylor pulled away slightly to look at Hobie. She lifted the vet's face and wiped the tears from her cheeks. "Okay, calm down. All right? I don't understand. You're probably the most successful woman I've ever met. You're an MD and a DVM, for God's sake. What do you mean when you say that you're a failure?"

Hobie took a deep breath. "Can we sit?"

"Absolutely."

Once seated, Hobie didn't look up at Baylor. She didn't feel as though she could admit to that part of her past with those soft gray eyes looking at her. It touched her heart when Baylor gently grasped her hands and silently waited for her to begin.

"I was pretty idealistic as a kid. I guess it really intensified after Dad died. I had a pretty rough time with it, but I hid that from everyone. Inside, though, I promised myself that I would never let some other kid go through what I had to go through. Like I said, pretty idealistic."

"I don't have a hard time picturing that," Baylor responded.

Hobie smiled. "I guess I'm not too terribly different than that little kid that everything came so easily for. Maybe I was too smart for my own good. I suppose I thought I could do anything I put my mind to. Maybe it didn't help that I graduated from high school at sixteen and a half."

"You really were a whiz kid, huh?"

Hobie smiled. "Yeah, I was one of those pain-in-the-ass kids you read about. Studies came too easy to me. I sped through my education and when it came time to choose my career path, I went with a branch of medicine that completely suited my character. I wanted to become a surgeon. I had no idea I would turn into such a failure."

Baylor could only stare at the woman seated next to her. "How did you do it?" she asked. "How were you able to change so much, Hobie? You seem so happy and self-confident. You say you failed. Do you mean at medicine?"

Those questions made Hobie feel much better. Baylor hadn't judged her or dismissed her, but simply accepted what Hobie had told her as the truth. Accepted and desired the same sort of change in her own life. To Hobie, that was the most beautiful part.

"It started my third year of med school, when I was actually seeing patients. I started to realize that it wasn't about me. It was about the patients and their families, and I could make a difference. I could save these people, keep them from going—"

"Keep them from going what you went through," Baylor said, squeezing Hobie's hands. "That's a noble impulse."

"Yes, it was, at first. But after my surgical rotation, when I really did start saving lives, I felt like—like I was God, almost. I held people's lives in my hands. I could choose whether they would live or die. I thought I could cheat death." She laughed bitterly. "Can you imagine the arrogance?"

"I'm sure that's not uncommon among surgeons," Baylor said.

"No, it isn't. But then I gave up. I came home. I had just finished my first year of residency when I started to feel...I don't know exactly. I think it was about the time I lost my first baby. We did everything for her, but she was just too small and weak. She got a postoperative infection and died in the middle of the night. I failed at the one thing I swore I would be good at. I finally had to accept that no matter how hard I worked, I couldn't save everyone. I started to see the faces of patients I lost, and I heard their families crying in the waiting rooms."

"So that's when you gave up medicine and came back to the island?" Baylor asked.

"No. I changed over to a family practice residency program. I thought it would be better there and it did help for a while, but then I had a terrible month I went on code after code, and unfortunately that's when I started to drink. At first, it was just a cou-

ple of glasses of wine when I came home at night, something to
relax me. It escalated to the point where I would just drink until I
could look at myself in the mirror, look at myself and not see a
complete failure staring back. That usually meant until I passed
out. It didn't last long enough to become a major problem. It was
only a couple of months before I realized I didn't want to live that
way. I finished up my residency and then I came home."

Baylor smiled in understanding, having undergone some
amazing changes herself since living on the island. "It was Ana
Lia, wasn't it? That changed you."

"I guess that's as good an explanation as any. I felt so lost by
the time I got back home. I had no confidence or ambition of any
kind. I was in a kind of limbo. I think it was a gradual process.
The kind of thing where you can't really look back and identify
the exact point where it all changed. I started to get involved in
people's lives, listening and accepting. Goofy little things like
starting a flower garden or helping out at the grade school. One
day I woke up and realized that I liked myself. I also had a few
conversations with Rebecca Ashby."

Baylor grinned. "The key to happiness."

"Yes. How did you know?"

"I've talked to her a little bit about that very thing. Not that
I'm any closer to figuring it out, but it's an interesting concept."

"It took me a number of years to put it all together. I started
working with Mary Thigpen, a visiting veterinarian. One thing led
to another and here I am today. I can't say it was one thing—it
was a hundred—but I know it wouldn't have happened if I hadn't
come back to Ana Lia. The icing on my cake was having Noah. He
was the only thing I felt I was missing in my life."

"So what is your key?"

"Home. I mean...Oh, this sounds goofy when I say it out
loud."

"No, it doesn't. Really, I'd like to know."

"Well, it doesn't matter where. It's more the *notion* of home,
what it represents. I guess it could be a shack on the beach, but if
what you love, what you care about more than anything is there,
then it's home. For me, that became the key to my happiness. I
realized that as long as I had someplace to think of as home, I'd
never be alone and I'd never be a failure. I'd always have somewhere to go. Right now, that place is Ana Lia. Because even if I
had no family here, I'd still have people who care. I'd always have
a spot on this earth to return to and know that I was loved, that I
don't have to be perfect and that my best will always be good
enough."

"So now your life is just great, eh?"

Hobie let out an ironic chuckle. "Yeah, except for the times when I go off on the people I care about."

"I guess I kind of bring that about, huh?"

"No, Baylor, well, I mean—"

"Hobie, it's okay. You can be honest with me."

"I suppose you don't *help* all the time." Hobie stroked the smooth skin of Baylor's cheek. "I don't blame you, though, because it's not your fault. I'm responsible for me—and my actions. I won't go blaming my behavior on someone else. You're trying; I see that a little more every day. I see how hard you're working at fitting in here, Baylor, and I'm proud of you for that."

"That's why I find your story, your past, so interesting, I guess. I didn't really try, Hobie, not at first anyway. It's something about this island and these people, something...I don't know what, but I know that this place changed me. Of course, now I'm trying, but at first..."

"It just happened. I know. That's exactly the way I felt."

Baylor smiled and leaned in to place a gentle kiss on Hobie's cheek. "You're a wonderful woman, Hobie. I don't really want you to know the person I used to be. I'd prefer you just know the woman I am now, and I want that door to swing both ways. You don't have to be afraid of the way you were or of losing it now and again. I love who you are now, and that's all I really care about."

Baylor took a deep breath. She wondered why she wasn't experiencing the same intense anxiety she had before. If anything, this was an even more profound moment.

"I love you with all of my heart, Hobie Lynn."

Suddenly Hobie's expression changed. Her hands grew cold. She pulled out of Baylor's grasp and stood, quickly walking a few feet away.

"What's going on?" Baylor asked.

"I—maybe we should just think about this."

"I thought you said that you loved me, too," Baylor said.

"I did. I do. It's just—"

Baylor tried to keep the hurt out of her voice. *Just what is she afraid of when it comes to me?* "Hobie, I'm not going to hurt you," she said gently.

"It's okay, never mind," Hobie replied.

Hobie turned back to face Baylor, but her face was an emotionless mask.

"God, you are so frustrating! Why are you so—so...guarded?" Baylor had to struggle for just the right word. "It's like you have all these walls built up around you and you only let me in so far."

"Oh, right. I think telling you my life story, what I used to be like, was a pretty good invitation."

"No. No, it's not. You're guarding yourself like Fort Knox. You let me on the front step, or through the door, but no further. You're acting like you're scared to death of something, and for the life of me I can't figure out what it is."

"I'm not scared."

"You are! What are you afraid of, Hobie?" Baylor placed a hand on the vet's arm.

Hobie pulled free and moved away. The tears made their way down her cheeks. "I am not afraid. Nothing scares me!"

"Bullshit!" Baylor reached Hobie in two strides. "You're terrified and I want to know why. Look at you!" She gestured toward Hobie's nervously intertwined fingers. "What are you so afraid of, Hobie Lynn?"

"You!" Hobie brushed her sudden tears away. "All right? *You* scare me!"

"Me?" Baylor questioned in a soft voice. "Hobie, why do I scare you?"

"Because at first I didn't like you. It didn't matter what you did or how you acted because I didn't care, and then all of sudden you became...nice, and...well, before you could treat people like shit and walk all over them because...because I didn't like you!" Hobie lowered her head as well as her voice. "And now, I like you. I love you. I really love you."

"And that scares you?"

Hobie nodded.

"Why does it scare you to be in love with me, Hobie? I mean, aside from the fact that I'm a loathsome and generally detestable character." Baylor smiled, but couldn't get Hobie to reciprocate.

"I'm thinking of Noah." Hobie lowered her gaze again.

"Noah? But I love Noah, and I thought he was kind of crazy about me, at least—"

"It's not that. It's just that, well, he *is* crazy about you."

"Then the problem would be?"

"Because he likes you, he'll begin to trust you. Trust that you won't lie to him or treat him badly. Then, pretty soon, he'll come to depend on you. Depend that you'll always be there for him and that you'll love him just as much as he loves you. And then one day...one day you'll leave."

"Hobie, you're not really talking about Noah here, are you?" She gently wiped a lone tear from Hobie's cheek. "You're talking about you, right?"

Hobie nodded and fell into the embrace that the writer

offered.

Baylor had always thought of Hobie as a strong woman, one who could take care of herself. At that moment, however, Baylor felt that she wanted, even needed, to protect Hobie. Hobie's father had left her with one lasting impression: he had loved her, and then he had left. It didn't matter that it was death that took him away. To a young girl, things like that didn't matter. What Hobie had always remembered was that things she loved left.

Baylor kissed Hobie's forehead and smoothed her hair. "Hobie, if you're afraid of loving me, well...knowing me the way you do, you have every right to be afraid of that. I can be selfish and controlling. I can act like a child some of the time, and loving anyone other than Tanti and Jules is really new to me." She lifted Hobie's chin. "Frankly, I'd be more worried about your sanity if you weren't afraid."

Hobie returned Baylor's smile with a hesitant one of her own.

"But, if you're afraid of something else, something like—like me leaving, all I can say is that I have some other attributes that you may not know about yet. For one, I'm very loyal. Jules and I have been through some major rows, but I've never thought twice about watching her back, even during our worst fights. I'm faithful, Hobie, honest to God I am. I haven't even been able to think about anyone else since I met you, and I don't see that ever changing. And I know that thinking of someone other than myself is new to me, but I do love you...and Noah. I get a sick kind of feeling in my stomach when I think about anything happening to either one of you. I love the both of you, Hobie Lynn, and I'm not going anywhere."

"It could happen, even if you didn't want it to," Hobie said in a frail voice.

Baylor closed her eyes and prayed she could convince Hobie otherwise. "I know that's what happened to your dad, but that doesn't mean it will happen again. Please, don't live in fear of that. If there's one thing I've learned from being here, from loving you, it's that I can't let my past unhappiness dictate my future. If I do, then I just keep making the same mistakes over and over. Even little kids learn not to touch a hot stove once they've been burned."

She wondered if it was only her imagination, but she thought that Hobie began to look at her differently. She no longer clung to Baylor quite so desperately. The writer didn't think one statement from her would change Hobie's life, but she did hope that the frightened woman would be able to get a sense of what was in her heart.

"I can't predict the future, Hobie, but I do know that I love you and that I have no intention of ever leaving you. I want to be with you, and I don't mean just while I'm on the island or for any sort of affair. I want there to be a commitment between us. It can be here, on the island, or on the moon for all I care. Wherever you and Noah are is where I want my home to be. My question is, do you want the same thing?"

"I'm not any picnic to live with, Noah will tell you that," Hobie said.

"And you think I am?" The writer breathed in a sigh of relief. Hobie was smiling and she looked more like the lovely woman Baylor had come to know.

"I know my fears are unreasonable—"

"Hey, aren't everybody's? If they were reasonable, we'd call them expectations instead of fears. Honey, we've both got some issues, but the best way I can think of to deal with them is to be honest and talk to each other."

"Baylor Warren being open and honest?"

"I didn't say it would be easy, but I'm willing if you are." Baylor waited patiently for the answer that would change her entire life.

Hobie stood on tiptoe to place a soft kiss on Baylor's lips, smiling as she pulled away. Hobie had no idea how she did it, but Baylor Warren had become a complete enigma to her. She couldn't help wondering if their chance meeting in Chicago had been fated from the start. She had no idea how the woman she detested not too long ago could affect such change in her. The idea was one of the many strange occurrences on Ana Lia that Hobie refused to question.

"Yeah." Hobie nodded. "I'm willing, too."

No one knew who was more surprised when Baylor and Hobie walked hand in hand into Evelyn's room. Baylor and Hobie looked at one another as Evelyn and her guest, Rebecca Ashby, exchanged their own looks.

"See, Evie, I told you they would come back together," Rebecca said. "It is together, is it not, ladies?"

Baylor and Hobie nodded.

"Let me guess," Baylor said. "You're the head witch."

Hobie elbowed her in the ribs.

"Wiccan. I meant Wiccan," Baylor added as she rubbed her side and glared at Hobie.

Rebecca chuckled. "I do like this one," she said to Evelyn.

"Baylor, Hobie Lynn, come in and sit, please. I have some information that I think you'll be interested in hearing."

Once they seated themselves, Rebecca began. "I understand, Baylor, that you have some concerns regarding how you came to visit Ana Lia."

Baylor felt the edges of her ears begin to burn.

"Well, we kind of sorted that out," Hobie said.

"Yeah." Baylor winked at the vet. "We pretty much agreed that I overreacted and acted like an idiot."

"Maybe I can help Evelyn in answering some of your questions anyway," Rebecca replied. "I had a feeling I might be needed."

Hobie's brow furrowed. "Mrs. Ashby, how did you get here so fast? Did Evelyn call you and tell you we had an argument?"

"In a manner of speaking, I suppose she did. Like I said, I had a feeling you needed me, and here I am."

"You *are* a witch—damn, I'm sorry, Wiccan," Hobie said. She looked over at Baylor, who wore a smug smile.

"Let's start at the beginning so we don't get confused. Shall we?" Rebecca suggested.

"I think it's already too late for that, but give it your best shot," Baylor answered.

"I think I should start off by saying that you ladies are correct. I'm the present leader of our coven, and it's true, we prefer 'Wiccan,' mostly because of the connotation that other name has. It may help to know that we don't worship the devil and we don't drink blood. Actually, most of us are vegetarians." Rebecca paused.

"It's perfectly acceptable to laugh," she said as Baylor tried to cover a giggle by clearing her throat. "We ought to at least be able to laugh at ourselves. We can talk more about our beliefs later, if you're interested. I thought I'd attempt to ease your minds. Now, Baylor, there are two important things that you should know. The accident that Hobie Lynn and your grandmother were involved in was an accident and nothing more. Are we clear on that?"

"Um, yeah. Thanks," Baylor said. "I guess it was just a little of my paranoia showing through. When I'm thinking clearly I know that there's no way you can really bring two people together."

Baylor's chuckle froze in her throat with Rebecca's next words. "Yes, well, about that..."

Baylor and Hobie each raised an eyebrow.

"Please don't tell me that we're under some kind of spell," Hobie said.

"Heavens, no, my dear. Even if we could do something of that sort, we simply don't play with people's lives that way. We serve nature, not things that go against nature."

"There's more though, isn't there?" Baylor grew suspicious. "I see it in your eyes, Tanti."

"We don't put spells on people, but we do believe in the Fates. We're students of human nature. We simply...coordinate."

"And what exactly does that mean in regards to us?" Baylor questioned.

Rebecca took a long breath. "That's the second thing I was going to tell you. We never manipulated either of you in any way, but we did arrange to have you, well, meet one another, spend time together."

"And you don't call that manipulation?" Hobie asked. "Starting when? All the way back to Chicago?"

"What?" Baylor chimed in. "Honey, that's impossible."

"Not so impossible. Cheryl, my office assistant, makes all my travel arrangements. That includes booking my hotel rooms and recommending restaurants to eat at."

"That could just be coinci—"

"And Cheryl belongs to the Ladies Guild," Hobie finished.

Hobie and Baylor looked to Rebecca for an answer.

"Yes, all the way back to Chicago," Rebecca admitted. "But we never did anything other than arrange for the two of you to be in the same area at the same time. Anything more has always been up to the Fates, I promise you that. We never could have *made* the two of you love one another, or even like each other, if it hadn't been a part of your destinies already."

"I don't believe what I'm hearing," Hobie responded angrily.

"Wait a minute. Are you trying to say that Hobie and I were destined to be together? That sounds like one of Harriet Teasley's plotlines," Baylor added with a smirk.

"Can I ask why you did all this in the first place?"

"To save our island." Evelyn finally spoke. "To keep its power alive, at any rate."

"Okay, this is starting to get a little too ooh-ooh for me," Baylor said.

"I think we need to tell them everything, from the beginning," Evelyn said to Rebecca.

"What a refreshing change," Baylor responded.

"We're all ears." Hobie folded her arms across her chest.

"I'm going to ask only one thing," Rebecca said. She quickly continued when neither woman responded. "I'm going to ask that you listen to this with a completely open mind, no preconceived notions about witches, spells, or anything of that nature. When I'm through, simply ask yourselves if what I have told you *feels* right. Agreed?"

Baylor shrugged, which surprised Hobie. "Okay, go for it," she replied.

"I think it would be easiest to tell you how Ana Lia Island came to be, before anything else. In 1702, Spain controlled a large portion of the area we now know as Florida. Ana Lia, which had another name back then, was just one of many small islands that existed in the Gulf. Native Americans mostly inhabited the islands at that time. It was then that the Count Alejandro Santiago and his new bride arrived. The count's job was an easy one—protect Spain's interests in the new world. Spain always searched these new territories for gold to fund their wars."

Rebecca paused to take a sip of water. "The count's new bride, Countess Ana Santiago, was only seventeen, but she had a grace and a dignity about her that few women her age knew. She didn't love the count; neither did he love her. Their marriage brought two powerful families together, and that's all that was important in those days. Ana didn't like the role that society forced women to play, but she accepted it as her mother before her had done. What was worse for Ana was that the count was three times her age. Ana did her best, however, to be a good wife. She was different from most women of her time. She loved to learn, especially to write. Her solitude on the island did at least afford her the time to pursue such studies.

"It was during their first year on the island that the count became ill. The fever lasted for weeks, then months. Ana would have taken him back to Spain had she thought he could handle the long ocean voyage. The count's doctors were perplexed by the illness. They worried that the raging fever would eventually prove fatal.

"One day, a girl approached Ana. She was a native girl, a Seminole Indian. She and her family worked for the count's household. Her was Lia, and she explained that her people knew her as a healer. Ana and Lia spent the entire day talking, and eventually Lia convinced Ana to allow her to see the count."

Rebecca stopped for another sip of water. Baylor and Hobie's attentive expressions encouraged her to continue. "To make a long story a little shorter, Lia's herbs and teas worked. Unfortunately, the fever had taken its toll on the count. He never fully recovered, and day after day he lingered in his sickbed. It's now believed that the fever caused seizures or a stroke. Now, the other side to this unfortunate circumstance was that the countess and Lia became good friends. Because of her husband's condition, Ana spent more and more time with her new friend, and she taught her Spanish. Lia took the countess to the island where her people lived and taught her what she knew about healing. It surprised them both on the day that they discovered they were in love with one another.

"Because the countess was an honorable woman, she told Lia that she could never be with her as long as she was married to Alejandro. Lia understood and even though it broke her heart, she expected nothing less from the woman who had captured her heart. Their love grew stronger as the days and, eventually, the years passed."

"Well?" Hobie asked when Rebecca stopped talking. "What happened? Did the count die? Did they—"

"I didn't know you were such a closet romantic."

"Very funny," Hobie said. "I just wanted to know if they ever got together."

"Honey, the island's called Ana Lia. I think that's a good indication."

"Oh, yeah."

"Actually," Rebecca said, "the count did die, but not for another twenty-four years."

"Years?" Hobie asked. "Good Lord. What happened to the two women?"

"They stayed together, and their love grew stronger with every day that passed. Ana begged Lia to find someone who was free to commit to her fully, but Lia could love no other. So they lived through the years on the island, spending their days together, but never their nights. Until the day that Count Santiago died.

"It was another three months before Ana's mourning period for her husband had ended. Ana wrote a letter of explanation to her mother, then left the estate that had been her home for twenty-five years. She left with Lia and together they sailed to the island where Lia's family lived. They lived there for the rest of their lives.

"On the night that the two women came together to commit their hearts to one another and consummate their love, a miracle happened in the skies above the island. On that first night, two stars that had burned brighter than any others came together in alignment. Until the sun rose in the sky the next morning, those two stars looked to be as one. Fifty years later, both women died peacefully in their sleep. From then on, the island became known as Ana Lia.

"Now, in the years before their death, the two women lived lives that were full of love and happiness. Their island developed into a mystical place, a place of power. In the 1800s, people even looked there for the fountain of youth—to no avail, of course. In later years it lost some of its magical properties, but even to this day people do experience a certain...I'm not sure how to put it."

"I think we know precisely what you're trying to say," Hobie answered.

"Okay, so even if we believed the story and the possibility that Ana Lia has some sort of...weird stuff going on, what does this have to do with getting Hobie and me together?" Baylor asked.

"That brings us to our last area of discussion," Rebecca said. "The order that we belong to," she indicated Evelyn with a nod, "the Ladies Guild, has existed since just before the deaths of Countess Ana Santiago and Lia. We are responsible for maintaining the unexplainable power of Ana Lia Island. You see, ever since that first night when Ana and Lia came together, the stars prepare us for the event's reoccurrence. It happens every fifty years. Members of the Ladies Guild receive...visions, for lack of a better term. These visions speak of two women with the potential and the strength to take the place of the two lovers, Ana and Lia."

"Uh-oh. I think I know where we come in now," Baylor whispered to Hobie.

"So you saw us?" Hobie asked.

"We weren't certain because of...shall we say, the animosity you initially had for one another. The signs are unmistakable, though," Evelyn answered.

"Signs?" Baylor and Hobie both asked.

"There are only three real qualifications," Evelyn answered. "Of course, you must be in love..."

"Check," Baylor grinned and looked at Hobie.

"One of you must be skilled in healing, and the other must make her way in the arts..."

"Check again," Baylor said.

"Finally, you must be the ages that Ana and Lia were when they came together. Ana was 42 and Lia was 38."

"Che—oh, wow," Baylor said. "Wait a minute. What exactly are you saying, that we're some kind of reincarnations of these women?"

"No, not at all," Rebecca answered. "I'll say it in the simplest way I can. For hundreds of years, this island has had some sort of power associated with it. The Ladies Guild passes on the knowledge that this power comes from love."

"Love?" Hobie looked at Baylor and was surprised at her expression. "You're not buying into all of this, are you?"

"I know it sounds crazy, and you know me. Usually I'm the first one to tell people that they're wacko, but this feels...I don't know what it feels like, but it's kind of weird."

Hobie rolled her eyes. "Part of me wants to believe. It was a beautiful story, but things don't happen that way in real life. Do they?"

"Hobie, can you explain us? Didn't we both just admit that some sort of power changed the two of us? For some reason, I'm just not convinced that an emotion like love doesn't have that kind of power. Look at us. Love nearly destroyed our lives, mine from the lack of it and yours from the fear of losing it. I don't know about you, but I was a mess. My whole life was a complete and utter bust right up until the point where I met you. Now, if love has that much power, couldn't it happen as they say? Couldn't it have an even stronger power when used positively?"

"Okay, now I don't know what to think," Hobie responded. "I figured you'd be more skeptical than me."

"Maybe it's the island." Baylor chuckled as she nudged Hobie.

"Very funny. When I hear you, it makes sense, but when I start to think about this whole thing—"

"Ah, there's your problem. Mrs. Ashby said to listen with your heart, not your head. Does all of this *feel* right to you? Well, does it?"

"I guess..."

"Then there you are. Don't think it to death, Hobie Lynn."

Hobie suddenly grinned. "What, and lose my membership in Skeptics Anonymous? Oh, all right, you win. Yes, it does *feel* right, and if I think with my heart and not my head, this all sounds perfectly plausible. So, what is it exactly that you want from us?"

"I'm glad you asked," Rebecca said. "The power of Ana Lia, which comes from a love unlike many others, changes hands every fifty years. Every fifty years since the first night that Ana and Lia spent together, when the stars became as one, the stars repeat that miracle if the selected women commit to one another in a ceremony on that evening. Only once was the guild unable to find the right couple. During that cycle, Ana Lia's power was noticeably depleted."

"Do we have to live here for fifty years? What if we need to—"

"No, no, not at all," Evelyn answered. "The guild found that it was the coming together that brought out the power in the island."

"So, all you want us to do is to have, like, a wedding cere-mony on one particular night?" Baylor asked.

"Correct. Well, um..." Evelyn looked uncomfortable.

"What Evie is trying to say is that the ceremony goes hand in hand with the physical expression of your love."

"Ohh," Baylor and Hobie answered in unison, both blushing.

"I don't know. Hobie? I mean, we did already agree to..."

"Yeah, I know. I guess. I mean, it's not like we have to drink blood or bite the heads off of chickens or anything. Right?" Hobie asked Rebecca.

"We tend to prefer champagne and pâté at these functions, but I suppose allowances could be made if you have a preference."

Baylor laughed aloud. "I believe she has a sense of humor," she told Hobie.

Hobie couldn't think of a witty enough response, so she set-tled for sticking her tongue out.

"Oh, that's attractive."

"You are such a comedian all of a sudden," Hobie replied, but she couldn't help smiling. "Just one more question. What if we don't believe it, not completely, anyway? Will that affect this power?"

"Not at all, my dear," Rebecca answered. "You don't neces-sarily have to believe in the magic. All you really have to do to make it work is to believe in one another."

Hobie smiled at the answer. "That I can do. I guess the next logical question is when does all this have to happen?"

"In three days," Rebecca and Evelyn answered.

"Three days!" It was Baylor and Hobie's turn to respond as one.

The room was silent for a few moments. Finally, Hobie looked up at Baylor. "Were we really going to do it anyway?"

Baylor smiled gently and then lifted Hobie's hand to her lips. After placing a light kiss upon Hobie's fingers, she responded. "Absolutely," she said. "Absolutely." There was conviction in the repeated word.

"Then I guess we're to be married," Hobie said at last.

Rebecca and Evelyn quickly began discussing plans for the ceremony. The other women didn't mind. Actually, it was proba-bly a good thing, because Baylor and Hobie were in the middle of a kiss that looked as though it was going to last for quite some time.

Chapter
16

Hobie put the cast saw down on the sturdy metal tray and pried the rest of the plaster off Baylor's leg. "Voilà," she said with a flourish.

"Oh my god!" Baylor cried out.

"What? What is it?" Hobie asked.

"I have a toothpick for a leg. What happened to it?"

"Baylor, you've had a cast on it for over ten weeks. It's just a little muscle atrophy. It'll come back as soon as you start using it again."

"I kinda liked the way it looked before," the writer said with a pout.

"And you'll grow just as attached to this new and improved version. Now, remember, I want you to take it easy today and continue to use your cane. Come on, let's take a few practice walks."

"I think I know how to walk," Baylor said as she swung her legs over the side of the examination table. "I've actually been doing it quite successfully for a number of years and I find it surprisingly easy."

"What a comedian you are today."

"Thanks. Whoa!" Baylor's leg gave out on only the second step. "I thought you said it wasn't broken anymore?"

"It's not, but you also haven't used it in a couple of months, not without support anyway, Miss I've been walking all my life."

Baylor looked up at Hobie with what she hoped was an intimidating expression.

Hobie continued to gloat.

"You know, a smirk that big is not very becoming on a lady of your position."

"I don't get to do it too much anymore. Humor me." Hobie went to the door. "Hey, Lor, give me a hand, will you?"

Once Laura arrived, Hobie told her what she wanted her to do. "Okay," she explained to Baylor. "Put one arm around my shoulder and the other over Lor's."

"This position has possibilities."

"Don't you wish," Hobie replied.

Baylor winked. At first, she winced with every step, but after she had worked some of the stiffness out, she found that she could walk quite well using her cane.

"You're a new woman," Hobie declared. "Okay, get dressed and out of my exam room. I have a pregnant Saint Bernard who needs the bed."

"Oh, I see where your priorities are." Baylor got dressed as Hobie put away some of the instruments. "Man, I've got to get to the drugstore," she said.

"What's wrong?"

"My leg looks like it belongs to a gorilla. I need to get some razors." It felt good to finally wear her favorite old jeans. "Okay, I'm outta here. Thanks, hon."

"Wait just a minute," Hobie called out. "Forget something?" She waggled Baylor's cane.

"Oh." Baylor chuckled nervously. "Yeah, how could I forget?"

"Baylor, remember what I said about taking it easy at first?"

"Sure, sure," Baylor answered distractedly. "You said not to walk too much today."

"No, what I said was to go home and put your foot up for a couple hours, then take a short walk, maybe five minutes. After that, put your foot up again and repeat the walk every three or four hours."

"Sure, sure. I will," Baylor added defensively at Hobie's exasperated look.

"Sweetheart, I don't mean to be a rag. Please remember that pain is your body's way of telling you something."

"I know, I won't forget." Baylor kissed Hobie's forehead and turned to leave once more.

"Baylor." Hobie still held the cane.

"Aw, shit, I forgot! Well, it's because you're confusing me."

Hobie closed her eyes and shook her head. "Tell me again, what is your leg saying to you when it hurts?"

Baylor stood at attention as she repeated the instructions in a steady monotone. "If my leg starts to hurt, it's saying to me, 'For God's sake, Baylor, sit down, put some ice on me, and have another margarita.'"

Hobie's brows scrunched together and she pushed her glasses up. "I don't remember saying anything about margaritas."

"No, I added that," Baylor said with a quick grin. "It sounded very medicinal."

"God, I worry about you."

"Who, me?" Baylor put a hand on her chest. "Just think, hon. You get to do this for the rest of your life."

"To some people that would be a threat. Go on. Out." Hobie pointed. She couldn't stop her laughter. Baylor might have been a giant pain in the ass at one time, but nowadays she was downright lovable. Her charm and sense of humor reeled Hobie in, just as they had done on that very first night in Chicago. "I love you, go home."

"Love you, too. Don't forget the barbecue tonight. Tell Noah to bring his trunks and he can swim before dinner."

"Deal. He'll love playing in the pool with you."

"Don't get his hopes up on that count."

"What's that mean?"

"We'll, um, talk about that later. Jules is going to go pick up Tanti and bring her home. I find it extremely odd that she recovered so quickly after hearing we were together. It's probably just my own paranoia showing again, but I wonder if there was any hocus-pocus involved in Tanti's illness. Aside from her broken hip, that is."

"Nope, it's not just you. I have a sneaky feeling that we don't *even* want to think about what the Ladies Guild might have had to do in order to pull that one off."

Baylor rubbed her hands together once more. The evening had finally arrived, and her palms got clammier as the moment of their ceremony grew closer.

"You look a little wobbly, mate." Juliana affectionately slapped Baylor on the back.

Baylor made a halfhearted attempt at a grin. "Most of me thinks this is the best day of my life, but there's a tiny piece of me, Jules, that just feels like throwing up."

"Actually, that sounds pretty normal, considering this is your wedding day. Or night, as the case may be. Pretty nice of Mrs. Ashby to have the ceremony here at her house. It's beautiful by the water like this."

"Yeah," Baylor answered distractedly. She looked over Juliana's shoulder to the woman who just had come outside. In Baylor's eyes, Hobie looked better than any woman had a right to.

"Hey, you two look cute. She's wearing a dress and you've got on slacks. You two plan this little butch-femme thing?" Juliana asked.

Baylor graced her with an arched eyebrow and a flat expression. "With that sense of humor it's no wonder you're still single," she finally said.

Juliana laughed and walked away. Hobie met her halfway across the large lawn, obviously on her way to where Baylor stood. She gave her a hug.

"You look absolutely wicked. This is your last chance, you know. You can still dump that girl and take a shot with me." Juliana's smile was infectious and Hobie found herself laughing.

"Please, Jules. Are you *trying* to start a fight? If Baylor hears that, it'll be World War III."

"Well, I thought I'd send you over Baylor's way to calm her down, but by the feel of these ice-cold hands of yours, it seems you're a bigger bundle of nerves than she is."

"Oh, very funny. Don't even think of lying to me, Jules. The prospect of spending the rest of your life with someone would make you a little goofy, too. Admit it."

"A little?" Juliana winked. "I'm really just jealous as hell. You do know that, don't you? Well, jealous of Baylor, at any rate. You I simply feel sorry for."

"Is she really that nervous?" Hobie asked, glancing in Baylor's direction. The brunette stood tall and straight, staring out at the ocean, her stance almost regal as twilight descended around her.

"You'd never know it to look at her, but right there stands a quivering tower of jelly."

Hobie chuckled and shook her head. "She looks like she's a million miles away. I think I'll go ease her fears."

Juliana could see the excitement mixed with the trepidation in Hobie's eyes. *They have no idea what they've found in one another,* she thought.

Baylor watched as Juliana met up with Hobie, laughing and teasing her just as she had Baylor. She had a feeling they were talking about her. She turned away and looked out at the water.

So many changes, Baylor mused. She wondered at the future and how her life would change with the ceremony. Any number of people would have told her that she was crazy to think it would last. Most of the acquaintances that still tolerated her played the same games she had. Straight or gay, they went from relationship to relationship without really thinking they would last. Baylor had never thought long term before Hobie. That would all change. Baylor just knew, in the same way that she knew which of her stories would sell, that if she went through with this ceremony, it would be forever. It was a scary prospect; terrifying, if the truth were known. So the question became, did she even want to back out?

She smiled to herself, glad nobody could see her face. Everyone thought she was strange enough as it was. Of course, for most of them "strange" was a relative term. The last two days had been a whirlwind of activity, mostly planning for the very future that she now pondered. Their first serious discussion had been about where they should live. Ana Lia had been good to Baylor and Hobie, and Baylor had never even thought about going back to Chicago for longer than the few weeks it would take to pack up her life. School was out, so they decided to take Noah with them and make it a vacation. Even though Hobie had told her it wasn't necessary, Baylor was rather looking forward to sharing with Noah some of the places that had impressed her as a child. Wrigley Field, Lincoln Park Zoo, and the Art Institute were all places she wanted to share with him, and she just knew that having a hot dog and watching the Cubs play at home would mean the world to Noah.

Baylor also wanted Hobie with her. She was afraid of what might happen to her once she left the island. Would she return to her old ways? Even though Hobie assured her that it hadn't worked that way for her, Baylor didn't want to take that chance.

They finally decided they would build a house on Ana Lia and live in Hobie's guest-house in the meantime. Hobie's family was happy about the arrangement, and it worked to Evelyn's advantage, too. As much as she adored having her granddaughter, Hobie, and Noah close, she was a private person and enjoyed living surrounded by the quiet of her greenhouses.

Baylor looked up at the evening sky. The two stars her grandmother had pointed out the previous evening certainly didn't appear any closer. She wondered what would happen during the ceremony and if there was actually any truth to Rebecca's tale. She looked down at her watch. It wouldn't be long before she found out.

"Hey, lady, does the bus stop here?" Hobie asked as she came up behind Baylor and slipped an arm around her waist.

Baylor smiled as she placed her own arm around Hobie's shoulder. "If it doesn't, I'll make it happen for ya."

"I believe you would. So, are you standing over here thinking, worrying, or a little of both?"

Baylor looked out over the water again and took a deep breath. "Wondering," she answered at last. "But no worries, especially today."

"What a con artist you are, Baylor Warren. You mean to tell me that you're not the least bit nervous?"

"I didn't say that. I'm scared to death, and I'll admit there's not a bone in my body that isn't screaming at me to turn around and run as fast as I can."

"Oh?"

"Now who's conning who? Do you mean to tell me that you don't feel the same way?"

Hobie chuckled and studied the ground for a moment. "Okay, I give up. I thought about playing the part of the gingerbread man, but it was only temporary."

"Don't worry, baby, mine was, too. I'm still scared—scared as hell—but there's one thing I'm not, and that's worried over the prospect of spending my life with you."

"I just hope you're not setting yourself up for a fall. You know, some idea of me as the perfect woman."

"I think I pretty much know better than that."

"Thanks a lot!" Hobie slapped Baylor lightly on the stomach.

"Hey, you stepped into that one," Baylor responded. "I don't think I have too many illusions, honey. You and I, we're like fire and ice. I'm almost certain that, given enough time, we'll run into areas where we disagree. Now, if I know the two of us as well as I think I do, then those disagreements are probably going to lead to some damn good fireworks. Just like real fireworks, though, they'll explode and then burn out quicker than anything."

"When you want to, you sure can put some nice words together. Do you know that?"

"I don't even have to work hard at it when it comes to you."

The two women embraced. No one appeared to be paying any attention to them; it was as if they were all alone.

"We can do this, right, Baylor?"

"Yes, baby, we can," Baylor answered before placing a kiss on the top of Hobie's head. She looked up at the two bright stars overhead. "Tell me, do they look any closer at all to you?"

"Well, maybe if I try real hard..."

"Do you believe any of this? I mean, I know these old gals are all pretty trustworthy, but I'm having a hard time with this. How about you?"

"I believe that they believe. I'm with you. I'm not sure I can be a staunch supporter just yet. But like they said, we don't have to believe in order for it to work. Whether it all comes together or not, I feel like we've helped a small bit."

"Ditto. Well, shall we?"

"I'm game if you are."

They had nearly reached the spot where the ceremony would take place. Noah rushed up to them.

"Baylor!" he called out as he jumped into her arms.

"Hey, Bubba, don't you look sharp in your suit and tie."

"Are you guys gettin' married?" Noah asked.

Baylor looked at Hobie, who silently nodded her head. "Um, yeah," she answered.

"Good. Then I can have a dad."

Baylor looked back at Hobie again and swore she saw Hobie smiling just a tiny bit. "Well, Bubba, um...you do know that I'm a girl, right?"

"Yeah."

"I'd be more along the lines of a mom, then."

"But I already got a mom."

"I guess I see your point, but what do you have if you go get an ice-cream cone and they decide to give you two chocolate cones instead of one?"

Noah shrugged.

"It'd be better, wouldn't it?"

"Two chocolate cones, all for me?" Noah asked. His eyes widened and a smile began to take shape.

"All for you, Bubba. Great, huh?"

"Great!"

"Now, I bet all your friends only have one mom. How do you think it would be having two moms, instead of just one?"

Noah's smile widened. "Great!" he exclaimed.

"You know it," Baylor agreed. "Okay, you go on and keep Jules company till we get started. She'll give you the rings. Okay?"

"'Kay, Baylor." He paused once she set him on solid ground. "You guys look beautiful," he added before running away.

"Nice save," Hobie said.

"Oh yeah, thanks for pitching right in there."

"You did better than I could have. You're a natural as a mom."

"I sure hope so. Parenting isn't exactly the kind of thing you get a do-over on."

Baylor looked past Hobie. A tasteful archway of small red and white flowers was the main stage for their ceremony. A long table was set up in front of the arch, and a number of women from the Guild stood around the table, preventing the couple from seeing what was on it.

"What in the world are they doing?" Baylor asked.

"God only knows. Maybe it's the sacrifice," Hobie replied.

"Don't make me crazier than I already am about this whole thing."

"Sorry," Hobie said through her light laughter. "You're about to find out. Mrs. Ashby is waving us over. Ready?"

"If you are."

"Baylor?" Hobie reached for Baylor's arm just as she took a step away.

"Hmm?"

"I do love you and I would have married you anyway, you know."

Baylor smiled, reminding Hobie that there was another woman behind that prickly outer shell. "I love you, too. Actually, it was probably a good thing. The Ladies Guild forced me to wait a couple of days."

Baylor and Hobie arrived just as Hobie's mother gave Noah and Juliana their last-minute instructions. Noah was taking his job seriously, listening intently to his grandmother. Hobie had wanted both her friends from the office—Laura and Cheryl—to stand up with her. That left Baylor short a friend, but she thought of Noah immediately. He was thrilled by the news.

"Baylor, Hobie Lynn, are you ready to begin?"

Both women nodded. The guests took their seats in the white garden chairs as the members of the wedding party arranged themselves, giving Hobie and Baylor their first real look at the table.

"What the hell is that thing?" Hobie beat Baylor to the punch by asking.

They stood staring at a metal monstrosity that took up most of the tabletop. Baylor had the strangest feeling that she had seen the object somewhere before. "Is that an orrery?"

The object did indeed appear to be a brass model of the solar system. Each ornately formed planet was mounted on a rod that moved independent of all of the other rods, connected in the center to what appeared to be the sun. However, there appeared to be more than a few extra planets, and simple round brass rings topped two of the rods. The center area had a flat top that supported two empty crystal champagne glasses. Hobie and Baylor looked at each other again.

"I suppose you're wondering what this is?" Rebecca asked. She was elegantly dressed, as always, and leaned slightly upon her walking stick.

"It may just be me, but I've always thought flowers made a good centerpiece," Baylor said.

Hobie nudged the tall woman with her elbow.

"I know it must appear terribly odd to you, but you'll both

have to trust me. The Pentasium is a three-dimensional planetary map. It's essential to the ceremony and its use will become quite clear in a short while. Let's begin, shall we?"

"It's probably a way to communicate with the mother ship," Baylor whispered to Hobie.

The ceremony proceeded as smoothly as if they'd all performed it every day of their lives. Rebecca, along with two women from the Guild, attended to the candles on the table. They lit the long line in order, from the outside in. Rebecca read a number of short passages, one in a language that neither Baylor nor Hobie recognized.

Finally, she stood before Hobie and Baylor. "It's time for you to say a few words, Baylor."

"Huh?" Baylor didn't remember anyone saying anything about vows or telling her that she had to speak in any way. She looked at Hobie, who shrugged as though she didn't understand either. "Say something?" she questioned in a low voice.

"The stars request a petition to show that you're ready."

"The stars?"

"The stars will only come together upon confirmation of your love for one another. All you have to do is make a statement regarding your love, your commitment to Hobie Lynn. Tell her what she does for your life, how loving her affects you."

"You guys didn't say anything about talking in front of everyone," Baylor responded under her breath.

"It doesn't have to be the Gettysburg Address, Baylor. Simple is good," Rebecca answered. A few more moments passed in silence. "Baylor?"

"I'm thinking!" Baylor felt a tug on her slacks. She looked down to see Noah's earnest face staring back at her.

"You can do it, Baylor. Come on." He smiled.

Baylor couldn't help smiling back. She loved the youngster who seemed to have so much more courage than she herself did. She winked at him and took a deep breath. She had no idea what to say, but the moment she turned and looked into Hobie's eyes, the words were there. "I'm probably going to sound like a real idiot here."

Hobie reached out to quickly grasp Baylor's hand.

It only took one squeeze to ground Baylor. She focused her attention on her heart and listened to what it had to tell her. "Hobie Lynn, the best thing I can think of to say about you is that you make me want to be a better person. I suppose the funny thing is...when I'm with you, I think I am."

"I think that's the sweetest thing anyone's ever said to me,"

Hobie replied.

Rebecca nodded appreciatively and Baylor breathed a small sigh of relief.

"Hobie Lynn?"

Smiling nervously, Hobie looked at Baylor. She loved so many things about the obstinate, sometimes eccentric, woman. To pick just one would be difficult, so Hobie concentrated on the one thing that had made the strongest impact on her.

"Baylor, you know I love you. You've made me feel very well loved in the short time that we've known one another. Since we decided to be together, I'm not afraid anymore. That sounds so silly, I know."

She looked down at her shoes before returning her gaze to Baylor. "I used to wake up in the morning afraid of what the day would bring, terrified of the smallest things. I don't feel that at all now, and it's all because of you and the love you've shown me."

"Wow," Baylor responded. She was unable to say more. Such a simple declaration, yet the words had such power.

"Ah, the timing couldn't be better," Rebecca said. She smiled brightly and gestured toward the Pentasium.

"Did you see that?" Baylor asked.

"Maybe," Hobie said slowly. "You tell me what you saw and I'll tell you if it's the same."

"Hobie, it's moving."

"Yep, that's what I saw, all right."

They watched in fascination as the arms began to move, slowly at first, but eventually picking up speed. It only took a few moments for the contraption to look like a wild carnival ride. As they revolved around the sunlike center, the planets also rotated on their brass rods.

Baylor chose that moment to look up into the nighttime sky. "Oh my god."

Hobie followed Baylor's line of vision. She took in a sharp breath as she watched the two stars that were the focus of the evening. "I don't believe it," she whispered. "They're closer."

"They're *really* close," Baylor echoed. The bright stars appeared to be on a collision course with one another.

A loud pop caused Hobie and Baylor to jerk in surprise, and Hobie held her hand to her chest once she discovered that Rebecca had opened a bottle of champagne. Carefully maneuvering around the rods, Rebecca poured the champagne into the two glasses. She didn't even have to look up to see how close the stars were. She remembered the previous ceremony as though it just taken place.

Just as the two rods bearing the brass rings came into perfect alignment, Rebecca picked up a small bowl that had been hand carved from a solid piece of jade. She lifted the lid and placed it to one side. Inside the polished green bowl was a small mound of white crystalline sugar stars.

"To love, long life, and Ana Lia." Rebecca held the bowl up to the sky at the exact moment that the two stars collided overhead.

The impact caused the two stars to explode into one. Their light shot down to earth in a single beam, passing directly through the open rings of the Pentasium and culminating in a brilliant explosion just as Rebecca dropped two of the crystal stars into each glass. Whether it was due to the light or the sugary stars, the champagne frothed and foamed over the sides of the glasses.

"To Ana Lia." Rebecca offered a glass to Hobie, then to Baylor.

"To Ana Lia," the ladies of the guild echoed.

Stunned into silence, Hobie and Baylor drank to the toast. They knew they would discuss the subject at great length one day, but at that moment, all they could do was stare at the sky and one another.

Chapter
17

"How long will they stay that way, Tanti?" Baylor asked.

"Until dawn," her grandmother answered. "Tomorrow evening, when the stars come out again, your two stars will appear exactly as they did before."

The women sat in a pair of comfortable chairs set far back on the expansive lawn. Evelyn's walker rested beside her chair, but she swore that she wouldn't need it for too much longer. Beside the walker lay Arturo, sound asleep. Noah and his friends had worn the poor pup out, and he lay on his back with all four paws in the air, snoring pleasantly.

Rebecca Ashby had spared no expense. The Cove had arranged a beautiful buffet that spread across three tables, and it seemed as if everyone on Ana Lia stopped by to wish Baylor and Hobie well. There was even a small string quartet set up on the lawn playing Vivaldi.

Baylor studied her grandmother's profile. Evelyn looked almost sad as she stared out over the ocean.

"Aimee used to love that sound," she said distractedly. "The sound of the waves breaking onto the shore."

Baylor watched as her expression grew even sadder. "You must miss her so much." She hadn't really comforted her grandmother very much after Aimee died, not that her grandmother was one to allow anyone to hover. Baylor deeply regretted the depth of her self-involvement, which had prevented her from seeing what was evident to everyone else.

Evelyn turned toward Baylor. "We had so many more years together than anyone ever anticipated, dear heart. When the doctors first diagnosed Aimee's cancer, they told us she only had a year or two to live. She lived for another twenty after that."

"That's incredible. I had no idea." Baylor smirked at the old woman. "More Ana Lia magic?"

Evelyn chuckled and held her hands up in a "who knows"

gesture.

Baylor couldn't even imagine the pain she knew would follow should anything happen to Hobie. "Weren't you angry about any of it? Mad that she was taken away from you?"

"Those twenty years we always considered a gift from Ana Lia. How could I be angry when we were given so much more time than we expected?"

"It was you—the two of you, wasn't it?"

"Hmm?" Evelyn turned from her introspection.

"You and Aimee. The stars came together fifty years ago for the two of you, didn't they?"

"Yes, it was us, all right. I meant it when I told you that I understood what you were going through. Aimee had to practically drag me kicking and screaming to our ceremony. I'm more like you than you know, dear heart," Evelyn added with a wink.

"I suppose I should have known." Baylor shook her head and smiled. "You know, I'm going to want to hear about it all. Actually, I want to hear about a lot of your life, Tanti. It's my own fault, but I feel like I've missed a lot of it."

"Agreed. We'll have our time, but you have other things to do tonight."

"Hey, you're right. It's getting late, too. Do you want me to take you home?"

"On your wedding night? No, I'm staying here with Rebecca for the night. Did you set everything up like you wanted for you and Hobie?"

"Yeah." Baylor grinned. "I'm glad I found out she likes your tropical atrium at the hospital so much."

"She'll be very pleased. I know it."

Baylor stood and stretched her legs. "I better mingle or folks are gonna think I'm antisocial. Besides, I saw Hobie giving me that 'why are you hiding in the corner' look."

"I think I'll sit here and listen to the waves for a little bit longer."

"You sure?"

"Absolutely. Go on now."

Baylor started to walk away, then stopped abruptly. She turned to face her grandmother once again. "I'm glad I could finally do something to make you proud of me, Tanti."

The older woman reached out and squeezed Baylor's hand. "Baylor Joan, I may not have always been proud of the things you did, but I have always been proud of you."

Baylor, her eyes full of tears, bent at the waist and gently kissed Evelyn's cheek. She couldn't speak for fear of breaking down completely.

"I didn't mean to make you sad," Evelyn said. "Not tonight of all nights."

"Not sad, Tanti. Between you and Hobie, you make me feel better than I ever have. All my life I'd been told that I was less than nothing, and now I find out that I was something all along."

Baylor kissed her again and quickly walked away. She saw Hobie standing by one of the drink tables, pouring a glass of iced tea. Baylor easily slipped up behind her. "Hey there, beautiful," she said as she put an arm around Hobie's waist. "Why don't you run away with me?"

Hobie leaned back against the tall body and chuckled lightly. She rested one hand on Baylor's arm. "Well, I am a married woman."

"I bet she's not half as good as I can be," Baylor whispered into Hobie's ear.

"Oh? Bold talk."

"Trust me, I can back it up."

There was a brief silence and then both women broke into laughter.

"I love you, Hobie."

"Love you, too." Hobie turned to share a gentle kiss with her new partner.

"I was halfway serious—about being ready to leave, that is," Baylor said. "You about ready to go home?"

"More than ready. Wait a minute. Where do you mean when you say 'home'?"

Baylor smiled. "I mean Tanti's. She's spending the night here and Jules is baby-sitting Noah at your place. I have something special arranged for us back at Tanti's."

"Well, you thought of everything."

"Hey, somebody had to."

"I was busy, you know." Hobie earnestly defended herself. "I had to deliver a breech foal this afternoon. I was up to my armpits in places you don't want to know about."

"Oh, lovely. I have a nice romantic vision of you on our wedding day now." Baylor laughed at Hobie's serious expression. "I'm just teasing you, Doc. I know you had to work. Besides, Mrs. Fazzini already told me how you saved the life of their $200,000 mare, not to mention the baby horse."

"Foal."

"Yeah, whatever. Wait a minute, I thought baby horses were ponies?"

"Something else entirely. Don't worry, you'll learn all about animals soon."

"Just be patient with me. We don't get a lot of wildlife on Lake Shore Drive. Besides pigeons, I mean."

"You enjoy giving me a hard time, don't you?" Baylor's smile reminded Hobie of her son's hearty, childish grin.

"Yeah, I kinda do," Baylor answered.

"Just be careful, my dear, and remember what happened to the young lady from Niger."

"Ooh, is that a threat?" Baylor grabbed Hobie a little tighter and moved to tickle her.

"That's a promise, tough girl," Hobie replied as she squirmed to elude Baylor's wandering hands. "Okay, okay," she laughed. "Uncle!"

It was at that moment that they looked up to see Juliana carrying a limp Noah in her arms.

"What happened?" Hobie rushed toward them.

Suddenly, Noah raised his head and opened one eye just a small bit. "Mom, don't. I'm dead." He then returned to his limp position in Juliana's arms.

"Jules, what are you doing?" Baylor asked in an exasperated tone.

"We're playing the part where the mummy carries his victim to the tomb," Juliana answered enthusiastically.

Baylor and Hobie exchanged a look.

"And I asked *you* to baby-sit *him*," Baylor said to her friend.

"Aw, Baylor, I don't need no baby-sitter," Noah rose up to complain.

"Did I say baby-sitter? I meant buddy."

"Yeah," Noah smiled and nodded. "Buddy."

"Come here, you living dead thing you." Baylor scooped Noah up. "Do you mind spending the night with Jules while your mom and I go someplace special?"

Noah shook his head. "Nope, Jules said married people go somewhere alone so they can do kissin' and stuff." His cheeks suddenly turned pink and he buried his face against Baylor's shoulder.

Hobie hid her smile, but Baylor chuckled at Noah's loveable innocence. He apparently got over his embarrassment in a hurry, because his mind was already on a new thought.

"Can I stay up late tonight?"

"It *is* late," Hobie answered.

"Then more late?"

"*More* late, eh?" Hobie chuckled. "Well, it is sort of a holiday, so okay."

"Yeah!"

"You go say goodbye to your grandma and Tanti. Okay, Bubba?" Baylor directed.

"'Kay," Noah answered before speeding off in the other direction.

"Don't worry, Jules. He'll probably fall asleep as soon as he gets home," Hobie said.

"No worries, love. I don't mind. After all, if I can live with Baylor, a six-year-old should be a breeze, right?"

"That's very funny," Baylor responded. "How'd you like to sleep next to the pool for the rest of your visit?"

"I guess that's my cue to go and collect my charge for the evening. Have fun you two. As a matter of fact—"

"Say good night, Jules," Baylor commanded.

"Right. Good night, Jules, and congrats, you two. I'm dead chuffed about this whole thing."

"Happy," Baylor translated.

"Oh," Hobie replied.

Juliana gave them each a hug before she left in search of Noah.

"I worry so much about your friends," Hobie said.

"This is very nice," Hobie said as she took in the champagne bottle sitting in a silver ice bucket. "Is this the surprise you said you had planned?"

"No, this is just sort of a precursor."

"Wow, it's still cold. How did you manage that?" Hobie asked when she placed her hand against the bottle.

"That was Tanti's handiwork."

"How did she do it?"

"She cast a spell." Baylor enjoyed the wide-eyed expression that greeted her remark. "Just kidding. She asked one of her friends to stop by on her way home and set it up."

"A spell, huh?"

"Sorry."

"You're not either."

"Sorry you don't think it's funny," Baylor replied with a pout.

"My poor baby." Hobie moved closer and wrapped her arms around Baylor's waist. "Hey, the water looks kind of inviting, huh?"

"What?"

"The water in the pool," Hobie explained. "Let's take a dip. What do you say?"

Baylor looked at Hobie's enticing expression, then down at the pool. "Uh-uh."

"Come on, sweetheart. I promise I'll make it worth your while," Hobie said seductively. She kissed Baylor's neck as she undid the top button of Baylor's blouse.

"Oh," Baylor groaned. She looked from Hobie to the pool once more. "Uh-uh." She shook her head vigorously.

"Okay," Hobie said, pulling away. "What is it with you and this pool? You wouldn't go in with Noah the other day, either, and all I keep getting from you is that we'll discuss it later. Well, it's later. Is it something about the pool? Did you see an alligator in it, or what?"

Baylor slowly shook her head. "It's not just the pool. It's all water, everywhere. Taking a bath gives me a weird feeling."

"Did something cause it? I mean, what are you afraid of?"

"Sinking, mostly. A fear of sinking. Actually, I had a—a bad experience in the water."

"Honey, people only sink when they fight it. If you relax and—"

"Nope, I pretty much always sink. Hell, I should have gotten over it and taken classes or something a long time ago, but I never did. It was one of those brilliant ideas my father had. Throw her in the water and she's sure to learn how to swim or tread water or something, right? Wrong. I sunk like a stone and passed out. I nearly drowned, and that bastard still acted like it was some failing on my part."

Baylor halfway expected Hobie to laugh. At the very least, she expected Hobie to calmly talk to her, attempt to get her to look at the whole thing in an adult manner and put off her childish fears.

"That goddamn son of a bitch!" Hobie began to pace alongside the pool. "That bastard ruined it!"

"Ruined what?" Baylor asked uncertainly.

"Things! He ruined things in your life, innocent things that are supposed to mean something or be fun. That sick bastard screwed it up for everyone that came after him. I hate him, and I hate the terrible things he did to you, the way he treated you. I'm the one who's never going to ever treat you that way, but he's already fucking ruined it all."

"Honey, honey..."

Baylor came up behind Hobie and wrapped her arms around her. Hobie was nearly rigid with anger and her whole body trembled. Baylor hadn't been prepared for Hobie's passionate response, and the display touched her in a place few had ever been able to reach. With the exception of her grandmother, no one had ever stood up for Baylor before, and certainly never against her father. She was sure that if she had met Hobie years ago, the feisty redhead would have been the one to give him a run for his money. Just knowing that helped Baylor more than ten years of therapy ever had.

"It's okay, honey. He can't hurt me anymore, not unless I let him, and I'm not going to let him."

Hobie was still quiet, but Baylor could feel her body began to relax. She heard a muffled sound and thought Hobie was crying. "Hobie, you okay?" When the vet turned, Baylor could see that she was laughing.

"God." Hobie shook her head. "Well, I think our wedding night is going good so far, how about you?"

"You are crazy, do you know that?"

"I know. I warned you, but you wouldn't listen. I'm sorry for going off like that."

"Don't be. I was pretty impressed, actually."

"Impressed that I can turn into a raving lunatic at the drop of a hat?"

"Well, I was thinking more along the lines of being thankful that I have someone who loves me enough to turn into a raving lunatic on my behalf."

"Thanks." Hobie furrowed her brow. "I think."

"I love you, Hobie Lynn, just as you are, all your frailties and faults included. I've always believed that it is a person's flaws that make them so lovable."

"Really? Well then, I should be damn near irresistible."

"You are, baby. You are," Baylor replied, punctuating her answer with a passionate kiss.

"Same goes for you." Hobie returned the kiss with equal fervor. "When you said that you weren't going to let your father hurt you anymore, does that mean you might," Hobie gently placed a line of kisses from Baylor's jaw to her collarbone, "give the pool a shot?"

"Um..." Baylor nervously looked at the water. She figured she could be brave if she had to, but was her wedding night the time to be closing old wounds?

Hobie continued her seduction exactly where she had left off before her meltdown. She unbuttoned two more of the buttons on Baylor's blouse and thoroughly surprised her by gently massaging her breast. Hobie could feel the nipple harden immediately under the thin silk blouse.

"Oh God," Baylor groaned. She wanted to speak, but her

body was enjoying the experience too much. She was sure her brain was making a conscious effort to keep her voice from messing up the entire experience.

"Because I was thinking..." Hobie continued. She had completely unbuttoned Baylor's blouse. Her fingers easily slipped inside the silky bra to tease Baylor even further. "You've got this negative experience on your mind, and maybe..." She lightly, pinched the hardened nipple, making Baylor gasp in pleasure.

"Maybe you just need a positive experience in the water to push that old memory out. What do you think?" Hobie nuzzled the skin of Baylor's neck and sucked, gently at first, then gradually increasing the intensity of the sensation.

"Good God!" Baylor answered.

"Hmm?"

Baylor finally received the message from her body that this was a good thing and that she shouldn't mess around and ruin it. "Oh, yeah. Positive is good. I could do positive." Her head bobbed up and down.

"I'm glad you feel that way." Hobie forced herself to separate from Baylor and walked over to the table. "Are you going to open this?"

"Now?"

Hobie nodded. Baylor made quick work of the wire and cork. She turned with a full glass to catch Hobie unzipping her dress. The redhead pushed the dress from her shoulders and carefully stepped out of it, then folded the garment over the back of a nearby chair.

"What are you doing?" Baylor asked the question that really needed no answer.

"Oh, I know you're smarter than that," Hobie replied with a devilish smile. She unhooked her bra.

Baylor had once again lost her ability to produce speech. She emptied the champagne glass in her hand in three swallows. Her eyes widened and her brows became lost in her hairline when Hobie tossed the undergarment onto the chair with her dress. "Holy shit!"

"I wondered what you'd say." With her index finger, Hobie touched the tiny gold hoop that hung from her left nipple.

"Holy shit."

"Is that all you're going to keep saying?"

"Well, I—I mean...I wasn't really prepared. God, didn't it hurt?" Baylor moved closer to inspect the piercing, having temporarily put her passion on hold.

"Not at all," Hobie replied dryly. She slapped Baylor on the arm. "Are you insane? I think I took Vicodin for a week just to get my bra on."

"How does it feel now?"

"Well, it has been several years. Why don't you tell me?"

Baylor didn't waste any more time. She slipped one arm around Hobie's waist, drawing her into a kiss, and her other hand found its way to Hobie's chest. She brushed the warm metal with her thumb and forefinger, tenderly massaging the area.

"Mmm." Hobie's eyes closed. "I'd say it feels very good."

"Very, *very* good," Baylor responded. She kissed Hobie until they were both breathless. "God, you feel good," she whispered as she ran her fingers across Hobie's skin.

Hobie's hands moved under Baylor's open blouse, finally coming to rest upon her strong back. She slid her hands upward and, with the skillful movement of two fingers, quickly unhooked the white silk bra.

Hobie took especial delight in the sounds coming from Baylor as she moaned into their kisses. Gently pressing her palm against Baylor's breast, she only allowed the barest contact as she tickled her palm by rubbing it against the stiff nipple. She repeated the action on the other breast.

Baylor's hands were similarly busy, and Hobie seriously considered just letting go and exploding into orgasm at that moment. She'd never experienced such intense emotions before. They excited and unnerved her at the same time.

"I have to say that you're slightly overdressed for the occasion," Hobie said.

"Your wish is my command," Baylor replied with a grin. She stepped back and took off her jacket. The rest of her clothes quickly formed a pile on the ground. With one last smirk, she bent to remove her panties.

Hobie hoped the gasp she just heard hadn't come from her, but she had a feeling that was wishful thinking. She still couldn't quite believe that this incredibly beautiful woman belonged to her, and that *she* wanted *her* as well.

"Better?" Baylor asked as she returned to wrap her arms around Hobie.

"You have no idea."

"Now who's wearing too much?" Baylor ran the tip of her finger along the top edge of Hobie's panties.

"Oh." Hobie offered a crooked smile. She made a move to remove the garment in question, but Baylor stopped her.

"I'd like to do that," Baylor said softly. She didn't wait for an answer. She tenderly kissed Hobie's lips, and then moved her hands to the sides of the panties, sliding them downward. She dropped to one knee and waited for Hobie to step out of them.

Baylor ran her hands up the backs of Hobie's legs, stopping to rest on her backside. She gently touched her lips to Hobie's thigh. The urge to touch her reddish-brown curls was almost too great to resist. The scent of Hobie's arousal tugged at the loosely held strings of Baylor's control. She forced herself to go slow and placed a soft kiss on Hobie's belly, just above the hairline. Then, as she stood, she allowed her lips and tongue to trail across the soft skin, all the way up to eager lips that met hers in a breathless kiss.

"Come with me," Hobie said a little hoarsely. She took Baylor's hand and directed her to the steps that led down into the pool.

Baylor paused as soon as her foot hit the water. Her breathing became shallow and she swallowed hard.

"It's all right, sweetheart. Let's just sit on the steps. The water isn't deep here."

Baylor nodded, but didn't appear entirely convinced that water and making love could possibly be a good combination. "It's okay," she answered. "I can do this and we *will* have a good time damn it."

"Okay." Hobie drew the word out. She couldn't help her amusement at her lover's unusually vehement approach to their lovemaking. "We may have to work on the 'tude a little, though."

They were on the top step, in a mere four inches of water, when Hobie began to whisper in a low, seductive tone.

Baylor's eyes widened at the language Hobie was using to entice her. She felt herself become wet at the images Hobie's words created in her mind, her wildest fantasies and secret desires. Baylor held her breath at some of the scenarios, risqué positions, and toys that Hobie promised.

Baylor pulled the smaller woman close and kissed her roughly. Her hands touched and teased as they declared possession of Hobie's body. Before she knew it, she was seated on the steps of the pool. Hobie straddled her and as they kissed, they proved that breathing really was an unnecessary function during lovemaking.

Some moments later, Hobie stroked Baylor's face with her fingertips. She found a light sheen of perspiration on her lover's brow. "Are you okay?"

Baylor seemed a little preoccupied as she nuzzled Hobie's neck. "Mmm, yeah...great."

"Baylor, you're sweating."

"The water's warm."

"Not that warm. Honey, we don't have to do this if it's freaking you out this bad." Hobie moved as if to pull away, but Baylor stopped her by locking an arm around her waist.

"Oh, no you don't. Now that you've got me going, we are definitely not stopping because of a little water."

"Is that so?" Hobie smiled when she saw the passion mixed with determination on Baylor's face.

"Yeah, that's so."

"Then I guess you don't want me to stop this." Hobie slowly pressed her lips to Baylor's for a deep kiss. "Or this." She moved her kisses to the writer's neck, nipping lightly at her flesh. Baylor leaned her head back and groaned, loving every minute of it.

"And I suppose that you don't, under any circumstances, want me to stop this." Hobie moved to straddle Baylor's thigh, sliding along her leg until they were once more pressed together. Hobie's tongue teased Baylor's earlobe with the same soft strokes that her fingers used to caress Baylor's nipple. The double action caused Baylor to shiver in delight, followed by another low groan.

Baylor usually took the lead in love play, but she was rather enjoying her new wife's efforts at seduction. The water now came to her waist, but her lover's actions quickly dispelled any remaining fears. Baylor couldn't believe the sensation the warm liquid, coupled with Hobie's sensual touch, caused against her skin.

"Oh, yes..." A slow moan escaped Baylor's throat. She looked down to see Hobie's mouth cover her nipple. The hard flesh immediately reacted, sending currents of pleasure straight to the spot between her legs. She lifted a hand and ran her fingers through Hobie's hair and pulled her closer, encouraging her actions. Hobie's tongue worked the stiff flesh, its strokes increasingly rough. Finally, seemingly encouraged by Baylor's response, she sucked hard.

Baylor braced herself with one hand on the edge of the pool. "God, woman!" she exclaimed. "So good."

Hobie moved over to the other breast and repeated her assault. By the time she straightened up again, Baylor was breathing rapidly. The writer captured Hobie's mouth in a kiss that communicated unbridled passion and a certain urgency. Hobie couldn't wait any longer and she interpreted Baylor's kiss to mean much the same.

She ran the flat of her hand down Baylor's belly and into the dark curls. Baylor gasped when she felt the electric touch between her legs.

"Right here?" Hobie whispered.

"Yes...yes," Baylor struggled to form just that one word. She didn't usually have such reactions to simply being touched. It was as if Hobie had complete command of her. Baylor had a feeling that what she had written in her novels all those years was true after all. Perhaps love did make all the difference.

"Don't stop," she managed to utter. She kissed Hobie's shoulder, wrapping her arms a little tighter around her.

"You feel wonderful. So wet," Hobie said as she stroked the length of Baylor's sex. She paused to circle the sensitive clit and Baylor groaned as if she were in pain.

"More. Please, baby."

Hobie realized that they'd both waited long enough. She easily slipped one, then two fingers inside of Baylor. The writer involuntarily opened her legs and Hobie slid her fingers in deeper. She began a continuous motion, sliding in and out. When she pressed in, Hobie made sure to rub her thumb in a circular motion against Baylor's clit. It didn't take long before she could feel the trembling begin within Baylor's body.

"I love you, Hobie. God, I love you," Baylor whispered breathlessly against Hobie's neck. She held tightly to her.

Baylor felt as if she were swimming against the raging current of a whirlpool. Certain that she would do something to mess it all up, she held back her release out of fear that this would never come again, that these feelings would never be duplicated and that she would only have this one time within Hobie's arms.

"I love you, Baylor. You'll always be safe with me," Hobie whispered into the trembling woman's ear.

That was all it took. A strangled moan escaped Baylor's throat as she tilted her head back. She could see herself giving up against the strength of the current. Her body relaxed and she began to swirl along with the water in a downward spiral. The closer she got to the whirlpool's center, the hotter the fire burned within her own body.

Suddenly, Baylor saw stars. They were the stars that had come together for them during their ceremony, but this time she was flying with them. Surrounded by shooting stars and the blue-black night, the two stars raced toward each other. At the most intense moment of her pleasure, as her release shot through her entire being, the two stars collided. The resulting explosion caused rings of color to burst forth.

Baylor gasped as she opened her eyes. The vision was gone. She still held tightly to Hobie, her heart pounding so hard she could hardly catch her breath. That's when her tears began. Baylor couldn't understand it; sex had never been this emotional before.

"It's official," she whispered after she brought her breathing under control. "I'm pathetic."

Hobie smiled in understanding. "It's okay, sweetheart. I've got you."

"Then I guess all I can say is thanks for having me."

They both smiled at the double entendre.

"No, don't move," Baylor held Hobie's hand where it was between her legs. "Not yet. It feels too good."

"You're telling me."

Eventually they realized they had to get out of the water. "Stay here, I'll be back in a sec with some towels," Baylor said.

True to her word, she returned moments later with two over-sized bath towels. The women wrapped themselves up in the warm terrycloth and sat beside each other on the side of the pool. They held hands and dangled their legs in the warm water, feeling like teenagers in love.

After a while, Baylor situated herself so Hobie could sit between her legs and lean back against her chest. They sat that way in silence with Baylor's arms around Hobie, listening to the breeze as it rustled against the palm leaves overhead.

"You are incredible, I want you to know that. I've certainly been around the block, but no one's ever made me feel like this. I know I sound all sappy and cliché, but it's the truth."

"I'm so there with you, sweetheart. I feel like I'm sixteen and in love, and I've never felt like that with any lover before."

Baylor's arms tensed. "Um, have there been many...you know, lovers?"

"Don't go there, Baylor Joan. Not tonight." Hobie turned in the embrace and touched her fingertips to the crease in Baylor's forehead. "It doesn't matter anyway, anything that came before. I feel like I've been living my life in a black-and-white movie and now, here we are in Technicolor."

Baylor instantly brightened. "Thanks for the reminder, and you're right. It sounds like something Harriet Teasley would write, but I feel like I've been transparent all this time. Now I meet you and suddenly I can see myself, others can see me. I'm whole."

"I think I like the way Harriet thinks." Hobie smiled and the women shared a tender kiss. "Thanks for tonight, for making it special," Hobie added.

"Well, I think for the evening thus far, I should be thanking you," Baylor replied, wearing a sheepish grin. "However, your special surprise is waiting in that building right there."

"In the greenhouse?" Hobie's voice took on an excited, childlike quality. "I've always wanted to know what Evelyn grew in that big one there. Guess I was too polite to just ask. To tell you the truth, I thought it might be pot."

Baylor laughed. "Well, it's nothing that exciting. I have a little spot all set up for us. Have you been eating right today?"

"As a matter of fact, I did skip a little. I was kind of nervous today and, well...Thanks for checking. You know it's the first thing I forget."

"I know, baby, but no more. Now you have someone to harp at you every day. I'm gonna make your mom look like she didn't even care." Baylor chuckled. "I've done a lot of research on the Internet about hypoglycemia, and I'm prepared to make your life a married hell."

Hobie laughed at Baylor's earnest vigor, feeling secure in the fact that someone was looking out for her for a change. "You'll probably drive me completely bananas, but I'll love every minute of it," she said.

"So, are you hungry?"

"Mmm, what did you have in mind?" Hobie fingered the spot between Baylor's breasts where she had her towel knotted together.

"A lot." Baylor jokingly slapped at Hobie's hand and then kissed the tip of her nose. "But later. First, you're going to eat some dinner. We're going to go on a picnic."

"A picnic? Isn't it a little late at night?"

"Nope. Not where we're going," Baylor answered cryptically. "I think you'll love it. Plus, I want you to eat plenty of high-energy food."

"Am I going to need it?" Hobie asked with a suggestive look.

"You have no idea, my love. Your evening is just getting started."

Hobie lay on her back upon the soft blankets and raised her arms above her head, stretching like a contented cat. She grinned sheepishly when she caught Baylor smiling at her.

"Never in my wildest dreams would I have ever guessed all this was in here," Hobie said. "It's like an entirely different world."

"You should have seen the look on my face when I first got here. I thought it was the beginning of a bad *Twilight Zone* episode."

The women, still in their towels, lounged beside the waterfall, surrounded by oriental grasses and tropical plants with dark glossy leaves.

"Get enough to eat?" Baylor asked as she gently patted Hobie's belly.

"Absolutely. How did you know I love Greek food?"

"Your mom."

"Well, these are the best dolmades I've had in years," Hobie said. "Where did you go for them?"

"Go, hell. I made them," Baylor said with a satisfied smirk.

"You made them? All of this?" Hobie peeked into the wicker basket, which was still half full of food. "Were you planning on a few more people showing up?"

"Very funny, and yes, I made everything. It's one of my hobbies, actually."

"Have I told you lately how much I love you?"

"Let me guess. You don't know how to cook."

"Do peanut butter and jelly sandwiches count?"

Baylor dropped her head in false dismay.

"Wait! I can make macaroni and cheese, too—well, the kind that comes in a box—so there. And I can make pancakes. From a mix, though."

Baylor couldn't hold in her laughter any longer. She leaned over Hobie and kissed her soundly. "You are as impossible as you are beautiful," she said after pulling away to look into Hobie's eyes.

"I try."

Baylor leaned down for another kiss. This time, Hobie felt an odd sensation. The only way she was able to describe it later was to say that she felt her destiny click into place. The kiss was soft and passionate, tender and hungry all at once. By the time she parted her lips to let Baylor's inquisitive tongue enter her mouth, their bodies were pressed tightly together. Hobie moaned at the warm softness of Baylor's tongue. She regretted that they had to eventually come up for air.

"Good Lord, Hobie Lynn. Where did you learn to kiss like that?" Baylor asked breathlessly. She didn't wait for an answer. "That's what I remembered, you know. As humiliating and embarrassing as it is to admit that I forgot your face, I remembered that kiss."

She took Hobie's face in her hands and kissed her again. She went even slower this time, lingering over every subtle nuance of Hobie's mouth.

"Baylor, touch me." It wasn't a command, more like a whispered plea, and both women knew it.

"And where would you like me to do this touching?"

"Anywhere." Hobie captured Baylor's lips with her own. "Everywhere."

They kissed for a very long time. Eventually, Baylor allowed her hands to roam, and when she cupped Hobie's breast through the towel and let her thumb brush back and forth across the nipple, Hobie groaned as if she were in pain.

"God, Baylor! That feels so—"

Baylor pinched the hardened nipple lightly through the soft cloth.

"God, so...so good!"

Baylor retreated slightly. Hobie pulled her back and nuzzled her neck, kissing the taut skin there. "Baylor...please, don't stop," she pleaded.

Baylor looked down at Hobie and gently touched her lips in the lightest of kisses. Lifting her body for just a moment, Baylor removed her towel, then reverently opened the towel wrapped around Hobie. She laid her body down on top of Hobie, and both women gasped at the feel of skin on skin.

"Hobie, I can't even believe that a woman as beautiful as you would want to be with me. Do you have any idea, my love, how beautiful you are?"

Hobie could feel her skin flush a deep pink.

"It's true. You are so beautiful," Baylor continued as she let her hands explore the smooth curves beneath her. "I want to make love to you. I want to be the only person to ever touch you this way. I want mine to be the name that you cry out when you come."

"Oh, yes."

Hearing that answer, Baylor moved her hands over Hobie's skin as she pressed her mouth against Hobie's lips. She sucked Hobie's tongue rhythmically, matching it to the tempo of her movements against Hobie's thigh. She could feel her own wetness as she rubbed her clit harder against the firm muscles.

Hobie enjoyed the feel of Baylor's body on hers. When the writer's kisses turned hungry, Hobie's passion increased until she was growling with need. Baylor's kisses ran along Hobie's jaw, and she pressed her head back into the blanket, giving her entire being over to her lover, instinctively knowing she would be safe and loved within Baylor's embrace.

Baylor ran her tongue in a random design along Hobie's shoulders and down to her chest. She took little nips of skin, and Hobie gasped in pleasure and surprise with each tiny bite. By the time Baylor's lips wrapped around a very aroused pierced nipple, Hobie felt every pull directly between her legs.

The first touch was exquisite, enough to send both women out of their minds with lust. Baylor used her lips, tongue, and teeth to drive Hobie higher and higher. She alternated between breasts, and when she had her mouth on one, she used her hand to knead and massage the other. Slipping the tip of her tongue into the small gold hoop, Baylor tugged gently, pulling harder once Hobie's breathless moans encouraged her.

Hobie's body trembled constantly. "Baylor...please. Please, don't stop. Don't ever stop," she moaned.

"I don't think you need to fear that, love." Baylor smiled down at her lover. Once she'd touched every inch of Hobie's skin with her lips, tongue, or fingers, Baylor ran the tip of her tongue down Hobie's belly. She slid between Hobie's legs, which parted instantly.

The sweet, musky scent of her lover aroused Baylor even more. "Perfect," she whispered, kissing the soft skin of each inner thigh until she reached her reddish curls. She laid numerous kisses on the soft triangle of hair.

"Oh God!" Hobie cried out, thrusting her hips up to meet the mouth that lingered so close to her center. "Oh, Baylor," she groaned, spreading her legs wider still.

Hobie almost climaxed at the very moment when she felt Baylor's tongue press against her needy flesh. She lifted her hips again so she wouldn't break contact. Her excitement increased as Baylor moved her tongue slowly, but relentlessly, sometimes teasing the folds with the tip of her tongue, other times pressing against the slick opening.

Hobie rotated her hips in a counter-rhythm to the persistent caresses. She pressed her clit as hard as she could against Baylor's tongue as the writer slowly picked up speed. Baylor's moans as she went about her pleasurable task did nothing to quench the roaring fire in Hobie's belly.

Feeling her lover's increased wetness and the quick shudders of her muscles, Baylor eased one finger inside her, never slowing the movement of her tongue.

"Yesss. Just like that." Hobie relaxed into the exquisite touch, letting the flames of their passion carry her to her destination. After a moment, grasping Baylor's shoulders, then her hair, Hobie forced her to increase the pressure of her tongue. "Baylor...Oh, Baylor, yes...please...more," she moaned.

In one fluid movement, Baylor slid another finger inside. Hobie's hips froze for a few interminable seconds, and the vet tried to catch her breath at the sensation of penetration as, at the same time, Baylor wrapped her mouth around the sensitive area of nerves and sucked it in gently.

Hobie's hips resumed their motion, now with an intensity that surprised even her. Baylor slid her fingers almost all of the way out and moved them in again. She repeated the action as she sucked harder on the bit of flesh between her lips. Finally, the Hobie shivered and her legs parted as wide as they could go. Baylor sucked harder and flicked her tongue quickly across the tiny area that would bring her lover the most pleasure. Hobie's back arched and she took in a deep breath. One shout of pleasure escaped her lips.

"Baylor!"

Suddenly, Hobie saw stars. She opened her eyes and looked through the ceiling of the greenhouse. Stars surrounded her. The two brightest were the stars that had come together during their ceremony, but this time she was flying with them. Surrounded by shooting stars and the blue-black night, the two stars raced toward each other. At the most intense moment of her pleasure, as her release shot through her entire being, the two stars collided. The resulting explosion caused rings of color to burst forth.

She gasped. When she opened her eyes, the vision was gone. She cried out again as one orgasm blended into another. She felt Baylor's tongue replace her fingers and slide deep into her. Just when Hobie thought she could take no more, Baylor pulled away and once more entered her with two fingers, causing even more waves of pleasure. Slowly, she came back to reality. She felt the gentle touches of Baylor's tongue as she lapped up the juices Hobie's excitement had created.

Baylor slid her fingers from her lover's satiny warmth and felt Hobie tremble with aftershocks of desire. She licked at Hobie's sweet juices, taking care to avoid the too sensitive area at the top of her cleft.

It was gentle and relaxed, and Hobie couldn't help becoming aroused again. Almost unconsciously, and with the vision of the stars still floating before her, she gently rolled her hips in an easy rhythm against the strokes from Baylor's tongue.

"Oh, yes," she soon murmured as Baylor feasted again on her more than willing flesh. Hobie felt Baylor's strong arms wrap around her parted thighs, and the writer's tongue replaced her fingers. There was less of a rush for Hobie this time; instead of racing toward her climax, she waited for it to come to her. It was slow, almost luxurious, and she cried out as another release engulfed her.

Baylor moved up and wrapped her arms around her still-trembling lover. She whispered her love as Hobie cried. Baylor understood the tears, as well as Hobie's inability to articulate the reason behind them. She couldn't explain them any better than Hobie could.

"Okay." Hobie wiped the tears away. "It's official. We're both pathetic."

Baylor laughed and held Hobie tighter. "You okay?" She didn't know quite how to phrase it. How did one ask if one's partner just had the most mind-numbing sex of her life, or was it just a "that was very nice" on the sex-o-meter?

As with most of Baylor's abbreviated language, Hobie understood exactly what she meant. "It and you were and are incredible."

"Really?" Baylor brightened considerably.

"I wouldn't have thought you, of all people, would have doubts about your abilities in that area."

"Well," Baylor's cheeks showed an uncharacteristic flush, "we're going to be doing this for the next fifty or sixty years. It would really suck if we'd waited till now to find out that we're no good together in bed."

Hobie laughed and shook her head, then pulled away from Baylor and leaned on one elbow. "The things you find to worry about scare me. And what do you mean fifty or sixty years? You sure do plan to be an active old broad, don't you?" She laughed again. "That will put us pushing a hundred."

"Funny you say that," Baylor responded as she settled comfortably on her back.

"Say what?" Hobie sat up and reached for the picnic basket, having worked up an appetite. She grinned in embarrassment when she saw Baylor smiling at her.

"Can I get you any more?"

"No. These are fine," Hobie answered. She popped a piece of cheese into her mouth. "So, what was so funny?"

"Actually, it was something Jules mentioned today. Then you just made the comment about how old we'll be in fifty years."

"And?"

"Did you know that Tanti and Aimee were the last—well, I don't know what to call it, but the supposed saviors of Ana Lia? Like we did tonight. They had their ceremony fifty years ago."

"I had no idea. Is it significant in some way?"

"That part really isn't, but I found out about it before we left Rebecca's and forgot to tell you. No, what Jules pointed out was the average age of the members of the Ladies Guild. I know Tanti's ninety-two and I think JoJo said Rebecca was, what? A hundred?"

"I think I heard Mom say that Rebecca was ninety-five or ninety-eight."

Together they came up with a half-dozen names of women in their nineties.

"Now, let me ask you the same question Jules hit me with," Baylor continued. "Do any of these chicks look over seventy or even eighty to you?"

"Well, I'm not sure, but once you're that age I guess it gets harder to tell, right?"

"You're the doc. You tell me. Do any of these gals get sick much? Aside from Tanti's hip, has she ever really had anything wrong with her?"

Hobie stopped eating to seriously think about Baylor's question. With the possible exception of childbirth, she could hardly recall *any* of the local women being ill. Doc Elston had always spent more days in his fishing boat than in his office. There was the usual kid stuff and accidents, but the women of the island were a surprisingly healthy bunch.

Hobie sobered until she realized that she was acting as paranoid as Baylor. She laughed and shook her head to dispel the niggling doubts. "Oh, please. I'm sure there's some rational explanation for it."

"Hey, weirder things have happened."

"Oh, come on. You don't seriously think that the women of this island have some special power that keeps them young, or from ever getting sick, do you?"

"Hey, all I'm doing is bringing up the possibility that there are, I don't know, *forces* on this island. Look at you and me. I drank like a fish before I got here. I think I've had a few beers and two margaritas all summer. That's not counting the champagne I had tonight. Didn't you have the same problem before you came back home? I've never even *wanted* a drink since I've been here. Okay, there was the party at the library, but I consider that an extreme time. How about you?"

"Oh, Baylor, that's just—" It was too crazy a scenario to even consider. Wasn't it? "What? You think we have the fountain of youth on Ana Lia? That Ponce de León was right all along?"

"I was thinking more along the lines of, you know...*spells* and...stuff."

"Excuse me?" Hobie asked with laughter in her eyes.

"Oh, you heard what I said, Miss Smarty-pants."

"I heard it, I'm just not sure I believe you said it." Hobie chuckled. "Look, whatever they're doing, it's working, and I, for one, am not about to question *how* they do it. Besides, we're a part of the whole thing now. What with our ceremony and the stars coming together, I expect that if they live to be five hundred, so will we."

"Oh my god," Baylor cried out. "We're witches, too!"

"Baylor!"

"Sorry. Wiccans."

"Being politically correct wasn't why I was yelling at you." Hobie laughed even harder. She didn't mean to make light of her lover's worries, but Baylor's paranoia exceeded anything Hobie had ever known. "I'm yelling at you because it doesn't work that way. It's like any other religion, so to speak. You have to make a conscious decision to follow it. You can't just become one of them without knowing it. I'm pretty positive there are no such things as Wiccan pods that they slip under your bed at night."

"Right. Okay, I know that." Baylor pouted, embarrassed at having the thought in the first place.

"Can we move on to something else that will probably freak you out?"

"I'm glad you're so amused with your own wit," Baylor said as she quickly stole a piece of cheese from Hobie. She popped it into her mouth and lay back down, munching contentedly.

"I am, thanks and—hey, that was mine!"

"Ya snooze, ya lose."

"Okay, can I be serious for a second?"

"I don't know, can you?"

Hobie arched an eyebrow.

"Sorry. Go ahead."

Hobie pushed the basket away and lay down beside Baylor. Leaning her head in the palm of one hand, she did indeed look as though she was about to begin a serious discussion.

"Something...well, odd happened to me while we were making love. Not so much during, but right when...you know. The moment when I..."

Baylor appeared rather amused. "Climaxed."

"Yeah. Geez, talking about it and doing it are really different, huh?"

Baylor chuckled. "I don't know. You didn't seem to have too much trouble verbalizing while we were doing it."

Hobie slapped the writer's stomach.

"What was this odd thing that happened?" Suddenly Baylor appeared interested.

"Okay, now remember that I had champagne, I was in the throes of great sex, and I was probably oxygen deprived. Okay?"

"Check."

"I saw stars."

"It's all just part of the service, my love," Baylor answered smugly. She looked at Hobie and realized she was serious. "What kind of stars?" she asked slowly.

"Well, it was like right before our stars came together tonight. They—"

"Slammed into each other."

"Yes! But—"

"You were right there—"

"Surrounded by them," Hobie finished.

They looked at each other for a long, silent moment, just staring into each other's eyes.

"You?" Hobie asked.

Baylor nodded.

Hobie explained further. "When they exploded into one, there were all these—"

"Colors, and they spread out in big circles."

They lay beside each other in silence.

"Okay, I'm pretty freaked out right about now. How about you?" Hobie finally asked.

"Oh, yeah."

"Is that even possible? For that to happen to both of us?"

"Maybe there's one of those rational explanations you're so fond of."

"Very funny."

Hobie chuckled aloud, then her laughter grew louder.

"You're not losing it on me, are you?" Baylor asked.

"No, sweetheart. Ironically enough, I think I'm finding it."

Baylor rolled to her side in order to look at Hobie. "I'm afraid to, but I have to ask. What in the hell are you talking about?"

"It's just some thoughts that struck me. First, what weird things are going to happen to us now, and I'm not saying they ever will, but what if they did? What if we only age every other year from this point on? What if Rebecca Ashby has the fountain of youth buried in her back yard? What if the witches of Ana Lia live down the block from us, or if we see visions of stars every time we have sex? Does any of it really matter?"

"Of course it matters," Baylor quickly answered.

"Why?"

"Well, because...in order to...I mean, they..." Baylor looked blankly at Hobie.

"See what I mean? We know none of it will ever hurt us. Frankly, the benefits have helped us more than anything else. It reminds me of something Evelyn said to you when you first got here. It was right after you met Albert at the Dilby sisters' shop. Remember?"

"There's not much chance I'll ever forget that day. I'm not sure what Tanti said, though."

"She said that we continue some things in life because we've grown comfortable with them that way. She said that change was hard on the soul and that sometimes you just accept things, and people, the way they are."

"My Tanti said that?"

"Baylor Warren, you were sitting right next to me."

"I was in my pre-Ana Lia selfish phase. Sorry."

"No need for you to be sorry. I was just as thick about it all, or self-involved, whatever you want to call it. That's the second point I wanted to make. I've lived here all my life and all these subtle things were just as invisible to me. I don't know how, but they were. It's almost as if I couldn't see them because I wasn't ready. Does that make sense?"

"Sometimes people tell us all sorts of things, and it's not that we're not listening, just that we're not quite ready to hear," Baylor said, a faraway look in her eyes.

"Wow, that's pretty profound."

"Don't get too excited." Baylor smiled affectionately. "Rebecca Ashby said it to me when she was doing my tarot reading."

"That's kind of what I mean. If you think about it—now, I could be reaching here—but I get the oddest feeling they were trying to tell us about all of this way back then. I know hindsight is 20/20, but I think of the things that these ladies said to us and it's as if they know a whole lot more about life, and us, than we realize."

"You know," Baylor grinned, "that all of this sounds like something Harriet Teasley would say."

"I see an easy book out of all of this."

"Now that you bring it up, I kind of already started a new novel. As a matter of fact, I'm about halfway through the first draft."

"That's wonderful. My mother will be thrilled to death. You know how she loves those—"

"It's not a Harriet Teasley novel," Baylor said softly, avoiding Hobie's eyes.

"Not by Harriet Teasley? Then who?"

"Um...Baylor Warren. It's a romance, but I sort of decided not to hide behind the *nom de plume* anymore. I also decided not to hide behind straight romance. It's the story of two women."

Hobie smiled brightly. "Good for you. Whatever and however you decide to write, though, you know I'm always behind you 100 percent."

"Well, it's been so many years that I have grown rather fond of old Harriet. I may have to write one once in a while to make the fans happy."

"As long as you're doing what you want to do, Baylor. I think if you do that, you can't go wrong. So, what's the name of this new novel?"

"I was thinking about *Rebecca's Cove*. I asked Rebecca Ashby and she thought it was a hoot."

Hobie laughed and settled back against the blankets. "Go figure." She snuggled against Baylor. The writer pulled a blanket over them and they lay there, looking up into the sky. The blackness had changed to the pale pre-dawn color that heralded sunrise.

"We've been up all night and I'm tired, but not *that* tired," Hobie said.

"Probably Ana Lia's fountain of youth at work."

"More likely is the fact that I'm simply happier than I've ever been in my entire life. I love you, Baylor, and I promise to spend the rest of my life proving that to you."

Baylor looked down and stroked Hobie's cheek. "In my whole life I never thought I'd ever be able to make anyone that happy. What surprises me even more," she said softly, "is that I never thought I'd be that happy, either. I am, though, Hobie Lynn. I'm in love for the very first time in my life and I promise that I'll try never to do anything to mess that up."

They lay together, winding down and waiting for sleep to come. Suddenly Baylor chuckled.

"Hmm?" Hobie asked sleepily.

"I was just thinking..."

"Mmm, always dangerous."

"Very funny. I was thinking about the Cove. More to the point, the sign outside the restaurant. 'Rebecca's Cove, the Golden Key of the Gulf.'" Baylor yawned and her eyes felt too heavy to keep open. "Who would've thought that a restaurant could be the key to so much of my happiness?"

She listened to Hobie's deep even breathing and realized that she was already asleep. With an easy smile on her face, she gave up her own struggle to remain awake and slipped into the land of dreams.

Epilogue

From: BJW
To: J Ross
Sent: Wednesday, December 25, 2002 5:33 PM
Subject: Hey there, woman!

Jules,

Hey, woman, Merry Christmas!

I know you were just here for the weekend, but you know I can't let the holiday go by without harassing you. Gotta love e-mail, huh?

First off, Hobie says hi. She said to tell you that the vertical blinds for your living room came in and she sent them back. Something about the wrong length...okay, I wasn't listening real good, I admit. She starts showing me swatches and my eyes have a tendency to glaze over. I do remember her muttering something about mainlanders not being able to use the brains God gave them. She hopes you don't mind, but she cancelled the order & the Dilby sisters have some on the way for you. Knowing those broads, you're probably getting a 50 percent discount. I figure you could live with that, eh?

Last on the list was the furniture for the office, and Hobie's mom said it all came a few days before Christmas. Hobie said it looks great. Mom says the guest-house is ready to move into, so get your butt down here. I say don't forget to bring me Marconi bread when you come. Geez, what the hell are we gonna do once you're all moved in permanently down here? We'll have to bribe your secretary to send us our Chicago eats.

Let's see...oh, before I forget, Noah just ran in and said thanks for the Harry Potter set. He loves them. Hobie's a little worried because Noah wants us to build him a little room under the stairs. Plus, he asked for an owl for Christmas. God, I love that kid! Hobie doesn't understand kids the way we do. Mack tells me she was one of those girls who played with dolls instead of GI

Joe. There's no accounting for taste.

I signed the contracts for *Rebecca's Cove.* They're in the mail...I dropped them in the box the day before yesterday. Tell James I appreciate him taking a chance on this one. Can you believe how quickly I punched out that third draft? Must be the gulf air out here. Whatever it is, I love it.

Hey, did I tell you that we have a new puppy? Yep, Tanti set up Arturo with some lady's Bichon bitch on the mainland. Arturo didn't act too thrilled about it...I think he's gay. Hobie says I'm nuts, but you know how many times a day she says that to me. But, he did his duty and we just got his baby boy, Harley. I named him in memory of the bike Hobie made me sell. Oh, I know she didn't really *make* me sell it, but trust me...She looked at me, folded her arms, and did that arched crooky thing she does with her eyebrow. Even I'm smart enough to know what that means. Of course, I wanted to name him Bubba, but Hobie said she wouldn't know if I was talking about Noah or the dog. I gotta admit, this little cotton ball is a heartbreaker, although if you repeat that to a soul, I will completely deny it. I have a reputation to keep up and I keep threatening to put him in the dryer on fluff.

Tanti sends her love. She's in the other room with Hobie right now. Hob took up photography, so she's getting some pointers from the expert. Tanti loves talking about the old days and Hobie loves hearing about the jungle expeditions, so they're in heaven.

Tanti did say to apologize to you. She said she never had a chance to thank you properly for everything you did for Hobie and me in the beginning. Just what does she mean? All I have to say is that when you get here...we're gonna have a talk, mate!

Well, Hobie's—wait a sec.

hi aunt jules this is noah are you ok

Okay, bet you can guess who that was. The guy types faster than I do, providing you don't mind doing without little things like punctuation and capitalization. He's in my lap and reminding me that I promised to help him set up his new telescope once it got dark. Yep...the life of a mom!

Oh, did I tell you that the Ana Lia Board of Education asked me to teach high-school English next year? Me, a teacher...wild, huh?

Okay, call me and let me know for sure what date you're planning on for the big move. I love you, mate, and can't wait until you live just down the street again. You and I will have a ball. I don't agree with Tanti & Hobie...I don't see us getting into any

trouble at all down here.
     Later,
     B.

Other LJ Maas titles available from
Yellow Rose Books

Meridio's Daughter

Tessa (Nikki) Nikolaidis is cold and ruthless, the perfect person to be Karê, the right-hand, to Greek magnate Andreas Meridio. Cassandra (Casey) Meridio has come home after a six-year absence to find that her father's new Karê is a very desirable, but highly dangerous woman.

Set in modern day Greece on the beautiful island of Mýkonos, this novel weaves a tale of emotional intrigue as two women from different worlds struggle with forbidden desires. As the two come closer to the point of no return, Casey begins to wonder if she can really trust the beautiful Karê. Does Nikki's dark past, hide secrets that will eventually bring down the brutal Meridio Empire, or are her actions simply those of a vindictive woman? Will she stop at nothing for vengeance...even seduction?

ISBN: 1-930928-53-X

Tumbleweed Fever

In the Oklahoma Territory of the old west Devlin Brown is trying to redeem herself for her past as an outlaw, now working as a rider on a cattle ranch.

Sarah Tolliver is a widow with two children and a successful ranch, but no way to protect it from the ruthless men who would rather see her fail. When the two come together sparks fly, as a former outlaw loses her heart to a beautiful yet headstrong young woman.

ISBN: 1-930928-05-X

Prairie Fire

A dying Shaman whispers a cryptic message..."The buffalo must run free..." In this sequel to *Tumbleweed Fever*, we continue the story of Devlin Brown, an ex-outlaw and Sarah Tolliver, the woman of her heart. The Shaman's words are translated by a Choctaw Medicine Man and now Sarah and Dev must convince the ranchers around them to destroy the wire fences that contain their cattle in order to avoid certain calamity.

Amidst the beautiful and, sometimes unforgiving, land of the Oklahoma Territory, the two women begin a new life together. Adventure and Mysticism abound as they revisit the Choctaw camp where Devlin grew up. Sarah must decide whether she will undergo the Clan rituals that will allow her to join with the former outlaw in a ceremony that will bind their hearts together forever.

ISBN: 1-930928-36-X

None So Blind

It's been almost 15 years since Chicago writer, Torrey Gray has set eyes on the woman she fell in love with so long ago. Taylor Kent has become one of the most celebrated artists in the country, and has spent the last 15 years trying to, unsuccessfully, forget the young woman that walked out of her life, stealing Taylor's heart in the process. Best friends forever, neither woman was ever able to find the courage to speak about the growing passion they felt for one another.

Now an unusual, but desperate request will throw the old friends together again, but this time, will either of them be able to voice their unspoken desires, or has time become their enemy?

ISBN: 1-930928-46-7

LJ Maas is the author of *Tumbleweed Fever, None So Blind, Meridio's Daughter, Prairie Fire*, and *Rebecca's Cove.*

Originally from Chicago, LJ now resides in Oklahoma with her partner of almost 7 years. They have an eight-year-old daughter (a blonde-haired, lab/retriever mix who simply refuses to believe she's a dog). Along with writing full time, LJ teaches computer graphics, web design and a variety of writing classes at a local college. Her online works can be located at:: http://www.art-with-attitude.com.